Items should be returned on or before the last date shown below. Items not already requested by other borrowers may be renewed in person, in writing or by telephone. To renew, please quote the number on the barcode label. To renew online a PIN is required. This can be requested at your local library.
Renew online @ **www.dublincitypubliclibraries.ie**
Fines charged for overdue items will include postage incurred in recovery. Damage to or loss of items will be charged to the borrower.

**Leabharlanna Poiblí Chathair Bhaile Átha Cliath
Dublin City Public Libraries**

Comhairle Cathrach
Bhaile Átha Cliath
Dublin City Council

Brainse Dhromchonnrach
Drumcondra Branch
Tel. 8377206

Date Due	Date Due	Date Due

Also by Lesley Lokko

Sundowners
Saffron Skies
Bitter Chocolate
Rich Girl, Poor Girl
One Secret Summer
A Private Affair
An Absolute Deception
Little White Lies
In Love and War

The Last Debutante

LESLEY LOKKO

First published in Great Britain in 2016 by Orion Books,
an imprint of The Orion Publishing Group Ltd
Carmelite House, 50 Victoria Embankment
London EC4Y 0DZ

An Hachette UK Company

1 3 5 7 9 10 8 6 4 2

A CIP catalogue record for this book is
available from the British Library.

ISBN (Trade Paperback) 978 1 4091 4254 6

Typeset at The Spartan Press Ltd,
Lymington, Hants

Printed and bound in Great Britain by Clays Ltd, St Ives plc

www.orionbooks.co.uk

For my sister, Debbie

Acknowledgements

Without a doubt, the biggest thanks of all must go to my fans who have waited *so* patiently for this novel to come out. Your wonderfully polite messages ('er, when can we expect ...?') have kept me on track over the past three years. Thanks, too, to the two Kates – editor and agent – for their patience and understanding. Juggling two careers isn't easy at the best of times but I hope the detour has enriched both. The list of sources consulted for *this* novel would run to several pages, but Andrea Levy's *Small Island* ranks top. A wonderful read. As ever, my deepest thanks to all my family and friends who put up with yet another move with such grace. I promise this will be the last one. For a while.

Timelines

PROLOGUE (September 2014)   1

PART ONE War (1938–1939)   7
Kit
Chapters 1–9

PART TWO Loss (1939–1940)   57
Kit
Chapters 10–16

PART THREE Joy (1941)   85
Kit
Chapters 17–32

PART FOUR Grief (1942)   159
Kit
Chapter 33

PART FIVE Peace (1957–1958)   167
Kit/Libby
Chapters 34–39

PART SIX Escape (1958)   197
Kit
Chapters 40–44

PART SEVEN Revolution (1958–1959)   215
Libby/Kit
Chapters 45–51

PART EIGHT Sex (1961)   241
Libby
Chapters 52–55

PART NINE Betrayal (1963)   271
Kit/Lily/Libby
Chapters 56–66

PART TEN Truth (2014)   303
Kit/Libby/Ro
Chapters 67–68

EPILOGUE (September 2014)   317

Main Characters

KATHERINE 'KIT' ALGERNON-WATERS
DOB: 9 September 1923

ELIZABETH 'LILY' ALGERNON-WATERS
DOB: 27 May 1920

KIT'S SON
DOB: 23 November 1939

EARL HIGHTOWER
DOB: 4 April 1917

ELIZABETH 'LIBBY' KENTRIDGE
DOB: 25 November 1942

ELUNED KENTRIDGE
DOB: 13 December 1956

MAEV KENTRIDGE
DOB: 10 April 1961

RO KENTRIDGE
DOB: 9 October 1964

PHOEBE KLEIN
DOB: 9 October 1999

In their earliest form, debutantes were presented as both girls on the cusp of womanhood, and as eligible bachelorettes. In fact, some scholars contend that 'debbing' surfaced at the same time that historically entrenched upper-class families were losing economic traction to the rising bourgeoisic. The debutante, as a commodity, fulfilled a basic economic function by infusing her cash-strapped noble family with 'new' money.

Robert Weir, *Class: An Encyclopaedia*

Prologue

Crabtree Wood, Kent – September 2014

Libby Mortimer stood still for a moment, watching the car's rear lights fade away as it disappeared from view. She heard the deep-throated purr of the engine as it accelerated up the hill and then the house and the countryside sank once more into soft silence. She pulled her cardigan around her, listening to the night sounds – an owl whooshing past, something rustling in the flowerbeds, the thin whine of a lone car coming down the hill out there beyond the fields. The house stood some way off the main road, hidden from view by a tall line of poplars. It had once been a country manor with several acres of surrounding woodland, but a succession of buyers had whittled the woods away until only the gardens and the orchard remained. In the autumn she picked apples and pears with whichever grandchildren happened to be visiting.

She turned around to look at it. Even after thirty years, its quiet elegance still took her breath away. Her home. She'd brought up her four children in it, turning it into the warm, safe haven that her own mother, Kit, had never quite managed to provide. Its pale yellow stone façade looked out across the driveway to the poplars, but the real face of the house lay on the other side, across a sloping garden of flowers and bees and moths to the long Kent valley. She could hear the dogs moving restlessly around in the kennels behind the garage. Someone had had the sense to switch off the stereo in the living room. For an hour or so before the port and the cigars they'd danced to the music they thought they'd forgotten – the Beatles, the Rolling Stones, the Clash – Kit looking on in mock horror.

'Come on, Nana, come and dance with me!' That was Tim, Maev's eldest.

Kit's mouth worked half humorously against itself. 'Don't be ridiculous! At my age?'

'Come on. It'll do you good!'

'Stop it at once, you devil. Stop it at once!' But Tim ignored her protests and pulled her to her feet. She was remarkable. A year short of ninety, shapely legs still elegantly narrowed at knee and ankle, picking up the beat with slow but careful ease. They'd all looked on indulgently. It was good to see Kit enjoying herself.

She stopped to brush her fingers against the lavender that grew in large terracotta pots next to the front door. She inhaled the peppery fragrance, nostrils prickling pleasurably as the scent overwhelmed her. She shivered slightly. It was nearly midnight and the air had abruptly turned cool. September. Autumn, glimpsed in the turning of a leaf from green to gold, was a whisper away. She pushed open the heavy wooden front door and left it partially ajar. It would take Toby the better part of an hour to drop Kit off, make sure she was settled in for the night and drive back. She opened the kitchen door and looked around. The long oak table was covered in half-full glasses and empty bottles of wine, one or two plates of half-eaten tarte tatin and that awful pudding that Eluned had insisted on making – something light and frothy on top and gelatinous and muddy underneath – which no one had touched. She pulled a quick, silly face – no one around to see! – and closed the door firmly behind her. Katie, her cleaning lady from the village, would come in the following morning and tackle it with her customary gusto.

The house was quiet, breathing softly the way old houses do: the odd creak of a floorboard; the gentle click as a bathroom door somewhere on the floor above was pushed shut; something – a stone, an apple? – falling on the ground outside. She counted all her guests off: Eluned, Luc and Loïc, their seventeen-year-old son, were there in the converted barn next to the orchard; Maev and her husband Bill were in the guest room on the first floor; Tim, their eldest, was sharing the small box room at the end of the landing with Cameron, his older half-brother from Bill's first marriage; *their* two little girls, Daisy and Zoë, were in the tiny box room that had once been a storage room on the second floor; Trin was in her old room; Emily was in hers, with Declan, the man she'd brought unexpectedly to the party; finally, Ro and her thirteen-year-old daughter, Phoebe, were in Ro's old bedroom. Only Duncan was missing. He was in Thailand, teaching English to gap-toothed, dark-haired children who stared politely into the camera alongside his girlfriend, Pim, who didn't look much older than the kids they taught. Libby half feared he would never return.

Fourteen guests: a full house but it had been months since she'd had everyone over to stay and she basked in the pleasure of it. She would leave Maev to organise brunch for everyone the following morning – Maev loved doing that sort of thing – and she and Ro would slip off to Rye for a spot of shopping, lunch and maybe even a walk down by the river. She smiled at the thought. It had been ages since she and Ro had had any time to themselves. They talked on the phone every week, of course, but it wasn't the same. None of her four children lived nearby. Ro was in Hammersmith, in a box of a flat that wasn't much bigger than the hallway, but which she insisted was enough for her and Phoebe. Jake, Ro's ex-husband and the father of her only child still lived in New York, where Phoebe was born. She still carried with her the trace of an American accent even though it had been nearly five years since Ro walked out on Jake, taking just two suitcases and her seven-year-old daughter with her. Jake had Phoebe every summer and every other Christmas – one reason her accent had never quite disappeared, perhaps, although Libby privately thought there were other, deeper reasons. But Jake was off-limits as far as Ro was concerned. The subject of Phoebe's lingering and persistent American accent was never broached. She sighed suddenly. Three children, two divorces. Already. What had gone wrong?

Her eyes suddenly fell on the box of photographs that Kit had handed to her, just before leaving. 'Put them into one of those lovely albums of yours,' she'd said, holding Libby by the arm, her grip surprisingly strong.

'What are they?' she'd asked curiously.

'Oh, nothing much … just a few old pictures. Found them the other day when I was clearing out one of the cupboards. Won't you put them into some sort of order for me, darling? The children might find them interesting. Show them what dancing's *really* like.' Her eyes twinkled mischievously.

Libby had nodded absent-mindedly and set the box down, forgetting it immediately afterwards in the wake of their other guests' departures. She picked it up now and was surprised at its weight; there were clearly more than a few old pictures in there. She carried it over to one of the sofas and sat down. There was a half-full bottle of wine on the side table. She picked it up and peered at the label, fumbling for her glasses. A

Bordeaux, probably one of the bottles Eluned and Luc had brought with them from France. She looked around for an empty glass and poured herself a half glass. It would help her sleep. She took a small sip, the velvety richness curling pleasurably against her tongue. She lifted the box onto her lap and opened it. The scent of old photographs, musty air and the trace of L'air du Temps and cigarettes that was unmistakably Kit rushed up to meet her. She closed her eyes for a second. It was the scent of childhood, of *all* their childhoods. Then she picked up the photograph that lay on top of the pile. It was of Kit as a little girl – aged perhaps six or seven – astride a pony. She recognised the paddock, which lay beyond the woods at Chalfont Hall. The photograph was black-and-white, of course, but even at that distance and across all those years, she could still make out Kit's piercing eyes, staring out at the world in that artful combination of curiosity and bold-faced accusation that was specifically hers.

She tipped the box carefully upside down – there were perhaps forty or fifty yellowing, sepia-tinted prints with a few more recent ones thrown in – and spread the contents on the rug at her feet. She bent low and rifled through them quickly, already thinking ahead to the album she would make: the choice of leather; thin, vellum insert sheets; the exact lettering. It was the sort of task she loved doing. She set the empty box down but as she did so, felt something else inside it move. She frowned and shook it against her ear. It was completely empty but there was something hidden in it somewhere. She peered inside it and noticed that the paper lining had come away in places. Using a fingernail, she carefully peeled it to one side, trying not to tear it. The box had a false bottom; there was something concealed in the narrow gap between the two layers of cardboard – a thick, padded envelope. She pulled it out slowly. It was unsealed and the flap opened as soon as she touched it. Two photographs slid out from between the sheets of crinkled thin blue paper. She turned them over, recognising the penmanship immediately – it was a younger, firmer version of Kit's hand. *18th December 1958. Muscat.* There was a sentence scribbled across the back of one of the photographs: *Driving down to Daghmar with al-Said to meet Eden and old Glubb.* She could hear Kit's voice, girlish yet commanding with the perfect enunciation and diction of her time and class.

She picked up the letter and began to read. It was long, nearly five pages, and it had been written recently.

There are things I've wanted to tell you, my darling Libby. So many times I've started, then stopped. I lack courage, I know. I expect you'll find that odd, coming from me, but it's true. I've been cowardly, especially with you.

Her heart started to accelerate. She turned the pages over, one after the other, incredulity rising in her chest and throat.

It was well after midnight by the time she'd finished reading. She sat in the armchair, too stunned to think.

Kit. Oh, Kit. Why did you wait so long?

PART ONE

WAR

1938–1939
Kit

1

There was a car winding its way slowly up the long drive towards the house. From where she stood on a chair, turning slowly, an inch at a time, waiting for the dressmaker to finish, she was able to chart its progress through the line of stately cedars that ran up the incline from the river to the house. She stood on tiptoe, craning her neck as the car swung in a wide arc into the forecourt, scattering gravel left and right. Somewhere, far below in the servants' quarters, she could hear the faint ringing of a bell and the slam of a door. Someone of importance had arrived.

'For goodness' sake, Kit, stand up straight. She'll never get the hem right if you keep fidgeting like that.' Her mother spoke up sharply from the corner of the room. The dressmaker's mouth was full of pins so she herself couldn't speak. Snips of the material like small shards of glass lay across the floor. The dress was pale green with an Empire waist and long, puffy sleeves. Kit didn't much like it. The material was stiff and unyielding and she thought the colour unflattering. It made her look like a corpse. (Not that she'd ever actually seen a corpse, of course, but the description of the unfortunate Ratchett in *Murder on the Orient Express* was terribly graphic and for a while she *thought* she'd actually seen it. Pale, with a bluish tinge, skin like marbled fat.) She shuddered then turned. Again. *Slowly.* She looked out of the window once more. The sky was clear and perfectly blue. It was June and the weather was hot, the days long and seemingly endless. But instead of escaping to the pond at the bottom of the valley with her books and a jam sandwich, she thought resentfully, here she was, standing on a chair in the drawing room whilst a pasty-faced French woman on her knees stuck pins in her calves. It was all on account of Lily, her older sister. Lily was eighteen and about to be presented at Court. For weeks the household had been in a frenzy of excitement, no one able to speak or think of anything else, certainly not Lily. She could think of nothing else.

'Oh,' she declared a dozen times a day to anyone in earshot, clasping her hands to her chest in an exaggerated pose of impatience. 'I cannot *wait*! I positively cannot *wait*! It's going to be *so* much fun!'

Kit was beginning to hate the sound of the word. How could standing around in some draughty hall in clothes that took two hours to get into, shoes that hurt and a silly smile plastered across your face listening to some half-witted young man with pimples, who was only there because *his* parents knew *your* parents, possibly be construed as fun?

'Kit! Pay attention, will you? Turn around. Slowly, *slowly*.'

'How much longer, Mama?' Kit sighed.

'Until it's *finished*. Lift your arms up, over your head. Otherwise your dress won't hang properly. Isn't that right, Mademoiselle Founard?'

'*Oui, madame.*'

It was all Mademoiselle Founard ever said. The dressmaker scrambled to her feet and at last Kit was allowed to climb down off the chair. She wriggled out of the pale green confection and quickly pulled on her pinafore, hoping to slip out of the room before another excuse was found to pin, tuck or squeeze her into shape … any shape. At fourteen and three-quarters she was still a beanpole – as flat as a pancake, unlike Lily, who spilled out of her dresses in the most alarming way. Kit couldn't imagine ever spilling out of anything, let alone a dress.

'Kit?' Her mother's voice stopped her just before she reached the door.

'Yes, Mama?' She turned, her hand hovering impatiently over the handle.

'You're to have supper in the nursery tonight. Lily will be joining Papa and I for dinner.'

Kit's mouth opened on a note of protest. 'But that's not fair! You said yesterday that—'

'No "buts". You're to have supper with Nanny and that's that.' Her mother's face had quickly taken on the distant coldness that Kit hated.

She swallowed her protest. 'Yes, Mama,' she said meekly.

She opened the door and shut it behind her. The grandfather clock in the hallway chimed loudly. It was five o'clock. If she were quick about it, there was just enough time to run down to the stables and feed the ponies before it was time for her solitary supper.

She marched down the hill at the back of the house, her feet thudding in a satisfyingly mutinous way. Maisie, her mother's long-eared cocker spaniel, trotted along obediently behind her, turning moist, anxious eyes up towards her every few seconds in hope of an instruction of some sort. Kit stomped along, distracted, torn between her recent irritation with Lily and the fuss she was making over coming out, and trepidation that the same fate might await her in three years' time. Part of it had to do with money. Everyone was quietly desperate for Lily to make what they called 'a good match'. She knew that much, even though no one spoke openly about it – least of all to her. In everyone's eyes, especially Lily's and her parents', Kit was still a child, not old enough to understand anything of importance, least of all the world of adults. But Kit had long understood that the only way to get to the heart of anything was not to ask, it was simply to listen, and she was very good at it. Unlike Lily, who was all talk – principally about *her* – Kit hung back. Even as a very young child she'd learned how to make her silences comfortable. Where Lily ate up everyone's attention, unable to bear it if all eyes in the room weren't directed at her, Kit deflected it neatly. When people talked, she *listened*, not just to the words but to the other, more hidden signs – the way a face might redden suddenly, or a quick, sideways glance that betrayed nervousness, or the way someone might cross their arms against their chest or develop a sudden itch. The *real* conversation, Kit surmised at a surprisingly young age, was invariably conducted somewhere else, buried in the myriad little giveaways that the body gave out, irrespective and sometimes ignorant of words.

She'd overheard her mother once saying, 'Oh, Lily'll be no trouble at all. She'll be married by eighteen, you mark my words. But Kit ... I don't know. Kit's ... well, she's *different*.' She gave a little laugh. 'Difficult. Mama always said she was *fey*.'

Kit hadn't waited to find out whom her mother was talking to. She hurried away from the door and made straight for the library. She hauled down the enormous leather-bound dictionary that was very nearly her favourite book and eagerly looked up the mysterious word.

From Middle English fey (fated to die), from Old English fǣge (doomed to die, timid), from Proto-Germanic faigijaz (cowardly, wicked), from Proto-Indo-European *pAik-, *pAig- (ill-meaning, bad). Akin to Old Saxon fēgi, whence Dutch veeg (doomed, near death), Old High German feigi (appointed for death, ungodly), whence German feige (cowardly), Old Norse feigr (doomed), whence the Icelandic feigur (doomed to die), Old English fāh (outlawed, hostile).

She'd closed the dictionary with a snap, frowning. All the 'whences' were making her head spin. Doomed to die? That didn't sound very nice.

She pushed open the wooden gate that led to the stables, making sure it was closed firmly behind her. Only the other week Lily had decided on a whim to go riding and instructed Benny, the lad in charge of the horses, to saddle up her favourite mare. At the last minute, typical of Lily, she'd changed her mind and made them saddle up one of Papa's mounts. She'd left Midnight standing in the yard and galloped off, leaving the gate open. Midnight, seeing her chance, bolted, of course. It took Benny and Mr Hinkley, Papa's gamekeeper, the better part of the evening to find Midnight and bring her back.

'Did she really?' was Lily's only comment at breakfast the next morning. 'Ooh, the naughty *thing*.'

Kit held her breath, expecting Papa to roar at her from behind his morning paper. He didn't. He rustled the paper once, twice ... and nothing further was said. Kit sat opposite, marvelling at the way Lily got away with everything. She wasn't resentful; luckily for both, they wanted such different things – even as young children – that there was no real competition between them. Kit admired Lily – when she wasn't irritated by her – but she'd also long grasped their fundamental difference. She, Kit, was terribly, intently interested in the world and everything it had to offer – good, bad, horrid, gay. Lily was not. Lily was interested in one thing only: Lily. The world – insofar as she noticed it – was simply *there*, a generally agreeable backdrop to her passions, which centred chiefly around parties, clothes, young men and fun. That word again.

She walked into the cool dampness of the arcade where the horses were stabled, which held a climate all of its own, dank and sweet-smelling. She lifted the lid on the barrel where Benny stored the leftover over-ripe apples that had fallen in the orchard and picked a few out. Maisie ambled along beside her, her nose twitching uncontrollably in excitement. Kit stopped beside Hands-Down, one of her favourite ponies. He must have sensed her arrival; as soon as she opened the upper door to his stall, his long, handsome face was thrust out to meet her, his eyes going impatiently to her pinafore pocket.

'There you go,' she said, smiling, as she pulled out the small, rosy apple. It disappeared immediately. For a few moments, the sound of crunching was the only audible noise in the stables. Kit watched him munching away contentedly. Her mind drifted back to the house and the arrival of unknown guests. She wondered who they could be. Someone important, she decided. Why would she be banished to the nursery otherwise? It was a good thing they were having guests; the atmosphere in the house had been gloomy for weeks. There was a great uncertainty in the air that even the animals seemed to have picked up on. It was expressed in the way Father pulled on his pipe – desperately, as though he were sucking the curved wooden handle deep down into his lungs along with the pungent smoke. It was in Mother's face every time the phone rang or she noticed that Father had left the transistor on in the dining room and forgotten to turn it off again. Their expressions were pinched, tense, as though waiting for some dreadful announcement to be made. Kit could sense it too downstairs in the kitchen whenever she came in, especially amongst the men. Caruthers, her father's valet, had fought in the Boer War in some distant, far-off past and land, and she'd come across him practically shouting at Billy Marchmont.

'If there's goin' t' be a war, I can't wait t' get over there,' Billy said just as Kit opened the door.

'My lad, there's nowt glamorous about it,' she heard Caruthers say sternly. 'There's nowt glamorous about war, I can tell you that for free. And those that think there is are either plain ignorant or stupid, or both.'

'I'm only just *sayin'*—' Billy began, his voice suddenly full of aggrieved exasperation.

'Don't,' Caruthers interrupted him. 'You don't know what you're talking about and neither do you, Bignell. Now, have you finished polishing them boots I gave you this afternoon? No? Well, what are you waiting for? Come on, look lively, Bignell! His Lordship doesn't pay us to stand around gossiping.' Caruthers marched off, his heels clacking loudly on the stone floor.

Kit hung back for a moment or two, wondering if she would hear what Billy Marchmont and Bignell really thought about war, but they both walked off without saying anything more.

By five thirty, she'd emptied her pockets. All the apples were gone, cores, pips, skins and all. She patted Hands-Down once more and called Maisie to heel. They set off back up the hill at a brisk pace. It was nearly suppertime and there'd be no pudding if she were late. As they hurried past the walled garden and the greenhouse, she saw a long, black, shiny car snaking its way along the driveway, then another. She stopped. Maisie stopped too and anxiously looked up at her, waiting for instruction. She scooped her up, feeling the dog's excited heartbeat against her stomach.

'Come on, Maisie,' she whispered, nuzzling Maisie's blonde, shaggy hair. 'Let's go and see Cook. Let's find out who's here.'

Maisie's ears pricked up, though for other reasons. Cook could always be counted on for titbits. Kit hurried up to the back door, struggling to hold onto Maisie and narrowly avoiding the two footmen who were rushing out to meet the cars.

The kitchens were a hive of frenzied activity.

'Who's here?' she asked Cook, her eyes wide with astonishment. She'd never seen the thirty-odd staff in such a tizzy. Cook was shouting at three of the scullery maids almost simultaneously; Doyle, the butler, was inspecting the wines as though his life depended on it; three footmen were furiously polishing the silver trays. Maisie, excited by the bustle and the noise, started to bark.

'Get that dog out of here!' Cook turned around and shouted at her. 'Go on. You know how I feel about dogs in the kitchen!'

Kit scooped Maisie up guiltily.

'I'll take her upstairs.' Sophie, Mama's housemaid, appeared suddenly in the doorway, a pile of floaty, diaphanous garments in her arms. 'Come on, Maisie.' She turned and hurried up the stairs, Maisie hot on her heels.

'Who's here?' Kit asked Cook again. There was a fraction of a second's awkward pause. Cook and Mrs Baxter, the housekeeper, exchanged a hurried, furtive glance. Kit frowned. Something was up.

'Never you mind,' Cook said finally, brusquely. 'Now, run along, wash your face and tidy your hair. Her Ladyship says you're to have supper in half an hour. In the nursery,' she added sternly.

'But—'

'No "buts". Run along now.'

Kit bit her lip. Better not to argue. It was a toss-up as to who was more fearful when angry – Mama or Cook. She turned away. Well, if *they* wouldn't tell her who was coming to dinner, she knew one person who would. The one person at Chalfont who was incapable of keeping anything to herself: her sister.

*

She pushed open the door to Lily's bedroom, which was twice the size of Kit's and nearly as big as Mama's – on account of her 'clothes and things', Lily told their cousins on the rare occasion they drove down from the Borders. Glenda, the eldest cousin, declared she'd never seen so many gowns, 'not even in the shops in Princes Street'. Lily, Kit remembered, was ridiculously pleased by the comment.

'Don't you ever *knock*?' Lily said crossly, looking behind her in the mirror. She was sitting in front of her dressing table, her face dreamily occupied with her own image as her housemaid stood behind her, endlessly fixing and refixing her hair.

'Sorry,' Kit mumbled. Why was Lily in such a bad mood?

'Well? Spit it out. What *is* it?' she said impatiently.

Kit sat down gingerly on the edge of the bed. Although she and Lily had never been particularly close – too different in their tastes and interests to share much beyond the fact that they were sisters – now that Lily was about to be presented, the likelihood of her swift departure from Chalfont was slowly becoming a distinct possibility – a probability, even – and Kit wasn't quite sure how she felt about it. The truth of the matter was that life at Chalfont was lonely. There were few children their own age anywhere in the vicinity. She and Lily had shared the same nursery and schoolroom for as long as she could remember. They'd moved through the same landscapes, lived in the same two bedrooms on the second floor of the house that had been in their family for generations, and had spent hours together, especially when they were very little. She didn't much *like* Lily – she'd long understood that it wasn't an automatic precondition of family that you actually liked one another – but she loved her sister all the same. She thought there would never come a time when Lily would move off into some adult space and world, beyond hers. But now Lily had. Kit felt it keenly, watching her sister stare at her own image in an even more distracted way than Mama, losing herself in the same silent contemplation of her own beauty. There was no getting away from it, either. Lily *was* beautiful. It began with her hair: thick, dark and auburn, that cascaded down her back in a shimmering waterfall of glossy waves. Green, almond-shaped eyes with thick black lashes and a small, perfectly shaped retroussé nose, a 'darling little button of a nose', as their grandmother, the Dowager Lady Wharton, always said. The comment was invariably followed by a sideways glance at Kit's nose, which wasn't in the slightest bit retroussé. The opposite. Kit had inherited her father's features: a strong, square jaw and piercing grey-blue eyes, thick, dark blonde hair – handsome enough in a man but a little unnerving in a teenage girl.

'Still,' as Grandmamma was wont to add, 'can't be helped. The child must learn to work with what she's got.'

Kit wasn't quite sure what that was, or might be, but it seemed to placate Mother.

'Why are *you* going down to dinner and *I'm* not?' she asked Lily finally. 'Who's here? And why's everyone making such a fuss?'

'Because.' Lily answered in that new, maddeningly grown-up way of hers.

'Because *what*?'

'Because it's a grown-ups' dinner.'

'But *you're* not a grown-up! You haven't come out yet!' Kit burst out.

'In three weeks' time I will. Besides, Papa's making a special exception for tonight. It's a very important dinner. Papa said it's *very* important that I'm there.'

'But *why*? And why won't you just tell me who it is?'

Just then another car pulled up on the driveway below, noisily scattering gravel. Kit slid off the bed and walked over to the window. There were now six or seven chauffeured cars forming a half-circle in front of the house. She glanced back at Lily, who was still deciding which necklace to wear. Her housemaid stood patiently to attention. Kit shook her head. She would get nothing further from her. Lily was lost to herself and the perfection of her looks.

'I'm going,' Kit said dramatically, her hand on the door handle. Neither Lily nor the housemaid even looked up.

But Kit wasn't beaten. She closed the door behind her as loudly as she dared and hurried down the corridor. There was a broom cupboard halfway down that connected to the servants' stairs, but before she could reach it, she heard voices in the hallway below. She stopped, flattening herself against the wall, her heart pounding. If Mama caught sight of her she'd be lucky to escape without a sharp smack. If there was one thing Mama couldn't bear, it was an eavesdropper.

'It's *so* good of you to come, Minister. We've been looking forward to your visit for *weeks*.' Her mother's voice, silky and welcoming.

'Indeed.' Her father spoke, establishing his presence and authority with just a single word.

'Why, thank you, Lord Wharton. Most kind.' A deep voice, a foreign voice. *Lord Vorton.* Kit frowned, recognition slowly dawning. A *German* voice.

'And Baroness von Riedesal … *so* delighted you're here with us.' Her father.

There was a pretty little tinkle of laughter. 'Thank you, we are also delighted to be here. May I present my cousin, Hans-Georg Schmidt von Altenstadt.'

'De*light*ed to meet you. Please, gentlemen, Baroness, do come this way. Dinner will be served in an hour, but first you must make yourselves comfortable. I trust the journey over was smooth?'

'*Ja, ja.* Everything was fine. Via Paris. Crossing was not too bad.'

'Still, it's a long way from Berlin. Do come this way.'

Kit pulled a face. So they *were* German, after all. Was it possible the visit was connected to the speech she'd heard the prime minister make over the wireless a few days earlier? Something to do with Hitler and the violation of the Treaty of Versailles. She'd asked Miss Frogworth, their teacher, what it meant but she was either unwilling or unable to tell her.

She waited until the sounds of their footsteps had died away and then she carefully opened the door to the broom cupboard, which opened onto the servants' staircase on the other side. She hurried down the stone steps, her mind whirling with a dozen unanswered questions.

Supper was a dismal affair. Everything about the nursery reinforced her sense of having been banished from the exciting world of grown-ups. Even the cake that Cook had sent up – clementine cake, decorated with icing and thin ribbons of lemon zest – failed to improve her mood.

'Don't you want any?' Nanny asked, cutting herself a generous slice, which she quickly polished off without waiting for an answer.

Kit shook her head mutinously. 'No.'

'It's delicious,' Nanny said, cutting another slice. 'Really delicious,' she added, just in case Kit might have missed the point.

'Can I go now?'

'Go where?' Nanny looked up nervously.

'To bed. I'm going to read my book.'

It wasn't even half past seven. The dinner gong had only just gone. Nanny was torn between putting her feet up and finishing off the rest of the cake or trying to coax a conversation out of a sulky teenager.

'Very well, then,' she said at last, the temptation of cake having clearly won out. 'I'll ask Mary to draw you a bath.'

'I had one yesterday,' Kit said hurriedly, already nearly at the door. 'Mummy said I don't have to have another one until the weekend.' She could see the hesitation flit across Nanny's face. There was no way to verify the matter.

'Very well,' she said again. She opened her mouth to issue another rule but Kit was already gone. She closed the door firmly behind her and took off down the corridor at full gallop. She was determined to find out why her parents had invited *Germans* to Chalfont Hall and why they were so insistent on having Lily join them. She knew exactly how to find out. As drastic and distasteful as it seemed, there was only one way to understand what was going on – and that was to spy on them. It was underhand, granted, and a little sneaky, but under the circumstances, it was the *only* way to find out what was really going on. And that, in itself, seemed reason enough to do it. In her search for the truth, nothing could – or should – be ruled out. What was it she'd read the other day? '*"Beauty is truth, truth beauty," —that is all; Ye know on earth, and all ye need to know.*' Keats. It seemed to her as perfect a pronouncement on life as any she'd ever read. Although she did rather like Lord Byron. He possessed a wry, humorous wisdom that appealed greatly to her, especially his descriptions of women. '*Man's love is of man's life a thing apart; 'Tis woman's whole existence . . . In her first passion woman loves her lover; In all the others all she loves is love.*' She remembered precisely the day Miss Frogworth had given Byron's slim volume of poetry to her and Lily to read. She'd opened it on the fourth or fifth page and smiled widely as she devoured the words.

'Do you find him funny, Kit?' Miss Frogworth asked, a trifle icily.

Kit looked up, surprised. 'No, not funny at all. I think he's perfectly right.' She glanced at Lily, who was staring out of the window, her chin cupped in her hand. 'Don't you, Lily?'

Lily turned around and blinked slowly. The book lay unopened on her desk. 'Don't I what?' she asked, puzzled as to why anyone would address her.

'Don't you think it's true?'

Lily shrugged. 'I've no idea what you're talking about and I don't care, either. Can't we go, Miss Frogworth? We been shut up in here for ages.'

Miss Frogworth opened her mouth to say something – in protest, perhaps? – but then clearly thought better of it. 'Yes, you may go,' she said resignedly.

Kit looked from one to the other. As ever, it seemed to matter little what she thought, if she were enjoying the lesson or not. It was Lily's view that counted and the supreme irony of the situation was that *she generally didn't have one.*

Kit picked up the offending book and trudged disconsolately out of the nursery. Lessons were over. When she got back to her room and flung herself onto her bed, the book opened accidently on a poem that had been penned for her, only her. *'If I could always read, I should never feel the want of company.'*

Now, waiting for her moment, she listened until the two footmen had disappeared down the stairs and then ran across the hallway, quick as a flash, and slipped into the library. Her heart was pounding as much with exhilaration as with fear. She hurried over to the bookcase behind her father's desk, pulled out the two books that covered the latch to the revolving shelf and pushed. It opened with a creak and a fusty cold breath. She inhaled sharply. She pulled the door shut behind her and swallowed down on a hard little knot of fear. It was pitch-black inside, and tiny, little more than a cupboard between the dining room and the library. She hated the dark but her fear was a small price to pay, she reasoned with herself sternly. If she pressed her ear tightly against the wall, she'd be able to hear everything that was said at the dinner table, almost like being in the room herself. She inched her way closer to the wall and pressed her face against it. There was a sudden burst of laughter and the sound of a chair being scraped backwards.

'May I propose a toast?' It was the same voice she'd heard before, greeting Father and Mother.

'Hear, hear.' There were all-round murmurs of approval. How many guests? It was hard to tell… Six, eight perhaps?

'To our hosts, Lord and Lady Wharton. We wish to thank you – all of *Germany* wishes to thank you – for your marvellous hospitality. It's good to know we have friends in these difficult times.'

'Indeed.' That was her father. 'Solidarity's the thing. Especially now.'

'Solidarity.' The word echoed up and down the table.

'And, if I may be permitted, another toast.' The German-inflected voice commanded attention. 'This time to your lovely daughter, Lilliane. To Lilliane.'

'To Lilliane.' Again, there was another murmured echo down the length of the table.

Kit pulled a face of disbelief. Her name wasn't Lilliane; it was Elizabeth! She could hear Lily's new laugh, that high-pitched polite little tinkle, which was nothing at all like her real laugh. A flush of embarrassment flowed through Kit. It was so … silly!

Her father's voice came booming through the walls. 'Shall we?'

It was the signal for everyone to leave the table. The ladies would go through to the front parlour room where Lily, if she were asked, might play the piano and the men would follow her father into his library for port and cigars. There was a great deal of chatter as the party broke up and the dining room emptied. She could hear the men coming through to the library on one side and the servants hurrying into the dining room on the other. She crouched down, sandwiched between the two worlds, listening to both.

'…Magnificent home you have here, Lord Wharton. You must come to visit us in Germany when this is all over.'

'I should like that very much indeed. I haven't been back to Germany since, well … for some time now.'

'…Eddie! Look lively, lad! You're not here to gawp at the paintings.'

'Sorry, Mr Edwards, just coming, Mr Edwards.'

'Who's coming in with me to serve the port? Annie, have you got the ladies' drinks?'

'Yes, Mr Edwards, I've got the tray right here.'

'…On that other matter, Lord Wharton … perhaps we could …?'

'Ah, yes … yes, of course … Why don't we talk over there, by the window? Won't do to have everyone listening.'

'…Hurry up, James. We can't keep his Lordship waiting…'

It seemed to take the servants an age to clear away the remains of dinner but at last Kit heard the sound of footsteps in the long corridor dying away. She opened the cupboard door and stuck her head cautiously out. The library was completely empty. She hurried to the door, checked that the hallway too was clear and then made her way as stealthily as possible to the stairs. She was almost halfway up when she heard Lily's voice. She crouched down and peered through the bannisters. Lily was standing below, half hidden by the enormous palm tree that stood in the hallway. She was talking to someone who was hidden from view. Her voice was high with excitement.

'Do you *really*? Oh, I'd *love* to see it!'

'Well, we must arrange a visit. I will be very happy to show it to you.' *I vill be heppy to show it to you.*

Kit drew in a sharp breath. He was German! Lily was talking to one of the Germans! There was a moment's prolonged pause. She craned her neck but caught a glimpse only of a pair of highly polished boots before the door to the library was opened and he vanished. For a second, there was complete silence. Through the palm fronds, Kit saw Lily's hand move upwards, as if in slow motion, to her lips: she'd been kissed. Then the door to the library opened, there was a flurry of apologies as one of the servants came upon the teenager, who stood as if she'd grown roots, and then Mother's voice: 'Lily? Where *are* you? We're waiting to hear you play!'

'I'm coming, Mama. Coming.'

Kit's breath came in short spurts. Suddenly, the line she'd been waiting for had come upon them and was crossed. Lily was gone.

2

Chalfont Hall – 1939 (six months later)

Why was it, Kit wondered, hurriedly spooning another dollop of mashed potato onto her plate before Mother noticed, that all the important facts about the family were always gleaned from others' conversations, never, ever told to her directly? In the six months since Lily's abrupt marriage and equally abrupt departure for Germany, almost everything she'd heard about her sister and her new life had come to her via someone else's recollection or recount. Why didn't anyone, including Lily, think it important to tell her what was going on? Why did no one think it mattered?

'What on *earth* do you mean?' Father's voice broke into the silence at the table.

Kit watched, her spoon halfway to her mouth, as Mother struggled to read to the end of the thin parchment paper. 'I ... I don't understand it,' she said at last. Her voice sounded very far away.

There was a second's pause before Father's fist came down on the table with an almighty 'whack', causing the glasses and the cutlery to jump. Out of the corner of Kit's eye she saw Bignell flinch. 'Say it, goddammit! What has that blasted girl gone and *done*?'

'I ... I'm not ... I'm not sure,' Mother stammered. It was the first time Kit had ever seen Mother lost for words. She, who was usually in command of everything, especially her own words, was stammering. 'She ... it seems as though ... she's met someone, a friend. Another English girl.'

'Who? Goddammit, woman! Tell me what's going on!'

'I ... she went with U—'

'Katherine. Leave the room.' Father's voice was suddenly – and dangerously – quiet.

'But—'

'Kit, do as your father says.'

'But—'

Another fist came down upon the table, louder this time. Even Bignell, doing his best to stand still and to attention, jumped.

Kit didn't wait to be told a second time. She slid off the chair and slid as unobtrusively as possible out of the room. She hurried across the hallway but instead of heading for the stairs, she opened the door to the library and hurried to her trusted hiding spot at the far end of the room. She yanked open the door; the cold air rushed out to meet her. She slipped into the darkness and crouched down. Mother's voice drifted through the walls.

'I think she's really gone and done it this time.'

'Spit it out, woman.'

'She's ... she's with that blasted Mitford girl. They've gone to see ... Hitler.'

There was a sudden silence. 'Bignell. You'd best leave.'

'Yes, your Lordship.'

There was the sound of the door opening and closing almost silently. Kit's breathing was harsh and loud in her ears.

'So, what do you propose? Should we ... send someone?' Mother asked.

Father snorted. 'Whom do you suggest? And to do what, exactly?'

'Bring her back!' Mother's voice was anguished.

'She's *married*, for goodness' sake! To that insufferable Kraut. Have you forgotten how keen you were on the whole damn thing? Now look where it's got us.'

'That's not fair, Harold. *You* were every bit as keen. Besides, what else could we have done? He was absolutely smitten! And once the news got out... well, who'd have wanted her on *our* side? No one.'

There was another tense silence. 'Well, no use going over *that* sorry business now,' her father said finally, tetchily. 'Point is, there's nothing we can do. She's his problem, not ours.'

'Harold! How can you say that? There's Kit to think of... If word gets out that she's with the Mitford girl—'

'Word's already out, woman!' Father snapped. 'Trust me, Liddell already knows. And if *he* knows—'

'We can't just wash our hands of her! She's our daughter, Harold. And as I said, there's Kit to think of. We've *got* to think of Kit. What are her chances if—'

'Oh, for goodness' sake! Haven't we got enough to worry about without thinking about that blasted girl? It's not as if she's doing anything to improve her chances, either. Moping about that long face. She's beginning to look like those damned horses she spends all day with. How's she ever going to—'

'Harold!' Mama interrupted, sounding horrified.

'Well, it's true. Oh, for God's sake, let's talk about something else.' Kit heard her father pick up and ring the bell angrily. 'Ah, Bignell. There you are. Was beginning to think you'd forgotten us.'

'No, your Lordship.'

'Right. What's for afters?'

And that was that. That part of the conversation was over. Kit waited tensely, but nothing more was said. There was only the sound of cutlery clinking against porcelain as Father polished off both his and Mother's helping of sticky suet pudding. Kit had watched Cook prepare it the night before. No jam, of course. It was 1939 and sugar was in short supply. 'I'm not wastin' half a pound on pudding!' was Cook's dismissive reply. ''E's to learn to like it without.' It amused Kit no end to hear Cook talk about His Lordship when he was safely out of earshot. Neither would have so much as dared lift an eyebrow or change expression in his presence.

She could hear Bignell creeping around the dining room, removing plates. The atmosphere was as tense and sharp as one of Cook's long-handled knives.

'Thank you, Bignell.'

'Thank you, your Lordship.'

Nothing more was said. Mother and Father pushed back their chairs and left the dining room in silence.

Kit sat back on her haunches, too puzzled by the conversation to leave just yet. She picked up the thick, fat end of her plait and brushed it against her lips. None of it made sense. What was the 'sorry business'? 'That Mitford girl' had to be Unity Mitford. She'd read about her in Father's copy of the *Daily Mirror* that he'd left in the dining room. It was all about a list of names she'd supposedly given the German leader of people who she thought ought to be shot. Naturally, it had caused an outcry in Britain. But how on earth had Lily gone and got herself mixed up with it? Lily didn't have a political bone or interest in her body. She *hated* politics! Well, whatever was going on, it was infinitely more interesting than the other thread to the conversation: *We've got to think about Kit. She's beginning to look like one of those blasted horses.*

She often wondered if they knew just how little she cared. The story was always the same. She was aware of the delicate but complex relationship between her 'future' – whatever or wherever that might be – and her looks. Nothing else seemed to matter. Least of all the fact that, aged fifteen, she was already the county's most competent horsewoman or that she'd read practically every book in Father's library. She could – and frequently did – hold forth on practically any topic someone cared to throw at her. Only a month ago, it had prompted Miss Frogworth to throw up her hands in despair, claiming there wasn't anything else she could teach the girl.

'I don't know where she gets it from,' Kit once overhead Mother saying to Lady Wendham, their neighbour on the estate across the river and one of the very few visitors to the house these days. 'Certainly not from me. Harold says I shouldn't encourage her, but what can I do? I can't ban her from reading, can I?'

'Better put a stop to it before it's too late,' Lady Wendham muttered cryptically.

'I think it's *already* too late,' Mother said, sighing.

Too late for what? Kit wondered. Now, sitting with her knees hunched painfully up to her chest, straining to hear the last bits of conversation that might shed some light on what was happening to Lily a thousand miles away, it was clear that things were becoming ever more complicated. It was all beginning to blur: Lily; the 'Mitford woman'; Germany; the talk of impending war; Kit's 'chances'. The facts and snippets were beginning to merge into one another until she could no longer distinguish between them and figure out for herself what was worth listening to and therefore acting upon.

She inched her way out of the cupboard, pausing only to make sure there was no one on the other side of the door, before standing up and dusting herself down. She scraped her thick blonde hair back into its habitual plait and made sure her dress wasn't dirty. She had to talk to Mother. There was something she needed to find out.

'Where did you hear that name?' Mother looked up from her cards in alarm.

Kit paused. She hadn't thought of that. 'Um, I... I heard it on the wireless.'

'*What* did you hear?'

'Nothing, really,' Kit lied. 'Just... just the name. I thought I knew... I mean, I thought it might be someone you know.'

'No, well, I know the *family*, of course. A *very* good family,' Mother added quickly.

'What did she do?'

'Who?'

'Unity. The Mitford... girl.'

There was a moment's awkward silence. Mother looked down at her cards, arranged her hand more decisively and then looked up. 'She's gone and introduced your sister to Hitler. Odious little man.'

'That's what they said.'

'Who?'

'The radio presenter. On the news. They said... that she – they – were at Nuremburg, at the party rally. There's even a photo, apparently.'

'Oh, dear God.' Mother's face turned a chalky shade of pale. 'That's it, then,' she said tightly, after a moment. 'She's sealed her fate.'

'What does *that* mean?'

There was another painful silence. Then Mother turned her face up towards Kit. There was a look of such anguish on it that Kit took an involuntary step backwards. She'd never seen Mother look so frightened before. Beneath the powdered cheeks was a pallor that spoke of emotions foreign to Chalfont Hall. Mother belonged to the generation and class of women who kept their feelings very firmly to *themselves*: tightly bound, locked behind clenched teeth, deep sighs and the occasional – very occasional – sharp intake of breath.

'Look, there's nothing for it, I'm afraid. You'll have to go and get her, Kit. Bring her back. Back home. Before something terrible happens and she won't ever be able to leave.'

Kit stared at her mother. This wasn't what she'd been expecting. '*Me?*' she said, with a degree of incredulity that would ordinarily have earned her a rebuke. 'I'm only fifteen!'

'You speak German, don't you? *And* you can go with Uncle Faunce.' Mother spoke as if she hadn't heard her. 'Yes, that'll be best. It's no use sending Father to fetch her. They'd only fight and then she'll refuse to come home. But you and Uncle Faunce could do it. You could both try and persuade her. I know you and your sister don't always get along but it's different now. There's going to be a war. You do know that, Kit, don't you? Everyone says so.'

'But my German's not really *that* good,' Kit said, so alarmed by the suggestion that she couldn't even hear what her mother was saying about an impending war. 'Why me?'

'Why, you're her *sister*,' Mother said, glaring at her. 'What other possible reason do you need?'

3

'Now, have you got everything? It'll be cold, you know. Colder than it is here, that's for sure. I'm not sure those Germans have heating.' Nanny looked on sourly as Kit finished putting the last of her clothes in a small leather suitcase, embossed rather grandly with the initials *H.L.P.G.A-W.* The case had belonged to her grandfather and, judging by its silky smooth patina, probably to his father before him. All first-born sons in the Algernon-Waters family bore the same names – Harold Lawrence Peregrine Gordon Algernon-Waters. Father was the 2nd Baron of Wharton in the County of Dorset, just as his forebears had been the 1st Baron or the 11th Earl, whatever the titles might have been.

'Of course they've got heating,' Kit protested mildly. 'Didn't you read Lily's last letter?' She looked up at Nanny, who was still scowling.

'No, I did not. Now, where's your coat? No, not *that* one. The blue one. The one with the brass buttons. It's warmer and I keep telling you, it'll be cold over on the crossing.'

Kit said nothing. In spite of the gravity of the situation and the air of impending doom that had settled over everyone, including the servants, she was excited. The crossing. She and Uncle Faunce would go by train to London's Victoria Station, where they would change trains and head to Folkestone. From there, they would embark on the said crossing, taking a ferryboat across the English Channel. *La Manche,* as Mademoiselle Founard called it. At approximately four o'clock in the afternoon, they would be in France, the first entry into Europe. From Paris, they would go by sleeper train to Munich, and then on to the small town in Bavaria, where Lily and her new husband lived.

Kit hadn't been able to sleep properly for days. The whole mission was clouded in secrecy. Mother had absolutely forbidden her to tell Lily the real reason for their visit.

'You're *not* to warn her that you're bringing her back. It's better this way. You'll have to persuade her in *person*. She won't be able to say "no". Not to you, at any rate.' Kit's look of disbelief went unnoticed. 'You must just say you decided to visit her on the spur of the moment. I'll leave it to you to invent a reason why she's to come home at once. You're good at that.'

Now Kit's mouth dropped properly open. Since when had Mother noticed what she, Kit, was good at?

Mother ignored her. 'Now, I must get on. Lady Helmsley's coming to dinner and she's bringing that awful bore of a husband with her.'

Only Mother could make the seamless segue from Lily's predicament to the prospect of a boring dinner with such ease, Kit thought, half admiringly. *Segue.* It was her favourite word *du jour.* How would you say 'segue' in German? she wondered.

'Kit?' Nanny's voice brought her back to herself. 'You're a million miles away! I asked you if you'd remembered to put an extra pair of woollen socks in.'

'Oh. Yes, yes I did. I've got two pairs.' She pointed to the thick woollen socks that she knew she would never wear. Her mind was still on the crossing. It spoke of movement, of escape, of getting away from the monotony of daily life at Chalfont, which, now that Lily was gone, consisted mainly of lessons with Miss Frogworth in the chilly school-room and her beloved horses. No one her age ever came to Chalfont. It was true that she and Lily had never been close, but it was only when she was gone that Kit realised how lonely life was without her sister. Whatever else one might say about Lily Algernon-Waters, she was at least *entertaining*.

Kit had actually grown to miss Lily's opening lines at dinner every night. 'Mama, Papa … you'll never *guess* what happened … !' She was right. No one ever did. But her light-hearted prattle chased away the gloom that might otherwise have prevailed between their parents, who never seemed to say anything to one another that might be of interest or even relevance. Lily had a way of settling upon something quite ordinary and nondescript and lighting it up with her attention. If she hadn't looked at it in that way, no one would have noticed it. It used to irritate Kit; Lily made her feel as though she expected something, a response that Kit just didn't have. Half the time she didn't know what to say to Lily and would feel frustrated that she'd let her down. And then Lily's attention would wander and all the fuss would die down … and you'd realise, after all that, it hadn't been worth the bother in the first place. But it made a difference to the silence, she realised now. If it wasn't for the library and the thousand-and-one escapes that the books provided, she didn't know what she'd do. Books were her sole companion and her only entertainment, aside from the horses, but she couldn't really talk to *them*, even though she'd found herself doing it more than once. As often as she could, she would slip away from the table of the schoolroom and push open the door to the library. Once inside, she would lean against the door, taking the sweet, cigar-scented and faintly musty air down deep into her lungs, as though inhaling the words, sentences, stories, whole *worlds* contained in the thousands of tomes stacked neatly in alphabetical order on the shelves.

She couldn't say precisely what it was about the library that enchanted her so. It wasn't just the discovery of another life beyond her own: there was something more. She was freed into something that was both discipline and rule – the alphabetical ordering of authors' names, for one thing, but also the way books were grouped according to subject:

travel, philosophy, art, botany … Roaming freely amongst the shelves she discovered order and system, which curiously freed her into the happy, dream-like state with which she opened every book anew. She wandered into unchartered territory, not just of subject matter, but also of place. Boundaries were notional: one minute she might be reading about the life of a peasant in Tsarist Russia; the next about the Malabar grey hornbill of southern India. The thousand-strong collection of books had been handed down from father to son in the Algernon-Waters family for generations. Only this time, there *was* no son. Three miscarriages: and all of them potential heirs.

'It's no use,' she heard Mother say once, though she didn't know to whom. 'I'm incapable. I can't even give him an heir.'

Kit was too young at the time to understand the significance of the admission. She understood it now. It was connected in some mysterious way to Father's perpetual frown and his worries about money and who would inherit what. There was a distant third cousin – the nearest male in line to the estate – only the way Father went on about it, it was a bit of a wonder there'd be *anything* left for *anyone* to inherit, least of all the distant third cousin.

'Kit!' Nanny was glaring at her again.

'What?'

'Don't you "what" me, young lady. "I beg your pardon", if you please. Now, show me your gloves.'

Ten minutes later, after Nanny having gone through the entire contents of the suitcase not once but twice, she was finally pronounced ready.

'Right, that'll do,' Nanny said, adjusting Kit's hat, setting it more firmly on her head. 'Come along. I heard a car come up the driveway. That'll be your Uncle Faunce, I shouldn't wonder. Come along now.'

'Ah! There she is! My favourite niece!' Uncle Faunce got to his feet as soon as Kit entered.

It was quite true, if only because Lily didn't much like Uncle Faunce and she wasn't at pains to hide it. 'There's something fishy about him,' she always declared, but, typically, was unable to say exactly what she meant.

Faunce was the youngest of Father's three brothers, two of who had been killed in the war. Uncle Faunce had never married. Kit had overheard Cook muttering something darkly about the fact to Nanny, but neither would repeat what she'd said.

'Hello, Uncle Faunce,' she said, suddenly shy.

Father was standing stiffly to one side; Mother was sitting, her legs elegantly crossed at the ankle, as always, looking on brightly.

'Goodness, what a pickle your sister's gone and landed herself in.' Uncle Faunce was deliberately keeping his tone light, Kit saw with relief. He had obviously decided to treat the episode as 'an adventure'. She entered into the spirit of it willingly, gratefully.

'Yes, hasn't she? Silly Lily,' she retorted, quickly resorting to Lily's childhood nickname.

'Yes, quite. Indeed. Now, are you ready? No sense in dragging the goodbyes out any longer than necessary, I shouldn't think. Come along, niece. We've a long way to go. Right, Harold, I think we'd best be off.'

Father made a funny little sort of bow, almost like the one Lily's husband, Hans-Georg Schmidt von Altenstadt, had made when he was most emphatically *not* yet her husband but simply a houseguest. Kit looked on, half expecting Uncle Faunce to click his heels the way she'd seen Baron von Riedesal do when they left. Nanny said it was a German thing to do, wrinkling her nose in the way she did whenever Germany was mentioned. Nanny's adored and only brother had died in the First World War, Mother had told Kit by way of explanation.

'But Uncle Peregrine and Uncle Charles died in the war and you don't hate the Germans,' Kit replied, frowning, but Mother didn't say anything.

She looked at her mother now and was alarmed to see her lips pressing together until the flesh whitened to a cleft on either side of her nose. Mother was crying! The fact of it washed over her in a mixture of incredulity and embarrassment. Mother *never* cried.

Father seemed equally nonplussed. 'Oh, for goodness' sake, Delphine! Pull yourself together! They'll be back before you know it. With Lily too.'

'I know, I know,' Mother said, dabbing daintily at her eyes. 'I'm just being ... silly.'

'Don't *you* start,' Uncle Faunce said in his cheerful, bantering tone of voice. 'Can't have *two* silly billies in the family. It's exactly as Harold says: we'll be back before you know it, won't we, niece?'

Kit nodded vigorously. She liked the way Uncle Faunce addressed her as 'niece', implying there was only one. In his eyes, at least, she was special.

'Come along. Car's waiting. We've got a train to catch, a continent to see... someone to bring home. All very jolly and exciting, I know, but we'd best get moving. Come along, come along.'

They drove past the dark green cedars, their wide, generous branches spreading towards the horizon, past the high garden wall that separated the house from the vegetable garden, past the ivy-covered oak trees that marked the descent to the river...

Kit pressed her face against the glass, stiffly conscious of her prickly overcoat and her hands already sweating inside her woollen gloves. Uncle Faunce fumbled around in his tweed jacket for his pipe, lighting it with a great sigh of satisfaction. The interior of the car – 'Wolseley 14/60, Series II,' Uncle Faunce told her, smiling benevolently – was immediately filled with the sweetly pungent yet acrid smell of tobacco. It was oddly comforting. A lit pipe brought back unexpected memories. Long ago, when visitors to Chalfont were a more regular and frequent occurence, Father would sometimes retire to the library after dinner with a large glass of brandy and his pipe. Once, when she was very small, she'd crept in after him and – to her astonishment, even then – he'd allowed her onto his lap whilst he read and smoked, and she'd drifted off to sleep, the feel of his sweater pressed against her cheek and that scent filling her nostrils. It came back to her now, strongly.

4

Victoria Station was all noise. Screeching whistles; screaming brakes; young boys shouting at the top of their lungs; babies yelling their heads off whilst anxious nannies and young mothers were chaperoned from this carriage to that, this platform to that. Uncle Faunce clearly knew his way; he strode ahead, threading smartly between gaps in the crowd, not bothering to turn and check that she was following.

Finally they arrived at the correct platform and climbed aboard. A private carriage had been arranged; the porter pushed his way importantly in front of them, showing the way. There was another loud scream of a whistle as the doors clanged shut up and down the length of the platform, and then they began slowly to move. The station slipped past; the train gathered speed. The grimy London streets were quickly left behind as they moved south and the city began to thin. It was nearly lunchtime and Kit's stomach was rumbling.

Uncle Faunce lowered his copy of *The Times* and smiled at her over his spectacles. 'Luncheon'll be served shortly. We can have it in here or in the dining car, if you prefer?'

'Can we have it in here? Really? Like in a hotel?' Kit nearly clapped her hands. She thought: I'm leaving England. She'd been abroad before, of course. Once to Vienna, when she was so little she could scarcely remember it, and twice to Paris. And a few years earlier, they'd been to the Amalfi coast with their cousins. And was Scotland actually 'abroad'?

She closed her eyes momentarily and in the confusion that came with the felted darkness of her own eyelids, images of their car journey up to London came back to her. She smiled inwardly, privately at her choice of words. *Up to London.* It was one of Father's phrases. To him, London was at the top of the world. Hence every journey made was 'up to' London. Those images now began to dissolve in a jumble, like pieces of a broken mirror: Mother's crumpled face; the cedars lining the drive; the glint of the river as the car swept through the wrought-iron gates; the slow build-up to the city through miles of small villages come upon in a blur and left behind.

She went back to the last image she had of Lily, departing from Chalfont much as they had just done, her dozens of cases packed carefully into a second car that followed them. Her long auburn hair was carefully hidden underneath a soft grey wide-brimmed hat. She'd had a whole wardrobe specially made for her departure. Endless fitting sessions with Mademoiselle Founard, Lily pirouetting slowly and dreamily in front of the mirror as yet another bolt of chiffon, silk or tulle was pinned against her slender frame. Lily. Lily Algernon-Waters, eldest daughter of Lord and Lady Wharton, was now Gräfin Lilliane Schmidt von Altenstadt. A bona fide countess, whose rank now surpassed Father's. It was hard to believe. In her letters, she sounded as she'd always done: girlish, full of high spirits, gossipy. She called Kit 'dearest' and 'darling', implying a closeness in their correspondence that they'd never achieved in real life. When the letters first began to arrive, surprisingly regularly,

Kit was astonished to realise she actually missed her sister. She fished for her last letter, written some four months earlier, which she'd shoved into her pocket at the last minute, and pulled it out.

Schloß Gattendorf
Hof, Bavaria

9 December 1938

Dearest Kit,

Well, I <u>have</u> to tell you, I had lunch with Wolf today! Hans-Georg sulked all the way through. We went to this pretty little osteria just outside the village, just the three of us, in Hans-Georg's new car! It was super. Wolf looked <u>so</u> handsome in his uniform! You should see them, my dearest little sister. They all look so smart and dignified, not at all like the men at home. I've asked Hans-Georg to give me driving lessons. Can you imagine me, driving! The scenery here is so pretty, you'd love it, darling Kit. I know you would. I do so wish Mother and Father would let you come. We saw the Führer in Berlin last week, by great good luck. It was ever so thrilling. We were driving along and he was driving in the opposite direction and everyone rushed out shouting 'Heil!' as he passed. It was <u>so</u> exciting. Nothing like that ever happens at Chalfont!

Oh, before I forget, will you tell Mother to send me some silk stockings, if she can lay her hands on a pair? And do you remember that cream Worth dress that Mother said she didn't want any more? If you could have it cleaned for me I would be ever so grateful. We're going to a ball in Vienna in January and it would be <u>super</u> to wear it.

Well, darling Kit, I long to see you. I don't know if Hans-Georg will let me come to England, especially not now, what with all the fuss over Rhineland, but I do hope so.

Best love from Lily.

P.S. Your last letter was the nicest I've had for ages. Please tell Father to write.
P.P.S. Oh, I do so miss you all terribly!

Kit smiled. It was hard to imagine Lily missing anyone, least of all Kit, but she sounded happy and, in her own strange way, contented. Who was Wolf? she wondered. On the flimsiest of hunches, she decided she didn't like him. Even his name sounded sinister, especially the way Lily wrote it, with a huge looping 'W' and a long, curved 'f'. And why would Hans-Georg sulk? She did hope Lily wasn't being silly. The requested cream chiffon dress was in one of the large leather trunks that the porter had wheeled away as soon as they arrived at Victoria Station. Kit hadn't managed to get hold of any silk stockings, though. Lily would be upset. She hated disappointments; always had. Kit folded away the letter. She stole a look at Uncle Faunce but he was engrossed in his newspaper and did not look up.

Presently he summoned a waiter by ringing the little brass bell just above the door and within half an hour, a perfectly respectable tray of sandwiches, cold chicken drumsticks and something that looked like pink blancmange, but was, in fact, salmon mousse, appeared, which they devoured in short order. There was lemonade for Kit and a glass of red wine followed by a silver pot of coffee for Uncle Faunce. It was all very thrilling.

Kit's mind drifted back to the letter. *We saw the Führer in Berlin last week, by great good luck.* It was very worrying. She'd overheard Father talking to someone on the phone a few days before their departure that Neville Chamberlain was an even bigger fool than MacDonald. She'd had to hunt through several weeks of newspapers to find out who Ramsay MacDonald was and why Father had such a low opinion of him.

'Uncle Faunce,' she said suddenly, surprising herself. She hadn't intended to disturb him.

He looked at her over the top of the newspaper and winked conspiratorially. 'Full?'

She nodded hurriedly. The food wasn't what she wanted to talk about. 'Yes. The egg sandwiches are rather good.'

'Good. We'll have dinner in Calais. I've booked the most terrific little hotel, not far from the train station. I stayed there last year. We'll be catching *Le Train Bleu* tomorrow morning. Heard of it? No? What on earth do they teach you these days? It's very smart. Did you bring something suitable to wear?'

Kit looked down at her sensible woollen skirt and jumper with its starched white collar and bit her lip. 'Isn't this suitable?'

34

Uncle Faunce shook his head. 'Not really. You look like a schoolgirl.'
'I *am* a schoolgirl.'
'Hmm. Touché.'
'Uncle Faunce... can I ask you something?' Kit began again hesitantly.
'You can ask me anything, niece.'
'Is... is it true what they say about Lily and Unity Mitford?' she asked in a rush. 'Did they really go to the Nuremburg rally?'
'How did you hear about that?' Uncle Faunce lowered the paper and looked at her intently.
'I heard it on the wireless,' Kit said quickly. It wasn't *entirely* untrue. She'd heard it on the wireless, but she'd also heard Caruthers and Bignell discussing it endlessly too.
'Ah. I *told* Harold that wireless was a mistake.' He pursed his lips thoughtfully. 'No, not a mistake, that's not exactly true. Just a bit risky, especially with someone like you around. You're such an inquisitive little thing, aren't you? Ever so observant, though.'
'How do you know that?' Kit asked, surprised. Neither Mother nor Father would ever have commented on a thing like that. Mother's remarks seldom evoked more than: 'Oh, really?', 'Fancy that' or 'That is of no interest to anyone, Kit'. She wasn't unkind; just not terribly interested.
'I'd have thought it rather obvious, don't you? You're a terrific little mimic. Mimics *have* to be observant. That's their skill.'
A warm flush of pleasure rose in Kit's face. She couldn't remember the last time she'd had a compliment from anyone. Not only was she always found wanting in relation to Lily, she'd been reprimanded for so long for being *different* from everyone else that she'd long given up the expectation of ever being recognised for anything. The idea of Uncle Faunce admiring her for a trait everyone else considered 'dangerous' (or, worse, 'unbecoming') was quite unsettling. 'Don't be so nosy', or 'Why are you so interested in everyone else?' were much more likely responses than 'You're a terrific little mimic'. Although you could hardly call her 'little', she thought, pulling a face. She was taller than both Mother and Lily, and by some considerable margin, too. Even her height came in for approbation. 'Goodness me,' she'd overheard Mother saying to Cook once. 'I do hope she's not going to get any taller. She'll never find a husband. Still, at least she's not *fat*.'
Fat or not, tall or short, finding a husband seemed an arbitrary and largely unpredictable business. Just look at Lily: one surprise visit from

a bunch of Germans and *poof!*, she was gone. The courtship had lasted six months, and it had largely been a courtship-by-letter at that. It didn't deter Lily. She was *in love*, and that was all there was to it. Hans-Georg was a count, richer than anyone could ever have imagined, and more sophisticated than anyone Lily had ever met. He was fifteen years older than her and a man of the world. He was *going* places. In the six months since their marriage, Kit understood that he was part of Hitler's inner circle of loyal, trusted officers. She'd shuddered when she read Lily's letters. But back then, in the days and weeks after their visit, Lily could talk of nothing else but love. 'Being in love is just so thrilling!' she exclaimed half a dozen times a day.

Kit rolled her eyes. She could see nothing thrilling about it. 'You only met him once,' she pointed out, exasperated.

'Yes, but I *knew*. I knew straight away. Oh, Kit ... he's a *count*! He's fabulously rich! He sent me a picture of his castle. Just imagine! I'll live in a proper castle, just like a princess! I can have whatever I want! I can do whatever I want! I won't have to worry about a *thing*, not like Mama!'

'You'll be bored,' Kit said dourly.

'No, I won't. You're just jealous. You never want me to have any fun.' The statement was so patently untrue it had the effect of temporarily silencing Kit.

Now, looking at Uncle Faunce who sat opposite her, reading but indulging her every now and then with a glance or a wink, she had the odd sensation of momentarily being aware of herself as a stranger, as someone else would see her. A little prim, sitting upright, her woollen coat buttoned sensibly up to her chin. A tall, thin, serious-looking girl, well behaved and unobtrusive in the way she'd always been, always. What did Uncle Faunce see when he looked at her? she wondered curiously. What did anyone see? The sensation passed slowly, but its trace remained throughout the remainder of the journey, lingering in her mind like a puff of lightly scented smoke.

5

It doesn't look like a castle at all. That was Kit's first thought as the taxi pulled through the gates. To her, it looked more like a large, forbidding prison. The walls were a strange shade of deep, pinkish ochre, unlike any building she'd ever seen. The roof was dark grey slate and pitched forwards alarmingly, in all directions, culminating in a single tower to the left-hand side of the façade. The windows were uniformly small and rectangular: poky little apertures that did little to break up the monotony of all that *pink*.

'Well, well, well. Schloß Gattendorf,' Uncle Faunce murmured. 'At last.'

Kit could only nod. The taxi pulled up in front of the entrance, a plain, severe-looking doorway with none of the ornamentation that Kit associated with grand houses. There were no columns; no balustrades on either side of the plain stone steps; no portico; it was austere to the point of hideousness. She thought fleetingly of the front door to Chalfont with its graceful neoclassical columns and enormous stone planters, ornately carved front door and shiny brass handles and knocker that Bignell polished every morning.

A movement to her right caught her eye. There, in the far corner of the forbidding façade, was a flag. It fluttered and a crumpled wing emerged. It was the swastika of the National Socialists. She gulped.

'Ah, *guten Morgen*.' Uncle Faunce tipped his hat to a young woman in uniform with a puzzled look on her face, who had just appeared in the doorway. Behind her, a darkened hall stretched into the unknown interior of the house. Kit gulped again. In surprisingly fluent German, Uncle Faunce enquired if the '*Gräfin*' was indeed '*zu Hause*'.

The maid looked nervously at them both. '*Wen soll ich sagen, bittet für sie?*'

'*Ich bin ihre Schwester,*' Kit broke in quickly, in her best German.

'*Einen Moment.*' The maid turned and disappeared.

Uncle Faunce and Kit looked questioningly at one another. A much older woman, also in uniform, suddenly appeared in front of them. She looked equally uncertain but led them into the hallway. It was freezing inside, just as Nanny had predicted. Kit pulled her coat more closely around her and looked up at Uncle Faunce. His expression was hard to read. Her heart sank. Their arrival had turned sour.

The two maids ushered them into a small, chilly reception room with a collection of high, hard-backed chairs. There was an empty fireplace in one corner and an assortment of gloomy paintings looked blankly down on them from the darkly painted walls. Tall, shuttered windows gave the impression of austere watchfulness that sent a surreptitious shudder down her spine. The maid bade them sit down and retreated, closing the door quietly behind her.

'Well. Not quite the welcome I was expecting,' Uncle Faunce said cheerfully. 'Perhaps they've got the date wrong? I expect we've taken them all by surprise.'

It was nearly three o'clock in the afternoon. The train journey from Munich had taken almost the entire morning, then there was the business of finding a taxi to drive them to the castle. The skies were already beginning to darken; the light was fading as the day began to draw to a close. Kit was hungry and tired. A feeling of despondency began to sweep through her and she found herself ridiculously – and embarrassedly – close to tears.

'Steady on, niece,' Uncle Faunce said quickly, sensing her distress. 'Everything's going to be fine. I promise.'

Kit nodded, not quite trusting herself to speak. Suddenly they heard footsteps approaching. Her heart began to race. It had been almost a year since she'd seen Lily. Would she have changed? From her letters, it didn't appear so, but with Lily, it was always hard to tell.

The door swung open. Kit looked up. There was someone standing in the doorway, staring at them as if she couldn't quite believe her eyes. Kit's mouth dropped open. Was *that* Lily?

For a few moments after they'd set eyes on each other, Kit couldn't bring herself to speak. The woman standing in the doorway looked nothing like her sister. The long auburn hair was gone, replaced by short blonde waves plastered close against her skull. Lily had always been slender but now she was rake-thin, so brittle she seemed almost breakable. Her china-blue eyes, once so lively and expressive, were enormous blank saucers that took up most of her tired-looking and drawn face.

'Lily!' Kit exclaimed finally, unable to keep the shock from her voice.

'Kit?' A frown appeared between Lily's eyes. 'Uncle Faunce? What on earth are you doing here?'

'Don't you remember? We wrote to you! You asked me to bring you some stockings! Oh, Lily! We've come to take you home!' Kit couldn't stop herself from blurting the news out. 'Mother and Father sent us. They said—'

'Kit,' Uncle Faunce broke in hurriedly, putting a restraining hand on her arm. 'My dear,' he said, walking towards Lily. 'You're looking *marvellous*. I love the new hairdo, don't you, Kit? Suits you.'

Lily put a hand up to her hair distractedly. 'Does it? Do you think so? I don't know. Hans-Georg—' She stopped. She frowned at them again, as though struggling to remember something. Then the penny dropped. She clapped her hands. 'Of course! You said you were coming to visit! Of *course* you did! What am I *thinking*? You must come upstairs! Come and have something to eat, to drink. Maria!' she yelled. 'Magda!'

The two maids who'd let them in appeared in the doorway. '*Zu Ihren Diensten, Gräfin*,' they chimed in unison, lowering their eyes.

Kit looked on incredulously. Lily was all animation now, throwing her arms around wildly, gesticulating at the maids as though it was their fault no one had been on hand to welcome them.

'We must go upstairs *at* once! They must be fed! They must be *starving*!' Lily practically screamed in fluent, if heavily accented, German.

Kit's mind was whirling. Lily hadn't even come forwards to embrace her. She turned on her heel and marched into the hallway with the servants scurrying behind. Uncle Faunce looked at Kit, raising a quizzical, conspiratorial eyebrow. With a sinking feeling that this was only the beginning of something she couldn't quite fathom, Kit walked behind Uncle Faunce, concentrating fiercely on the patterning of his tweed jacket, desperately trying to keep her burning tears of disappointment in check.

The drawing room to which Lily took them was more in keeping with what she'd imagined: spacious and elegant, a pale blue high ceiling with ornate plasterwork swirling and curling above them, a set of narrow windows that opened out onto a view of the Bavarian countryside, now fading swiftly to night. Lights from the village in the valley below twinkled like stars in the blackly opaque sky. Heavy silk and damask curtains tied in elaborate swags on either side framed the disappearing view. It was all very beautiful and tasteful but it had the appearance of a stage-set, a room in which no one sat, no conversation ever took place, no words were ever exchanged.

All three sat stiffly together. Lily's earlier burst of energy seemed to have dissipated as fast as it arose. She was nervous and distracted, her eyes darting around the room but not settling on anyone or anything, least of all her sister. Every so often, she barked out an instruction to one of the maids. *Light the fire. Bring in some wine. Is there no bread?* Finally, a tray was brought in to the room and carefully laid out on the table by the window: cold cuts; slices of thick rye bread; a brandy for Uncle Faunce; and apple juice for Kit. They helped themselves; Lily declined everything, including a glass of wine.

The room had begun to warm up at last. Kit nibbled at a piece of bread, not trusting the translucent dark red ham – nothing like the ham at home. Lily and Uncle Faunce sat at opposite ends of a pale grey velvet sofa, with a bank of cushions stacked between them. They talked in low voices, their conversation veering towards channels that excluded Kit, leaving her at the edges of her comprehension. They talked of people Kit didn't know; places she didn't recognise; events she'd never heard of. *Die Reichspartei*; someone called von Blomberg, who had resigned earlier that year; something called *Fall Grün*. What did it all mean? Kit was too tired to even try to follow them.

Outside, night had settled over the countryside. It was bitterly cold – too cold to snow, Uncle Faunce had remarked – but the threat of it had settled in the pregnant clouds, a heavy load just waiting to fall. Sitting there, listening to their talk, Kit felt as though the world had begun to dissolve into half questions that would never be asked; dark ribbons of intuition that couldn't be verified in the faces opposite her. She tucked her feet under her, her right foot dancing a little tune of impatience mingled with apprehension. All three appeared to be waiting for something to happen, but did not yet know what it might be.

Suddenly, a noise made her start. The door opened. Kit had dozed off for a moment or two, lulled by the crackling fire and the murmuring conversation, which made no demands of her. She looked up. There were two men standing in the doorway. One was Hans-Georg, whom

Kit recognised at once. Unlike Lily, he hadn't changed a bit. He was in uniform: a fitted black jacket with its distinctive red Swastika armband, black jodhpurs and impossibly shiny, knee-high black boots. The man standing behind him was hidden in the shadows.

'Ah, there you are, Lilliane. I was wondering where you'd got to.' His voice, too, was exactly the same.

'Darling!' Lily's voice hit a false note of surprise. 'Look who's here! Can you believe it?' She sounded out of breath, as though she'd been running. She clearly hadn't told her husband about her sister's impending visit.

'Yes, I see,' Hans-Georg said drily, sounding not in the least bit surprised or pleased. He made the same funny, formal little bow that she'd seen her father make. His eyes flickered over them both. 'How are you, my dear sister-in-law?' He turned to Uncle Faunce. 'And you, sir?' There was something strange in the way he greeted Uncle Faunce. There was a familiarity in his voice, as though they knew one another well. But they'd only met once, at Lily's wedding.

'*And* darling Kit, this is *Wolf*!' Lily interrupted Hans-Georg, sounding even more out of breath. Kit's eyes slid past Hans-Georg to the even taller figure behind him. The man moved forwards into the firelight. He was white-blond, though his hair was hidden mostly under his stiff-peaked cap. His face was cold and impassive, with an impossibly square jaw, lips a narrow line in the otherwise expressionless face, and his eyes were pale, pale blue.

'Well?' Lily asked archly, presenting the two men as though they were a gift of some inexplicable kind. 'What do you think? Aren't they both the most handsome men you've ever seen?'

Kit felt a liquid flash running through her, an inexplicable feeling of panic, shuddering lightly over her face and neck. She began to tremble slightly, as though she'd walked into a spider's web and the strands had settled themselves invisibly all over her skin. There was a beat of silence. Something flashed between Lily's face and the stranger's, something she couldn't quite catch hold of. She turned to Uncle Faunce, seeking tentative assurance, but his face too was closed. An extraordinary distress came over her. She felt again the panic she'd once experienced walking along the cliffs at Mupe Bay, by the coast, when they'd gone to visit Granny. She'd taken Lupo, Granny's old black Labrador along, dismissing Mother's concerns.

'You'll get lost, darling!'

'No, I won't,' she'd shouted back, confidently striding to the edge of the garden, Lupo lolling along patiently.

She *did* get lost. One minute they were walking along the pebbly path that skirted the white-faced cliff; the next, a dense white mist rolled in and the world disappeared. Land, sea, horizon, cloud – all had become one. Some instinct in her made her stop and stand still. Lupo must have sensed her unease; he flopped down on the pebbly path, his tongue hanging out, breathing ragged, tail thumping weakly.

When the mist finally cleared she saw they had stopped only inches from the cliff's edge. Sound returned: the soft, drawn-out yawn of waves rolling in six hundred feet below. A single step more ... The descent was terrifying, a brutal, dramatic sweep to the rocks below. She inched her way carefully backwards, as if afraid to disturb the view.

That same sense of urgent, inexplicable panic was in her throat now.

6

The room was cold, despite the fire roaring in one corner. The air was stale and smooth, like the air of a church. A small brass bed stood in the centre of the room. Kit shivered in her nightdress, the soles of her bare feet barely touching the ground as she hopped from the dressing table, where she carefully laid down her brush and comb, to the bed. She drew back the covers gingerly and slid between the cardboard sheets, ironed so fiercely that the central crease stood proud. She pulled the covers up to her chin and lay back, exhausted from the effort of trying to keep up with the mercurial shifts in mood and meaning that crackled through the air all evening. Several times during the course of dinner, she'd caught a glance exchanged between one or more of the other guests, including Uncle Faunce, that made her feel as though she were part of an audience watching something she wasn't expected to fully grasp.

There were eight people to dinner that evening; three others had joined their odd party of five. All the men, save Uncle Faunce, were in uniform: the same smart garb with the puffed-out trousers and collarless jackets. The women wore evening gowns of the sort no one in England could afford to wear any more: silks, furs, pearls... Everything was ornate and exquisite.

She watched her sister closely all evening but Lily had moved far away into her own world, a world of suppressed sighs, raised eyebrows, exaggerated expressions and coy, flirtatious gestures that Kit couldn't follow. She could find no connection to the high-spirited, gregarious young girl she'd been at Chalfont. She appeared almost drugged, as though her real personality had been drained out of her and a slower, deadened version of herself had been poured back in. Yet every so often, a flash of her former brightness showed through in her laugh or the wild clapping of her hands, and Kit found herself even more bewildered than ever. What was going on? Uncle Faunce, too, was strange. There was again that odd familiarity between him and Hans-Georg that seemed out of place. At dinner, Kit was on the periphery of a three-sided male conversation between Uncle Faunce, Hans-Georg and Wolf, but once, somewhere in the long pause between courses, she laughed at something one of them said, and they all became aware of her with such surprise and distaste that she felt as though she'd been eavesdropping and withdrew into herself.

The fireplace changed from near-invisible flickers of liquid colour to brilliantly focused tongues of light. She watched it, her body underneath the sheets finally beginning to warm. Somewhere outside, several floors below, there was the clang of a metal gate and the sound of wheels scraping across the cobbles. There was a muffled shout and then the squeal of brakes. She heard the heavy front door downstairs being opened. Someone had clearly arrived. An answering door opened and closed somewhere further down the corridor. She had no idea how many guests were staying the night. She didn't even know where in the draughty castle Uncle Faunce might be sleeping. A maid had appeared as soon as dessert was over and led Kit away from the grown-ups, up through several flights of stairs and down long, cold corridors to the room in which she now lay, struggling to make sense of where she was.

There was a noise almost directly outside her door. She lifted her head, anticipating a knock. But none came. She waited for a few seconds. Someone was outside, she was sure of it. She opened her mouth but found she couldn't speak. Instead she carefully peeled back the covers and slipped noiselessly out of bed. She crept to the door and stood against it, poised, like an animal, ready at any moment to take flight.

There was someone on the other side of the door; she could almost feel his breath – and it was a man, she was certain – through the thickness of the wood. Nothing moved, neither he nor she. She felt the shifting of weight from one foot to the other, communicating itself through the floorboards that ran under the door. There was a creak, then another, and another... Whoever was on the other side had begun slowly, almost soundlessly, to retreat. Footsteps were soft tremors, tingling against her toes. At last, when she was sure whoever had been outside her door was gone, she grasped hold of the handle and slowly pressed down. The door gave way soundlessly. The corridor was in complete darkness. She stepped outside and was enveloped in the eerie quiet.

A wind had come up. As she crept down the corridor she could see the curtains on the floor below billowing gently in the light that spilled from the hallway. Beyond the long windows on one side she could just make out the trees in motion. As she passed one of the windows, she saw that the moon was up, even though this side of the castle was shrouded in darkness. As she neared the end of the corridor, she heard the distinct murmur of voices. She stopped, looking around her to find the source. There was a door at the end, and as she stared, it opened a crack.

She moved instinctively to one side, her gaze narrowing. A man's figure appeared, paused for a moment, and moved on, out of sight. It was him. It was Wolf. She could tell by his stance. Gathering her courage into a tight little knot that she held somewhere in the pit of her stomach, she crept towards the doorway, propelled by something she couldn't yet name. Something was driving her, some hidden, banked-down, inexplicable desire to see something – but what? She was only aware of one thing: the wish to be confronted by whatever was behind the door. To force herself to look at it; to believe it, whatever it was.

She crept up to the crack of light and peered in. She could see Wolf's shape poised at the window, his body so upright and alert that she could feel the energy of it like a kind of heat in the room. He was staring at a point out of her line of vision but there was something in the way he regarded it that spoke not so much of looking as of setting himself apart, like an animal preparing to catch a scent. There was a hard-edged quality to his outline, a kind of awareness of himself that made her think of something. Like a cat, she thought suddenly, clearly. She too was trapped, with her heart beating fast. She heard someone sigh on the other side of the room. He was in profile to her, his face looking straight past hers to something on the other side of the room. There was a faint smile on his mouth. What light there was – no more than the reflection of the fire and the moon through the curtainless window – was full on him. But what she was looking at was beyond him, beyond the thin smile and the grey-blue pupils and the look on his face. She caught her breath, realising that she was looking past his face to another face, hidden and concealed behind the façade of icy dispassion he'd worn all evening.

She stood shivering in the doorway, trembling again with the emotion that had come over her earlier. The edge of the bed was just visible. Someone's leg was directly in line with her eye. A bare leg, tied with something that bound it to the bedframe. She shifted her gaze upwards a fraction. There, sitting at the head of the bed, dressed only in a silk slip, was one of the women who'd been at dinner. Bettina someone-or-other. She was smoking, raising a languid hand to her mouth, drawing hungrily on her cigarette before letting her arm fall again. The scent wasn't tobacco; it was something else, something sweeter and sharper. Someone across the room, whom she couldn't see, spoke and there was a general murmur of laughter. There were six or seven people in the room; everyone who'd been at dinner, it seemed. Kit swallowed hard. She had seen more than she could bear, more than she could understand. Quietly, as carefully as she could, she backed away from the door. As she turned, she thought she saw a sliver of light coming from a room further down the corridor, but when she peered into the darkness, it was gone.

She made her way back to her room by feel, her hand reaching blindly in front of her, groping her way. At last she reached her door. She grasped the handle and pushed. The same strange scent from the room she'd just spied upon was in her own room. Her nostrils pricked uncomfortably. There was another, deeper note to the smell, but she couldn't place it. Her heart hammering, she crept across the floor and slid into bed. The fire had gone down but the room was still warm. She pulled the covers up to her chin and lay there, forcing herself to breathe calmly, normally. Her teeth were chattering, but out of fear, not cold. A fit of trembling seized her. Although she hadn't seen anything – not really, not properly – the sense of having escaped something too dreadful to name was upon her, thick as fog, as dense as cream.

7

'Home?' Lily looked at her as though she'd said something too ridiculous to be true. 'What on earth do you mean? This is my home. All of it.' She waved a hand in the general direction of the estate.

'No, I mean ... you *know* what I mean,' Kit said earnestly. 'Home to England. Mama and Papa are desperate to have you back. They say there's—'

'Don't you understand *anything*?' Lily interrupted her angrily.

They were in one of the many rooms on the ground floor that overlooked the long valley, now covered in a hoary, freezing fog. A ring of mountains lay to the south of the castle; their sharped, jagged peaks punctured the mist like accusatory fingers, pointing to the sky. It was so unlike the soft smoothness of the Dorset countryside that Kit couldn't take her eyes off the landscape. How had she ended up here?

Lily pushed back her chair and stood up. Breakfast had been laid out for the two sisters but neither had been able to eat a thing. Kit didn't drink coffee and the tea the maids had brought was nothing like the tea at home: dark and bitter and they'd left the leaves in the pot!

Lily walked to the sideboard and picked up a packet of cigarettes. She lit one, folding her arms protectively around her tiny waist. She was wearing a long, flared tweed skirt with a silk cream blouse, ruffled at the collar with long, billowing sleeves. Her style had changed; it was hard to believe she had just turned nineteen. She looked – and behaved – like someone much, much older, an infinitely tired-looking and jaded version of her former self. Kit looked down at her hands, which were folded in her lap. She felt immensely young and foolish and utterly out of her depth. Why had Mama insisted she be the one to come? The situation in front of her demanded the intervention of adults, not her. And where was Uncle Faunce? She hadn't seen him since she was led out of the enormous dining room the night before. It was nearly ten o'clock in the morning. Where the hell was he?

Lily came back to the table, still smoking. That was another unfamiliar sight. She knew Mother occasionally smoked a thin cheroot cigar, like many of her friends. But they smoked in the evening, after supper, not at breakfast and not when they hadn't eaten a thing! She looked up at her sister. She'd pushed her shirtsleeves up to the elbow. Kit stared at her arms. There were bruise marks around her wrists, ugly, bluish welts that stood out against her porcelain-white skin like ink stains. There were bruises further up her arms, too, smudges in the soft, delicate hollow of her elbows and dozens of tiny black pin-pricks, where something seemed to have punctured her skin. Kit swallowed. Lily, catching her sister's stare, angrily pulled down her sleeves. She ground out her cigarette with great force.

'I'm not coming back,' she said briskly. 'Never. And if you had any sense, you'd stay here. We're going to win, you know. I'm surprised you haven't worked that out, you being the clever one and everything.'

'What do you mean?' Kit was startled by the sudden venom in her sister's voice.

'Oh, don't play the innocent with me. It won't wash, you know. That was your little game, wasn't it? Silly Lily and Clever Kit. Always trying to please Papa. Sucking up to him with your silly little bits of nonsense. Look at me, Papa, look how *clever* I am! We all know he wanted a son and if Mama couldn't manage that ... well, you always wanted him to see how clever *you* were, and how stupid *I* was. It didn't work, do you hear me? Everything's going to change and you'll—'

'What are you *talking* about?' Kit's voice rose in distress. 'I never did any of those things!'

'Didn't you? Oh, Papa,' Lily's voice took on a mocking tone. 'Guess what *I* just read. It says in the encyclopaedia that—'

'Stop it! Stop it at once!'

'Why? It's the truth, isn't it? You were so happy to see me married and packed off to Germany. You didn't even buy me a *wedding* present! Can you imagine how that felt? Not even my own sister! You couldn't wait to get rid of me so that you could have Papa all to your*self*! Don't think I don't know you, Kit. I know you better than you know yourself. You were always jealous of me, always! And now, just because Papa's too afraid to face the future, he's sent you, Little Miss Goody Two-Shoes, to try and get me back. Well, it won't work! I'm staying here! When we conquer England, you'll see how misled you've all been, how wrong you are. It's going to happen, make no mistake about it. And *then* you'll be sorry you weren't nicer to me!'

Kit's mouth dropped open at the same moment the kitchen door opened. It was Uncle Faunce.

'Hello, you two,' Uncle Faunce remarked pleasantly. 'I heard voices … so I thought I'd come and see who was up.'

Kit struggled to hold back her tears. She couldn't bring herself to speak, not just yet. A whole torrent of emotions swirled dangerously around in her chest, from incredulity to anger. How *could* Lily have said those things? Had she gone quite mad? Lily looked from one to the other, her face flushed and animated in a way it hadn't been since they arrived, and then flounced out of the room, her heels clicking ominously on the stone floor.

'Oh, dear.' Uncle Faunce came forwards and took the chair Lily had just vacated. He sat down heavily and took Kit's hand in his. 'I heard a little bit,' he began quietly.

Kit looked across the table at him. His Adam's apple pulsated impatiently, like the throb of a bullfrog. He seemed about to say something of grave importance. She waited, her own heart beating fast beneath the scratchy wool of her undergarments. Unlike her father, Uncle Faunce was one of those men who weighed no more at sixty than he had at twenty. His fine, bright skin was wrinkled all over but had remained incongruously taut, rather like a piece of paper that had been crumpled then lovingly smoothed out. He appeared to be studying her, but she knew it was his easy way of giving attention whilst he withdrew into the privacy of his own mind and thoughts.

'You're a little young to be taught this lesson *now*,' he said carefully. 'But Lily's right. You *are* the clever one. And with that extra dollop of intelligence comes an additional burden of responsibility, I'm afraid. Harsh, but true.'

'What lesson, Uncle Faunce?' Kit asked, hoping her voice was steady.

He paused for a moment. His Adam's apple throbbed again. She fixed her eyes on it, avoiding his own.

'Come, my little schoolgirl niece. Why don't we take a short walk? It's freezing, I know, but wrap up tightly in that terrible blue coat of yours. Come on, I think we could both do with a bit of fresh air.'

She looked up at him. He seemed to be saying something else beneath the cheery words.

'I'll just get my coat,' she said quietly.

*

He was right. It *was* freezing. She belted her offending coat more tightly and hunched her face into her scarf. Uncle Faunce tucked her arm in his and together they walked slowly through the enormous archway that led to the vegetable gardens and the barns to the rear of the castle.

'Things aren't . . . always as they seem,' he said finally, just when she thought the silence between them had to be filled, somehow.

'What things?'

'Everything. This.' He waved a hand languidly to take in all of the landscape surrounding them. 'And this. Us being here. *Me* being here, more to the point.'

'But . . . aren't we here to bring Lily home?'

'Well, yes, that would be a happy consequence of our visit. But, no, it's not my primary purpose.'

Kit swallowed. 'Then what is? Why *are* you here?'

Uncle Faunce let go of her arm and stopped. He turned to her. 'I don't suppose you know very much about me,' he said slowly. 'Other than the fact that I'm your father's younger brother. I don't suppose you've ever given a thought to how or where I live, what I do, where I go every morning when I'm in London. Why would you?'

'I do know a little bit,' Kit said carefully. 'I know you're not married.' She hesitated. 'No one's ever said anything, but . . . I . . . I *think* I know why.'

Uncle Faunce nodded. 'I dare say you do. Lily's right, in one way. You are a clever little thing. But she's wrong. About Germany, I mean. Oh, there's going to be a war, no doubt about it. Hitler won't be appeased, no matter what the idiots back home – your father included – think. No, there's only one thing to be done with Hitler and that's to stand up to him.'

Kit said nothing. Her head was spinning. She was right. Uncle Faunce was trying to tell her something. She turned to look up at him. 'Uncle Faunce,' she began carefully. 'There's something I . . . I want to ask you. You've been here before, haven't you? When we arrived last night, I . . . I just had that feeling . . . I don't know why.'

Uncle Faunce regarded her thoughtfully. 'You're very observant,' he said finally. 'I told you so before we left.'

Kit blushed deeply. 'So . . . is that why we're here?' she asked slowly. 'Do you really think Lily ought to come home?'

Uncle Faunce hesitated, then smiled. 'Tenacious little thing, aren't you?'

49

'Uncle Faunce, please stop calling me "little". No one ever does. Besides, I'm nearly as tall as you.'

'Yes, I know. Silly of me. I'm talking to you as if you were an adult, my age … I know it's wrong of me but I can't help it. And I suppose I throw in the word "little" every now and again to remind me of it. Sorry, my dearest niece. Unforgivable of me to burden you with all this. I really shouldn't.'

'It doesn't matter.' Kit spoke earnestly. 'Really, it doesn't. And it's better this way, anyway. It'll make it easier.'

Her uncle looked at her sharply. 'What are you talking about? What will be made easier?'

She turned her full grey-blue gaze on him. 'Me helping you. What is it you need to know?'

8

She pushed open the door a crack. It was dark and quiet inside. The only sounds came from the dining room two floors below. It was their fourth night at Schloß Gattendorf and, like the three nights preceding it, each day was taken up with preparations for the nightly dinner. Tonight there were a great many guests, too many to count. All afternoon cars had been arriving, passing under the great stone archway to the east of the main door, before being whisked out of sight. Guests trooped up the great staircase to the handsome salon on the first floor for afternoon tea, whilst maids scampered in and out, carrying great armfuls of bedding to the castle's numerous bedrooms.

Lily had announced imperiously that afternoon that Kit's company wouldn't be required at dinner. 'It's a very important dinner,' she pronounced loftily. '*Much* too important for you, Kit. You can have supper in the kitchens with Maria, just the way you do it at home.'

Kit said nothing. Since her talk with Uncle Faunce, she was determined not to rise to Lily's bait. She had other, much more important things on her mind.

Like now. She pushed the door open a little further and waited. There wasn't a single sound. The room was empty. She slipped in and closed the door behind her. She knew what she was looking for: the list.

'What sort of list?' she'd asked Uncle Faunce.

'It's a list of names. Names of British sympathisers. Unity Mitford drew up a list of traitors, but we're not interested in those. It's the sympathisers we're after.'

'What makes you think Lily's got it?'

'She's the one who drew it up. We overheard her boasting about it to the Mitford girl. I personally think it's been handed over to Wolf von Schuppler already.'

'So you think *he's* got it? But where?'

Uncle Faunce shrugged. 'Somewhere in the castle, I imagine. Probably in his room. I'll have to think about how to get hold of it. He's staying until Saturday, and from here, he goes directly to Berlin. My guess is that he'll take it with him and hand it over in person to Hitler.'

'I'll get it.' Kit spoke firmly, as though the decision was hers alone.

'Don't be ridiculous. I'd never allow it. It's absolutely out of the question. If your father ever found out that I'd so much as breathed a word of any of this to you, he'd have me shot, I guarantee it. No, you're to stay out of this altogether. We may need you in helping us get your sister back, but that's the extent of it. I shouldn't have said a thing.'

'It'll be easy for me. He doesn't even notice me. I'm the last person he'll be looking out for.'

'No, Kit. And that's final. Not another word.'

She leaned against the door for a moment, switched on the light and quickly looked around. A large four-poster bed stood in the centre, its velvet drapes immaculately swagged and pinned. The walls were a deep, dramatic blood red and there was an enormous, oversized fireplace opposite the bed. A small door led to a bathroom and every square inch of floor was covered by thick oriental rugs. The effect was both rich and oddly feminine, quite at odds with the austere furnishings she'd seen everywhere else in the house. A writing desk was placed just below the window; there were papers scattered across its surface. She walked over quickly to take a look. Most of the papers were official memos, in German. She picked up one or two, scanned them quickly, and put them down again. She opened one of the little drawers, but there was nothing of interest inside: a button; a small badge; a pen; a little gold brooch... She shut the drawer and turned to the bed. She saw it almost immediately. A thin sheaf of papers held together with a clip. She recognised Lily's handwriting straight away. She hurried over and picked it up. There were three sheets of crinkled blue paper, covered in Lily's still-childish script: *Lord and Lady Fane-Bertie; the Earl of Shaftesbury; the Earl of Denbigh; Viscount Torrington (but not his wife – she's extremely anti-German!)*. There were perhaps thirty or forty names on the list, covering two and a half pages. She took a deep breath. She had no other way to copy the names; it was too risky to remove the list from the bed. She had to memorise them, quickly. She immediately began grouping the names alphabetically, repeating a trick she'd learned from Father. There were four 'As' – *Arscott, Arbuthnot, Alderton, Ashkeaton*. Then she moved on to the 'Bs'. Only one: *Lord Bagshawe*. She went down the list, seeing in her mind's eye the imaginary notepaper on which she'd written everything down. She stopped at 'M' and ran over everything in her head. Yes, she had them all... nearly all. She'd missed out *Lord Matthiesen*. She went back, repeating it to herself until she'd got everything right. Then she went on to the second sheet. There were more names here, more densely crowded together, and Lily's comments were more frequent: *Son not to be included. Too Liberal*. She stopped at 'W', her eyes widening in shock. There they were. Their parents. *Lord and Lady Wharton. But <u>not</u> Katherine Algernon-Waters. Young, but has Communist tendencies*. She stared at the comment.

A noise outside suddenly brought her back to her senses. It was an owl or a bird of some sort, swooshing past the window. She hurriedly finished reading the names, committing them to memory. She laid the sheets down carefully, exactly where she'd found them, and crept back to the door. She switched off the light, waited a few seconds, then opened the door a crack. The corridor outside was empty. She slipped out, shut the door behind her and made her way in the shadowy gloom to the staircase. Her own bedroom was on the floor below. The dinner party was still going on; she could hear the sounds of animated chatter and laughter coming from the first floor. A clock chimed somewhere in the vast corridors. It was eleven o'clock. She ran lightly down the first flight of stairs, her heart thudding fast, her mind still full of the names she'd just memorised. As soon as she got to the safety of her room, she would write it all down. She couldn't wait to see Uncle Faunce's face when she presented it to him. It was the singular most important thing she had ever done in her life. Some higher courage had closed in on her when she stood in Wolf's room, looking around for the thing that Uncle Faunce sought. She wasn't afraid; she knew, as soon as she saw it, that there was only one thing to be done – and she'd done it.

She had almost reached the first staircase that marked only a few doors remaining until her room, when she heard footsteps coming towards her. Someone was coming up the stairs. She had only a second to react. She reached for the handle of the door closest to her and pushed. The door gave way with a loud creak. She stepped inside but it was too late. As she shut it behind her, she caught sight of the face of the man coming up the stairs. It was Wolf. And beside him, clutching his arm, was Lily. She had only a second to register her sister's look of angry suspicion before she shut the door in their faces. She stood inside the room, her teeth chattering. If she hadn't felt fear before, she felt it now. She heard them walk up the few remaining steps in silence and then stop. She hadn't switched on the light. She had no idea where she was, into whose room she'd stumbled. She waited in the thick darkness, just as she had on her first night, sure as anything that the person standing on the other side of the thick wood that separated them was a man. But this time, he wasn't alone. There was a soft creak as the handle began to move slowly downwards. It swung wide open. Light spilled in from the hallway. Wolf and Lily were on one side of the threshold; she was on the other.

'So, what do we have here?' Wolf murmured, stepping inside. Lily remained where she was. She seemed to have trouble focusing. Kit stared at her. Her eyes were enormous black holes in her face. Her whole expression seemed unable to settle, to be constantly sliding off her face.

'I ... I was just on my way to bed,' Kit stammered, looking from one to the other.

'Ah, but your room is in the other direction, *mein Kind*. You've been snooping, haven't you? *Du bist ziemlich neugierig auf die Dinge, nicht wahr?*'

Kit swallowed. She shook her head. 'No ... not at all. I ... I was just on my way to bed.'

'What are we going to do with her?' Wolf turned to look down at Lily. She was leaning against the doorjamb, one hand draped above her head as she coolly contemplated her sister, standing trembling in front of them. For a few moments, no one said anything. Despite the sounds coming from the dining room below, it was as though they were all three holding their breath, waiting for the next move, the next command, the next act.

'Teach her a lesson, Wolf,' Lily said finally, lowering her eyes. 'She was always such a nosy little thing. Always snooping around. Made me quite angry, you know. Yes, that's it. Teach her a lesson. You're good at that.' She nodded firmly, as though to herself, and then turned away.

Kit drew in a breath of terror; it stuck in her throat. She felt as though she couldn't breathe. Wolf smiled at her. It was the same, dispassionate smile he wore at all times, but as he moved towards her and let the door behind him close shut, she saw again that she was looking past his face to his other, hidden face – his real face.

'*Kom,*' he said, reaching out a hand. '*Kom.*' He held Kit by the wrist, gently at first. Then he tightened his grip and pulled.

9

She stumbled across the floor in the dark, her hands in front of her, feeling her way. She did not dare switch on the light. Her knees bumped against the bed. She lifted the covers and climbed in. She was trembling from head to toe. She pulled the sheet up to her chin and lay there, conscious only of the ferocious pain between her legs. She was breathing fast, as though something inside her were racing, struggling to get out. As soon as he touched her, her mind had emptied itself, gone blank, as though trying to protect her by forcing her to forget before it had even begun. She knew what he was about to do – she wasn't naïve – but she knew too that something enormous had happened, bigger than her, or the dangerous Wolf or hard, cruel Lily... Something that would change her for ever. Her hand went out in the dark to the bedside table and the small notebook she kept there. She reached for the light switch to turn on the lamp but changed her mind. She felt for the pencil beside it and placed both on top of the sheet. There was just enough moonlight to see by. She sat upright and opened the notebook to an empty page. She wrote in bold, childish script: *The List* and underscored it twice. Then she began to write, her lips moving slowly, as she carefully emptied her mind, line by line, name by name, group by group. She tore the sheet carefully out of the notebook and slipped it under her pillow. Then she lay there, in the dark, listening to the muffled and distant sounds of the night.

In the morning, when it was light and the house was still quiet, she got up and bathed, carefully washing the dried blood from her legs and belly. She got dressed, wincing as she pulled her stockings on. She checked her face in the bathroom mirror before she left her room. Nothing. There was nothing to be seen.

She walked downstairs to the kitchen. For the past three mornings, Uncle Faunce had been up before her. She opened the kitchen door. He was sitting beside the window, a cup of steaming coffee in his hand. He looked up as she entered, his eyes quickly searching her face. She gave absolutely nothing away. She walked towards him, holding the piece of paper in her hand.

'What's this?' he asked, as she put it down on the table in front of him.

'It's what you were looking for. I found it.'

He looked up at her, his eyes wide with surprise. 'But... but this is *your* handwriting.'

She nodded. 'I know. I memorised the names. I wrote them down this morning. They're all there. Every single one.'

'But... how? When?'

'Last night. When you were all at dinner. It didn't take me very long.'

'He didn't see you? No one saw you?' Uncle Faunce picked up the piece of paper and hurriedly slid it into the inner pocket of his jacket.

She shook her head. 'No. No one saw me. I went into his room and it was lying on the bed. I just memorised it. Miss Frogworth taught me how to do it. No one saw me, I promise. But it's all there.' Uncle Faunce suddenly appeared to have difficulty breathing. 'Don't be upset,' Kit said quickly. 'It's all right. I remembered what you'd told me about being calm. I was calm. That's how I was able to remember all the names. And then, as soon as I got back to my room, I wrote them down.'

She saw then, from the look on his face, that although her own faith in herself had been absolute, Uncle Faunce's had not.

PART TWO
LOSS

1939–1940
Kit

10

It was quiet in the drawing room as the maid poured the tea. A large plate of scones, without butter but with a meagre dollop of jam, was placed in front of the two women, neither of whom so much as glanced at it. Lady Wharton and her guest waited until the maid had finished and withdrawn from the room before opening their mouths to speak.

As soon as the door had closed behind her, Lady Wharton burst out, 'Surely you're not suggesting she comes back *here?*' The words exploded out of her mouth before she could even think of stopping them. 'What on earth would we *say?*'

Margaret Arscott regarded Lady Wharton coolly. She reached for a cigarette, ignoring the pained expression on Lady Wharton's face. 'What do you mean, "What would we say?" She's your *daughter*, Delphine. Your youngest daughter. And if the newspapers are anything to go by, she may well wind up being your *only* daughter.'

'I do wish you wouldn't *say* that. I don't believe Lily could ever have done such a thing; I don't care *what* the papers say. She would *never* betray her own country, never! Oh, here, give me one.'

Margaret tapped out another cigarette from the pack and watched as Lady Wharton lit it, her trembling hands betraying her nervousness.

'And there's Harold's position in the county to think of. What would people say?'

'What's there to say? *You* sent her over there, don't forget. Both of you.'

'Faunce was supposed to look after her,' Lady Wharton began.

For a brief second, Margaret's expression softened. 'Has there been any news of Faunce?' she asked.

Lady Wharton shook her head. 'No. They... they say the last sighting anyone had of him was in Berlin, about two months ago. Why he didn't just come back with Kit I'll never know.'

'What a mess,' Margaret said slowly. 'What a *terrible* mess. So where is she now?'

'I don't know. The last letter I had was in March, just after Kit left—'

'No, not Lily. Kit. We *know* where Lily is. Where did you send poor Kit?'

'Oh, *Kit*. Yes, of course. Well, I sent her to Scotland. It was the furthest away I could think of. Do you remember Mrs Baxter? She was the housekeeper here before Mrs Hughes. Her sister lives out on one of those islands... I forget which. She runs a boarding house for girls who... well, you know, who have found themselves in trouble. It's perfectly nice, or so she told us. It's quite remote, and there's a village doctor on hand. In case... well, just in case.'

'And then what are you going to do? I should have thought one scandal in the family's plenty, don't you?' Margaret Arscott said tartly.

Lady Wharton looked down at her hands. 'Yes,' she said unhappily. 'One's quite enough. But she can't come back here,' she repeated, turning enormous, red-rimmed eyes towards her. 'We were lucky enough to get her out of here before it began to show. Oh, Margaret, I just don't know what to do.'

There was another long silence. Margaret Arscott sipped her tea. 'Very well,' she said at last. 'Let her come to me.'

'Would you really?' Lady Wharton said tremulously. 'I wasn't sure... I didn't know how to ask.'

'Well, *somebody's* got to take her in. She's *sixteen*, Delphine. I know you can't think of anyone other than Lily, but honestly... you're her mother.'

'I know, I know.' Lady Wharton's voice began to quiver. 'But there's the family name to think of. I just... I just can't think straight. And what about afterwards? Would you be able to find someone? You know, to take the child in? *You* know how it's done. You were always the practical one, Margaret. Always.'

'Hmm.' Margaret Arscott pursed her lips. 'And if I can't? Then what?'

'We could send her away, I suppose,' Lady Wharton said, her voice regaining some of its imperious strength as the idea came to her. 'Somewhere new, where no one really knows her. Ireland? Or America, perhaps? Harold's got family... you must know them. The Crichfords? Lord Dunboyne. They live somewhere on the West Coast. I can't remember exactly where. Los Angeles, or San Francisco, or some such. She could start all over again there.'

'Delphine, you cannot be *serious*. You've already lost one daughter to the Nazis and now you want to banish the other one? No, my mind's made up. I'll take her as soon as she's had the baby and she's well enough to travel. We'll see about finding a suitable family for the child. She can come to me in Norfolk. No one there will bother her and she can stay with me as long as she likes. It's 1939, Delphine, not 1839. The war's changed everything. I know you and Harold still cling to the past, but what's done is done. We've got to move forward. And, as I said, you've already lost one daughter. Goodness knows what's going to happen next but I'll tell you this: Hitler will *never* succeed. *Never.* And when this terrible war is over, you'll have the task of explaining just how someone brought up in Dorset could ever have contemplated throwing in their lot with *him*. Odious little man. Too despicable for words. How *could* Lily? How could she be so *blind*?'

Lady Wharton shook her head, reaching for a handkerchief. 'I don't understand it either,' she said. 'I don't understand anything any more. What did we do wrong? Both of them ... ruined. And Lily was so beautiful, too!'

Margaret Arscott rolled her eyes. Was there nothing else the silly woman ever thought about? 'As I said, Delphine, what's done is done. The most important thing is to bring her and the baby safely to me.' She stood up, her newly shorn hair swinging to just below her chin. She looked down at her friend. Lady Wharton was still slumped in her chair, as though the effort of getting up was simply beyond her. 'She'll be fine with me, Delphine,' she said softly, finally, her voice surprisingly gentle. 'Let's take it a step at a time.'

Lady Wharton was quiet. For a few moments, the two women remained in the slowly deepening gloom. The lingering scent of cigarette smoke mingled with the faint traces of their perfume, different but discernible. Then Lady Wharton looked up at Margaret Arscott, whom she'd known for the better part of half a century. Like so many women of their time and class, the ties that bound them to each other went long and deep. Their parents had been friends and their grandparents before them. Although Margaret was nearly ten years Lady Wharton's junior, they'd struck up a friendship in that far-off place called childhood that had remained long after childhood was over. In spite of her obvious disapprobation, she knew that Margaret had another reason for wishing the war was over and done with. She'd been married once, many years earlier, to a man much older than her. His sudden death at the age of fifty-four had shocked everyone. They'd only been married six months. She'd been a widow as long as Lady Wharton had been a wife and mother. She hadn't even had enough time with her husband to fall pregnant. She'd dropped Lewes from her name in her late thirties, Lady Wharton remembered dimly, along with her long hair, conservative clothes and the slightly old-fashioned airs of her parents. Although they'd been friends for almost their entire lives, once Margaret had dropped out of the London and Dorset circles, in which mostly married couples moved, they'd drifted apart a little. It was partly to do with circumstances, Lady Wharton acknowledged. Although it hadn't always been that way, Margaret's fortunes had risen in almost direct proportion to the decline of theirs. She didn't have to worry; her generous widower's pension and the enormous inheritance she'd received from her parents took care of that. She'd always been active, always busy with one philanthropic venture or another. She was bright, too, born at a time when the idea of a woman working for a living was so foreign to most of their peers that she wouldn't have known quite what to *do* had the opportunity presented itself. Perhaps that was what made her unusually sensitive, Lady Wharton thought. She'd known tragedy at such an early age and it had marked her for the rest of her life. No wonder she'd rushed down from Norfolk as soon as she'd heard the news. Odd, wasn't it, she mused as she watched Margaret gather her belongings – a very stylish handbag, she noted distractedly, as well as a rather fetching caramel-coloured coat and a red pillbox hat – Margaret was the first person she turned to, even after all this time.

'Marge,' she said slowly, looking up at her. She'd reverted to her child-hood name. 'You don't think I'm ... I'm an awful mother, do you?' She had difficulty releasing the words.

Margaret looked at her. It seemed to take ages before she shook her head. 'No, Delly, I don't. The thing is, though, sometimes you have to put your instincts before anything else. Before Harold, before Lily, before your friends and neighbours. Those ridiculous people you call "friends", anyway. Sometimes you just have to do what's right for you. Not for anyone else. Kit's having a baby. She needs your help. Who cares what all those other idiots think?'

'It's easy for you to say,' Lady Wharton replied sadly. 'You've *never* had to conform. You've always done things your own way.'

'That's not true, and you know it. Have you forgotten how difficult it was to get Daddy's permission to marry Donald in the first place? And all that fuss about dropping his name after he died? There was the most terrific row. Daddy threatened to cut me off without a penny, don't you remember? But he couldn't cut me out of his life, just the way you can't possibly cut Kit out of yours. Fine, you'd rather she were somewhere else for now and I expect you'd rather have to deal with Lily. I never understood why you preferred Lily to Kit. No, don't say anything. You've always treated them differently, ever since they were children. I'm not judging you. I'm just saying that Kit needs you now. Lily doesn't, at least not now, and at least not in the same way. Don't shut Kit out. And don't let too much time pass before you find a way to bring her back into the fold again. That's all I'm saying.'

'Of course I won't,' Lady Wharton cried suddenly. 'I'm not entirely without feelings, you know. It's just *difficult*. Kit's always been difficult. I never know *what* she's thinking. You know how she is ... she's not like Lily. And now there's *this* ... I don't know *who* knows.'

'Does it matter, Delly? Does it *really* matter? Let's just get her home. Let her come to me, with the baby. We'll take each step as it comes. This time next year the war will be over and Kit will be back here at Chalfont Hall. We'll have found a good family for the baby ... everything will work out, you'll see. Things will just go straight back to normal.'

'Normal?' Lady Wharton said slowly. 'Normal? I don't know what that is any more. I don't know if we'll *ever* know again.'

Lady Wharton wandered over to the window and stood in the shadow of the drapes, watching Margaret's car pull slowly out of the driveway. It was a long, dark green car – something new, no doubt. She shivered and pulled her cardigan around her shoulders. It was freezing in the drawing room. That was another thing they'd had to compromise on: coal. That and butter and jam and puddings and meat and petrol and God knows what else they'd soon have to cut out. It was all right for Margaret. She had Foulden Hall, which, at almost a third the size of Chalfont, was easy to keep, especially in these straitened times. There was the house in Belgravia and the pied-à-terre in Paris, not to mention the farmhouse in the south of France where she summered every other year. Oh, yes, it was all right for *her*.

As the shiny green car disappeared over the hill, she gave way to a long-suppressed moment of self-pity. Where had it all gone so wrong?

She lit another cigarette. Harold was in Portsmouth on business. He wouldn't be back until the following Monday. She had the whole damned place to herself and the thought filled her with dread. There was a time when the opposite would have been true; the thought of a weekend without Harold meant something else. She shivered again. It was a period of her life she didn't like to think about. Margaret's comment had struck a raw nerve. *I never understood why you preferred Lily to Kit. You've always treated them differently, ever since they were children.* It was true. But Margaret would never know the reason why. No one knew, perhaps not even Kit herself. How could she? She was too young to remember and even less likely to understand. She tried to stop herself from remembering that dreadful Saturday morning... but failed. The memory of it was branded in her, as if into flesh.

They were lying in bed in her room, her private room, across the hallway from the master bedroom where she sometimes slept beside her husband. Funnily enough, it was her mother who'd insisted they keep to the old ways.

'Don't give up your own bedroom,' she'd said, weeks before she and Harold were married. 'I know you young couples like to do things differently, but trust me, there'll come a time when you'll be grateful for your own privacy. A woman has to have her own sanctuary.'

It was the closest her mother had ever come to discussing anything about married life. It was doubtful that her mother had ever envisaged this, Delphine thought to herself as she turned around and into the warm, willing embrace of the man lying next to her. Yes, she was grateful for her own privacy, but for other reasons. Harold was 'up' in London. They'd been married nearly ten years. In that time, if he thought for one second that she didn't know what he got up to when he was away, he was an even bigger fool than he looked.

'That's just the way it is,' her mother said, looking bored when she brought it up. 'Men. They're all the same, darling. Never mind. You've got the girls. And the houses, of course. At least there's that.' And that was the end of it.

She didn't quite know how it happened. How it actually began. How she even dared think of it. One minute, it seemed, he was in the dining room serving breakfast, the next minute he was in her room. Naked. In her bed. He was young and strong and ridiculously good-looking for a servant. If the truth were told, it was the latter that made it all the more exciting. She had absolute power over him and they both knew it. In bed, however, it was another matter, and that made it all the more delicious. She had never, ever imagined herself capable of such thoughts, such acts. And it was in the middle of one of those such acts that she suddenly became aware of a movement in the room. She was lying face down on the quilted eiderdown, her arms and legs spread in a way that would have horrified every single person she knew had they been able to see her. The oval mirror above the dressing table by the window threw back a reflection every now and then: his pale, smooth skin; the bulge of muscles in his arms; the way her neck arched; and the tousled mess of her hair once he'd undone the pins. Something moved. A shadow flitted across the mirror. A sound escaped. She froze, rigid with fear. Peters didn't notice. He was too busy pursuing his own pleasurable release.

'Hey, what's the matter?' he gasped, as she tried to wriggle free. 'Steady on, no, don't move.'

'Get off me!' she hissed, jerking against the bonds. 'Untie me, quick!'

'What's the matter?'

'Just get off! There's someone here!'

That stopped him. Quick as a flash, fingers trembling, heart pounding, absolute silence. She clutched the sheet to her chest.

'Who's there? Who is it?' Her voice sounded as loud as thunder in her ears.

'There's someone behind the curtains,' he said, his own voice shaking in a way she'd never heard anyone's voice shake before.

'Come out at once!' If it was one of the maids, the situation was easily resolved. She'd be gone by nightfall. 'Come out, whoever you are.'

It was she who got up, the sheet still wrapped tightly around her. Peters was busy doing up his uniform, his lovely strong body already disappeared from sight. She pulled back the curtains. It was Kit. Her expression gave nothing away. She was holding onto her teddy. How the child had got into the room in the first place was beyond her. The two of them stared at the five-year-old, too shocked to speak. Then she turned and walked out of the room. Nothing was said.

Peters beat a hasty retreat, leaving her standing with the sheets draped ridiculously around her body, her hair cascading down her back, her mind gone completely blank with the horror and shame of it all. For the first time in her life, she had absolutely no idea what to do. Should she run after the child and somehow explain? But explain what? She was five years old! She wouldn't have been able to put into words what she'd seen, surely? In that way, she was safe. Wasn't she? If she did indeed say something, well... she'd quickly put it down to childish fantasy. But what child could possibly invent something like that?

In the event, nothing was ever said. When Nanny brought the two children down later that evening after tea, Kit calmly presented her cheek to her mother to be kissed, just as always. She was still clutching the same dog-eared teddy bear. Delphine watched them go, Lily skipping along, cheerful as you please, Kit quiet and self-possessed as ever. She let out the breath she'd been holding all afternoon. She'd got away with it. Just. It could never happen again.

To this day, she'd never been able to rid herself of the mixture of shame and resentment she felt whenever she looked at her youngest child. Margaret was right. She did treat them differently. But not out of love, one loved less than the other. Out of shame. It came as a surprise to her to understand that of the two emotions, it was shame that lingered on, shadowy, destroying everything, including love.

11

The weather rolled in from Canada, many thousands of miles away. Some force of nature out there over the vast, high seas caused a drop in pressure and a storm began, crossing the Atlantic by way of Ireland, landmass, then the Isles – Tiree, Coll, Rùm, Uist – all the way up to Lochmaddy. Miles out, the storm paused, gathering breath, and then it swept up the sound, veering towards one side of the island, bending the few trees until their thin branches touched the ground, first this way, and then that. It changed tack, sweeping towards the east, a battering rain that beat down mercilessly on the mirrored surface of the inland loch, smashing tiles and slamming windows, hammering at doors. It went on all day.

'A good rain,' Mrs McPherson remarked. 'We're needin' it after the summer.' The ground was parched, or so she said.

The young girl, standing at the doorway, looking out over the low water to the fingers of land that marked the island's edges, did not notice. She moved awkwardly, her long coltish body at odds with the weight it carried. The rain continued all night and into the next day.

*

'A "set-in" rain, that's wha' we call it up here,' Mrs McPherson said the following morning, as she bustled into the girl's room, a plate of glistening poached eggs and toast balanced on a mahogany tray. She set the tray down upon the dressing table and strode across the room.

The girl raised herself on her elbows, the distended mound of her stomach momentarily obscuring her face.

'How're ye feelin' this mornin'?' Mrs McPherson asked, pulling aside the curtains to reveal a thundery sky.

The girl swallowed. She appeared stunned, though whether by the weak light coming in from outside or through some lethargy brought about by her own condition, it was hard to tell. She levered herself upright, but gingerly.

'I … I'm fine,' she said finally, as though the words had cost her some effort.

'Ye've no' long to go now,' Mrs McPherson said briskly, eyeing her with a semi-professional gauge. 'It'll be over afore ye know it.'

The girl said nothing. Her eyes were drawn to the patch of sky that was holding, a tender area of glare underneath which the sun was buried. 'Could I … could I have some tea?' she asked politely.

'Aye, there's a pot right here.' Mrs McPherson pointed to the woollen cosy, incongruously jolly in a room that seemed swaddled in sadness. 'I'll leave ye to it, shall I?'

The girl nodded. There was a moment's awkward silence as the two women looked at each other from opposite ends of the spectrum of female experience, then Mrs McPherson dropped her gaze with a murmur of no consequence or meaning, and left the room.

It took the girl a few minutes to negotiate her way out of the tangled mess of sheets and eiderdown cover, and for her feet to find the slippers she'd discarded beside the bed. She got out carefully, putting one foot down before the other, then rose, one hand hugging the bulge that made a mockery of her young face. She walked to the window and peered out. The rain had started again, forcefully. She watched as a man in yellow oilskins staggered across the road below, his arms out, struggling to keep his balance. He staggered back, having changed his mind, his arms stretching towards the shelter from which he'd come. She looked beyond him to the choppy grey sea, heaving from side to side. The line of hills rolled on until they blurred, dissolving in the rainy light.

And still the rain went on.

12

'It's yer waters. They've broke,' Mrs McPherson said briskly, surveying the sodden sheets. 'Right ye are. I'll call the midwife. It'll no' be long now. Come away wi' ye. I'll get the sheets changed but they'll get just as wet in no time.'

'Am … am I dying?' Kit asked fearfully. The pain in her lower abdomen was like nothing she'd ever experienced.

Mrs McPherson chuckled. 'No, ye're no' dyin', lass. Ye're givin' birth. Come away now … that's it. Up ye get. Bridie!' she yelled out to the girl downstairs. 'Put the kettle on and find some pans. We're goin' to need all the hot water we can get!' She helped Kit out of bed. 'That's right, ye hold on to me, lass. Remember, it's the most natural thing in the world. Dinnae fear.'

She was conscious throughout, but the real work was being done by her body. She was aware of voices, shapes, hands … At one point, she thought there were half a dozen people in the tiny room but later realised that she'd been delirious with the pain. It felt as though something were being torn from her body. Some*thing*, not some*one*. She could no more think of the baby as a person – a living, breathing being – than she could think of it as a 'thing'. A thing that had been done to her. The moment Wolf had reached out to take hold of her arm, something inside her had snapped. She knew what was coming. She wasn't as innocent of the facts of life as another in her place might have been. She had her father's books to thank for that. But, at that same moment, another memory had drifted in, replacing what was going on in front of her and mercifully allowing her to escape into another, distant past where the horror of what was happening was happening to someone else. She couldn't have said precisely when it was; in her jumbled up, reconstructed way, she knew she'd seen her mother caught in some guilty act. The body covering her mother's wasn't Father; she knew that much. But there was something desperately shameful, not just about the way she'd seen them together, but more tellingly, in the way her mother behaved towards her afterwards, that repulsed her. She understood, somehow, that she could never think about it. She could never move around safely in the crumbling shadows of the past. She had to banish the images, block out the sounds... retreat from what had been shown to her. It was the same instinct to protect herself that saved her then, as it did now. That was how Wolf was able to avail himself of whatever it was he sought.

When the fact of the baby revealed itself, several months later, she had almost managed to convince herself that none of it had ever taken place.

Until now. Now the pain was so immediate and real that it had broken through the protective veil of her own memory and mind, catapulting her into the present, where the sound of screaming drowned everything out to the point where she couldn't tell whose voice was struggling to be heard above the noise, the newborn's or hers.

13

The countryside opened itself up to her, mile after mile of snow-covered fields, damp, narrow lanes and frosty verges, scenes from another life before the present one. Even in the grip of what everyone held was the worst winter for years – in living memory, some went so far as to say – there was something gentle, almost feminine about the slow rolling hills and hedge-fringed country roads. The hedges were lacy silver and green screens, sometimes overtaken by low stone walls, the barns sat squarely atop rises, not huddled from the rain the way they were in Scotland. There the weather was less an element than an enemy; all life centred on protecting oneself from its whims and vagaries. Blue skies the colour of a duck's egg one day, a sea that rose to meet the thundery sky the next. She'd spent a month in that little room on the isle of Uist, the last sliver of barren hills and craggy valleys before the expanse of ocean that was so wide and complete it was hard to fathom there would ever be land again. The sound of the language was still ringing in her ears. English? Gaelic? She wasn't even sure. After the baby was born there was another noise filling her head: his cries, sniffles, whimpers, burps

69

and, lately now, something that sounded like laughter. But it couldn't be. They had little to laugh about, she and him. She looked down at the bundle in her arms, some distant part of her brain marvelling at the way she held him. Naturally. Protectively. Mrs McPherson had said to her a few days afterwards that she'd never seen anyone take to it so naturally.

'Ye're only a wee slip o' a thing,' she'd said, looking down at her. 'You're no' much bigger 'n him, to be honest. But ye've taken to it like a duck to water, aye, ye have.'

Kit didn't know what to say. She had the baby in the crook of her arm, just as the midwife had shown her, and with the other she held the warmed-up bottle of milk to his lips.

'Dinnae worry, lass,' the midwife had said, shaking her head firmly. 'Ye'll no' be wantin' to breast-feed the wee lad, no … That's no' a guid idea. Morag here says ye'll be givin' him up just as soon as ye're able. No, lass. Best ye don't start.'

'She's right,' Mrs McPherson chimed in. 'Best no' to.'

'Yer milk'll dry up soon enough,' the midwife said briskly. 'It'll make it easier for ye when the time comes.'

When the time comes. It was a phrase she'd heard all too often in the past year. When the war comes. *When the baby comes. When the time comes.* It felt as though her life was nothing but a series of perpetual 'whens'.

The baby whimpered suddenly and in an instant her focus was restored. He was a strong little thing, pudgy hands gripping the blanket that covered him, even in his sleep. It was an hour since his last feed but to her immense relief he hadn't woken since they'd boarded the train at King's Cross.

Bridie, Mrs McPherson's niece, accompanied her all the way from Uist to Mull and then to Oban, where they caught the train to Inveraray. All Kit could remember of the journey was the clanging and banging, the terrible grind of metal on metal, the high, piercing shriek of the guard's whistle and the strange moment when the train began to move slowly out of whatever station they'd arrived at. The figures on the platform began to dissolve into one another; here and there a hand was raised in a half-wave and then the engine picked up speed and the platform and the waving strangers were left behind. As they rolled south towards the border, the baby slept in Bridie's arms, seemingly content. There were one or two older women who looked curiously at the trio as they staggered down the narrow passage to the compartment that had been reserved for them under the name of 'Arscott'. A knowing glance, the merest lift of the eyebrow, the sudden tilting of the head. What must they look like? A tired-looking girl-who-wasn't-a-schoolgirl, a young, anxious-looking woman and a sleeping baby... and not a shred of resemblance between them. Bridie Stuart was a redhead, Kit had blonde hair and the baby was dark-haired, oddly enough. No wonder people stared.

She turned her head to look out the car window. Norfolk began to slip past. No sooner was a sign come upon than it was left behind. *Swaffham 15. Hilborough 4. Foulden 1.* The roads were almost empty. It was 29th December. They were in the no-man's land of the week between Christmas and New Year, desperate to be rid of 1939, yet dreading what 1940 would bring. It was no time for celebration. Only days before, two British ships had collided off the coast of Kintyre, with the loss of more than a hundred lives.

She'd given Mrs McPherson the slip the morning after the news was announced on the wireless and gone down to the beach with the baby swaddled so tightly it resembled one of those Egyptian mummies she'd seen on a visit with Lily to the British Museum, back in the days of their by-now forgotten childhood. The waves frothed angrily at the shore; the sea and sky moved as one, a ponderous swaying back and forth that made her dizzy. She stood at the edge of the road in a light, misty drizzle that was both rain and fog and yet neither, staring out to where the ships had sunk. It seemed unfathomable. A ship was an enormous, weighty thing... all that steel and iron...

'One thousand, three hundred and fifty-seven long tonnes,' the news-reader's disembodied voice filled the small front room, where she and Mrs McPherson sat in the mornings and late afternoons with the fire and the wireless on, keeping time and company.

In the old days, as she now thought of her life before Germany, she'd have piped up immediately: 'What's a long tonne?' Someone would have answered her. Bignell, perhaps, though chances were he wouldn't have the answer. She could almost hear him: 'Well, milady, can't rightly say.' Or Caruthers: 'A long tonne is...' If the answer didn't satisfy her – and their answers rarely did – there was always Father or the library and the pleasurable anticipation of flicking through the tomes until the answer was come upon, the *right* answer... the one she'd sought and found. She felt the loss in the pit of her stomach like a hunger pang, an ache that threatened to swallow her whole.

She looked out across the misty expanse where colour and texture dissolved, disappearing before her eyes like the drowned sailors, making her newly aware of her own slightness. *A slip of a thing.* She lifted a hand to brush a strand of hair from her face. She'd rushed out without a hat. What if she just walked into the greyness? Carrying the baby who hadn't made a sound until now? No one would miss her. Mother and Father would be only too glad to be rid of her and she already knew she would never see Lily again. Mother had made it very clear that she would never return to Chalfont. In a few weeks' time, when she was 'well enough to travel', she and the baby would be escorted to Norfolk, to the home of one of Mother's friends, Mrs Margaret Arscott. Kit remembered her principally for her laugh. She laughed a lot. That was all she could recall.

'Mrs Arscott's going to take you in, darling,' Mother had said down the crackling telephone line. 'She'll arrange everything. It's all been decided. Just as soon as you're well enough to travel. You need to get your strength back.' They all spoke of her as though she'd suffered an unimaginable, unspeakable illness. In time, they all assured her, she would be 'well' again. No one ever referred to the baby.

Someone clutched her arm. Startled, she turned and found herself staring at Mrs McPherson.

'Come away in,' Mrs McPherson said softly, her voice unexpectedly gentle. 'Ye'll catch yer death o' cold. Ye've no' even got a coat on.' A sudden gust of wind picked up her voice, scattering the words.

Kit had allowed her to pull her away, back across the road and up the short hill that led to the farmhouse. Inside, she stood by quietly whilst Mrs McPherson fussed around her, covering her knees with one of the thick tartan blankets that lay permanently draped on any available surface in the room, waiting to be of service. The baby was being fed in the kitchen by Mrs McPherson's aunt – one of many women who dropped in at regular intervals throughout the day and who seemed equally adept at feeding a three-week-old infant as they did at making the tea.

'There ye go, pet. Right by the window, that's right. Aye … ye're awffy keen on the outside world, aren't ye? Goodness knows why … Nothin' out there but rain an' that dreary view o' the sea.' She stood there for a moment, contemplating the view, then shook her head. 'On a bonny day, aye … But who wants to look at the rain?'

'I like it.' Kit spoke up suddenly, surprising them both.

Mrs McPherson looked at her curiously. 'Aye, I dare say ye do,' she said finally. 'Well, I'll leave ye be for a wee while. I'll just be out back in the kitchen wi' the bairn.' She touched Kit very lightly on the shoulder – the first time she'd ever done that – and withdrew.

Kit could hear the two women chatting companionably as Mrs McPherson bustled about the small kitchen, no doubt making yet another pot of tea. She leaned her head against the prickly upholstery, hearing the rise and fall of their voices, rather than anything they actually said. The baby was quiet. There was a large puddle right outside the window and the whole world was repeated in it, upside down, the stone façade of the farmhouse dimpling as the pinpricks of rain punctured its surface. Her mind was still; the half questions that hovered there continuously, like the psychedelic light that burned on the inside of her eyelids long after its source had disappeared, were still. She was resting, the way babies – including her own – rest between one stage of labour and the next, thinking, perhaps, that they'd arrived.

'Miss? Miss?' The chauffeur's quiet but insistent voice broke through the silence that had enveloped her. She'd fallen asleep. She struggled carefully upright, praying the baby wouldn't wake up.

'Are we here?' she asked, peering out into the dusky afternoon. It was nearly four o'clock and the night was fast closing in. Back on Uist, it would have been pitch-dark already. She stopped herself from saying the word 'home' just in time. She'd read it once, somewhere – you only had to return once or twice to a place to call it 'home'. *A hotel room, a guest room, a spare room in someone's house. Or a room in which you'd been sent to have a child.*

14

Margaret Arscott had been up, dressed and waiting since before breakfast. She couldn't put her finger on quite why Kit's impending visit had made her so emotional. She felt sorry for her, of course, but there was more to it, there had to be. It had been over a year since she'd last seen either sister. If her memory served her right, it was in the week before

Lily's coming-out ball. The whole house had been turned upside down. Dressmakers came and went; the kitchens had been churning out cakes for weeks; there were visitors every other day... You'd have thought the girl was getting married. And then, of course, she *did* get married in a whirlwind of announcements and newspaper articles. That he was nearly twenty years her senior and German to boot seemed to make little difference to anyone, least of all Lily and Delphine. He was rich. That was all that mattered.

She remembered coming upon Kit one day, long ago, sitting in the window seat in the upstairs drawing room, reading. She was filled with a sudden tenderness for the young girl who'd been elbowed out of the way.

'Hello,' she said, crossing the richly patterned carpet to where Kit sat, legs tucked up underneath her. 'All alone?'

Kit looked up. She had the expression of a face in a high wind, nerve-tinglingly alive. Hers was not the dull, plastic beauty of her sister's; her attractiveness had to do with the quicksilver signs of life on the surface of her skin, like a flash of the sun or the shiver of wind on water. It was a quick, intelligent face; there was passion and vitality in the smooth sweep of skin from brow to cheekbone, the slick of glossy eyebrows surprisingly dark for someone so fair. It was a face that would come into its own later in life, Margaret thought as she settled herself into the comfortable seat beside her. As a child she was precociously awkward; later, as a woman, she would be commandingly beautiful, she thought, almost imperious.

'I thought I should never be alone,' Kit said, smiling. As usual, she held a book in her hands.

'Can I get you anything?' Margaret asked, inexplicably wanting to make amends, somehow, for the lack of attention everyone paid to Kit.

Kit looked at her, a frank, unflinching gaze. 'Like what?'

'Oh, I don't know... something to eat or drink, perhaps? Aren't you bored?'

'No, no, I'm not.' Then she added, 'But I know what you mean. Every now and then you notice someone and then you find you don't know what to say to them.'

Margaret was surprised by her answer and her astuteness. She laughed and saw that Kit had taken it as a sort of confession. The scene seemed to be set for an exchange of confidences between them.

'Yes,' she said slowly. 'I suppose you're right. As you get older, there seem to be more and more of them… other people. And then one day you realise you're one of them. Other people, I mean.'

How old was she then? Fifteen? She was still too young to know how to respond to a comment she didn't quite understand.

'Well, I'd best be going,' Margaret said finally, getting to her feet.

Kit didn't change the angle of her head over her book. Margaret had the ridiculous sensation it was she who had blundered somehow.

Now, watching Kit cross the hallway, she saw that the girl had the self-conscious gait and expression of someone who knows herself to be watched. As she came towards her, she had the sudden, curious certainty that what she saw on the girl's face was exactly what was on her own: guilt. She had one of those terrible contractions somewhere in her chest that almost brought tears to her eyes. What did the poor girl have to feel guilty about? It was *they* – the world of adults, including her own mother – who should be held to account.

'Darling Kit!' she exclaimed loudly, more out of an attempt to cover her own embarrassment than in welcome. Too loudly, she saw immediately as Kit flinched, although she did her best to cover it. 'My dearest girl,' she repeated, more gently this time. She opened her arms. Kit stopped, and stood perfectly still, allowing herself to be hugged. Hovering behind her, Mrs Wright, her trusted housekeeper of nearly twenty years, held the baby, who was the cause and centrepiece of all the drama, in a white basket, covered up so efficiently that all Margaret could see was a tuft of dark hair.

'Was the journey very terrible?' she asked solicitously.

Kit shook her head. 'No, it was fine. A little tiring, but he slept most of the way.'

'Come, my dear. Let me show you to your room. I've put you both in the wing that overlooks the park. It's quite lovely, especially at this time of year. Mrs Wright will stay with you for the first night.' She beamed at them both. 'Mrs Wright, will you see Lady Katherine to her room and get her settled in. Supper will be at seven. Mrs Wright will show you where it is, darling. No need to dress up. It's just us. Now, I don't want you to worry about a thing. You're here to rest and get better.' She gave what she hoped was a bright, cheery smile and watched as Mrs Wright briskly took charge, leading the way.

By the end of the week, everything would have been settled. A family had already been found through the parish church, a decent, hard-working couple with no children of their own. According to Mrs Wright, at least, they viewed the chance to adopt a month-old baby of 'high birth' as a miracle. No one had said a word about the paternity of the child. *Secrets and lies; the unspoken and the unsaid.* It was the way their class had always done things and would likely continue to. Respectability – or the appearance of it – was paramount. Women like Delphine accepted marriage and motherhood as social, rather than personal, relationships, content for their lives to revolve within the parameters they all understood. Coming out at eighteen was only the first step of many that settled the course of their lives. In another twenty years, or so, their daughters would perform the same and so it would continue. Occasionally, as now, a girl took a wrong step, faltered … made a wrong move.

The consequences could – and usually did – reverberate for decades.

15

Kit sat down gingerly on the bed and looked around her. In the next room, Mrs Wright was fussing with the baby. She could hear his whimpers, a prelude to full-throated screams. The first time he'd properly cried, she nearly dropped him. How could such a tiny little thing produce such ear-splitting noise?

'There, there,' she could hear Mrs Wright murmur. 'There, there.'

It was uncanny how women seemed to know what to do in the face of a whimpering or screaming child. But not Mrs Arscott. She'd seen the way Mrs Arscott had looked at her and the child, a mixture of distaste and guilt and pity. It was the same look she'd seen in her mother's face when she broke the news. Kit's eyes filled with cold, heavy tears, but it was not the place or time to weep. It was nearly six thirty. In half an hour, she would be expected to descend the long staircase and join Mrs Arscott for dinner. She would sit with her in the fusty dining room, just the two of them at a polished dining table that looked exactly like the dining table at home. The same silverware, unused crystal wine glasses, the orderly array of polished cutlery and the same tasteful paintings of inoffensive English landscapes in calm, pastel colours that were a sharp and uncomfortable contrast to the raging torrent of emotions that crashed around inside her own head, unable to find expression or peace.

She held in her mind for a moment all that belonged to the horror and hollowness of the past few months. She reached out a hand and clutched at the patterned bedspread, crushing the pink and mauve paisley print between her fingers. The storm inside her rose, like a breath drawn in. She could scarcely breathe.

'There, there,' Mrs Wright half sang from the room next door. 'Go to sleep now, there's a good little boy.' The throwaway phrase slowly began to restore her.

And then just as suddenly as it had erupted, its grip was broken. She took a deep breath and willed herself to return to the surface, to the sure facts. She was here with the baby in the house of her mother's friend, safe and warm. A family had been found for the baby, who was still unnamed. It made it easier not to have named him. There was no one to address; he hadn't yet *become* anyone. She would hand him over and in a few weeks' time she would return to pick up the thread of the life she'd left behind.

A gong sounded from somewhere deep inside the house. Her eyes fell on the little brass clock beside the bed. It was nearly seven. She pushed herself upright. All was quiet next door. Had she dozed off? There was no longer any sign of Mrs Wright. She tiptoed to the door. The baby was fast asleep in the crib that had been brought up – God knows from where – and placed in the centre of the small box bedroom. She peered cautiously over the edge. The gathering beat of her heart was in her chest and throat as she looked down at her sleeping child. Despite having no name, he was already a collection of identifiable marks – eyes, a snub nose, cheeks. She stared at him. Hers? She could no more think of him as belonging to her than she could think of herself as separate from *him*. The confusion she experienced deep inside her whenever she looked at him was too much to bear.

She turned away, shutting the door quietly but firmly behind her. She looked down at her dress. She'd been travelling in it for over a day. She walked over to the armoire in the corner of the room and opened the door. Her few dresses were already hanging on silk-covered hangers, three pairs of shoes neatly lined up. A footman had obviously whisked her cases from the car as soon as they arrived, and no doubt one of the maids had organised her clothes whilst she and Mrs Arscott stood downstairs.

She hurriedly pulled the navy blue dress over her head and stood shivering before the open door in her slip. Foulden Hall was exactly the same as Chalfont: unless you were standing directly in front of a fire, it was damp and chilly in winter. She took a pale cream woollen dress off the hanger and held it against her. There was a mirror on the inside door of the wardrobe. She scarcely recognised herself; pale, now thin again after those months where she'd looked and felt as swollen as the pregnant horses in the paddock at the bottom of the hill at home. Clumsy, awkward, heavy... that was what it felt like. In the few novels she'd read that touched upon such matters, women were always described as 'blooming' and 'blossoming' and 'glowing with health'. She'd felt none of that.

She glanced at the clock again. Seven minutes past. She hurried down the corridor to the stairs. Although it had been months since she'd gone 'down' to dinner, the habits of a lifetime of punctuality died hard. Father would rarely say a word but his frown spoke volumes. It was only Lily who got away with being late. 'Papa, I'm so *sorry* I'm so tardy!' she would declare excitedly, flouncing into the room and throwing herself onto her chair. She would ignore Mother, her feminine wiles reserved exclusively for Father. He would generally keep silent but the deep groove between his eyes softened visibly. 'I'm absolutely *fam*ished!' Lily would declare loudly, and then proceed to pick half-heartedly at whatever was put on her plate.

At the thought of her family, Kit's throat constricted. She had had a role, once. The youngest daughter, the younger sister, her place in the small domestic constellation assured. It should have been an easy graph of formative roles. Daughter, sister, wife, even? But now the true graph of her life lay elsewhere. She was a mother, even though she couldn't bring herself to name her child.

'Have you had enough?' Mrs Arscott looked dubiously at Kit's half-empty plate. 'You've hardly eaten anything.'

'I'm not very hungry,' Kit answered in that controlled voice of hers that Margaret had already come to recognise.

'But you must eat *some*thing. No? Not even a little cake? Cook made it specially and I must tell you, it might very well be the last piece of cake for a while. Everything's rationed now. I don't mind the bacon so much, but sugar *and* butter?'

Kit said nothing but continued to look down at her hands. There was something disconcerting about her silences, Margaret thought. In place of either the hysterics or the ineffable sadness she'd expected to find there was a stoic, almost passive acceptance of the facts that no sixteen-year-old who'd been through what she'd just endured could possibly be expected to display. She looked up briefly as her plate was cleared and for a second their eyes met and held.

Margaret drew in a breath, as though testing whatever would come next. 'Was it ... was it very dreadful?' she asked suddenly, surprising herself with her own question. 'What happened, Kit? What *really* happened in Germany?'

Kit looked down at her empty place. She picked up one of the small silver dessert forks – despite there being no cake in front of her – and ran her finger along the tines. 'It wasn't Lily's fault,' she said quietly. 'It really wasn't. I got caught doing something I shouldn't have done.'

'But where was Faunce?'

'He wasn't there. He was downstairs.'

Margaret swallowed. 'Who was it, Kit? Who did it?'

Kit looked away. 'It was a friend of Hans-Georg's. He was in the same regiment. He was staying at the castle.'

Margaret's mouth had gone dry. She couldn't bring herself to utter the word. 'Did he ... was it ... did he hurt you?' she asked finally.

Kit shook her head. 'No, not like that.'

'Was it ... just the once?' Margaret couldn't think of any other way to put it.

Kit nodded. 'Yes,' she said, her voice suddenly that of a child. 'Just once.'

'And that's all it takes,' Margaret said slowly, quietly. 'Just once. It's so unfair.' Her heart was thumping as she looked at the girl who returned her gaze without flinching. Her awkwardness grew until it sounded loud in her ears.

'Am I to go back?' Kit asked. 'Back home, I mean.'

Margaret put a hand to her throat, catching the single strand of pearls she always wore. She felt she had to do something with her hands. 'Well, I ... I suppose so. Once everything's settled,' she lied quickly. 'Why? Don't you want to go back?'

Kit paused, as if considering the question. She shook her head slowly. 'No, no ... I don't think so. I'd rather do something else.'

Margaret was surprised. 'But what will you do? You're still so young. You've got your whole life in front of you. I *know* it seems absurd to go on as if nothing ever happened, but that's what you must do, darling. That's just the way it is. You'll go on and do everything you ever wanted, what everyone expects of you—'

'That's just it,' Kit interrupted her. 'I don't want to do what everyone else expects.'

'Whatever do you mean?'

'I don't want to be the kind of person you all think I should be.'

'But what else do you want to be?' Margaret was genuinely puzzled.

Kit turned her eyes upon her. There was a small, taut fold of skin beneath each eye that hadn't been there the last time she'd seen her, Margaret thought. The girl – young woman, almost – had aged, changed. The blue eyes regarded her curiously, as though expecting her to know her answer before it even came.

'Useful,' she said slowly, considering the word. 'I want to be useful again.'

16

She woke just before dawn. It was still dark outside, though a faint, weak light was beginning to break. She had lain awake the night before, unable to sleep. At one point, she'd climbed out of bed and gone to the window, drawing back the curtains to look out onto the moonlit gardens. She'd forgotten to close them again; now light began to show as threads of brilliance in the blanket of cloud. She sat up, properly awake, and it came flooding back. Today was the day. Everything had been arranged. Just after breakfast, the couple Mrs Wright had found would come up the driveway and collect their new child. At lunch, she would sit down with Mrs Arscott and it would be all over, as if it had never been. There was a dull, leaden ache in her lower stomach. She slid a hand cautiously down her abdomen and touched something warm and sticky. She brought her fingers up to her face, squinting to see. She was bleeding again. A sign. Her body knew before she did that it was time to return. She looked at the blood on her hands and suddenly, without warning, her eyes filled with tears. She tried to stop herself but it was too late. The ache in her throat was too great to contain. There was nothing for it but to give into desolation and wait for the storm to pass.

Half an hour later, washed and dressed, she looked at her reflection in the mirror. Her reddened eyes were the only outward sign of the distress that had come over her. She splashed a little cold water over her face and pulled her hair back into its neat ponytail. She took a deep breath. It was time to say goodbye.

A hoary fog rolled in from the sea, hovering above the snow-covered fields and obscuring anything above eye level. It gave the landscape a blunt, cut-off air, lowering the sky and flattening everything for miles around.

Her breath scrolled out before her as she walked quickly across the forecourt to the waiting car. Mrs Arscott had gone to great lengths to find the petrol necessary to take her to the station. Her feet couldn't carry her towards the car fast enough. Instead of returning to Dorset, she would go to London, to the Belgravia home of a mutual friend of her mother's and Mrs Arscott's, Lady Fiona Harrington.

She did not look back, not once. Behind her, she could hear Mrs Arscott's footsteps, anxiously keeping pace.

'Don't forget to phone,' she said loudly, pressing her face against the glass as Kit got in and closed the door after her. 'Lady Harrington will be at the station to meet you. You've been so brave, darling, I—'

'Could you please go?' Kit said to the driver, who was waiting patiently, cutting Margaret off. 'Please just go.'

'Yes, *m'lady*,' the driver said hurriedly, revving the engine. Kit turned briefly as the car jerked forwards. She saw Mrs Arscott's worried-looking face, saw the soft, pale stone of the west wing slide by and then they were clear of the house, surrounded by the frosty, misty fields. She huddled into the seat, pulling her coat around her as tightly as it would go. Was it really only a fortnight since she'd been driven up this very lane with the baby asleep beside her? She couldn't bring herself to answer her own question.

The car swung around a corner and the fog closed in behind them. All of a sudden, the smell and feel of Foulden Hall washed over her: the oily smell of the furniture polish that permeated the corridor leading from her bedroom to the stairs; the metallic smell of the hallway as she descended; and the smell of frying eggs and toast in the morning. Of the room next to hers where the baby lay, there was nothing… no memory, no scent, no trace. It lay empty, like the fact of the baby itself, put out of her mind with a determination that frightened her, had she had the courage to examine it. She was alone. She had the queer sense of seeing herself as a stranger, erasing not just her own past but the way she'd been within it, passively accepting whatever came to pass. She closed her eyes. She had no wish to see anything, let alone her own memories.

The station at King's Lynn was crowded. There were soldiers everywhere, rucksacks strapped to their backs, gas masks dangling, weapons slung over their shoulders. There were hundreds of children, too, being hurriedly shepherded onto the carriages by harassed-looking women in uniform. They were the evacuees, London children who'd been sent to the countryside for safety. From the snatches of conversation she heard blowing around her, she understood that a lucky few hundred had gone back to London for Christmas and were now returning to the counties that were their temporary home. The mood was tense and anxious; many of the children were in tears. She watched them, curiously detached. It came to her that although war had been declared some six months earlier, she'd been at such a remove from it both mentally and geographically that she'd watched it all unfold from afar, preoccupied with the momentous changes going on inside and around her. Aside from the sinking of the ship off the coast of Mull, which now seemed so long ago it was hard to fathom it had ever happened, the war was something distant, far-off and remote. Even the anxious talk of imminent rationing seemed to be happening to someone else, somewhere else.

A whistle shrieked loudly, piercing the din around her. A uniformed guard was shouting orders. 'Stand back! Stand back! All aboard the London train! All aboard!'

With her little overnight case held firmly in one hand, she pushed her way through the people, murmuring apologies. She made it to the carriage marked 'D' just in time and clambered aboard. Since the outbreak of war, the first- and second-class distinctions on trains had ceased to exist. She balanced her way carefully down the aisle, looking for a free seat. The train had begun to rock back and forth as it jerked its way out of the station, gathering speed. She found one at last – a window seat – and slid into it gratefully, unnoticed. No one so much as glanced at her. She held onto the window frame as she stowed her case under the seat and sat down. The door at the end burst open and a conductor appeared, snatching at tickets in a sea of waving hands. She passed hers and received it back in return. She slipped it into the pocket of her navy blue dress-suit and carefully unwound the thick woollen scarf from her neck. She arranged it on her knees, fussily, the way she'd seen her aunts and her grandmother do. She was on her way.

PART THREE
JOY

1941
Kit

17

Her route was always the same. She came out of 3 Ecclestone Mews by the side entrance, walked up the cobbled lane to the archway at the end and turned left onto Ecclestone Street. She walked all the way down, past the sandbagged entrances to the grand houses on either side of the wide road, now mostly empty since their owners had either fled to their country homes or had sold up and left altogether, though it was hard to imagine where they might have gone. America? It seemed the only country left in the world not touched by the war.

In the hallway of the office where she worked, a large map showed the state of the Allied forces and Axis powers across the globe. The world was divided into blue, red and black blocks of power. Almost all of central Europe was a consolidated swathe of black with outposts of neutral blue, like Norway and Denmark. There was the huge red rump of West Africa, 'belonging' to the Allies, and then on the other side of the continent, Madagascar and Somaliland, which the Germans controlled. The whole world had been brought together in a never-ending succession of air strikes, ground manoeuvres, bombing raids … She could barely remember a time when the shriek of the air raid siren *didn't* go off every night.

Every morning on her way to work, she passed the gaping hole on the other side of Eaton Place, where an entire terrace of shell-pink mews houses had been ripped apart one winter night by a single bomb. She'd been working late that night and came home to the wail of ambulances mingling with the scream of the air raid siren. Mrs Arscott had come down to London for a visit but, luckily, she too was out when the hit happened. Lady Delamere, their neighbour, told them the following day that the pavement afterwards had been littered with 'bits'.

'Bits? What sort of "bits"?' Mrs Arscott asked nervously, her hand at her throat.

Lady Delamere looked around her, as if afraid to speak. 'Body parts,' she said eventually.

Mrs Arscott looked as though she might faint. Kit sipped her tea and looked straight ahead.

She waited for a bus at the corner of Ebury Street, which took her most of the way towards work.

Work. Even after a year she couldn't get used to the sound of it. *Work.* She had a job. She went to work every morning. Sometimes, for the sheer improbability of it, she practised saying the words out loud. *I'm a secretary. I have a job.* In her narrow circle of friends and relatives, she didn't know any woman who worked. Marriage and motherhood were the height of ambition and aspiration. She thought of her cousins in Scotland, or of Arabella and Antonella Musgrave, their neighbours in Dorset, who lived a few miles from Chalfont in a stately home that was every bit as empty and austere. Work? They wouldn't have understood the term. Fathers had jobs; mothers did not.

As usual, it was Mrs Arscott who'd suggested it. 'It'll be the best thing for you,' she'd said briskly, on a visit to London a few months after Kit had left Norfolk. She'd left the rest of the sentence unsaid. 'Get you out of the house, for one thing, and I imagine you'll be quite good at it.'

'But what would I *do*? I'm not trained to do … well, anything.'

'What was it you said to me in Norfolk?' Mrs Arscott asked, though they both knew she already knew the answer. 'Useful. That's it. You said you wanted to be useful. Well, here's your chance. You ought to learn how to type, at the very least. You speak a couple of languages, don't you?'

Kit looked at her. Her pulse quickened. She no longer considered herself capable of *any* kind of emotion, let alone affection, but there was something about Margaret Arscott that she admired.

She nodded carefully. 'Yes. French … and … and German.' She said it with some hesitation.

'Jolly good. Well, I'd say Pitman's is where you ought to start. In six weeks you ought to at least be employable.'

And that was that. She completed her Grade 1 and Grade 2 courses in typing, shorthand and basic bookkeeping at Pitman's Secretarial College. To celebrate, Mrs Arscott came down from Norfolk for the weekend and took her to Claridge's. There hadn't been a raid for a fortnight and the beleaguered capital suddenly came up for air. Mrs Arscott insisted on 'taking tea', a ritual that seemed to belong to another age. For almost two years, the East End of London had been pummelled nightly by the Germans, flattening the streets east of Aldgate to rubble. The West End, where the wealthy lived, had been spared. But the illusion of protection didn't last long. A pilot had targeted Buckingham Palace towards the end of 1940 and dropped five explosive bombs, shattering the calm. Now the whole city was a target. No one was spared, not even the Royal Family.

But Claridge's was still safe. Inside the domed hall, with its magnificent glass cupola and the black-and-white chequered floor tiles that she remembered from childhood, society matriarchs and their daughters still took tea. The café still looked like a real Parisian café, with wicker chairs and tables draped in snowy white linen. The menu was still the same. Across from them, a group of ladies who were beautifully turned out in smart coat dresses and fur stoles had entered to take their seats. Drinking, smoking, laughing ... wide slashes of bright red lipstick revealing white teeth ... the soft gleam of a string of pearls or the hard glitter of a diamond ring ... That afternoon, Claridge's was the place of resurrection. It brought women in elegant outfits to sit and smoke in the café; and it brought men in sober suits, who, after a decent interval had passed, could slip off to the bar where a good cognac could still be bought.

Kit glanced down at the plate of daintily cut sandwiches and éclairs oozing with real cream in front of her. It was so long since she'd tasted either chocolate *or* cream ... She reached for another one. Mrs Arscott looked on, smiling indulgently. She sipped elegantly at her glass of champagne and lit up a cigarette. The packet lay on the table between them. Kit looked at it for a second, then boldly reached for one herself. Mrs Arscott raised her eyebrows but said nothing, offering her the lighter instead. It was Kit's first cigarette. She took the smoke cautiously into her lungs, just the way she'd seen her mother do, and was rewarded with a burning sensation in her throat that made her want to cough, but was invigorating as well. She caught sight of herself in the mirror across the room. In her neat navy blue suit and patterned silk scarf that Mrs Arscott had insisted on loaning her, she looked like any other young woman: grown-up, self-possessed, elegant. Mrs Arscott was impeccably dressed; they could have been any wealthy middle-aged mother and grown-up daughter. She was a little shocked by the image, but oddly pleased too.

It was as if her inner self, wise beyond her years, had just caught up with her outer self; the two sides of her, which, ever since Germany, had rubbed along awkwardly together, suddenly merged. She stole another glance. It felt strange to sit there in contemplation of her image. That was Lily's way, not hers. She felt again the little sharp stab of pain at the thought of her sister. But for the first time in her life, she began to see what it might 'all' be about: the clothes, the style, the make-up, the hair … It was all about disguise. Style was something you could put on and take off, as and when you pleased. Style was a barrier. It was a way of keeping the world at arm's length. An added layer of protection. Beauty was different; it acted as a magnet, pulling people *towards* you, even those whose attention you hadn't sought. You couldn't control it or them. She'd seen it in Lily. Her looks were everything. She was enslaved by her own face and body, terrified of losing the one 'thing' she possessed. But it was no possession. Style was different.

That's it, she thought, as she finished her cigarette. Stylish. That's what I'll be.

She was toying with the idea of helping herself to the last éclair on the plate when a shadow suddenly fell across the table. She looked up. A tall, lean man with a leathery, weary-looking face was standing in front of them, smoking a pipe. The fruity, pungent scent of it wafted down, bringing her father sharply and poignantly to mind.

'Dennis! How *lovely* to see you. Is Marion with you?' Mrs Arscott looked up, evidently pleased to see him, whoever he was.

'Hello, Margaret. No, she's in the country. Prefers to avoid London. Especially now.'

'I know, I know. I only come down rarely myself. Give her my best, will you? It seems as though we haven't seen each other in years. Once this is all over … Goodness, where are my manners? This is Katherine Algernon-Waters. Lord and Lady Wharton's youngest.'

'Ah. Harold's daughter?' He looked down at her keenly. 'The youngest one, did you say?'

Kit nodded self-consciously. He seemed to be able to see straight through her.

'Visiting, are you? Up for the day?'

She shook her head, but before she could answer, Mrs Arscott interrupted.

'Darling girl's up with me for the *entire* duration. She's determined to make herself useful, and why not? God knows when it'll end. Still, we're making the most of it, aren't we, Kit?'

Kit nodded, but again, before she could formulate a suitable answer, the man asked abruptly, 'Useful? What do you mean by "useful"?'

'All *sorts* of things,' Mrs Arscott said smoothly. 'Aside from her languages, she's just finished her typing course and she's learned how to drive. Ever so useful, don't you think?'

'Languages? French and German, I suppose?'

'Yes, sir.' Kit nodded, slowly going red. There was something strange about the whole conversation, as though he and Mrs Arscott were rehearsing lines they already knew. There was something about his abrupt yet piercing manner she found uncomfortable, as if he knew more about her than he should.

'Why don't you come round and see me?' he said after a moment, his eyes narrowing, as though trying to see beyond her careful, wary expression. He turned to Mrs Arscott and spoke as though Kit wasn't there. 'I'll be at the War Office all of this week. Let them know I asked her to come.'

'What an absolutely *splendid* idea!' Mrs Arscott exclaimed loudly, turning to Kit. 'We'll do just that. Monday, shall we say? We'll get there nice and early.'

'Assuming there hasn't been a raid,' Kit said suddenly, speaking up for the first time. Both Mrs Arscott and the man looked at her in surprise. 'There were two last week,' she said, feeling a warm flush spread across her cheeks. 'It took them ages to clear the streets and none of the buses were running.'

'Quite. Well, nine o'clock, shall we say?'

'Splendid.' Mrs Arscott beamed. 'Absolutely splendid. Do give my love to Marion. And the children, of course,' she added quickly.

'Yes.' He gave them both a quick, formal nod and moved on.

Mrs Arscott was looking at her queerly, Kit saw. 'Don't you know who that was?' she asked, as soon as he was out of earshot.

Kit shook her head.

'That was Lord Hamilton,' Mrs Arscott said triumphantly.

'Who's he?'

Mrs Arscott looked at her witheringly. 'First Lord of the Admiralty.

I'm surprised you haven't met him before. Six daughters. You remind me of his eldest, Daphne. A lovely girl.'

'But where would I have met him?'

Mrs Arscott opened her mouth to say something, then obviously thought better of it. 'Never mind. Well, then, that's settled. We'll go round first thing on Monday morning. Don't look so surprised. You wanted to be useful, did you not?'

Back at the office, an hour or so later, Lord Hamilton paused for a moment to light his pipe. Beneath his famously bushy eyebrows, his eyes were narrowed, his expression both thoughtful and watchful at the same time. Across the table, Sir Evelyn Gore-Brown, Parliamentary Secretary to the Minister of Food – his official, public role – was equally thoughtful. In his hand he held an airmail letter, crinkled blue paper covered in Faunce Algernon-Waters's famously neat, precise script.

'How long was she there?' Sir Evelyn asked, twitching his elegant, patrician nose as the sharp acrid tobacco filled the air.

'Just over a month. She left rather abruptly, it seems. Not quite sure if there'd been a row with the sister, or something along those lines. It was she who got the list for us, so Faunce says. Just marched up to the officer's room, found it and memorised it. He seems to think she'll be the most terrific asset.'

'Hmm. And where's Faunce now?'

Lord Hamilton made a weary gesture. 'France, apparently. It's gone quiet at the moment. Germany was thought to be too dangerous. The letter's almost a month old.'

'Hmm.' It was one of Sir Evelyn's favourite expressions, covering all manner of emotions from exasperation to hope. 'Well, what do you think of her?'

'In principle, yes, I think she'll do very well. She's young. A year or two younger than Daphne, I'd say.'

'Keen?'

'Mmm. I think so. Faunce seems to think she'd be ideal, what with the sister being so close to the inner circle. Reports seem to indicate she's even closer to the Führer than the Mitford girl ever was.'

Sir Evelyn nodded. 'Fine. Well, let's bring her in.'

'They're coming in on Monday. I'll get one of the secretaries to take care of Margaret and you can interview her.'

'Fluent in German, you said?'

'Like a native, or so Faunce says.'

'Good. Let's see.'

'Odd business, this,' Lord Hamilton said, suddenly getting up. He walked over to the window. He stared down at the Holborn Viaduct, at the slow line of cars snaking their way towards the City, the sandbagged entrances and the gaping holes where the wrought-iron railings had recently been removed. Every scrap of iron and steel had been requisitioned for the war effort. The buildings looked like his youngest daughter, Belinda, all those years ago, when she'd lost her baby front teeth. At the thought of his daughters his stomach tightened unexpectedly. He wasn't a man much given to emotional excesses, least of all those that had anything to do with his family. He was a Royal Navy man, from a long line of distinguished lords and naval officers, and was descended on his mother's side from Charles Grey, the 2nd Earl Grey, whose government abolished slavery throughout the British Empire in 1833. He had his ancestor's strong moral convictions, a rigid, unbending sense of discipline and abhorrence of emotional outbursts, particularly of the female sort.

Yet there was a side to him that few of his colleagues, if any, ever saw. For the first time in six or seven generations, there was no Hamilton male heir. 'Failing male issue' was the correct historical term. He and Marion had six daughters, one after the other, bright, splendid little girls... but no son. Aside from the question of inheritance, particularly of the handsome Northumberland estate that had been in the family for almost a century, there was another, deeper question that had yet to be properly articulated in his own mind: ambition. He was sixty-six years old and heading for a much-anticipated and comfortable retirement when war broke out. On 10 May 1940, Neville Chamberlain resigned and, after a top-secret and hasty meeting to which he was called after the agreement between Chamberlain, Winston Churchill and Lord Halifax had been reached, there was no question of retirement, comfortable or not. He grasped the mantle of power as required of him and became First Lord of the Admiralty, a century or so after his forebear had. In some ways, the appointment of the two men – Churchill and himself – both men in their sixties, with a combined military history and experience of nearly the same length of time, was exactly what the country needed. Wisdom as well as power, experience as well as expertise. The sense that the War Cabinet was in good hands was palpable, even if the outcome of the war was not.

But the responsibilities of his new role weighed unexpectedly heavily on him. It brought the question of the lack of an heir sharply to bear. Daphne, their eldest daughter, had been married the year before. Splendid fellow – army officer, of course – but her departure from the household had suddenly made him aware of how much she'd filled a hole in his life without him ever realising it. She was easily the cleverest of their six children, with a sharp, keen intelligence that was a combination of his own analytical mind and his wife's much sharper emotional intuition. She read voraciously and refused to allow her gender to get in the way of things. Although he was careful not to show it – and certainly not to his other daughters – Daphne was by far and away his favourite. At thirteen, she clamoured to be sent away to boarding school – almost unheard of in their circles, where girls were largely educated at home. He and Marion gave in, and she was duly enrolled at Badminton School for girls in Bristol, on account of one of Marion's great-aunts, who taught science at the school. Daphne flourished and came home during the holidays, her head bursting with new ideas, new friendships and new possibilities. Some of his favourite memories were of the two of them sitting in the quiet, book-lined library at home, debating on topics that could range anywhere from the price of coal to whether or not a certain butterfly that had been spotted in the garden was native to Northumberland.

In his rare, private moments, he admitted to a sharp sense of disappointment when Daphne simply went along with her mother's demands and gave in to the whole nonsense of being presented at Court. It was spring 1938 – the last season, as it turned out. She seemed to enjoy the fuss and pomp, which surprised him. For weeks the house was full of female relatives, dressmakers, Daphne's friends, flitting about excitedly. He realised then that he'd had other hopes for her, though he found them hard to articulate. And it wasn't as though he held the system in disregard – after all, it was through the very same network of events, parties and people that he'd met Marion. After twenty years of marriage, most of them exceedingly good, who was he to complain?

And then, of course, the inevitable happened. Almost a month to the date after her presentation to the King and Queen, Captain Alasdair Wyse began 'calling'. Six months after that, Daphne Hamilton became Daphne Wyse. And that was that.

It took him a further six months to realise the enormity of the hole she'd left behind. He no longer looked up facts in the leather-bound almanacs that lined the walls of his office, or bought trinkets on shore leave in places as far-flung as Oman and St George in the Caribbean, wondering what she'd make of them. He missed terribly the quizzical look she often gave him when he lit his pipe after dinner and the two of them sat in the drawing room discussing the political manoeuvres of the week. She had a way of pursing her lips when he recounted something particularly outrageous or hard to swallow, the expression on her face mirroring his own innermost thoughts which, after years of maintaining a stiff upper lip, were often hidden, sometimes even from himself.

He looked out of the window. A lone bus came trundling down High Holborn, cutting into his thoughts. A soldier was leaning against the conductor's pole, shouting at a group of young women who'd just exited one of the shops. He pointed at one of them, a tall blonde with a red pillbox hat, and they began to laugh. He could see their faces, bright smiles that lit up the dreary spring morning, splashes of colour in the smoggy grey. He thought back to the brief encounter in Claridge's earlier that day. The look he'd seen on the young girl's face, he realised suddenly, was the same as the one he'd grown used to seeing on Daphne's. Hunger. Ambition. And something else, too, that he couldn't quite define. Courage, perhaps? He turned back to Sir Evelyn.

'Do you know, I've a feeling she's exactly what we're looking for. Faunce is probably right.'

18

'Morning, Katherine.'

'Morning, sir.' Kit smiled timidly at Sir Evelyn Gore-Brown, the rather grandly named Parliamentary Secretary to the Minister of Food, Sir Gwilym Lloyd-George, 1st Viscount Temby, who was coming down the staircase.

When she'd first started work in the imposing War Office, just off Horse Guards Parade, she'd been puzzled by the proliferation of secretaries: Parliamentary Secretaries, Under-Secretaries, Permanent Secretaries, Company Secretaries, Private Secretaries... and then, of course, plain old secretaries like herself, who ranged in rank from Miss Hodgson, a formidable woman who presided over the flock of young women in the Ministry like a particularly watchful mother hen, to herself, the youngest and newest recruit to the ranks. Within a few days, she understood that the term was misleading. What she and the dozen other young women in the large, open-plan office did all day had nothing to do with Sir Evelyn's job description, or anyone else's for that matter. They were the typists. They typed. That was all. Other people's words, other people's comments, other people's decisions. Their job was to note things down, as accurately as possible, and to have no opinion beyond the correct spelling of a particularly obscure word. She was good at that.

She hurried up the stairs to the typing pool on the first floor, stopping to quickly check her reflection in the large mirror on the landing before pushing open the heavy wooden door. She still couldn't quite get used to her new haircut. Short, like a boy's, with a long sweep-over from one side to the other. 'Suits you,' was Mrs Arscott's only comment when she returned from the hairdresser's. She'd been walking along Ebury Street late one afternoon on her way back from secretarial college when she'd stopped outside the salon. She'd never been to a hairdresser's in her life. Back in the mists of childhood, a woman from the village had come in every other month to 'do' Mother's hair; she would emerge at dinner with her hair carefully styled and waved. Every six months or so, she'd been entreated to chop off a few inches of Kit's hair. Lily, since the age of fifteen or so, had begged to be allowed to go to Portsmouth or Bristol, where her long auburn hair was cut and curled according to the latest fashions. Not Kit's. She'd had a simple ponytail for as long as she could remember. Not any more.

'Here, why don't you try this?' Mrs Arscott added, handing her a small black tube. It was lipstick. Bright red. 'It suits your colouring.' She'd tried it hesitantly. The face that stared back at her was unrecognisable. She was secretly thrilled and terrified. With every passing month, the old Kit receded further and further away. She smoked. She wore her hair short. She wore lipstick. In a few months' time, no one who knew her then would be able to connect the earnest, awkward teenager with the serious and careful young woman she'd become.

Mrs Arscott was thrilled with the transformation, mistaking its impetus. She thought Kit was 'growing into her own'. She was mistaken. Kit was running as fast as she could from everything she'd once imagined she would be.

She pushed open the door, leaning her full weight against it. All the doors in the War Office were the same: enormous, heavy oak doors capable of stopping the world in its tracks. She hurried over to her station and pulled out her chair. It was two minutes to nine. They began at nine o'clock on the dot, every morning, bombing raid or not, rain or shine. There were thirteen young women in the typists' pool. Kit knew everyone in the pool by name – Jane, Allison, Margery, Petronella, Rosie, Anna Tremayne and Anna Murphy, Louise, Diana, Caitlin, Peony and Sarah – though she could hardly claim to be friendly with any of them. They sat in a single row of desks set against the long windows overlooking St James's Park. Kit's desk was next to Sarah Norton's, a tall, willowy blonde with impeccable family credentials, whose mother had pulled a few strings to get her the job. It seemed to be a well-known fact that her mother's lover, Lord Dudley, had the ear of the prime minister.

'What on earth's the point of your mother having an affair with a minister if all you'll ever get out of him is a lousy secretarial job?' she often said, only half in jest. 'I mean, honestly! I thought I'd be doing something much more exciting! Anyone can type!'

Kit liked her. There was a warmth to her that Kit was reluctantly drawn to. Had the circumstances been different, they might even have been friends. But Kit had lost that facility. She returned a smile when it was directed her way, she occasionally joined in a conversation when she was addressed but she held herself apart.

Sarah was undeterred. 'I'll get to the bottom of you one day,' she said.

Alarmed, Kit turned away before Sarah could see her expression. She was a forthright, practical girl. Kit sometimes thought Sarah could see straight through her and wouldn't hesitate to voice what she saw.

She pulled her typewriter towards her and put on the headphones before anyone else could strike up a conversation. She had a file almost as long as her arm of meeting minutes to transcribe. Across from her, somewhat reluctantly, Sarah did the same. Within five minutes, the room was filled with the sound of clacking fingers, moving at lightning speed.

*

'Ah, there you are, Katherine. A word, please.'

Kit looked up from her typing. It was Miss Hodgson. A funny little man in a bowler hat and a rather ill-fitting suit hovered next to her. His spectacles – enormous round tortoiseshell frames – gave him a myopic, owlish look. He blinked rapidly, his dark eyes magnified by the distorting lens. Hoddy turned away and walked briskly back to her office. It was clearly a private meeting. After a second's hesitation spent looking around him, the funny little man hurried after her. Kit glanced at Sarah, who had taken off her headphones and was watching the proceedings keenly.

'Do hurry up,' Sarah murmured under her breath. 'You know how she hates to wait.'

Kit scrambled to her feet. Should she take in a notebook and pen? She quickly grabbed her stenographer's pad and hurried after them.

'*Würden Sie bitte die Tür schließen?*' The little man spoke as she entered Hoddy's office. She looked at him in surprise.

'*Die Tür?*' she repeated, confused.

'*Ja. Sofort. Und dann geben Sie mir Ihren Namen, bitte. Und wie alt sind Sie?*'

'*Ich heiße Katherine Algernon-Waters,*' Kit said, hurriedly closing the door. '*Und ich bin jetzt neunzehn Jahre alt. Ich wurde in 1923 geboren.*'

The man turned to Hoddy, who was watching them both closely. 'She's pitch-perfect.'

His English was impeccable, Kit noticed immediately, but there was the slightest hint of another language or accent hovering just beneath its surface.

'Good. This is Mr Bier. He's just come up from Buckinghamshire. Is there anything else you'd like to ask her?' She turned back to the funny little man.

'I see you visited Germany just before the war. How long were you there?' Mr Bier asked, lapsing back into German.

'A few weeks,' Kit answered, hoping she didn't sound evasive. He'd clearly done his homework. 'Not very long.'

'Indeed.' She saw from his expression that Mr Bier already knew the answer to his question. 'You know how to type, I take it?' he went on.

She nodded. 'Yes, I do.'

'Good. And would you be averse to report-writing?'

Suddenly, the tone of the conversation slipped a gear. 'No. Not at all.'

'Even if some reports stretched the definition of truth?'

She looked him straight in the eye. 'No, not at all,' she repeated.

Mr Bier turned to Hoddy. He allowed himself the tiniest of smiles. 'Well, I think we've found our candidate.' Kit looked from one to the other. It was the first time she'd ever seen anything like satisfaction on Hoddy's usually frowning face. Now her habitually peevish, dissatisfied expression was replaced by something else entirely: intensity. Kit had never seen such an expression on Hoddy's face before.

'You understand what's being asked of you, Katherine?' Miss Hodgson asked, her eyes fixed on Kit's.

'Yes, Miss Hodgson,' Kit said quietly, although her heart was thumping. 'Yes, I do.'

'You understand you may not disclose the nature of your job to *anyone*, not even your parents?'

'Yes, Miss Hodgson, I do.'

'Good. Report on Monday morning to Sixty-four Baker Street, Section D. You'll be told what to do when you arrive.'

Kit's mind was racing. 64 Baker Street was on the other side of town. Section D was in the basement. At least twice a day she handled envelopes clearly marked 'Top Secret' addressed to someone in Section D, 64 Baker Street.

'Will that be all, Miss Hodgson?' she asked.

'Yes, thank you, Katherine. Close the door on your way out.'

She did as she was told. Her heart was still thumping fast as she shut the door behind her and leaned against it for a second. Her most fervent wish had unexpectedly come true. She was to be useful again. At last.

19

She pulled open the wardrobe door and stood in front of it for what seemed like hours. It wasn't as though there was a huge range to choose from. Mrs Arscott had been generous enough to open her extensive wardrobe and say, 'take whatever you have a yen for', but Kit's own pride and a reluctance to wear another woman's clothes had kept her borrowing to a minimum. That, and the fact that Mrs Arscott was a good three or four stone heavier than she was. Still, she'd managed to find a tailor half a mile away on Sloane Square who had fashioned a wardrobe out of the six or seven outfits she'd chosen. Nothing elaborate but the fabrics were exquisite and her boyish, pencil-thin frame meant she could carry most outfits off with ease. She took a deep breath. It was her first day in her new job, whatever the job might turn out to be. She hadn't even had time to say goodbye to Sarah or any of the other girls in the typing pool. She wondered what Hoddy might have told them.

She reached in and took out a tweed A-line skirt and a simple white blouse. She pulled on a pair of stockings, fastened her skirt and did up the buttons on her blouse. At the last minute, she added a brooch. It had been her grandmother's. She looked at it for a second and then pinned it to her blouse. It was an unusual silver and emerald brooch in a vaguely Celtic arrangement; it would do. She brushed her hair until it lay flat against her scalp, smoothed a little Vaseline over her eyebrows and outlined her lips carefully in red. She stood back and looked at herself. She was ready. She slipped on her coat – a mustard-green fitted coat with a fur-lined collar that the tailor had fashioned out of another of Mrs Arscott's hand-me-downs – picked up her handbag and closed the door.

There was a young man in a dark grey suit waiting at the entrance to 54 Broadway Buildings. Without saying a word, he indicated she was to take the lift to the basement. At the foot of the stairs, she was met by a group of earnest-looking young men and women standing self-consciously to one side; no one seemed to know anyone else. There were about twenty of them. She looked around her as surreptitiously as she could. There were about six or seven young women, much like herself, though none in a dark green dress-coat with a fur collar. The rest were men of varying ages. No one spoke. The atmosphere was tense and nervously expectant.

At eight thirty on the dot, a set of heavy-looking doors opened and the group was ushered in.

'Take a seat, please, ladies and gentlemen. Mr Fennell will be along in a moment.' A young woman strode briskly amongst them, repeating herself in a loud, commanding voice. 'Please take a seat. Yes, anywhere. Close to the front, if possible.'

There was a general scraping of chairs as everyone did as she asked. Kit found it amusing. On the rare occasion they'd visited the local school in

Dorset, she and Lily had often been called upon to hand out a prize or read to the village schoolchildren, whom she secretly envied. They were behaving exactly like those obedient little pupils who got up when she and Lily entered the room and stood to attention, like soldiers nervously awaiting an order.

'Morning, boys and girls.' A man breezed into the room. He was tall and fair-haired, rather good-looking, supremely confident. There was something in his relaxed manner that seemed to settle the room. One or two of the young men visibly relaxed, as though recognising one of their own.

'Thanks very much, Marge,' he said, nodding at the officious-sounding woman who'd shepherded everyone in. 'You can leave me alone with this lot now. Nothing'll happen to them, I promise.' He turned to face them. 'Quite a serious-looking bunch, aren't you?'

A tremor of nervous laughter rippled across the room. Kit, who'd rarely ever been in such a large group of people, was fascinated. Already she could tell which of the young men were leader types. Some of the speaker's nonchalance had already rubbed off and their body language was beginning to mimic his own. The women were different. They all displayed a stiff, upright eagerness that spoke of governesses and years of sitting up straight at the dining table, minding their manners. There was one girl who seemed different, though. She sat a little apart from everyone, a solitary figure, sitting stiffly alert in the back row. She was dark-haired, with a sallow complexion and dark eyes. She was slight, with a long, slender neck, and she was older than most of the rest. Her dark hair just brushed her shoulder blades. She turned her head suddenly, aware that she was being watched. For a split second, their eyes met and held. The corners of the girl's mouth dented slightly. It wasn't a smile but rather an expression of wary confidence. They had seen each other.

'Hello, my name's Ruth.' She held out a hand. 'Ruth Mandelbaum.' She said it almost defiantly.

'I'm Kit.' She thought it pretentious to include her last name. 'Mandelbaum?' she said hesitantly. 'Isn't that a German name?'

'No, not German. Jewish,' Ruth said firmly. 'I'm Jewish.'

'Oh.' Kit was nonplussed. She'd never met a Jew before, much less a young Jewess who looked and sounded just as English as she did. She studied her curiously. It was their first break of the morning. They'd gone outside into the small basement courtyard. 'Would you like a cigarette?' she asked, more to cover her confusion than out of any real desire to smoke. She was surprised when Ruth accepted.

'So ... what are you doing here?' Ruth asked, taking a long, grateful draw. 'Or aren't we supposed to ask?'

Kit let her shoulders lift and fall. 'I'm not sure.'

'Which bit?'

She was quick off the mark, Kit noticed. 'Both. Either.'

'What was it he said?' Ruth murmured. 'A good spy is the person you *don't* notice. I think that rather rules us out, don't you?'

Kit smiled. 'He also said there are lots of way *to* spy. Not all of us have to be on the front line.'

'Oh, good. I've always preferred the back door. That's how we got in, by the way.'

'We?' Kit was momentarily confused.

'My family. We're from Germany. Or at least we were from Germany. Ironic, isn't it? Hitler couldn't wait to get rid of us and now you can't wait to send us back. *If* that's what's intended. I've no idea what they want, do you?' She indicated the room they'd just left with a jerk of her head.

'But you sound so English,' Kit said, puzzled.

'Well, we are. At least I am. My dad still sounds German. Or Yiddish, actually.'

'What's Yiddish?'

Ruth stared at her. 'Don't they teach you anything in school these days?' she asked, only half-jokingly.

Kit shrugged. 'I don't know. I've never been to school.'

'Never been to school? But what are you doing here? I thought this was only for the clever ones. You *look* clever,' Ruth said, regarding her keenly. 'At least to me.'

'What I mean is, I've never actually been to *a* school. We're taught at home,' she explained.

'We?' Ruth raised a quizzical eyebrow.

Kit blushed. She'd been caught out. *The upper classes.* 'I meant, my sister and me ...' she said lamely.

'Ah, of course.'

There was a moment's silence. 'So ... what is it?' Kit asked finally.

'What?'

'Yiddish.'

'It's a language, silly. It's what Jews speak. Even the aristocratic ones, though they'd be at pains to admit it. It's very similar to German, almost a German dialect, you might say. The more educated ones don't speak it, of course. They prefer *Hochdeutsch*. They think it makes them more German. Hitler thinks differently, of course. More fool them, that's what I say. Anyhow, my folk are hardly the educated sort. I'm the first person in the family who's had *any* sort of education, and even then it was cut short.'

'Me too,' Kit said suddenly. 'And it wasn't a terribly good one, either.'

Ruth cocked her head and looked at her. 'Well, well, well. And there was me thinking you'd come from a long line of scientists or botanists or something. You seem frightfully clever for someone who's never been to school.'

Kit smiled faintly. 'Well, we read a lot. The upper classes,' she added, this time without apology. 'The men, that is. We women mostly sit around, looking decorative. Sometimes we ride.'

'How old are you?' Ruth asked curiously. 'You can't be much more than twenty.'

'I'm eighteen,' Kit said reluctantly. 'How old are you?'

'Oh, I'm ancient. I'm twenty-seven. An old maid, in *our* parlance. My mother's given up hope. Would you like to come to tea?' she said abruptly.

Kit looked at her, surprised. 'Tea? Where?'

'At my house. We live in Soho. It's not so very far from here. It's only me and my parents. And Ludo, of course.'

'Who's Ludo?'

'My dog. He's a Jack Russell. You know, one of those loud, squeaky types. Papa was set against him for ages, but he's one of the family now.'

Kit thought fleetingly of Maisie, her mother's dog, and a sudden pang of homesickness flowed through her.

She swallowed. 'Why not?' she said suddenly.

20

The Mandelbaums lived in a house unlike any other she'd seen. In fact, it wasn't a house at all, but rather a flat, balanced above a tobacconist's on Old Compton Street. Ruth let herself in with a key, opening a door onto a narrow passageway that smelled as though spring had not yet made it past the front door. The smell of oil and fried food rushed down the stairwell to meet them.

'It's probably quite a bit smaller than you're used to,' Ruth said with a wry smile, leading the way upstairs.

Kit couldn't think of anything to say. It was the understatement of the century.

'Ma? I'm home.' Ruth stooped at the door to the flat to pick up a leaflet that had been left on the doormat. There was no answer. The door opened directly onto a small living room, dominated by a large, dark wooden table and six stiff, high-backed chairs. An enormous sideboard ran down the length of the room; above it, peering owlishly down from a pair of gilt-framed photographs, were the faces of a couple in whom Kit could see an immediate resemblance to Ruth.

'Who are they?' Kit whispered. There was something in the still, quiet atmosphere of the flat that made her want to whisper.

Ruth glanced up. 'Oh, my grandparents. Both dead.'

'Oh.'

'Come on, let's go to my room. It's on the next floor.'

Kit followed her up another narrow flight of stairs, past a shiny green sofa with worn cushions. Their footsteps sounded loud in Kit's ears. Ruth pushed open the door and there was an answering yelp from the bed. A tiny bundle of energy leaped towards them; it was the dog. Kit felt an unexpected rush of pleasure. She bent towards it, revelling in the long-forgotten feeling of a dog's muzzle being pressed into the palm of her hand.

'Ludo! No! *Her'auf!* Stop it!' Ruth admonished him immediately.

'No, don't worry... I like dogs,' Kit said, ruffling the short bristles behind his ears. She had to catch hold of herself. The sudden rush of love was too much to bear.

'He's not a dog, he's a pest,' Ruth protested, but there was a smile in her voice. 'He behaves as if he's starved of affection ... Just look at him!'

'He's very sweet,' Kit said, straightening up and forcing herself to turn away. She looked around the tiny bedroom. There was a single narrow bed in one corner, piled high with pillows and cushions and an incongruously placed rag doll. A bookshelf at eye level groaned under the weight of books, sagging precariously in the middle. There were books everywhere: on the chair by the window, on the dressing table ... everywhere one looked. Kit's gaze turned outwards, as if in a museum. Yeats and Byron; thick, heavy books on science; a stack of slim Agatha Christie volumes ... Ruth's reading taste was, if anything, even more eclectic than her own. A second wave of nostalgia for the library at Chalfont came over her and she had to sit down on the edge of the silky counterpane.

Suddenly a soft, hoarse voice interrupted them. 'Ruth ...?' It was a questioning voice, gentle and reluctant.

Kit looked up. A woman was standing in the doorway. She was short and round, with an apron tied around the solid mound of breasts and stomach. She looked at them both from under thick, rather beautifully arched eyebrows. It was Ruth's mother. Despite the differences in girth and appearance, Kit could see the resemblance, like faint, ghostly tracings, one face over another. She stood up, but the woman ignored her.

'Ruth ... I was just wondering ... did Papa say he was coming home for tea?' she asked hesitantly. 'Only I thought he might have gone to Finkelstein's ...'

'Finkelstein's? No, why would he have gone there? No, of course he's coming home for tea.' Ruth's voice carried with it the same mild irritation Kit often felt when her mother asked a question to which she already knew the answer. She smiled shyly at Ruth's mother, as if to excuse her appearance, but to her surprise, Mrs Mandelbaum did not appear to feel the need for anyone's forgiveness, least of all Kit's. She looked back at her with frank, unguarded curiosity.

'Why don't you bring the young lady downstairs?' she asked, looking around the room. 'Why've you stuck her away in here? It's not so nice, believe me ...'

She looked around her again as if to confirm her appraisal. She smiled. In her awkwardness, Kit found herself smiling back.

Mrs Mandelbaum led the way back downstairs, talking as if Ruth weren't there. 'She always does that. Hiding herself up there, like a ... how you say? *Wie sagt man? Eichhörnchen?*'

'Squirrel, Ma. It's a squirrel. And I'm not a squirrel. It's my room, that's all.'

'Come, sit down ... have a seat.' Mrs Mandelbaum fussed over her. Her movements were slow and heavy but she held herself with a solemn dignity, as though Kit's presence warranted a different kind of hospitality. She went over to the sideboard and opened the door. She took out a glass dish filled with foil-wrapped toffees.

'Here, you'll have something?' Kit hesitated before taking one. 'Perhaps the young lady would like some tea? Ruth? Would she like some tea?' She had a curious way of not addressing the person to whom her questions were really addressed.

Kit sat nervously on the edge of her seat, as though she were a child in the company of adults.

'You're a lady, aren't you?' Mrs Mandelbaum said, as Ruth disappeared, presumably to make the tea. 'A proper lady, I mean. Your father ... he's somebody, no?'

'Yes.' There didn't seem to be any other answer.

'And your mummy? Are you an only child?'

'No. I ... I have a sister. Lily.' Kit was surprised at her own words. It had been months since she'd heard Lily's name spoken out loud. 'She lives in Germany.' Suddenly the urge to make her life real before this woman came over her. 'She's married to a German. One of Hitler's aides. I hate him. I hate them both.'

Mrs Mandelbaum stirred slowly in her chair. 'So? She's your sister; we must love our family.' She got up and stood looking around the room for a moment. 'If you'll excuse me,' she said, as if Kit were not there. She went out slowly, withdrawing yet taking the atmosphere of the room with her. Kit remained frozen in embarrassment, both at her outburst and its implications.

Ruth came in a few minutes later with a tray of tea. She placed it on the ground and knelt down, busying herself with the cups.

'D'you want to wash your hands?' she asked, glancing at Kit's fingers.

'They're awfully sticky, aren't they?' she said, referring to the toffees. 'My mother does make them very well, though.'

There it was again, Kit noticed. Ruth had a way of saying exactly what she thought without embarrassment. She'd been forced to eat the sickly sweets out of politeness but far from being apologetic, Ruth commended her mother's skill. Kit, brought up on a diet of anxious manners that cared desperately what others thought, found it oddly liberating.

She stood up abruptly. 'I ... I'd better go,' she said, looking around for her coat. A curious feeling of distress had swept over her suddenly, leaving her inexplicably close to tears.

'But you haven't had your tea.' Ruth looked up at her in surprise.

'I ... I know. I'm sorry ... I forgot I have to be somewhere.'

There was a moment's pause. Kit looked away. She couldn't bear to be found out.

'Of course,' Ruth said quickly. She stood up as Kit slipped on her coat and belted it.

'I'm sorry,' she said again. 'But it was really lovely to meet your mother and—'

'Here.' Ruth held out a book. 'I saw you looking at it.'

Kit took it from her, surprised. *Mildred Pierce*. 'You haven't even opened it,' she said wonderingly, turning it over. 'I couldn't possibly ... No, you read it first. It's yours, after all.'

'Not at all. I've got loads of other books. No, go on. Read it and tell me what you think.'

So there it was. An offer of friendship, no less. Kit held the book out in front of her, absurdly reluctant to part with it. She looked at Ruth. There was that quick change of focus in her face that Kit had come to recognise. She stared at her for a moment, at the steely dark hair and boldly drawn features. Suddenly the bland, neutral quietness of the faces she'd grown up with all her life seemed to fade away. Ruth's dark brightness took on a sharp, clear quality, like metal.

'I will,' she said simply. 'On Monday.'

21

She didn't see Ruth on Monday, or for the rest of the week. When she arrived at 54 Broadway Buildings at eight thirty on the dot, a young, thin man in army fatigues escorted her down the corridor, past the room where they'd all gathered, into a small windowless office at the foot of the stairs.

'You'll be in here,' he said, opening the door and standing back to let her pass.

'What about—'

'Atherton'll be along directly.' The young soldier hurriedly cut her off, closing the door smartly behind him.

She turned around. There were two young men already sitting at desks. She recognised them from the group but didn't know their names. They eyed her warily, as if they couldn't quite believe her presence in the dark, airless office alongside them.

'I'm Kit,' she said after a moment, choosing the nearest seat and sinking into it. She was glad she'd taken extra care that morning with her outfit, choosing a plain dark blue woollen dress with a small white collar and white cuffs.

'Harry.' The taller of the two inclined his head.

'Charles.'

'Wh… what's going on?' she asked in a low, hurried voice. 'Why aren't we with the rest?'

'You're not supposed to ask so many questions,' Harry said primly. 'Besides, I've no idea.'

The door opened suddenly. A tall, striking-looking woman in uniform stood in the doorway, flanked on either side by two uniformed older men. Behind her, Harry and Charles got to their feet. Kit quickly followed suit.

'Morning.' The woman walked commandingly into the room, followed by the two officers. 'I'm Squadron Office Vera Atherton. I'll be your section head for the four weeks. If you pass muster, you'll be sent to

Scotland for basic training. From there, again, if you pass... well, who knows where you may end up. Any questions?'

Kit stared at her. She was possibly the most commanding-looking person she'd ever seen, male or female. Her short, dark hair was fashionably waved; she couldn't have been more than forty years old. Her voice was low and husky, with just the faintest trace of an accent. Like Kit, she wore bright red lipstick and her uniform was perfectly tailored to fit. She met Kit's incredulous gaze unflinchingly.

'I have a question,' Kit said.

'Go ahead, Miss Algernon-Waters.'

So she was already known to her superiors. 'What's happened to the rest of the group?' she asked, thinking of Ruth Mandelbaum.

'They've been assigned elsewhere.' One of the officers behind Vera Atherton spoke up.

'Will we see them again?'

'This isn't a prison camp, Miss Algernon-Waters. After hours, you're free to see whomever you like. I must warn you, however, that in my section, hours are both long and discretionary. You are to report for duty each morning at oh-eight-thirty hours sharp, but it's anybody's guess when you'll leave each night. Such is the nature of our work. Now, are there any *real* questions?'

Kit flushed. Behind her, Charles or Harry sniggered softly.

'Loyalty to one's colleagues,' Vera Atherton said crisply. 'You may be glad of it one day, Mr Stafford-Holms. Right, shall we begin?'

It wasn't until Thursday that she saw Ruth again. Vera Atherton wasn't joking. It was sometimes midnight before they left the office at the foot of the stairs.

'*There* you are,' Kit said, hoping she didn't sound too eager. She'd only just met her after all.

'Oh, hello. Where've you been? Coming for a fag?' Ruth's easy manner put her own shyness to rest.

She nodded and together they walked down the corridor towards the inner courtyard. It was nippy outside, and the air was damp with a fine, practically invisible drizzle. They huddled together as Ruth tried unsuccessfully to light both cigarettes.

'Here, quick, before it goes out.' Ruth handed her a lit cigarette. A weak sun poked momentarily through the clouds and for a second they were bathed in light. 'Got any plans for the weekend?' Ruth asked, drawing hungrily on her cigarette.

'The weekend?' Kit repeated, caught off guard by the question.

'Mmm. D'you like jazz?'

'Jazz? You mean . . . jazz music?'

'Yes. What other sort of jazz is there? A friend's invited me out on Saturday and he's asked me to bring a friend along.'

'Out where?' Kit asked, genuinely surprised.

'Does it really matter? A club. D'you want to come or not?'

'A club?' Kit was flummoxed. She'd never been to a club before. 'But . . . but why me?' she asked. 'Wouldn't you rather go with a friend?'

'Oh. I rather thought you *were* a friend.' Ruth ground out her cigarette under her heel. 'I just thought you might like to come, that's all.'

'I . . . I would,' Kit said. 'I've never been to a club before, that's all.'

Ruth looked at her and shook her head in mock despair. 'You've never been to school, you've never been to a club, you've never met a Jew before—'

'I didn't say that,' Kit said hurriedly, protesting.

'You didn't have to. It was written all over your face,' Ruth said slyly. She smiled. 'We'll pick you up on Saturday. Give me your address. And wear something nice. Joel likes a pretty girl. You're quite beautiful, you know.'

'Me?' Kit couldn't help herself.

'Yes, you. When you stop looking so stern, that is. You should see the expression on your face sometimes when you think no one's watching. It's quite . . . well, quite desperate. I often wonder if you're not guarding some dreadful secret or other and—'

'I'd . . . I'd better go,' Kit interrupted her.

'What's the matter?' Ruth looked at her sharply. 'Are you all right?'

Kit couldn't hear. She pushed past Ruth and yanked open the door. She stumbled down the corridor and blundered into the toilets. She shut the door behind her, drew the lock and sat down. Her legs were shaking. There was a hollowed-out, gnawing feeling in the pit of her stomach. She pressed her knees tightly together and put up her hands to the sides of her head. The tremors of shame and guilt that lay beneath the surface of her skin erupted all over her like a fever. She drew in gulping mouthfuls of air, waiting for the storm to pass.

'Kit?' Ruth's voice broke into the silence. 'Kit? Are you in there?'

The deep roaring in her head was suddenly arrested. 'I . . . I'll be out in a minute,' she called out weakly. Her heart was pounding and her palms were clammy with sweat.

'What's the matter? Did I say something wrong? I didn't mean to upset you, I—'

'I'm f-fine,' Kit stammered, interrupting her. 'I'll be out in a minute. I... I just felt a bit faint for a second, that's all.'

There was a minute's silence. Then she heard the creak of the door as Ruth left and the soft patter of footsteps retreating as she walked back down the hallway. Kit brought both hands up to her face. She could feel her heartbeat in her cheeks, its beat thudding lightly against her palms. Breathe, she commanded herself silently. *Breathe. In. Out. Steady, now. Breathe.* The stretch of smothering darkness that had spooled out in front of her at Ruth's words slowly began to recede.

She sat very still, her head on her knees, reaching for her own breath. At last, just when she thought she could bear it no longer, she found that her knees had stopped shaking. She waited for a few minutes more, then she got up slowly, opened the door and went to the sink. Her face stared back at her. Her cheeks were flushed. She turned on the tap and bent her head, her lips finding a coolness that was like a light in her skull. She lifted her head, smoothed back her hair from her damp forehead and opened the door. She made her way back down the corridor. There was no one about. She slipped into the office where Charles and Harry were waiting. She sat down, avoiding their eyes. She picked up her pencil, opened her notebook to a fresh page, moved her pencil case to the side, establishing the order that would make the afternoon lurch ahead on its usual course. In a few moments, the storm that had blown up inside her earlier would have been forgotten, thrust away and buried, as if it had never been.

22

A short, sharp blast of a horn announced their arrival. Kit drew back the curtains in the living room and peered down. A shiny, dark green car stood directly below the window, its engine purring throatily. With sparkling white wheels and a long shiny bonnet, it looked impossibly glamorous. She could just see Ruth's dark head in the front seat. She hurriedly picked up her coat and went into the hallway, automatically checking her reflection before opening the door. She'd taken one of Lily's old evening gowns to the tailor at the end of the road, and asked him to cut off the sleeves and alter it to fit her properly. It was made of dark burgundy silk, long, with a 'V' neck and an elegant, if slightly fussy, bow at the back. It wasn't quite her colour, she thought to herself as she pulled it out, but beggars couldn't be choosers. She had precious little in the way of evening garb and Mrs Arscott didn't seem to possess anything remotely suitable for a club. She doubted Mrs Arscott even knew what a club was.

Gloves? She hesitated. No. She would look like an eager debutante, which was the last thing she wanted. She shook her head ruefully. Already the very idea of a debutante seemed hopelessly passé. The last presentation at Court had been in 1938, almost four years earlier. The war had put a stop to all that ... Who knew if the season would ever return? She closed the door behind her and quickly ran down the stairs.

The door to the car opened as she came into the mews and a young, dark-haired man in uniform got out.

'Hello.' He smiled as she approached. 'You must be Kit. I'm Joel. Do climb in.' He held the door open for her.

Ruth turned as she got into the car. Her hair had been swept up in a chignon and she wore dark red lipstick. She looked transformed. Again Kit was reminded of the clear, steely brightness of metal; there was a look to her that was at once bold and appealing.

'Hello,' she said in that low, soft voice of hers that Kit had already come to know. 'Don't you look the part,' she said, smiling faintly. 'I thought you said you'd never been to a club before. D'you know,' she turned back to Joel, 'it's Kit's first time. She's never heard jazz before.'

'Really? Well, you're in for a treat.' He started the engine.

The car smelled luxuriously of leather and cigarette smoke. There was a sense of expanding excitement in the air. Ruth was smoking, her arm rested lazily, protectively across the back of the seat, not quite touching Joel's uniformed shoulder. Kit felt momentarily awkward, as though her presence had interrupted something between them. But then Joel swung the car around into Ecclestone Street and they joined the line of cars heading towards Pall Mall and her awkwardness faded. She was on her way to a club!

'We're going to Café de Paris,' Joel shouted above the sound of the engine. 'David's meeting us there.'

'Who's David?' Kit asked, shouting to make herself heard. Café de Paris! Even the name sounded impossibly glamorous.

'Joel's best friend. They're on leave,' Ruth answered for him. 'Ten days.' She reached up to ruffle his dark hair. 'David's Joel's best friend, and Joel's mine. Aren't you?' There was a strange wistfulness to Ruth's voice.

'Oh, do stop,' Joel said good-humouredly. His eyes briefly met Kit's in the rearview mirror. 'Just because we went to *shul* together, aged nine. She never lets me forget it.'

'What's *shul*?'

'I told you,' Ruth said to Joel, laughing. 'She doesn't know anything.'

'Stop teasing her,' Joel said, his eyes meeting Kit's again. He was a good-looking young man, with the same olive-toned complexion as Ruth. 'She's a dreadful tease, had you noticed?'

Kit shook her head. It seemed impossible that she'd only known Ruth for a week. 'No, not really,' she murmured.

The girl sitting in the front seat with her hair swept up elegantly and a pair of long, dangling earrings seemed a million miles away from the quiet, serious-looking colleague whom she'd spotted sitting to one side on their first day. She wondered if Ruth thought the same about her.

The street lamps, which were darkened all the way down Park Lane, were abruptly lit up again. To their right was the dark swathe of St James's Park, but all along the left-hand side it was as if they'd suddenly left the war behind. The shops were lit, people were walking along the pavement arm in arm ... It was a Saturday night and in defiance of the perpetually screaming air raid sirens, Londoners had come out to play.

Kit felt a strange tightening of her stomach. She had a sudden premonition of the evening ahead: dancing couples, loud music, the faces of strangers sweaty with passion ... The simultaneous longing for warmth and excitement combined with a strange desire to be free of it all bewildered her and she was silent.

'Gosh, you *are* pretty!' It was the first thing he said as they walked towards him. He pronounced it with a laugh. '*Surprisingly* pretty, as a matter of fact.'

Kit looked up at the man who'd addressed her, astonished at his cheek.

It had to be David, Joel's best friend. He was waiting for them at the entrance. He was fair and tall, a good half a head taller than she was. He was lean and rather rugged-looking and, like Joel, his face was tanned and ruddy with health.

'And why shouldn't I be?' she asked, aware of a curious need to please him, to show off.

He laughed then, properly. 'Oh, because Joel's always saying, "you've got to meet so-and-so, she's awfully pretty", and then when I actually meet her... well, let's just say Joel's definition of the word sometimes stretches things.'

'Why does it matter?' Kit said, perhaps a little more sharply than she intended.

'Absolute rubbish,' Joel said easily, diverting her response and punching David lightly in the arm. 'Come on, then. Shall we go in?' He looked down at the two girls and smiled.

They turned and walked in together. Around them, the noise and laughter of the club rose and fell intoxicatingly. The air quivered with excitement. Kit was suddenly reminded of a summer picnic she'd gone to with her cousins once, down at her grandmother's beautiful home on the Dorset coast. All day the children had run free, Kit in her best shoes that made her feet big and noisy, tearing around the adults, wild with the excitement of it all. The atmosphere in Café de Paris carried with it the same whiff of deliciously tense unpredictability, as if anything could – and would – happen.

'It *does* matter.' David bent his head to her ear, answering her earlier question. 'It shouldn't, but it does.' He bent his head closer. 'We've only got so much leave. I know we're not supposed to say anything, but the thing is... anything can happen. You do see, don't you?'

Kit nodded slowly. She *did* see. She was about to say something when a great roar went up from the crowd. She narrowed her eyes, following a group of men as they emerged from backstage. She blinked in surprise. They were black. All six or seven of them. The first black people she'd ever seen. The light spilled around them, making their entrance even more dramatic. The beat quickened, and in the roar of applause that followed, her eye fell on the trumpeter who strode confidently out in front.

The music was so loud it was deafening, but no one seemed to mind. Couples danced so close together they might have been one. Amidst the men in black tie were men in uniform, young officers like Joel and David. They were both junior army doctors, she learned, stationed in Palestine, which accounted for their tanned faces. They were both Jewish, though David looked as if he belonged in the English countryside, just as she did.

She danced, conscious of his hand on the small of her back and of the warmth of his skin through his uniform, but her attention lay elsewhere. She couldn't take her eyes off the trumpeter, whose tawny skin seemed to give off a light and atmosphere all of its own. The sound of his instrument poured over the crowd like treacle, darkly smooth and deliciously sweet. She closed her eyes for a moment, and in the felty darkness of her eyelids, the lights blazed fluorescent and the vast ballroom faded to darkness. The tempo set by the band was hypnotic. The crowd around them receded until there was only her own body moving, not under David's direction, but another's.

David's grip on her back tightened suddenly. She opened her eyes and dragged herself back to the present.

'Sorry?' She looked up at him, dazed.

'Would you like something to drink?' he asked, looking down at her with an amused smile on his face.

'Oh. Oh, yes, please. It's quite warm in here.'

He pointed to one of the upstairs balconies. 'Why don't you go and find Joel and Ruth?' he shouted above the noise of the crowd. 'They're up there. I'll get us a bottle of something and bring it up. I won't be a moment.'

She nodded obediently and turned and pushed her way through the throng. Just before she reached the stairs, she stumbled over someone's feet and put out a hand to balance herself.

A man grabbed hold of her arm, quickly and powerfully righting her. 'Whoops. There you go, miss.' The voice was deep and bass and absurdly American.

She looked up and immediately felt the blood and heat rush into her cheeks. It was the trumpeter.

'Oh! I … I must've stepped on you … Did I step on your toes?' she gasped, her words falling over themselves.

He smiled and shook his head. 'No, not on mine, miss. But I think you may have injured the man behind you.' He looked past her to the shimmying dancers behind them. 'But he don't seem bothered, if you ask me.' He smiled. His teeth were very white.

I'm talking to a Negro. The thought flashed absurdly through her mind. She might have spoken the words out loud. She continued to stare at him, but shyly, as if waiting for permission to speak. They looked at each other for a moment like people looking across the gulf of a crowded platform or the water of a quay.

'Ah, *there* you are,' an exasperated-sounding voice behind her broke through the noise of the crowd. She turned, almost guiltily. It was David, holding aloft a bottle of champagne by the neck. 'I've been looking everywhere for you!' His tone was peeved. 'I thought I told you to go upstairs?'

She was taken aback by the rebuke. 'Sorry, I ... I was on my way but I nearly fell over someone and this gentleman here—' She turned to include the trumpeter in her account but he'd vanished. 'Oh, he's gone.'

'Who?' David was oblivious. 'Well, come on then. Let's go upstairs and find them. I've an awful thirst.'

Disappointed by the trumpeter's abrupt disappearance, she allowed herself to be swallowed up in David's wake as he purposefully cleared a path through the revellers and led her up the steps to the small balconies that lined the mezzanine. They spotted Ruth and Joel immediately. They were deep in conversation. Ruth's face was animated, her features even more clearly drawn than usual. They fell upon the champagne with gusto.

'Where d'you get *that*?' Joel grinned, holding it up to the light. 'Monopole. Heidsieck, thirty-nine. It's bloody real, too!'

Ruth lit a cigarette and made a space for Kit whilst David pulled up a stool and sat opposite her, his knee touching hers as they drank and smoked and shouted to one another over the noise of the music.

From where she sat on eye level with the balustrade, Kit could see all the way down to the stage. The trumpeter had rejoined the band and within minutes his music filled the air once again. She took a sip of lukewarm wine and closed her eyes, giving herself up to the pleasure of listening to him. She began to drift away from the chattering voices around her. All at once, she felt only the most tentative of connections to the trio with whom she'd come. Absurd as it seemed, she felt as though her *real* place was down there, on the stage, next to the trumpeter with skin the colour of milky coffee and those bright, liquid, aubergine-coloured eyes.

She opened her eyes. Ruth was looking at her quizzically. She flushed. Had she missed something? She looked at David, who was frowning at her.

'Sorry,' she mumbled. 'I . . . I'm just a bit tired all of a sudden.'

'Well, this ought to liven things up.' David grinned. 'I've got this friend – a friend of the warrant officer's, actually – he knows this club somewhere around King's Cross. There's an after-hours party tonight, apparently. Once the band's finished here, they'll head over there. It's a private thing but he says he'll get us in. Are you chaps in?'

'Oh, let's!' Ruth broke in. Her eyes were shining. She turned to Kit. 'We're perfectly safe with these two. Joel'll get us home safely. Do say yes.'

Kit hesitated. The heat and gay abandon of the evening had entered her body the way alcohol enters the blood. 'Won't we—' she began timidly, but Joel interrupted, regarding her almost fondly.

'Poor Kit. I've a feeling we've quite shocked her this evening, what with the Negro band and all the dancing and us suggesting we stay out until dawn.'

'She's quite the innocent, isn't she?' David agreed cheerfully, as if she weren't there.

All three looked at her expectantly, waiting for her answer. She regarded them all. How little they knew of her. Then and now. Her mind lingered on one fact. *The band would be there. Her trumpeter would be there.*

'Why not?' she said quickly. She turned to David and said brightly, recklessly, 'Didn't you just say it earlier? Anything can happen. Who knows where you'll both be next week, or the week after that. So let's go.'

David leaned forwards eagerly. His knee touched hers again and this time, it was anything but accidental.

'Capital,' he said proudly, as though he'd been the one to persuade her. 'Absolutely capital.'

They stepped out of Café de Paris into the cool night air, made sharper by the heat they'd left behind.

'Come on!' David cried, as they walked quickly to the car. 'To King's Cross!'

Across the road there were piles of sandbags in the doorway of the closed-down cinema. It was a rude reminder of the world outside the club. David took Kit's arm and tucked it possessively into his. She allowed herself to be pulled along in the slipstream of his enthusiasm. The evening had taken on an even more unrealistic air. She found it impossible to believe that she'd spent the past few hours in Café de Paris, listening to a black band in the company of two men who she'd only just met *and* the evening wasn't yet over. In fact, if David's excitement was anything to go by, it hadn't even begun.

'D'you like him?' Ruth whispered, her voice soft and buzzing against her ear.

'I suppose so,' she whispered back. To whom was she referring? She couldn't bring herself to say.

'Oh, *good*. It's *much* better if you actually like him. The first time, I mean,' Ruth murmured, managing to sound both conspiratorial and comforting at the same time.

Kit's mouth fell open in surprise but she closed it again, firmly.

They sped up Holborn towards King's Cross. David had been to the warehouse that served as a club once before but it took him several false turns down dark side streets before they finally came upon a sign that announced: *Busby Brothers – All Antiques Bought and Sold* in an incongruous scrolled script, and he gave a shout of recognition.

'Ah! That's it! See that door, the green one? Yes, that's it. Just park over here.'

Joel pulled up dutifully at the kerb and they all peered out rather dubiously. They were on Railway Street, just off York Way, a street full of smoky, grimy industrial buildings that seemed another world away from Belgravia and the West End. Apart from pulling into King's Cross Station by train, Kit had never ventured north of the Euston Road.

'Is this it?' Ruth asked nervously.

'Yes, this is it. Don't worry. It's perfectly fine. You wouldn't believe who comes here. I heard Prince Edward himself was here before the war broke out. It's perfectly all right.'

'If you say so,' Ruth murmured dubiously. She got out first, clutching her coat.

David and Joel led the way. The street was completely deserted, shrouded in darkness, but as they approached the green door with its peeling paint, light spilled out around its edges and a faint, rhythmic thumping noise could be felt beneath their feet.

'It's actually in the cellar,' David explained, and rapped loudly and commandingly on the door.

A man in a rumpled suit opened it, peering at them suspiciously. He wore his hat at a dangerously low angle, giving him a rakish, untidy air. David slipped him a pound note and the name of the warrant officer who'd sent them.

'Down the stairs, through the passage to the warehouse at the back,' he said grudgingly. 'Mind your heads.'

Down the rickety wooden stairs they went, the girls' heels clipping loudly on the stone floor at the bottom. The place smelled of sour wine and sawdust; the air down there was a good deal colder than at street level. They walked down the passageway as directed, the thump of music and voices and laughter growing louder with every step.

Kit's heart began to race. A woman was standing at the entrance to yet another doorway. She had the look of a gypsy, Kit thought, with a long string of pearls that looped several times around her neck and fell almost to her waist over the great shelf of neck and bosom. Her hair was pulled back off her face and her lips were painted a deep, shocking scarlet. She looked them over as they approached, smiled ingratiatingly and wished them a 'very good evening, ladies and gentlemen'.

She opened the door and all of a sudden they were in a place of light and music, cigarette smoke and warmth and the high, excitable sound of conversation. They were ushered to a table in one of the arched brick alcoves, where makeshift tables had been knocked together out of wooden pallets, adorned with thick, waxy candles whose fat, molten sides dripped down the wine bottles in which they'd been shoved, pooling at the base.

'Shall I get us a bottle of champagne?' David asked the girls, smiling broadly, proudly.

They nodded in unison, too busy staring at the scene in front of them to answer. The place was absolutely packed. At one end of the room, a band was playing, though without the excitement of the band they'd just left behind. Kit thought again of the trumpeter and felt a rill of tension run lightly up her spine. David had said the band at Café de Paris would head this way when they were finished. Would her trumpeter come?

She looked at the dancing couples squashed together on the small dance floor. The mood was one of wild, energetic abandon. Through a gauze of thin blue light she saw a girl turn her head to look at her friend who was dancing beside her, her back arched so closely into her companion's embrace it seemed unnatural. She saw a glint of teeth, like the hidden centre of a flower, and a shy smile of complicity passed between the two women. Men without partners stood hunched in the shadows, watching, their hands hanging limply from their sides as if something had just fallen from them. She followed Joel and Ruth to the alcoves at the edge of the dance floor, where the tables were packed together as tightly as the dancers.

David had secured a bottle of cold champagne and solemnly passed her a glass. She drank automatically, the sharp, fizzing bubbles tickling the back of her throat. They were sitting tightly squashed together on the banquette that ran in a curved half-moon around the alcove. David leaned in to say something to her and his hand pressed down firmly on her thigh. The gesture was at once proprietary but she made no move to draw away. She felt his grip tighten. He offered her a cigarette, which she accepted.

'You're a funny thing,' David murmured against her ear as they leaned back to smoke. 'I've never met a girl quite like you.'

'What do you mean?'

'Well, on the one hand you seem frightfully well brought up and all that.'

'I am,' Kit said mildly, wondering what he meant.

'Yes, I know. I mean I know *who* you are. Your family ... your sister and all that.'

Kit stiffened. 'I see,' she said carefully.

'Oh, I don't mind a bit,' he said cheerfully. 'Adds a bit of interest. Mind you, I'm not particularly Jewish. Not like those two.' He nodded at Joel and Ruth. 'They can't wait to leave.'

'Leave? Leave where?'

'To Palestine, of course. That's where we're stationed at the moment. He wants to move out there permanently. He's been trying to persuade Ruth to join him for ages. Me, I can't wait to come home. England's *my* home. They can bloody well keep Palestine, as far as I'm concerned. Nothing but trouble.'

Kit stared at him. 'I didn't realise,' she began hesitantly. 'I've only just met Ruth.'

'You work in intelligence, don't you?'

Kit blushed. 'I ... I don't think ... we're not really at liberty to say,' she said slowly.

'Oh, don't worry. I'm not going to tell anyone,' David said, taking another swig of champagne. 'Everyone's in intelligence these days. Even girls like you.'

'I don't know what you mean,' Kit said stiffly. Was he making fun of her? And how had he heard about Lily?

'You've no idea what sort of girls I usually meet. Nice girls,' he added hastily, in case she'd misunderstood him. 'I don't mean anything like *that*. It's just… well, no one's done very much. They haven't seen much of life, to be honest.'

'And you have?' She pulled back a little from him to give the question the emphasis of her look.

He shrugged. 'I suppose so. That's the thing about this damned war. You see and do things… things you weren't… meant to.' He seemed about to say something more but at that moment, a sudden wild burst of applause broke out across the room.

Kit glanced up. Everyone was looking towards the door. It was the band! The Negro band had arrived! Kit's eyes followed the clapping hands and the smiles of anticipation. They came into the room, one by one.

'It's Louie Lejeune!' someone shouted. 'They're here! It's the Chicago Set!'

She stood up to get a better look, craning her neck above the tightly pressed together bodies. At Café de Paris, everyone was glamorous, the women in silk, the men in black tie or uniform. But this place was different. Beyond the candlelight and cigarette smoke, it was probably grubby with dirt. Yes, there were ladies in satin and furs but there were others, too, working-class girls in cheap dresses and too-bright lipstick. In place of furs and silk theirs was a bold, defiant beauty that seemed somehow more authentic. There were other girls, too, young girls, waitresses, who carried bottles of wine and champagne, wriggling their way expertly through the crowd, a tray held aloft in one hand, a cigarette in the other.

Louie Lejeune was at the centre of the stage now and his band members were busy arranging themselves around him. They were the most extraordinary-looking group. There were eight of them, tall, well-built men with skin colour that ranged from deepest, darkest mahogany to the drummer, who was the palest shade of café au lait.

Kit saw her trumpeter straight away. He picked up his instrument and within seconds he began to carve out a rhythm that the others followed. The crowd clapped and waved and cheered encouragingly. Louie and his band were obviously regulars. Kit had the sensation again of having stumbled upon another world that ran parallel to her own, hidden and unseen.

'Do sit down.' David tugged at the skirt of her dress but she quickly moved out of reach.

She was filled with a sudden impatience to be rid of him, of all three of them. The music picked up and all around her people began to dance. She edged her way closer to the centre of the room, buffeted on all sides by blind shapes. Now and then someone said, 'Sorry!' and moved off, out of range. Her trumpeter – for she thought of him now as hers – joined Louie in front, throwing up his instrument and catching the golden light. The music was electrifying. His notes began to climb higher and higher, creating a space for himself upon which he landed momentarily, pausing for a long, drawn-out echo, only to establish himself on a higher note and then take off again.

Her heart began to thump wildly. The path of the sound was inexplicably painful to her; it tore at her nerves until her heartbeat became louder than the music. She felt as though she couldn't breathe properly, as though she were suffocating with emotion, yet there was such beauty and pain and poise in the notes that to stop listening would have been to collapse, right there and then, in the midst of the stamping, tapping, twirling feet. She heard the music – deeply, properly – for the very first time. She had no partner but it didn't matter; she couldn't bear the thought of sharing the experience with anyone, least of all David, whom she could no longer see.

She found her way to one of the columns at the edge of the room, around which a little space had been cleared, and she stopped. She leaned against its cool solidity, glad of the support. All the while, the frenetic, mysterious place moved around her and Louie's voice rose and fell, rose and fell, died away and then picked up again. She was still holding a glass of champagne. Her fingers tightened their grip. Between her and the eight black men on the stage, who held the crowd in the dexterity of their fingertips, a woman danced with her partner, her entire body draped, suspended from his neck. Her eyes were closed and her face sank inwards, away from the throbbing beat.

Love one another. The thought came to her irrelevantly out of the atmosphere of the place. But it didn't matter. Miracles and gods come like that, she thought. Not in the places we prepare for them, but randomly, amidst the rabble and the crowd.

She looked beyond the moving bodies to the man who held them all spellbound in the polished brass gleam of his trumpet. He was looking directly at her. Everything else suddenly ceased to exist.

23

Earl saw her straight away, almost as soon as they entered the smoky room. The girl he'd seen across the floor at Café de Paris. The girl whose arm he'd touched when she almost tripped over some clumsy fella's feet. She was wearing a dress made of material that moved like water. She'd looked up at him and he caught his breath. She had quick, expressive eyes and the alabaster whiteness of her delicately boned face caught the light in the same way her jewellery did. Darkness did not put her out the way it did some other women. In her, the full force of her personality shone through. He'd laughed a little to himself as he walked away from her. He was being fanciful, he could feel it. How much of anyone's personality could you get from a single encounter? But there'd been no time to stand and ponder the question.

Louie was frowning at him. *Get on with it.* Never mind that they'd been playing for almost six hours straight by then. But Mr Cunningham had promised them there'd be someone special in the crowd that night who might open doors… and man, were they ever in need of an open door. Two of the band members had run into trouble with the law, another had had his work permit suspended, and yet another was suspected of having entered the country under a false name. Jesus Christ. As if the mere fact of being a black man weren't trouble enough. He had no time to ponder that question either.

He picked up his trumpet, his mouth seeking the cool brass opening as surely as any woman's lips, and began to play. He could still see her over the heads of the dancers: shiny blonde hair, her tall, slim body encased in some shiny material that he couldn't name but whose feel under his fingertips he could already imagine. Soft and hard at the same time, slippery too, the kind of material that made a noise like paper when touched. He'd had to stop himself. He was getting carried away.

That was his romantic side, his grandmother always used to tell him. The nonsense side of him. The side that refused to submit to Jim Crow by upping sticks for New York, leaving behind his grandmamma and his six siblings in the cramped tenement on 35th and State that had been home for the first twenty-six years of his life. Only New York wasn't no different. Same as it ever was. 'Cept there he was one of thousands of young black trumpeters, rather than hundreds. Two years of scrapping for a living, playing in clubs he never wished to see or hear of again; playing for white folk, Jewish folk, even black folk who'd come into money or were hustling for it ... and all that time never making any himself. Wages, that's all he got. A night's wages handed over by some shark who claimed to 'represent' them – whatever *that* meant – and who took the lion's share for himself.

When he met Louie Lejeune, whose real name was Aloysius Jackson, it seemed an answer to a prayer he wasn't even aware of. *Let's get outta here.* It was 1940; the mood in America was jittery. The newly elected Roosevelt had just signed the Lend-Lease Act, which many assumed was a precursor to war. Louie was adamant and persuasive. *He* wasn't about to cross the ocean to fight white men on the orders of other white men. The only Germans and Italians he'd come across were neighbours to the south and east of South Side, Chicago, and they'd always been good to *him*. Besides, there were other ways to get to Europe.

'How d'you mean?' Earl asked, frowning.

'Here's the thing,' Louie said, warming up. 'You remember Morris Wasserman? The cat who owns the Harlem Club? Well, he's had this idea to send a big band across to London. They can't get enough of our music over there, he says.'

'There's a war going on,' Earl said pointedly.

Louie laughed. 'Since when did that stop anybody enjoying themselves? Shit, that's *exactly* the right time to start something new! Something they ain't never seen before.'

'Like a bunch of black men playing jazz? Come on, Louie. They got their own black men over there. Even *I* know that.'

'Sure they do. But they ain't got us. Wasserman wants us to take be-bop out to England. We'd be the *first*, man. I got me two fellas from Jamaica ... You ain't never heard nobody play the drums the way Charlie does. Stop by the club tomorrow night. You'll hear him. If I can get me one more trumpeter like you, we're set. We even got ourselves a new name.'

'What is it?' Earl's pulse had begun to race, in spite of his scepticism.

'Louie Lejeune and the Chicago Set. Like it? It's French. Classy, ain't it?'

Earl grinned. 'You speak French?

'Nope. But one of them Caribbean boys does. He's from one of them islands . . . I can't remember which one. Plays the piano like he was born to it. Come on, Earl. Whaddya say?'

'How would we get there?'

Louie smiled. Earl could see that by saying 'we' and not 'you', he'd begun to promise better material.

'Cruise ship, out of New York. We'd leave on eleventh of December, be there in time for Christmas. Place is hopping, Wasserman says.'

Earl's mind began to race. Europe! London! A chance to get away from the hateful segregation laws and the never-ending grind of trying to make it in a white man's world, one day at a time. The very word conjured up an image of timeless, elegant beauty – the charm he felt was utterly lacking in his everyday life. Still, he was no fool. He knew it wouldn't be easy. It wasn't as though black men didn't face discrimination over there; he'd read the stories, heard the tales, seen the films. But it would be different; a different kind of life. Louie was offering him a chance, a way out.

He took it.

'That was terrific. It was the best thing I've ever heard.'

He turned in surprise and almost jumped out of his skin. How'd she manage to sneak up on him like that? Although she'd only spoken to him once before, there was no mistaking the sound of her voice. He'd never heard a voice quite like it, each vowel carefully and beautifully expressed. *It was the best thing I've ever heard.* The trite phrase suddenly summing up his whole life. She looked up at him out of the smoky darkness that enveloped them, her eyes shining, and he was seized by the most alarming concentration of need. His entire being seemed to depend on her continuing to speak.

'Can I get you something to drink?' He had to say *some*thing and the banal phrase was as good as any other. He thought of the change in his pocket and fervently hoped it would cover the cost of a drink. She looked the type to drink only champagne, too.

But she surprised him. 'Not a bit of it,' she said firmly. 'I'm the one who should buy *you* a drink. What will you have?'

He was taken aback by her boldness. He liked the way she said it, all easy like, yet assertive, too, as though buying him a drink were the most natural thing in the world to do. He could sense people beginning to look at them. The fella he saw her with at Café de Paris was nowhere to be seen. Perhaps she'd come alone? He doubted it. Girls like her never went out alone.

'Yeah, sure,' he said slowly, smiling at her. 'A whisky, please.'

'Coming up.' She smiled back at him and turned to summon the attention of a passing waiter.

He watched her as discreetly as he could. Like many of the white women he'd known – even if only in passing – there was a confidence about her that attracted him. She summoned the waiter with a quick, impatient little lift of her arm, not because she was rude but because girls like her *expected* to be served. She turned back to him and again he experienced the whiff of perfume that seemed already to belong to her.

'What's your name?' she asked as the waiter handed them two glasses.

He took a sip, aware that they were being watched. The fiery liquid burned its way down his throat and chest, bolstering his nerves.

'Earl. Earl Hightower,' he said, and then laughed. 'Funny name, huh? Specially for you English.'

'Hightower?' She laughed too, shaking her head. 'That sounds terribly English.'

'Well, coulda been. I mean, some slave owner or other ... you know how it is.'

A small, pained dent appeared between her brows and he had to hold himself back from reaching out to smooth it. 'And yours?' he asked hurriedly, to cover his confusion. 'I bet you're called "Lady" something, right?'

She blushed a little. He could tell by the way her eyes shone. She was the kind of girl on whose skin all her emotions could be seen, ripe, blossoming ... like a fruit warmed by the sun.

'Well, I suppose you *could* call me that,' she said, smiling in semi-culpable acknowledgement. 'But no one does. I'm just Kit.'

'Kit. I like that.' He took another sip. 'So, Kit, you like jazz? Yeah, I think you do. No, I *know* you do. I could tell by looking at you.'

'You were looking at me?'

'Couldn't stop.'

She gave the low-voiced laugh that all females give when signalling what can't immediately be put into words. He felt it as surely as if she'd touched him. The sheer audacity of it thrilled him. He felt a sudden ridiculous pride in her beauty and the toughness he could sense lying just below the surface of her outward emotions.

One or two men were openly staring at them with unmasked envy or alarm ... maybe even disgust. He couldn't tell, didn't care. He took another sip of whisky. In half an hour or so, Louie would signal to him to get back on stage. There was no telling if she'd come back the following night, or if indeed he'd ever see her again. The drink made him bold.

'You want to get some fresh air? It's pretty hot in here.' His voice sounded hoarse with the effort of appearing natural and light.

She looked up at him. He was aware of the delicate but strong line of her eyebrows and the way the skin was pulled tight over her cheekbones. Her short hair framed her face in smooth curls. He wanted nothing more than to bury his nose in it, to take handfuls of it between his fingers and pull her close. He had to look away. He was afraid she would look through him, beyond the casual offer to 'get some air', to the other side where the contradiction and confusion of everything that he was – black, Negro, 'other' – shadowed his every moment.

When he glanced back at her, he saw that her face was open, but confused, too, as though something of his inner turmoil had transmitted itself to her, a consequence he hadn't foreseen. They stared at each other for a few minutes, neither willing to break the spell.

Finally she spoke. Her lips parted and he saw a flash of white teeth. 'Come on then,' she said, tossing back her drink.

Her blind confidence was intoxicating. He hurriedly swallowed the rest of his and followed her as she pushed her way through the crowd.

24

What was the secret signal in him that had communicated itself to her so directly across the dancing couples and the wildly waving hands? What was it in his music that spoke to her and her alone? The questions only broke the surface of her consciousness.

They pushed their way up the narrow stairs until they reached the darkened street. The gas lamps loomed dark and silent; all along the pavement were the ever-present sandbags, pushed up against doorways as if to hold the buildings in. Kit shivered. It had been a warm evening to begin with but now the air was turning cold. She wondered what time it was – past midnight! – and how she could have so callously left David and the other two behind. Ruth wouldn't mind, she knew that. What would she make of the fact he was black? she wondered. She pondered the question as they walked together towards the main road. They'd fallen into step, walking side by side, not touching, not speaking, but she felt the terrible thread of desire pull tighter with each passing second.

She had no answer to the question of what Ruth might think. The question was overlaid immediately by other, much more difficult questions. What was *she* doing walking along a darkened road in the small hours of the morning with a complete stranger? Feelings that she'd buried, or that she'd thought long dead, suddenly began to surface uncontrollably. That old, childhood fear of being left behind, left out of things, especially where Lily was concerned. Lily's relentless teasing. Her mother's disappointment in her looks and the terrible secret that had bound them together all through her childhood, right up until another, even more terrible secret had come between them.

She thought of the wet and windy coast of Scotland, where she'd gone to have the baby, and the devastatingly long days and nights that had passed since then where she dared not allow her mind to wander or break free of its chains.

She shivered again and slipped her hand into Earl's. His palm gave off a warmth and solidity that was beyond physical. Behind her eyes she felt the sharp tug of tears, but of relief, not sorrow. She couldn't have put what she felt into words, not at any price.

They emerged out of the alley and began the long walk down the deserted main road. A lone taxi was bearing down upon them. She lifted her arm to summon it and felt him stiffen beside her.

'It's quite all right,' she murmured. 'Nothing will happen to us.' She reached for the handle. 'Ecclestone Mews,' she said firmly. 'Just off Upper Belgrave Street.'

'Very good, miss.' If the taxi driver was surprised to see a girl like her in the company of a black man, he made no show of it.

They clambered into the back seat, still holding hands, and the cab lurched forwards. The quiet London streets flashed past, pavements slick with a recent downpour. A thick pall of smoke hung over the buildings and the air seemed dense with the threat of an air raid. It had been several days since the last one. There was no moon that night, only clouds that hovered close to the ground.

She leaned her head against his shoulder. He had one arm stretched along the top of the seat with the hand dangling only a few inches from her face. She looked at it in the dim interior of the cab. His salmon-coloured palm was turned towards her; she'd never seen a palm like it. She had an awareness of him unlike any other man she'd known. For the first time in months, she felt the dark, heavy shadow that lay upon her heart ease a little. She had no real thought of what might lie ahead.

She opened the front door cautiously, half expecting Mrs Arscott to be waiting in the hallway. There was no one, of course. The grandfather clock at the end of the narrow passageway chimed accusingly as they entered stealthily, like thieves. It was nearly two o'clock in the morning. Her heart was thumping and she could feel the heat in her face rise a notch as she closed the front door firmly behind her.

'Just in here,' she said softly, by way of breaking the silence.

'After you, ma'am,' he said, giving her an exaggerated bow.

She was grateful for his easiness and the way he made things light between them. She liked, too, the sound of his voice, the way his vowels stretched out lazily, like smoke. It was a foreign voice, belonging to a different place and time, and its very distance in terms of her own life made it possible to believe that anything could happen.

She led the way into the living room, telling him to mind his head as she walked through the doorway. The ceiling was low. She'd bumped her own head on it many a time and he was a good foot taller than her. She looked around hastily, wishing she'd had a chance to tidy it up before leaving earlier that evening. A pair of precious, discarded nylons hung over the back of one of the armchairs. There was mug of tea and a piece of toast with a bite comically taken out of it lying on a side plate on the carpet. She bent forwards hurriedly to retrieve it but he held her back.

'It ain't nothing,' he said gently. 'Nice place you got.'

'It's not mine,' she said hastily. Her arm was warm where he'd touched it. 'Would ... would you like something to drink?' She switched on a lamp, more to give herself something to do than to light up the room.

He shook his head. 'Nah, I'm good.'

She smiled at that. 'Only an American could say that. You must find us terribly formal.'

It was his turn to smile. 'Forward and formal,' he said. 'That's new to me. I'm not used to girls like you.'

In the faint light, his skin appeared darker than before. They were standing close but, again, not touching. There was a delicacy in the way he held himself. He reached out slowly, almost hesitantly, and caught hold of her arm, drawing her towards him. In a gesture that was electrifying, he suddenly put his hand on the flat of her waist. Her breath rose and fell shakily beneath the fabric of her dress.

'How do you mean?' she asked, her voice barely above a whisper.

She was now at eye level with his neck. She looked at the light brown smoothness of his skin, contoured by tendon and muscle. She had the sudden uncontrollable desire to taste him, to run her tongue along the crevice between chin and neck, which she knew would be salty with sweat. There was a hot welling in her throat and in another part of her body that she had never felt before. Automatically, her hands went to his shirt, pushing it up so that she could rest her fingertips against the padded muscle of his chest. His hands slid down her back, gathering her to him. He was looking at her so intently that she had to close her eyes. She was ashamed. He began to kiss her, fiercely, as though he couldn't get enough of her in his mouth and hands. After a moment's hesitation, she answered. They began to tease and please each other. If there was curiosity, there was also surprising passion, the solemn passion of two people who'd found something unexpected in each other and who were only now beginning to recognise it. This time was so different from the last time that it was as if it were two separate acts. *This* had nothing to do with *that.*

He laid her very gently on the floor and began slowly to unbutton her dress, pausing every now and then to ask a silent question with his lips and eyes. *Is this okay? Are you ready for this?*

At last she was naked. He stopped only to pull aside his braces and shirt and then he lay down, laying the full splendid length of his frame beside her. She smoothed the indentation of a rib with one finger, not pretending to ignore the contrast of his skin against hers. Unlike her pale nakedness, his light colouring was a covering. Under his touch, she felt the whole surface of her skin come alive. Fleetingly their eyes met and in hers was the question: *Is it all right?* He nodded and she heard the sound of a packet being torn open. She blushed from the roots of her hair to the tips of her toes. After what had happened the last time. Trusting him, she gave herself willingly, listening with unbridled pleasure to the sounds that now poured out of him as he drove towards his own pleasure without forgetting hers. He showed her a different profile; the tightly drawn lines she'd noticed on either side of his mouth relaxed as he settled into his own, steadily mounting rhythm. Just as it had been when she heard him playing, her emotions climbed from one dizzying space to another, every nerve screaming for pleasurable release. She felt herself pushed to the limits he'd discovered for her, over and over again.

They must have slept. She woke in one of those terrific starts, half fearful, half dreaming, and put out a hand to stop herself from falling. But she was lying on the carpet and her hand knocked against his. He mumbled something in his sleep, turning drowsily towards her, but she was awake now. She couldn't believe what had happened. She lifted a hand and peered at her wristwatch: it was nearly four o'clock in the morning. They'd barely slept.

'Whassa matter?' he mumbled against her ear, sensing her alertness.

'Nothing,' she whispered. 'I woke up suddenly.'

'Go back to sleep, baby. It's nearly morning.'

'It *is* morning. It'll be light any moment now.'

He grunted, shifting his weight. 'Can't a man get a decent night's sleep?' he spoke into her hair.

She shook her head, full of lazy delight. 'What about the band?' she asked, reaching behind her for one of the blankets covering the chair. She wrapped it over them both.

He groaned, this time in despair. 'Shoot. Louie's gonna *kill* me,' he sighed. 'It ain't the first time either. Not me,' he added hastily. 'The other guys. Happens all the damned time.'

She said nothing but let her fingers trail across his chest and up the salty neck she'd tasted earlier. An overnight beard had begun to sprout beneath his skin; it felt rough to her fingertips. Curious, she reached up and ran her hand across his short, neat hair. Like all the other band members, he had it cut quite close to his scalp, with a parting to one side and a thin moustache. It felt light and springy to her touch; it was unlike anything she'd ever felt before. *He* was unlike anyone she'd ever met before. In more ways than one.

25

'So where did you *go*?' Ruth hissed, her voice torn between suspicion and concern.

They'd met accidentally in the corridor. Ruth was hurrying to catch up with her group, who'd been sent upstairs to the library on the fourth floor; Kit was coming down on her way to one of the Nissen huts outside, which served as temporary offices.

'I'll tell you later,' Kit whispered back. 'Meet me after work?'

'All right, but I want the truth, Kit. We were absolutely frantic. The lady at the door said you'd left with someone but she wouldn't say who. She just said you'd hailed a taxi and driven off. It was all very cloak and dagger. David was beside himself.'

Kit swallowed. It was an unexpected kindness from an unlikely source. She remembered the woman at the door, a brassy redhead with a bust that was practically a shelf. Kit had smiled shyly at her as she and Earl escaped up the stairs. She'd looked at her, half expecting a reprimand of some sort. None had come.

'I'd better go,' she said, hoping her voice was steady. 'We've got some test coming up. I'll meet you here at five, all right?' She hurried off before Ruth could ask anything further.

What would she tell her? What *could* she tell her? She had no idea what lay in store. She knew she would see Earl again but beyond that... who knew? In just under a month's time, she would be sent to Scotland. Then what?

'Kit!' She looked up. It was Charles, gesturing forcefully. 'Come on! Vera's waiting.'

She needed no second reminder. She ran.

The expression on Ruth's face when Kit finished speaking would have been comical, if only she'd been in the mood to laugh. Her eyes were as wide as saucers.

'The *trumpeter*?' she squeaked finally. 'The trumpeter from the *band*?'

Kit nodded, holding her breath. They were sitting in the crowded front room of Sam's Café on Rupert Street, a few streets away from Ruth's home. She curled her hands protectively around her coffee cup. It was nearly dark outside.

'I... I don't know what came over me,' she said meekly, hoping Ruth would accept the half-truth for what it was: a feeble excuse.

Ruth shook her head. 'Well I never,' she said at last, lighting a cigarette. She looked at Kit appraisingly. 'Yes, you're the type,' she said after a moment, picking delicately at a fleck of tobacco that had somehow wound up between her front teeth. She took a sip of coffee. 'You're a giver. You'll throw everything on the bonfire, including yourself. But you can't marry him,' she said flatly.

'Marry him?' It was Kit's turn to look at her with widening eyes. 'Who said anything about marriage?'

'You don't have to. It's in your face, Kit. Oh, I know... you think *I* think it's because of your background. Nice girls like you and all that. But it's not. You're like me, Kit. You want... I don't know... to live. To *do* something. To *be* someone. That's why we're here.' She gestured at the café but they both knew she spoke of 54 Broadway Buildings. 'I could have gone to university, you know,' she said. 'Nothing would've made my parents happier. You've no idea what these *shtetl* Jews are like.'

Kit shook her head. She had no idea what a *shtetl* Jew was.

Ruth smiled. 'Learning. There's no higher goal, as far as they're concerned. I gave up my place at Oxford to work for the government. They couldn't understand it... They still can't. As soon as anyone in a Jewish family shows the slightest inclination towards learning, they all start nodding their heads. "Just like so-and-so," or, "So studious, just like her Uncle Solomon." The fact is, no one even knows who Uncle Solomon is, or was. Some Talmudic scholar or other, long dead. I don't want to end up like *that*.' She stopped and looked at Kit. 'The thing is,' she said slowly, tracing a pattern on the tablecloth with her fingertip, 'I want to be *useful*.'

'But that's exactly it!' Kit broke in excitedly, staring at her. 'That's it! That's exactly what *I* want to be.'

'And that's why I'm telling you not to marry him. It's not *him*. It's marriage. It'll be the end of you. It'll be the end of everything.'

'And that's why you don't want to marry Joel,' Kit said slowly. 'You do love him, don't you?'

Ruth nodded. 'I... I suppose so. I mean, we've known each other since... well, since for ever. His parents aren't like mine. They're both doctors, educated people. I suppose it was his mother who first gave me the idea that I could be... well, *more*. Don't get me wrong,' she said quickly. 'I love my parents, honestly I do. I'm not ashamed of them or anything. But I don't want *their* life. I want my own.'

Kit looked at her with a growing admiration. She loved her parents enough to accept their differences from her in a way that Kit could not. To break free from hers, Kit had had to suffer the guilt of severing her ties with those whom she ought to have loved most. Ruth, more mature than her, and more practical too, had not. She managed to hold the contradictions of her past and her life now in a balance that Kit suddenly longed for.

'Me too,' Kit said with a sudden uprush of emotion. Their backgrounds couldn't have been more different but she felt she understood exactly what Ruth meant. 'We're awfully alike,' she said slowly.

'Perhaps.' Ruth shrugged. 'I'm not as romantic as you, Kit.' She smiled faintly. 'Oh, I know you're going to say I hardly know you and so I oughtn't to say things like that. But I've seen you, I watch the way you put on this... this cloak... the clothes and the bright red lipstick and the air of not really giving a damn. I know something happened to you somewhere along the line. Don't worry, I won't pry. And I can see you're doing this not just because you're duty bound to king and country and all that. Yes, it's a job and it's a chance for young women like you and me to prove that we're capable of doing more than our families want from us. You, with your background and your titles and everything, and me with my parents' hope that I'll settle down soon with some nice Jewish boy and produce the grandchildren they've been waiting the past ten years for. No, the truth is we're both running away from ourselves. Perhaps the only difference is the lengths to which we're each prepared to go.'

There was a moment's silence. Kit felt her own eyes slowly fill with tears, a brimming she couldn't control. She looked down at her hands. She couldn't speak.

'Don't worry,' Ruth said, more gently this time. 'I said I wouldn't pry and I won't. But the thing is, Kit, I've got to tell you ... it's no use looking for someone else to do it.'

'Do what?' Kit's voice was barely above a whisper. She had never talked to anyone like this in her life before.

'Save you. SOE won't save you. Vera Atherton won't. And your black trumpeter certainly won't. The only person who can save you from yourself is *you*. You've got to decide what you want from life, how you want to live it ... even *where* you want to live. Just think, in a couple of weeks' time, we'll be leaving this place. God knows where we'll end up. We could be sent anywhere, anything might happen. You and I might not ever see each other again.'

'Don't say that,' Kit protested.

She suddenly felt childish in a way she hadn't been in years. But it wasn't the envious, impatient immaturity she'd experienced all her life with Lily; it was a naïveté of a different order. Ruth was eight years older than her but at that very moment, the difference in age between them could have been an entire generation, even more. She was reminded of Uncle Faunce and a terrible feeling of sadness swept over her. She felt she should apologise, though for what she wasn't sure.

'I'm sorry,' she said hesitantly.

'Don't be. We're on the brink of something. Something enormous. I don't know how they recruited *you* but someone, somewhere, noticed us and took a chance.'

'I was part of a typing pool at the War Office,' Kit said slowly. 'A man came in one day and asked if I spoke German.'

'Funny, I was in my father's shop. Someone overheard me speaking German to a customer and asked me if I wanted to work for the government. So you see, it all comes down to chance. If we'd been at war with the Americans, being fluent in German wouldn't have been much use to anyone and then who knows … I might be married to Joel by now. And you'd have been practising your curtsey. Isn't that what girls like you do?'

Kit nodded. 'I'd have been a debutante.'

'The last debutante.' Ruth smiled. 'Well, there you are. Aren't you glad that fate intervened?'

Kit couldn't speak at all. 'I'm so glad I met you,' she said finally, in a taut and trembling voice. 'And you're right. Something *did* happen to me but I'm sorry, I can't speak about it. I just can't.'

'Then don't. Use it in another way. Don't let it destroy you. Let it be the making of you instead.' She hesitated. 'I probably shouldn't say this, I know, but they're not who they seem either.'

'Who?' Kit looked at her, puzzled.

'David and Joel. Have you ever heard of the Palmach?'

Kit shook her head. 'What is it?'

'It was established last month. Fourteenth of May, to be precise. It's to be an elite fighting force, a strike wing of the Haganah. I bet you don't know what that is either, do you?'

Kit shook her head again. 'Is it something to do with Palestine?'

Ruth nodded. 'You're learning fast. Haganah is the Jewish paramilitary organisation. It means "the defence" in Hebrew. It's been going since the twenties. No one will ever admit to it – at least not now – but there's going to be another war in Palestine when this one is over. That's what David and Joel are really doing. They're in the Jewish Brigade, part of the British army. But the real reason they're both there is to join the Palmach. That's what Joel wants me to do. He wants us both to join up.'

Kit's head was spinning. 'And leave everything here? Your parents? Your job?'

Ruth nodded. 'People only rise to the occasion when there's about to be a change,' she said slowly. 'When there's a threat, or something big is about to happen. You only say to yourself "I'm alive" when you're facing death. Or "here" suddenly takes on a different meaning because you're about to leave. That's where we both are, Kit. In the middle of everything, right here, right in the thick of it.'

'What will you do?' Kit asked breathlessly. She felt as though her whole world was about to turn over again, only not in the way it had turned over before.

Ruth shrugged. 'What will you do?' she parried.

Neither girl spoke. Both unanswered questions lay before them amidst the discarded teacups and cigarette butts.

26

Only two weeks to go. It was her first thought on waking every morning. Only a week to go. Only five days to go. A fortnight had passed since the night she'd met Earl and not an hour went by where she didn't agonise over how to tell him she'd soon be gone. They were being sent to Scotland for basic training. No one knew exactly where. Rumour had it they'd be stationed somewhere on the coast, but beyond that, no one seemed to know anything more.

There was talk of different training camps – weapons, counterintelligence, sabotage, code-breaking . . . The list seemed almost impossibly covert, and endless. From the little they'd managed to glean from their trainers, basic training was supposed to last six weeks and from Scotland they'd be posted elsewhere in the country according to their proven capabilities. A whole host of stately homes up and down the length and breadth of the United Kingdom had been requisitioned by the government. Weapons research was housed in Buckinghamshire; forgery in Essex; camouflage units were trained just north of London, in Borehamwood. Wherever she'd be sent, it would mean an end to the idyllic cocoon in which she and Earl were temporarily suspended.

He appeared to have no idea what she did. 'I'm a secretary,' she told him in one of their precious late night talks.

'You seem kinda, I don't know, too *classy* to be a secretary,' he said, smiling at her. 'I mean, don't you people live in homes with a thousand servants, that kinda stuff?'

'Not any more.' She smiled back. That much, at least, was true. 'That was then.'

'So what's this?' he asked, tracing a lazy circle across the smooth, taut skin of her thigh. 'What's now?'

She was quiet for a moment. Now she would tell him. Now. But she couldn't. 'This is … this is now. This is different.'

'Because of the war, you mean?'

'No. Because of you.'

'Why me?' Like lovers everywhere, they were endlessly fascinated with each other's account of how 'it' had come to pass.

She was aware of a delicately, deliciously hollowed-out feeling within her body. She reached across him for the packet of cigarettes balanced precariously on the edge of the bed. She lit one and turned to him, propping herself up on one elbow, the better to study his somnolent frame. Her eyes wandered over his dark, smooth chest, past the rumpled eiderdown to the rest of her bedroom. Earl lived with three other band members in a shared house somewhere in the south of the city. It was unthinkable that he would take her there. Her little mews flat had become their haven, a place of escape that might, under other circumstances, have been claustrophobic in its smallness, its tightness. As it was, it was perfect. On the window was the potted plant she'd bought at the market around the corner from Ruth's flat in Soho. Its leaves were yellowing and a little bedraggled. It was June and there were days when the sun shone on London as fiercely as on any Mediterranean seaside town.

'Do you have to play tomorrow?' she asked.

'Nah, tomorrow's a day off, thank God. Louie's bin tryin' to get us a gig at some fancy hotel uptown. He's makin' sure we playin' every hour God sends, it seems like. Nah, we don't got to play until Monday night. Yes*sir*! I got me a whole Sunday off.'

'So … you're *completely* free tomorrow?' she said slowly, hopefully.

He turned to look at her, squinting in the dark. 'What you plannin'?' he asked with a slow smile. 'What's goin' on in that pretty little head of yours?'

'Nothing.' But it was a lie.

'Come on. What you thinkin'?'

'Have you ever been to the country? The *proper* countryside, I mean.'

He considered the question. 'No, I guess not. We docked in Southampton. D'you call that the countryside?'

She laughed. 'No, not really.' She hesitated, the idea still forming in her mind. 'I was just thinking … why don't we go somewhere? We could leave early tomorrow morning and be back on Monday afternoon. Where are you playing on Monday?'

'Café de Paris. Same place I saw you.'

'Well, then?'

He propped himself up on an elbow and touched her cheek with his free hand. 'Well then. Looks like you got it all planned out. So, where we goin'?'

She smiled, bending her head to kiss his palm. 'You'll see.'

She let her tongue trail over the salmon-coloured flesh, seeking the deep grooves, lingering on the fleshy pad of his thumb. Suddenly it was clear to her what she ought to do.

27

Hook. Basingstoke. Micheldever. Salisbury. Pimperne. The quaint English place names announced themselves as the train pulled into station after station. *Pimperne.* He had to laugh at that one.

'*Pimp*-erne? Now, what kinda name is *that*?'

Sitting opposite him, her stomach a churning mass of nerves, Kit forced herself to smile. The phone call earlier that morning to her mother had unnerved her.

'Katherine? Well, this is a surprise.' It had been months since she'd spoken to her mother. News of Chalfont generally came to her through Mrs Arscott, and vice versa. 'What's the matter?'

'Nothing's the matter. I ... I was thinking of coming down.'

'Here? When?'

'Today. Around lunchtime, in fact.'

'Why? Something's wrong, isn't there?'

'No, Mother, nothing's wrong. I ... I just thought it would be nice to visit, that's all.'

There was a suspicious silence at the other end. 'After all this time? Well, Father will be pleased. Why now?'

Kit sighed. Nothing had changed. 'It's just that I'll be starting a new job next week and it might be a while before I get the chance to visit again. I thought…'

'A new job?' Mother gave one of her high, disbelieving laughs. 'Well! You're *quite* the little career woman these days, aren't you?' She managed to sound patronising and disapproving in the same breath. One of her mother's singular talents, Kit thought to herself.

'We'll be coming down on the train,' she said, trying not to rise to the bait.

'We? Who's "we"?'

'I'm coming with a friend. Someone I'd like you to meet.'

There was a meaningful pause. 'A friend?' Mother asked. 'What sort of friend?'

'Just a *friend*, Mother. We'll stay the night and catch the train back on Thursday. I thought he could stay in Lily's old room.'

There was another meaningful pause as Lady Wharton took in the significance of Kit's words. 'Well, all right,' she said finally. 'I'll have the new girl make up the room. Bignell's not here any more, did you know?'

'Yes, Mother. Mrs Arscott did tell me. Look, I'd better go. I've got to get ready.'

'What's his name? Anyone we know?'

'No. It's Earl. Earl Hightower. He's American.'

'American?' Lady Wharton's voice rose to a disbelieving squeak. 'An American, did you say? What's he doing—'

'Mother, I've got to go. I'll see you this afternoon. We'll be on the two thirty train up from London.'

'Very well. I'll send Caruthers. He's now—'

'Yes, Mother, I know. He's now the driver as well as the butler. Mrs Arscott keeps me up to date. I … I'll see you later.' Kit put the phone down before her mother could say anything further. She paused for a moment, torn between a desire to burst into tears or burst into hysterical laughter.

She went into the living room. Earl was standing by the window, looking down into the cobbled mews below. He turned as she entered.

'Right, it's settled,' she said, smiling at him, as if in reassurance. 'We'll catch the train down to Dorset after breakfast.'

'And these?' He gestured at the clothes he wore. 'I ain't got nothin' fancy. You sure this'll be okay?'

She couldn't help herself. She went up to him and put her arms around his neck, drawing his face close to hers.

'It'll be fine,' she whispered. 'I'll get Father's butler to fix you up with a dinner jacket. Please don't worry. I want you to meet them.'

He drew back a little to look at her. 'You sure you know what you're doin', baby?'

She understood the question as he intended her to. She nodded. 'Trust me.'

'If you're sure?'

'I am sure.'

Now, as the train slipped out of Blandford, heading towards Dorchester, she wasn't feeling quite so sure. She turned to look out of the window. The pretty Dorset countryside rolled by, basking in the early summer sunlight. Puffy, fluffy green trees marked the edges of fields that were bordered with low walls of chalky stone. The barley fields she remembered so well from childhood rolled before them, their velvety heads blazing with the June morning sun. On another day, the particular vibrancy of the light might have given her a headache, or caused her to close her eyes. Today, the world around her shimmered.

Caruthers was there to meet them at Hooke Station. She could see his distant yet familiar figure at the far end of the station as the train slowed to a halt in a cloud of wispy white smoke and squealing brakes.

'We're here,' she said to Earl, who'd dozed off after Yeovil.

She'd been unable to stop herself from staring at him as he slept. They'd travelled down in a first-class cabin, which they'd had to themselves all the way from Paddington Station. The only time they'd left it was at lunchtime, when they'd joined the other first-class passengers in the restaurant car. It had been worth the price of the tickets just to see the looks on other people's faces as they entered. For the journey back home, she'd chosen a lilac-coloured dress printed with tiny flowers and a row of fabric-covered buttons from the bust to the waist. She'd spent an unaccustomed fifteen minutes in the bathroom, arranging her hair this way first, then that, finally landing on a side parting that matched his. Only his hair was short and black and hers was thick and blonde. She knew they made a striking couple, and not just because of the colour difference. At 5'10", she'd always been the tallest girl in the room, but Earl was easily 6'4". In the easy confidences of bed, he'd told her he'd played football in high school and might have gone on to make something of a career had he not been bitten by the 'music bug' and headed north. As he talked and she lay drowsily in his arms, she was hungry to hear more. He was the most beautiful, most fascinating, most other-worldly man she'd ever met.

His aubergine-coloured eyes flew open, and he stared at her as he focused, taking in his new surroundings.

'Here?' he echoed. 'Where's "here"?'

'Hooke. It's about a three-mile drive to Chalfont. The chauffeur's waiting. Come on.'

She pulled down the window impatiently and they stepped onto the platform amidst the noise and bustle of alighting passengers. Several people stared openly at them, but Kit feigned indifference. She hurried down the platform to where Caruthers stood. He was a little older, a little more stooped.

'Caruthers,' she said softly, coming up to him. 'How nice to see you.'

'Afternoon, miss,' he said, tipping his hat. 'Welcome back.' His eyes widened as Earl drew level.

Kit turned to him. 'Caruthers, this is Mr Hightower. He'll be staying with us for the night. Would you take my bag?'

Caruthers only just managed to close his mouth before dipping his head briefly in acknowledgement. 'Afternoon, sir. Just this way, miss. Car's parked in the forecourt.'

'It's awfully good of you to come and fetch us,' Kit said, following his lead. 'Did you have trouble getting petrol?'

Caruthers gave a little snort. 'Oh, no, miss. Her Ladyship's got her ways, if you know what I mean.'

Kit smiled faintly. She did indeed.

The car was the same one in which she'd left for Germany with Uncle Faunce. She swallowed down on the knot in her stomach as she and Earl got into the back.

'Nice car,' Earl murmured as they pulled out of the station.

She said nothing. The road led straight into the soft rolling hills surrounding the village, rising gradually towards the woods that appeared dark green at that time of the day. The wheat and barley fields were dulled every now and then by cloud shadows, as though an unseen hand were rubbing across the landscape with a cloth. Bright, hard glints of silver and gold shone through, and then disappeared again. Somewhere across the fields towards the sea, a shape lifted and fell, making lazy circles high in the sky. It was a plane, dipping and rolling, coming into view through the car window and then falling once more out of sight beneath the horizon line of trees. It couldn't have been an enemy plane: there was no shrill, high siren that followed the sighting of planes, as there usually was in London. She watched it roll once more, sending a vast flock of the birds who lived in the woods scattering into the patchy blue sky, and then there was silence, the only sound the steady drone of the car's engine as Caruthers motored them slowly home.

She began to picture the journey that she knew so well through Earl's eyes: the hedgerows and stone walls, copses of dark, mysterious trees and wide open fields of ripening wheat. What must he make of it? she wondered. It was a world away from London's sandbagged, grimy streets.

They rounded the last bend in the road, crossed over the little brook that ran along the estate's edge, and suddenly, there it was. Chalfont Hall. Home. They drove through the high wrought-iron gates, which still had the crooked brass plaque with the lettering so worn it appeared as Braille might, a delicate spidery network of lines and grooves.

'*This* is where you live?' Earl couldn't keep the disbelief from his voice.

'Used to live,' she corrected him quickly. 'You've seen where I live now.'

'This is like something outta some fairy tale! All you English folk live like this?'

'No, of course not.' Kit felt herself beginning to blush.

'So, you really *are* rich, huh?'

'No, not rich. Well, I suppose we were wealthy, once. Now we've just got land... loads of it. Too much, in fact. That's the thing with these country homes. No one can afford to keep them going, but we can't get rid of them either.'

'Why not? Why can't you just sell up and get the hell out?'

She shrugged. 'Because you can't. It's not... done.'

'And this is?' He took her hand. 'Even *I* know girls like you ain't allowed out of the house without a... what do you call it? A *chaperone*? Ain't that what you call it?'

In spite of her nervousness, Kit laughed. 'Yes, that's right, a chaperone. But the war changed all of that. No one has a chaperone any more.

You've seen how we live. We go to parties, we go to work … Everything's changed.'

Earl turned to look at her. 'That's where you're wrong, babe. Some things ain't never gonna change. You should know that.'

She couldn't answer. Caruthers brought the car to a stop outside the entrance to the house. The enormous front door was partially open. Kit could see her mother's figure in the shadowy interior. Her heart was thumping. They stepped down and onto the gravelled driveway. She looked across at the front door. He was wrong, she thought to herself fiercely. Things *were* changing.

'Katherine!' her mother's voice rang out across the driveway. She stepped out of the shadows and walked out onto the stone steps. She raised a hand to shield her eyes against the early afternoon light.

Kit was overwhelmed by the familiarity of everything: the touch of air on her skin; the sharpness of the light; her mother standing, waiting to welcome her home.

She tucked her hand into the crook of Earl's arm and moved towards her mother. For a second, her mother's gaze held them both in its grip. Her mouth opened, as if on an utterance of shock, then it closed again. Behind her, Kit's father suddenly appeared.

Kit felt Earl stiffen. They walked slowly towards the front steps and stopped. For a moment, all four simply stood and stared at one another. Her mother was no doubt aware of Caruthers behind them, pretending to polish the car bonnet as he watched yet another drama unfold at Chalfont Hall.

'You must be Mr Hightower. Good of you to come all this way.' Lord Wharton took a step down towards them, extending a hand. Half a century's worth of breeding rose to the fore.

'Sir.' Earl took his outstretched hand and shook it firmly.

'Journey all right?' he asked, turning to lead the way into the house. He might have been enquiring about a neighbour's trip down from London for the day. If he were shocked to see her in the company of a Negro, he hid it well. Behind them, Lady Wharton struggled to follow suit.

'Mighty fine house you have here, sir,' Earl said as they walked into the cool hallway. He stood for a moment, looking around.

'Yes, yes … we rather like it. Helluva expense to keep it all going, though. You can't imagine what these old piles cost to run.'

'No, sir. That I can't.' Earl smiled.

Kit watched her mother studying him in fascination. Lady Wharton was dressed as though for a country fair, in the most extraordinary outfit. Like a horribly ageing schoolgirl, Kit thought despairingly. Her face was painted whiter and pinker than it ever could have been when she was a young girl. In the months since she'd last seen them, both her parents had aged.

'Luncheon will be served shortly. You must join us for a drink,' Lady Wharton said finally, trying desperately to interject a note of gaiety into her voice. She'd obviously made up her mind that the best way to treat the unexpected arrival of what might – for all Kit knew – be the first and only Negro she'd ever encountered was as a thrilling excuse for celebration. 'We've been absolutely *parched* for company, did Katherine tell you? No one comes down any more. It's the blasted war. No one's got any petrol, that's the thing. Oh, I *do* wish it would end soon, don't you?'

Earl turned to her, picking up something of her mood. 'Yes, ma'am. Though I can't exactly say it will. Seems as if Roosevelt's preparin' to join in. That's what all the folks back home say.'

'And where exactly is "back home"?' Lady Wharton asked archly as she led the way into the front parlour. 'Shall we have cocktails, darling?' she asked her husband before Earl could answer.

Lord Wharton's eyebrows shot up. 'Cocktails? Before luncheon?'

'Why not? What does Althea always say? "The sun's setting some-where in the Empire." I'm right, aren't I?' Her girlish laughter rang out in the room.

Kit stared at her.

'Ah, there you are, Digby.' Lady Wharton turned as someone entered the room. 'Tell Cook to rustle up four Gin Bucks. She'll know what I mean. We had them only the other night. Have you ever had one, Mr Hightower?'

Earl inclined his head with a slow smile. 'I have indeed. Gin, ginger ale and lemon juice. That's a sharp drink right there. I used to be a bartender back in New York. Amongst other things.'

Lady Wharton's mouth dropped open but she recovered herself just in time. 'How utterly fascinating! Do come and sit next to me. I'm *dying* to hear all about New York. They do things differently there, don't they?' She patted the spare cushion on the seat next to her.

After a minute's hesitation, Earl sat down, leaving Kit standing awk-wardly next to her father.

'Everything all right up in London?' Lord Wharton asked hesitantly.
'Yes, perfectly fine, thank you, Father.'

'Work all right? What's Evelyn got you doing?'

Kit hesitated. *You do understand you may not disclose the nature of your job to anyone, not even your parents.* 'Not much, really. Typing and filing, that sort of thing. Keeps me busy, though.'

Lord Wharton nodded. He brought his pipe to his lips and struck a match. For a moment he seemed rather lost. 'Busy, yes, that's the ticket. Must keep busy. Well, I think those drinks have arrived.' He nodded at Digby, who had entered, balancing four glasses rather precariously on a tray.

Kit dimly remembered him from childhood. He'd retired when she was very young. But with so many of the young men away fighting, it seemed retirement was the only place to find replacement staff. She smiled at him to acknowledge the bond and accepted a glass. The gin was both sweet and fiery and she sipped it gratefully, relieved to have something to do.

As they rose and moved into the dining room, she heard her mother ask, with great conscious charm, if Earl would like to ride after lunch.

'Ride? Ride what?' Earl asked.

'Why, a horse, of course. You do ride, don't you?' she asked, sounding surprised.

Earl shook his head as he took his seat. 'No, ma'am. I ain't never bin on a horse before.'

'You don't say!' Lady Wharton regarded him disbelievingly. 'But how is Kit to show you around the estate?'

'We'll walk, Mother,' Kit said drily. 'It's perfectly fine.'

But Earl had other ideas. 'How difficult can it be?' he asked Lady Wharton. 'Get on, sit up straight, point the animal in the right direction ... Seems like that's all there is to it, wouldn't you say?'

Lady Wharton was amused. 'Well, I dare say Kit would beg to differ. She's an excellent horsewoman, you know. But if you're game, we'll certainly find you one of the more docile horses. Splendid idea.'

Earl continued to surprise her, she realised. She was charmed by his easiness where there might have been strain. He said what he thought and it was somehow not what she imagined. He had the courage to be himself without show or pretence. It was admirable, and in its own light-hearted way it was the opposite of her own nature, which tended towards opposition in order to test the validity of her own feelings or reactions. She had been ready to make it easy for him, to show him that it didn't matter to her what he thought of her mother. It was quite disconcerting to realise he didn't need her intervention, or even her concern. He took every encounter as it came, without judgement. The discovery unexpectedly freed her. It wasn't necessary to pretend.

In the end, it was decided that the two 'youngsters' would go for a walk, leaving Lord and Lady Wharton to sleep off the effects of rather too much gin before the sun had gone down.

'They always drink this much?' Earl asked as they donned waterproof jackets and wellington boots. The weather had turned swiftly.

'Here, use mine,' Father had said generously to Earl. 'It always rains in Dorset. Always.'

Kit looked up at him. 'No, they never used to. At least not that I remember. I expect it's the war.'

'Nice folks you have, though. Especially your father.'

'Really? I always think of him as rather dull.' Kit was surprised.

'Not at all. He knows a helluva lot about jazz music. Knows more'n I do.'

Kit stopped in her tracks. 'Jazz music? My *father*? When did you find that out?'

'When he took me to the library, after lunch. He's got some darn fine records, I tell you. Coupla Armstrong, some Charlie Parker, Ellington, Monk… All the greats. I don't know many folk back home who've got even *half* as many records as your old man.'

Kit was astonished. 'I've never even heard him play a record, let alone a jazz recording. How strange.'

Earl shrugged. 'Not so strange. I bet you didn't know your future king is a fan, now, did you?'

'Actually, I *did* know. Ruth told me. When she was trying to persuade me to come to Café de Paris. She said Prince Edward often goes.'

'Well, I don't know about "often",' Earl said, chuckling. 'But I *have* seen him there a coupla times. Been introduced to him, too.'

Kit's eyes widened. Was there no end to the surprises Earl Hightower could pull?

'Do you know,' she said, letting her hand run lightly along the tops of the roses that lined the driveway almost all the way down to the bridge, 'I've known you for less than a month. Imagine that – less than a month! Why do I feel as though I've known you for so much longer?'

'Just the way it is sometimes.' Earl shrugged off her surprise. 'It don't matter where you from, where you bin, how much money you got. It's all about how connected you feel to the other person. The rest of it don't matter. Least that's how *I* see it.'

'I see it that way too,' Kit agreed firmly.

She looked up at the sky. Father was right. It did rain in Dorset nearly every day. Over the low hills to the south of the estate a clutch of grey, thundery clouds was amassing, at the moment no more than a smudge on the horizon. It was nearly four o'clock. The sun shone on them in spurts, warming their faces, then disappearing behind the grey clouds. Happiness rose in her veins like a fever. Earl's hand lay slackly on her arm. When she thought back on their lovemaking of the previous night, a flush of erotic pride swept through her. She'd looked upon his exhaustion after it was over with a sense of wonder. How far away he was then from the tense frenzy in which he'd been snatched up only minutes earlier.

The road dipped towards the river. They walked across the stone bridge to the wild grasses that lay beyond the manicured lawn and stopped. Earl turned to her and took her face in both hands, turning her head gently, first this way, then that.

'You're real, ain't you? I didn't just make you up, did I?' he asked her, his dark eyes trying to see past hers to whatever might lie behind. 'You're for real, ain't you?'

'What a funny thing to say!' Kit exclaimed. 'Of course I'm real. Didn't you *feel* me last night?' She blushed as she spoke.

He was silent as he contemplated her. Her words seemed to fill him with an anxious delight. He kissed her, fiercely, and his lips sent an afterglow of sensuality through her. His face above hers came to life. The empty moments of falling terror that had haunted her for almost as long as she could remember were unexpectedly secured. She clung to him, taking in great gulps of the mysterious stranger whose entire being was foreign to her in ways she couldn't even comprehend. She saw it in everyone around her; in the way they drew back from him, instinctively recoiling, as if his very being staked out some invisible boundary that was impossible to cross. But when she was with him, those boundaries that everyone else seemed to notice simply blurred, melted, dissolved, leaving only the distinction of their sex, the most impenetrable boundary of all. Man. Woman. It was all that seemed to matter.

She looked at him standing against the backdrop of the woods, his expression both tender and proud. She thought of his strong, young body as it had hovered over hers the night before, tensely poised and waiting to enter hers. She remembered the tight whorls of hair on his chest tapering to that other hair that drew a crude crucifix across his abdomen and down to the base of his penis. Now, fully clothed, the lovely secret of his nakedness was hidden from her and it made her newly aware of what else must be hidden... A whole life lived without her; men and women with whom he lived it; women whose bodies he'd surely entered just as he had hers.

She was again aware of the hollowed-out feeling within her body, of the shaky newness of pleasure, like the trembling of unused muscles when put to a new task. Absurd as it seemed, he was hers, in all senses of the word.

This, then, was the answer. Here he was, the black man, the one everyone pushed away; the one no one else dared touch. Ruth was wrong. It *was* him. He was the one who had come to save her.

28

She heard their voices first, otherwise they'd have stopped arguing, aware they were being overheard. She stood on the landing, frozen to the spot, holding her breath.

'Don't be so bloody ridiculous!' It was her mother's voice, a piercing, angry whisper.

'Why not? He's as good as any other.' That was Father.

'How can you even *say* that?'

'Oh, for goodness' sake. He seems a perfectly decent chap to me. All right, it's obvious he's got no money, but then again, neither do we, Delphine. You *must* face facts.'

'Facts? Don't speak to me of "facts"! The *fact* is, we cannot – *cannot* – allow it to go on. Whatever will our friends say?'

'Which bloody friends? The ones who still whisper about our "other" daughter behind our backs? *Those* friends? You're concerned what *they* think? Do you know, Delphine, sometimes I'm ashamed of you. Yes, that's right, ashamed. I've not forgotten the way you treated her when she came back.'

'You've no right to speak to me like that! *I* was the one who—'

'What's that noise? Did you hear something?' Father interrupted her.

Kit pressed herself flat against the wall, her heart hammering so loudly she was sure they could hear it.

'No, there's no one there. You're avoiding the issue, Harold. I won't have it. I simply won't have it.'

'You've got no say in the matter. When I think of what Kit has been through ... I'm the one who's ashamed. If she's found whatever little happiness she can, leave her be, for God's sake. Is that what you want? To drive *both* our children away?'

Kit pressed her hand to her mouth. She was standing on the landing that led to the wing where Earl had been given a room.

'Just wait for me,' she'd whispered to him as Digby stood stiffly to attention, waiting to lead him upstairs. 'I'll come to you when they've both gone to bed.'

She wasn't sure she could bear to hear any more. She was filled with a sudden tenderness for her father, perhaps for the first time in her entire life. She was lost to them now, just as Lily had been lost. It was a consequence she hadn't foreseen. In their choice of men – whether as husbands or lovers – both sisters had embarked on a course that would take them away from everything they'd known, everything they were, the women it was decreed – by whom? – they should be. Yet, whilst there was a terrible sadness in her at the late realisation that perhaps Father was braver than she'd ever dared acknowledge, there was also a burning impatience to be gone from Chalfont.

Here in Dorset, the war seemed so very far away. But it was not. As soon as they returned the following day, they would both be thrust straight back into it. America was about to enter the war. Earl spoke of it as though it were already a fact. What would that mean? she wondered. Would he go back? Enlist? Die? She'd been planning to tell him she was going away; now that the hour was upon her, she couldn't. She couldn't spoil what might turn out to be their very last weekend together. She would tell him as soon as they were back in London the following day.

She turned and made her way blindly back to her room. The euphoria of the trip down from London and the day spent walking in the woods had evaporated. She pushed open the door, closed it shut behind her and walked over to her bed. Earl lay in Lily's old room, halfway across the house. There could be no thought of joining him.

She lay down, tightening the belt of her robe around her, and closed her eyes. The room was filled with an odd electricity, as if a storm had come up, setting everything in a new, harsh light. She felt panicky.

Is this what life will be like from now on? The question hovered in the air and on her lips. And then suddenly, without warning, she slept...

29

At Paddington the following morning there was no time to do anything other than kiss hurriedly, promising to meet again that evening. She had to go straight to work. She'd phoned Ruth from Dorset with an excuse about a family emergency. It hadn't satisfied Ruth, of course, but at least it would keep Vera Atherton from demanding her head on a plate. Standing on the crowded bus that took her from Paddington to Westminster, her handbag awkwardly squashed up against her face as she hung onto the overhead strap, the butterflies in her stomach that had quietened down over the past two days began to flutter again. She *had* to tell Earl. She held onto the overhead strap and tried to think only of the evening ahead.

At five o'clock that evening, having survived Vera Atherton's disapproving silence as she stammered out her excuse for having missed half a morning's work, the day was finally over. She didn't wait for Ruth but ran straight down the front steps. She could just hear Big Ben striking the hour. In a few hours, she would see Earl again. The thought of it obliterated everything else.

*

She opened the wardrobe door and stood in front of it for a long time. Finally she chose a pale blue silk dress. She held it against herself and looked in the mirror, trying to fathom how Earl might see her. She turned her head slowly, anxiously examining her profile. Was her nose not perhaps a little too large, her lips a little too wide? And her hair … how should she arrange it? To one side, as now, or pulled back? She looked down at her hands. Her nails were short and clean but terribly plain. She really ought to paint them. She looked at her watch yet again. She had just enough time. She wanted to be at the café by the time the band came on stage so that she would be the first thing he saw as he walked on.

A glow of sensuality washed over her, leaving her trembling. *Earl*. She whispered his name to herself. *Earl*. Only a few hours to go until she saw him again.

30

It all turned ugly. Real ugly. *Real* fast, too. He wasn't sure what happened, or why, only that it turned without either of them meaning it to. And then it was too late. Things were said. Voices raised and then the first punch. Who threw it? Who hit whom?

He went over the events time and again. He'd come back to the boarding house, his spirit light. He may have even swaggered a little. Kit was that sort of girl. Every time he thought about her he felt a surge of exaltation. He felt as though he'd been waiting his whole life for a moment like this, every nerve in his body told him that. Right from the start. As soon as they walked up those steps out of that basement club, he'd felt it. And unlike last time, he told himself fiercely, *this* time he wouldn't let the moment slip out of his reach. This time it belonged to him and if he didn't grab it with both hands, it would be lost, for ever. You didn't get a second chance at things. He knew that.

So when he got home that morning, he went up the front steps with a little spring, a little swagger in his step. Louie was at the top waiting for him. He must've seen him coming.

He wasn't sure what happened next. Louie must've said something. A passing comment? Whatever it was, he'd caught from the mere look of him a touch of the rebellious spirit he was carrying. He made to move past him but Louie put out a hand. And that's when things got a little bent out of shape. Next thing he knew, they were arguing. Where had he been? Why'd he just gone off like that without telling anyone? He'd been looking for him the night before; they'd had an invitation to play at a party. Where the hell was he?

'Because of some bit of white *pussy*?' In Louie's mouth the word was filthy.

'That ain't it,' Earl started to say. 'It's not like that—'

'The hell it ain't! I'm sick of cleanin' up behind you, boy.'

Maybe it was the 'boy' that did it. Some part of him went cold at the sound of it, but in another part, the swaggering part, he was glad. Because now they could finally have it out. That thing that had been building up between them ever since New York could finally be released. He was aware of the hair standing up on the back of his neck, all prickly-like, and of his body moving to close the space between them. He saw Louie's face right up against his. There was a look in it – hard to tell what. Disgust? Hatred? Fear? The possibilities went around in his mind. Then, in a flash, he had it. It was envy. Jealousy. *That* was what he'd been carrying all this time. He started to laugh.

'Don't you fucking laugh at me, boy,' Louie snarled.

Earl, with the lightness of the past two days still on him, stopped, turned, and his spirit acted in spite of him. He spat in Louie's face. And then a kind of madness between them set in.

There was an animal fury in him and he was suddenly in a place where anything could happen. Blood rushed to his head and into his throbbing palms. His body came down; he took the full weight of himself and could hear himself gasping for breath. He didn't feel the blows; didn't feel himself giving them. They were locked in a primal, savage dance. He heard syllables come out of his mouth that he didn't recognise, passing straight through him. Blow after blow, the sound of something breaking – chair? Table? Glass shattering, the hot, wet gush of blood – whose? His?

Somewhere, in another part of the house, a door opened. There was more noise and a woman's screams. It would pass, he kept telling himself. It had to. But for now he and Louie were outside all rule and order. He felt himself cut off entirely and yet at the same time, he'd never been so aware of himself, his own body, his physical presence that was more than the sum total of what he *should* have been. *Nigger. Boy. Know your place.* That was why he'd left Alabama. That was why he'd run. *That* was why he'd followed Louie, thinking it would be different somehow. But it never was. He should've known that. Even Louie – cosmopolitan, debonair Louie – who had the pick of almost every girl he wanted, even that wasn't enough for him. He couldn't keep the wolf from the door. Earl knew Louie had seen him with Kit that first night at Café de Paris. He'd caught his eye after he bumped into her that first time but he'd mistaken the quick look Louie gave him. He thought it was just one of those nods that men give each other, half in jest, when a pretty girl walks by and appears to notice you. A sort of mental thumbs-up, a 'good on you, man'. But it wasn't. He saw that now. Why had she looked at him and not Louie? That's what the look said. Why'd she choose you when she could've chosen *him*, so much lighter-skinned and so much more *refined*?

Earl hadn't seen it. Hadn't wanted to see it. But in the end, the nastiness had come flooding out. It was all a sham. The 'brother' this and 'brother' that. Pretending like they were in 'it' together. They weren't. The only thing they were in was competition.

But it shouldn't have ended that way. When it all calmed down, he knew he would be full of shame. But his body had the final word, as always.

31

She was late. Almost an hour late. And all because of her scarlet nails. She'd smudged two already because she hadn't waited long enough for them to dry

'Can't we go any faster?' She leaned forwards to ask the cab driver.

'Sorry, miss. Streets are crowded tonight. There's been heavy bombing out Shoreditch way. Heard on the wireless there's been at least three big 'uns.'

She leaned back in her seat and looked out the window at the snaking queue of cars. Londoners never ceased to amaze her. Since September of the previous year, the Germans had bombed London, night after night. High-explosive bombs – those over a hundred pounds in weight – were dropped from the skies, wreaking havoc. But Londoners refused to be cowed. Life went on. Buses and taxis started up again in the morning, trains ran on time. The government had allowed Londoners to use the Underground stations as shelters; as soon as the sirens sounded, surprisingly orderly queues formed and people went down into the bowels of the earth quietly, as if simply going about their business. People had got so used to it that they spoke about the bombing in the same way they spoke about the weather. 'Blizty today,' was a common phrase. If Hitler thought he could bomb the British into submission, Churchill declared, he was wrong.

She looked at her watch for the hundredth time. It was nearly ten thirty. She could have wept. Frustration mingled with unbearable anticipation swept through her. She stared at the road ahead. It would honestly be quicker to walk.

She tapped on the glass again. 'Listen, why don't you let me out at the corner ... right here. I'll walk the rest of the way.'

'You sure, miss? Something big must've happened. Them cars up ahead ain't movin' at all.'

'Yes, I'm sure.' She hurriedly shoved the fare through the window between them and opened the door.

It was a chilly night. Somewhere in the distance she heard the wail of an ambulance. Had there been a bomb? she wondered. There'd been no air raid siren. She pulled up the collar of her coat – it had suddenly turned cold again – and hurried up Piccadilly. As she drew closer to the roundabout, the crowd thickened. People were moving in the opposite direction, streaming towards her. She pushed her way through until she reached the statue. There were three ambulances parked next to the statue, blocking the way to Shaftesbury Avenue. A policeman was directing traffic away from the closed road, up Great Windmill Street instead. She hurried up to one of the ambulance men who was standing beside his vehicle, his face blackened with soot and dirt, smoking.

'Has something happened?' she asked, her eyes widening as she took in his blood-streaked overalls and the stunned expression on his face.

He gave a short, mirthless laugh. 'Yes, miss. You could say that. I've never seen anything like it. Been driving for a year. Never seen anything like it.'

'What? What's happened?' Her heart was beginning to thump. Someone jostled her elbow. People were running past, shock radiating from them in waves.

'Bomb. Fell down the ventilation shaft, so they say.'

'Where? Where?'

He ground his cigarette out with his heel. He jerked his head in the direction of Shaftesbury Avenue. 'Nightclub just up the road. You shoulda seen it. All them jewels and furs, splattered with blood . . . Sorry, miss. I do beg yer pardon.'

But she was gone.

32

It was filled with a gay crowd on Saturday evening, many in uniform. The lively band had opened its programme and the floor was crowded with dancers. 'Oh, Johnny' the band was playing, whilst outside the guns crashed, but were unheard against the accompaniment of cheerful music and chatter.

Then suddenly there was an explosion somewhere above, the ceiling fell in and all but one of the lights went out. The restaurant was filled with dust and fumes, which blackened faces and frocks. Couples dancing had been flung apart; those able to do so struggled to their feet, and many searched amidst the confusion with torches and lighted matches for their partners of a second before.

Many had been killed; others were seriously hurt. But accounts by many who were there all agree that there was the utmost coolness and much gallantry.

'Don't bother about me,' people with less serious wounds said over and over again.

Rescue work began almost immediately. Civil Defence workers were helped by passing soldiers, who brought out their field dressings. Girls in dance frocks were carried through debris and tended on the pavement or in nearby houses until motor-ambulances, which travelled quickly to and from hospital, could get all the casualties away.

There were many wonderful escapes, and a fair number of people were able to walk out of the damaged building with no worse hurt than a bruised back or some cuts. All nearby helped to ease the lot of the wounded. People living near made tea, and passers-by contributed handkerchiefs.

Prominent amongst the helpers were a young Dutch member of the Fleet Air Arm and a nurse from Chelsea, who was off duty. The nurse was able to get some colleagues quickly to the scene by taxicab.

All the girls due to take part in the cabaret escaped unhurt. They were in their make-up room, waiting to be called.

Kit put the paper down and looked blankly out of the window. He hadn't even been named. None of them had been named. *Band members killed.* That was all it said.

It was a direct hit. Thirty-four people died that night. If she hadn't seen the bodies – or what was left of them – she'd never have believed it. They'd been lined up on stretchers and put to one side. Not named, not identified, because there was nothing to identify them by.

She'd grabbed one of the nurses by the arm and forced her to show her where the dead band members lay. She'd recognised him by his belt. The same belt she'd unbuckled before.

It was raining outside. The summery weather of the past week had given way to thick, rolling grey clouds, swollen with rain. It made night-time bombing raids more difficult, the man reading the news on the wireless said.

She got up stiffly, walked over to the sideboard and picked up her cigarettes. Her fingers were trembling as she opened the packet. Downstairs in the cobbled courtyard a figure swam into view. It was a postman on a bicycle. She watched him cross to the other side and knock on the door. He took off his cap and stood stiffly, respectfully, to attention. Delivering war telegrams was the one thing the Post Office still did on a Sunday.

She lit her cigarette. She was breathing hard. Her heart was thumping as she waited for the door to open. She knew the woman who lived there. Mrs Milligan. She'd been a housekeeper in one of the big houses across the road, in Belgrave Square. She was widowed, with one son. Not any more.

The door opened slowly. Mrs Milligan stood in the doorway. The look of dread on her face said it all. Across the way, hidden by the curtains, Kit watched. Suddenly she became aware of herself. Her mouth was full of saliva. There were unshed tears hovering behind her eyes. Her blood was pumping and her heart felt as though it would burst. For the second time in her young life, her body was driving the message home to her again.

You won't die, my girl. Not of this. Not yet.

PART FOUR
GRIEF

1942
Kit

33

Bicester, Oxford – three months later

Kit threaded her way across the lane to the Churchill Road, heading back to her digs. She cycled over the cobblestones, teeth chattering as the wheels bumped over the pocked surface, then she hit the smooth tarmac at the end and stood up in the saddle going up the slight hill. She turned left into Bristol Road and parked her bicycle outside No. 29. It was a red-brick two-up, two-down worker's cottage that she shared with three other girls who worked with her in the barracks just behind the station.

Mrs Leonards, their landlady – an ancient, taciturn woman with the moral code and expectations of a Mother Superior – had lost her husband in the First World War and her two sons in the Second. Those terrible losses ruled their every waking moment. Her rules and regulations were shakily drawn handwritten notes pinned up in almost every room in the tiny house. It reeked of sadness but it was close to work. For Kit, the grief was simply an extension of her own. She had no idea how long she'd be stationed there and she didn't care. She simply did what she was told, when she was told to do it and kept to herself.

Grief. She was intimately acquainted with grief. As some people were said to attract luck, she attracted grief.

'Oh, *there* you are, Miss Algernon-Waters,' Mrs Leonards called out loudly as soon as Kit put her key in the lock and opened the door. 'You've a visitor. A *male* visitor.' Her tone was both disapproving and suspicious. 'Best take a look.' She indicated the kitchen at the rear of the house with her head. 'I've put him in the kitchen. I'd rather he were *there* than in the front room. *If* you don't mind.'

Kit stared at her. At her briefing meeting in London the previous week, no one had said anything about sending up a visitor. She unwound her scarf and hung it up on the peg marked: *Miss A-W. All coats and scarves should be hung in their indicated positions. Thanking you.* She pushed past Mrs Leonards and walked into the small kitchen.

*

He was sitting at the table holding a crumpled soft cap in his hands. He still had his coat on. He looked up as she walked in. For a few moments, they simply stared at each other, neither able to speak. She felt her legs wobbling, so she pulled out a chair and sat down abruptly opposite him. A thick, long silence spooled out in front of them. She suddenly felt raw, as though she were being cut open, sliced in two.

It was Louie. The band leader.

He saw the distress break all over her face, a dull, upward flush that stained her cheeks like a fever. 'I'm sorry,' he said hastily, getting up clumsily. 'I shoulda called. Warned you.'

'Louie? What … what are you doing here? I … I thought you were dead. I thought you were killed. With … with … the others. With …' She stopped, unable to say his name.

He shook his head vehemently. 'No. I wasn't there,' he said, screwing up his soft cap in his hands. 'I was the lucky one.' He gave a bitter laugh. 'I'd just left the stage. I went to the bathroom … next thing, I heard it right behind me. Loudest thing I ever heard.' He shook his head, as if he still couldn't believe it. 'Couldn't stop the ringin' in my ears for days afterwards.'

'How … how did you know where to find me?' she asked, her heart thumping.

How many times had she met Louie? Three? Four? It seemed inconceivable that he was standing in front of her.

'I followed you. No, no … not like that,' he added quickly, seeing her face. 'I was playin' in the bar at The Randolph in Oxford last weekend. I joined another band … had to. Ain't got no other way of makin' a livin'. I saw you come in with a bunch of girls so I asked the barman who y'all were. Said you were all working up here in Bicester. Said he'd seen you all a few times before. So I drove up here yesterday and just waited by the station. I saw you come out but you was with someone – brown-haired girl – didn't want to alarm you. Followed you all the way here and parked across the road. I was meanin' to come in but then you came straight back out again and walked up the street. So I just waited but by the time you came home yesterday, it was real late. I figured you'd be kinda upset if I came knockin' on the door at midnight. So I drove back to Oxford and came up again this afternoon. Knocked on the door. Your landlady let me in. Didn't want no Negro in her front room, though, so she put me in here.'

Kit couldn't speak. She stared at him. His presence evoked Earl so strongly that she could feel him in her mouth, in her throat, in her hands, in her *heart*.

Louie looked older, much older. And tired, too, like a man who had been through too much, *seen* too much. There was a tight, wary tension around the eyes and in the hunch of his shoulders. She'd seen it in Earl when he thought she wasn't looking, an awareness of himself in moments when his understanding of events hadn't quite caught up with him ... A sense of puzzlement at a world that made no room for him.

Louie turned away from her suddenly, pushing his hands roughly into his pockets. He walked to the window. She followed him with her eyes. It was his way of claiming a little space, a temporary breather from the turmoil she could see was raging inside him. He needed to put himself out of her reach, even if only momentarily.

'Look, why don't we go and have some tea?' she asked gently. 'There's a tea room just up the road.'

He looked at her quickly, gauging her reaction. He nodded, visibly relieved. 'Yeah, why not? My car's outside. Little noisy, but she goes.'

'I'll just get my coat,' she said, standing up. She left the room and ran quickly upstairs. She lifted her coat from the back of the door. She caught sight of herself in the mirror above the dresser and stood still for a moment. She stared at her pale, wan face, then pulled out a tube of precious red lipstick with shaking hands. She outlined her mouth, blotting it carefully. Then she slipped it back in her pocket, closed the door carefully behind her and ran back downstairs.

Mrs Leonards was hovering in the hallway, frowning. She ignored her and went through to the kitchen. Louie was standing by the window, his shoulders hunched in a way that made her see the truculence in him. For all his swagger, he was at a disadvantage. He'd come to tell her something, she could see that, but he was also telling her how hard things had been on him.

'Ready?' she murmured.

He turned and nodded at her, and together they walked out.

'I'll be back later. Don't make any tea for me,' she said to Mrs Leonards, her voice surprisingly commanding.

Mrs Leonards had no option but to nod. She stood back, glaring at them as they walked past.

'G'bye, ma'am,' Louie murmured, touching his cap.

'Goodbye ... *sir*.' It was wrung out of her at the last moment before they closed the door.

Kit saw from the way his mouth relaxed almost imperceptibly at the corners that although it was a small victory, it was just enough to set him more at ease.

'Car's over there,' he said, pointing to a rather racy-looking black sports car with a long, shiny bonnet. 'Ain't mine,' he added quickly, as he opened the door for her. 'Thirsty as all hell, mind you, but she's a beauty.'

Kit slid into the passenger seat. She knew – and cared – very little about cars but even she could tell it was – or had once been – a rather special model.

He started the engine. It was noisy, just as he'd said, and she could feel her neighbours' eyes on them as curtains were pulled back and landladies up and down the street, like Mrs Leonards, peered out.

'Let's not go to the tearoom,' she said suddenly. 'I've got a better idea. If you keep going along this road, we'll come to a little village called Garsington. There's a pub just before the village green.'

'You sure have some curious neighbours,' Louie said as he pulled away from the kerb. 'I guess it ain't every day that a black man appears on their doorstep.'

She smiled faintly. 'No, I suppose not.' She reached in her handbag for a packet of cigarettes. 'Do you smoke?'

He nodded. 'Helps the voice, would you believe?' He took the cigarette from her.

For a few minutes neither spoke as they drove along. She looked at his hands on the steering wheel. They were a light brown, chalky colour, much paler than Earl's. She'd never known there could be so many shades of black. He wore a thick gold signet ring on his little finger, which crooked it away from the others and gave his hand a rather dainty, almost ladylike, air.

She drew in a deep breath. A moment could – and seemed to – hold a lifetime. A day could contain a year. Time had lost its bearings when she met Earl. When he was gone, she realised it hadn't started again yet. Not until the moment she opened the kitchen door and saw Louie sitting there. In that moment, the whole of her life – all of it – came bursting through the hastily erected wall that separated her body from her emotions, her actions from her *self*.

*

He brought the drinks to the table, setting them down carefully so as not to let the thick, creamy slice of foam slide down his glass. Out of the corner of her eye, she could see one or two customers looking curiously at them.

'Cheers,' he said, lifting his glass to hers. 'I'm . . . I wasn't sure what . . . well, how it would be to see you, you know?'

She nodded slowly. She took a sip of her G & T. The gin burned its way pleasurably down her throat. 'You're the last person I expected to see,' she said. 'The very last person.'

There was an awkward silence, which neither seemed to know how to fill. 'Did he say anything?' he asked suddenly.

She looked up at him. 'When?' she asked. The dull ache that had lodged itself in the pit of her stomach as soon as she'd seen him sitting in the kitchen flared up again sharply. She winced.

'That night. When you saw him. He didn't say nothin' about what happened before?' he asked carefully.

She shook her head. 'No, I didn't see him. We were supposed to meet at eight. I was a bit late . . . I was in a taxi, coming up Piccadilly.' She stopped. Her hands and knees began to tremble. She forced herself to go on. 'There was a lot of traffic. It took ages to get down Park Lane. I . . . I didn't know it then, of course, but the bomb had already gone off.'

Louie frowned. He seemed to have difficulty taking it in. 'So . . . he didn't tell you about us arguin'?'

She shook her head again. 'No.' She looked at him closely. 'What were you arguing about?'

He looked quickly away. 'Nothin'. Just stupid stuff. Man-to-man stuff, y'know?'

'No, I don't know. What was the argument about?' she asked again.

He shifted in his seat. He was uncomfortable. He took a long draught of his beer, then reached up to loosen the collar of his shirt. He unbuttoned it until his throat was showing. He pointed to a faint puckered scar that ran diagonally across his Adam's apple, stopping just short of the sternum. It was pinkish and raised, as though someone – or something – had cut a line across his neck.

'What's that?' she asked, frowning. 'What happened to you?'

He dug into his pocket and put something on the table. She looked down at it. It was a thin gold crucifix. One of its legs was missing, snapped off. She stared at it. A wave of sorrow surged powerfully into her throat. She knew what it was. It was Earl's crucifix. His mother had given it to him before he left the US for Europe.

She felt the veins of her neck swell and the room around her lurched in a film of tears. She put out a finger and touched it as lightly as she dared. He was watching her closely.

'Still don't know how it happened,' he said slowly, shaking his head. 'One minute we was talking, then arguin', next minute it seemed we was all over each other. Somehow it musta come loose, come off him ... It was in his fist when he hit me.' He pointed to his scar again. 'Man, all of a sudden there was blood everywhere. It cut me, dragged right across my neck. Stopped us fightin', though. All that blood ... cooled us right off. He stormed off and I was left with this.' He pointed to the crucifix. 'And that's how come I wasn't on the stage with them. When it went off. I was still bleedin'. I could feel it through my shirt. I told Striker – remember him? Tall, thin fella? – told him to take over the song for me ... Just wanted to go clean myself up. So I left the stage and went to the bathroom in the back, behind the kitchen. I was just wiping my shirt when I heard it. The blast. Like a ... a thunderclap. Damn near split me in two. I can *still* feel it.'

She was quiet, struggling to keep her breathing even. 'They said you all died,' she said finally. 'I saw ... I saw him. And the others, too. They were all laid out ... just there, on the ground. They said everyone died.'

He shook his head unhappily. 'Everyone 'cept me. Not a scratch, least nothing anyone can see. And all because of this.' He pointed at the necklace still lying loose in her palm. 'Don't seem right, do it?'

She couldn't answer.

'Don't seem right,' he repeated. He drained his glass. 'You want another one?' he asked her. 'I need one. I ain't talked to nobody like this in a long time.'

She nodded and stood up. For a moment she thought he was going to clutch at her physically, not wanting her to leave him, but he gathered himself and the moment passed.

'I'll get us another drink,' she said, her voice hoarse with the effort of appearing normal.

She walked unsteadily to the bar. As she placed her order, she suddenly felt a twinge somewhere deep in her abdomen. She put a hand on her stomach. Her eyes widened in panic. She knew that pain. The deeply buried memory rose swiftly to the surface. No, it couldn't be. Please God, no.

PART FIVE

PEACE

1957–1958
Libby / Kit

34

'And *this*...' the woman from the Iraq Petrol Company intoned, peering at the young girl who stood before them, eyes downcast, from over the top of her pince-nez spectacles, 'is Miriam. She's here to do *whatever* you need.'

She might have been describing a chair, Libby thought, watching her through sulkily narrowed eyes.

'My advice to you is to get 'em young. *Much* easier to train.'

Or then again, a pet. Or a wild animal. Miriam stood quietly to attention. Libby watched her closely but there was no way of telling what Miriam might be thinking.

'Thank you, Mrs Clarke,' Mother said briskly. 'I think that's quite enough for today. We'll find our way around things, won't we, darling?' She looked meaningfully at Libby.

Libby nodded slowly, and then a little more vigorously, just to be on the safe side. Mother didn't like it when Libby sulked.

'Very well. I'll leave you to it.' Mrs Clarke's tone implied doubt.

'Libby, will you see Mrs Clarke to the door?'

'Yes, Mummy.'

'I'll take Miriam upstairs with Eluned.' She bent down and picked up the wicker basket that held the sleeping figure of the person Libby most hated in the world: her baby sister. She watched them go, her mother's high heels clipping out a brisk, staccato rhythm on the tiled floor.

'*Well!* I can see myself out,' Mrs Clarke said huffily. 'I'm *quite* familiar with the house.'

In her (braver) mind's eye, Libby rolled her eyes heavenwards, just as she'd seen her mother do countless times. It had been over an hour since they'd been introduced to Mrs Clarke, who was in charge of Housing & Resettlement, or Family Logistical Arrangements – or something equally vague-but-important-sounding – but she already knew she wasn't going to like her. Perhaps more crucially, Mrs Clarke wasn't going to like them, especially not her mother. That was the funny thing about her mother: although she knew literally hundreds of people, she seemed to like *anyone*. She didn't *dis*like anyone but she didn't really have any friends. Aside from the people they had to entertain as part of Father's job, there didn't seem to be anyone whose company she sought. She'd never heard her mother chatting away on the phone to friends, the way Libby's friends' mothers did. Back in Chelsea, in London, where they'd lived for the first eight years of her life, she'd never, *ever* seen her mother go upstairs, put on a frock or a coat and trip down the steps to meet a girlfriend with whom she might spend an afternoon or an evening.

'But, darling, *you're* all I need,' was all she would ever say if Libby asked, ruffling Libby's hair. 'Why should I spend the afternoon with anyone else when I can spend it with you?'

The rare show of affection thrilled Libby, but the fact of the matter was that her mother rarely, if ever, spent an afternoon with Libby. Most afternoons when Libby came home from school, she was already in her study on the second floor of their narrow house, furiously typing away.

'Is Mummy a writer?' she'd once asked Father.

He'd laughed and shook his head. 'No, not exactly. She's a translator. She translates other people's books into German and French. She's very good with languages, your mother. You ought to take after her, you know. They say it runs in the family.'

Libby was categorically forbidden from ever entering her mother's study. She'd been told it so often it had become ingrained; second nature, like eating with her mouth closed or making sure the tines of her fork never grated against her teeth.

Once, when she was about five or six, she'd sat outside in the passage-way, whimpering softly at first, then with increasing strength, until the door finally opened. She'd looked up, expecting sympathy, but what she got instead was a slap that still reverberated in her ears, even now.

'Don't you *ever* sit outside my study!' her mother hissed in a voice that was thick with anger and a face that was made momentarily ugly with anger. 'Never, *ever*! If I catch you sitting outside eavesdropping ever again, you'll wish you were never born!'

She'd never done it again. Until one day, when she was nearly eight and her mother had popped out to the shops at the end of King's Road and left the door open, she dared to enter. She slipped inside as soon as the front door closed. She stood in the doorway for a moment, breathing in the scent of her mother's perfume and her cigarette smoke, her heart beating fast. She wandered over to the desk that overlooked the street. There were lots of papers strewn around, some with the word 'Classified' stamped across the top. No books. She put out a cautious finger to touch one of the crisp white sheets and then she heard the front door slam. Her mother was back.

She only just made it back to her room in time before she heard the familiar *tap-tap-tap* of her mother's high heels on the stairs.

Her mother was the most mysterious person she knew. She was beautiful, in the way of film stars and famous people. She was very tall and very slim, with the sort of loose, languid figure that made Libby think of the inert models in shop windows who looked so haughtily onto the world from their petrified perch. She had short, platinum-blonde hair that was always perfectly cut, piercing blue eyes and a long, narrow nose. Her nails were always short and painted bright red, and she usually wore bright red lipstick to match. She was frightfully clever and good at everything. Everyone said so. Cooking, playing tennis, swimming, making paper hats or fancy dresses out of nothing, and birthday cakes... everything.

She'd been at Oxford after the war, which was where she'd met Father. Deep down, Libby secretly knew her mother was much cleverer than Father, who hadn't actually *finished* university. His studies had been interrupted by the war, like so many men of his generation. He was a pilot – or at least he had been before his plane was shot down over North Africa. He'd spent seven months in a prisoner-of-war camp, which, Libby had to admit, was terribly brave of him. But all of that happened a long time ago and no one ever talked about it. Now he was the rather grandly titled Senior Distribution Manager at the Baghdad branch of the newly formed Iraq Petroleum Company, where, Libby supposed, bravery was no longer required. However, she still wasn't sure what he actually *did*. Unlike many of her friends' fathers, who had easily identifiable careers – doctors, lawyers, accountants, engineers – her father's job seemed, in the main, to consist of organising people.

'Is that what we ought to call you? An *organiser*?'

That earned her a smile. 'No, not exactly, darling. I'm a *manager*.'

Manager. It was no clearer to her than 'organiser'. When they lived in London, he left the house early in the morning with a bowler hat on his head, wearing a dark coat, like all the other men in their street. He got back late at night, mostly after she'd gone to bed. On Saturdays he played golf. Very occasionally on Sundays they went for a drive down to the coast. It was always just the three of them, which suited Libby perfectly. She had them all to herself, although even she had to admit sometimes it was a bittersweet victory. The thing was, with both of them, you never quite knew where you stood. Sometimes she was the centre of attention … and sometimes not. She'd never quite learned to read the signs, either. Sometimes her mother would pay her such piercing attention and ask so many questions about her day at school, her friends, her teachers, her *feelings* about this or that … and then, just when she began to relax and bask in it, Mother's attention would abruptly be cut. She would retreat into her study, sometimes for *days* on end, forgetting they even existed. She treated Father exactly the same way. Libby's heart ached with sympathy when he came home to an empty kitchen and no sign of dinner.

Mother's affections weren't to be trusted. *That* was the long and short of it.

And then, one day, everything changed. Mother's slim, upright figure transformed itself overnight. Suddenly she began to walk differently, holding her hands protectively over her stomach.

It was Carole, Libby's best friend, who told her what was happening. 'She's going to have a baby, silly. Can't you tell?'

Libby stared at her in utter disbelief. A *baby*? At her mother's age? How? But, if anyone, Carole ought to know. She had three younger brothers.

Almost a week to the day later, Mother and Father called her into the living room and broke the news she already knew. She was going to have a brother or sister.

A month or two later, her mother went into hospital. Her stomach was so big Libby secretly feared she would explode.

Carole was sanguine. 'Oh, that's *nothing*. You should've seen *my* mother. She looked like an *elephant*.'

Mother didn't look like an elephant. She looked exactly the same except for the bursting mound of her stomach.

One Thursday afternoon there was a strange woman waiting for her at the school gates. Her name was Mrs Ferguson. She was a friend of Mother's. Libby squinted at her suspiciously. Didn't she know her mother didn't *have* any friends?

'I've been sent to walk you home,' she said briskly. 'Your mother's in labour.'

It made little sense to Libby.

'Aren't you pleased?' she asked, taking hold of Libby's arm without being asked.

Libby hated that. She was fourteen, not four.

'Just think... in a few hours' time, you'll have a new addition to the family!'

Libby wanted to tell her that the family didn't need a new 'addition', thank you very much, but she didn't dare. She walked along beside Mrs Ferguson, torn between rage and curiosity. What would the baby look like? Like her?

In the event, Eluned Louise Kentridge didn't look anything like Libby. She didn't look anything like anyone – or any*thing* – for that matter. She was bright pink and horribly chubby, with a wispy mop of light brown hair and a face that seemed perpetually stuck in a scowl. She screamed all day long, her fat, dimpled face screwed up into a concentration of rage. Libby hated her from the minute she arrived in that silly wicker basket with all those pale pink ribbons.

She never saw Mrs Ferguson again. Luckily for him, Father was away on business the week Eluned was born. By the time he came back on Sunday evening, the screaming baby had already usurped his place in the master bedroom. Father moved next door into the spare room that had once held Mother's winter coats and the baby slept in a cot beside Mother. Now the rhythm of the house revolved around the baby's cries.

It slowly dawned on Libby that she hadn't actually paid much attention to what having a baby sister would actually *mean*. Well, now she knew. However infrequent Mother's attention might have been before the baby was born, now it was non-existent. Even when she spoke to her, Mother's real ear lay somewhere else. She was distracted all the time by the baby who never did anything other than scream.

Well, at least Eluned wasn't screaming now. The journey to Baghdad from London must have exhausted her, even though they'd done it in at least four stages.

Libby ran over them quickly, savouring the memories. First of all, there was the train to Dover, which was terribly exciting. They had a compartment to themselves and Mother ordered a small bottle of wine, allowing Libby to have the teeniest sip. It was horrible but she pronounced it 'delicious', which made Mother smile unexpectedly. And then there was the boat ride to Calais, which was even *more* exciting. She loved hearing Mother speak French. You couldn't tell her apart from a *real* French person. She seemed someone else entirely. At Calais, they boarded another train, which took them all the way across France and Italy to Brindisi. It was warm in Italy in a way that England never was, with glittering blue skies and green palm trees that fringed the sea. At Brindisi they boarded a ship that was really a floating city, nothing like the ferry that had taken them across *la Manche*. They had a cabin to themselves with a bunk bed and a special cot that had been fixed up for Eluned. The windows were round, not square, and they looked directly out onto a gently swaying sea, which set the rhythm of movement for all the passengers on board.

Mother was quite ill on the first day of the voyage. She lay in bed looking thin and wan and couldn't keep anything down, not even water. Libby was alarmed; she'd never seen her mother ill before – not even with a cold. But after the second day she perked up and 'found her sea legs', as she put it, which puzzled Libby until it was explained to her and they all laughed, including the man who'd joined them as they walked up the gang plank to board the ship on the first day.

At first Libby didn't pay him much attention. Lots of people were drawn to her mother before finding out, politely, firmly, that there was no friendship to be had. But this man was different. He was short and bald with a funny stiff gait. He seemed to know Mother but no introductions were made. Mother never said, 'Oh, this is so-and-so.' She didn't even mention him by name. He simply appeared whenever they were going to the dining room or joined them on deck.

One evening, Libby saw them talking together, leaning over the rail. Their heads were so close they were almost touching. Libby wasn't alarmed. She felt no threat from him. She knew enough of her mother's nature to know that there must be some reasonable explanation. If she knew the funny little man in the badly fitting suit, there had to be a reason *why*.

They docked in Cyprus two days later, but when the ship pulled out again the following morning, he wasn't there.

At dawn, she felt her mother moving about the cabin and opened her eyes. 'I'm just going on deck for a minute,' she whispered. 'I love watching the ship pull away from the land.'

'Can I come?' Libby was awake. She suddenly longed for a minute or two in her mother's company, alone. Eluned was fast asleep.

Her mother hesitated for a second. 'Well, all right. Come on. But we'd better be quick.'

Libby was filled with delight. She scrambled into her dressing gown, pulled on a pair of socks and followed her mother out the door, leaving it a little ajar, just in case Eluned woke up. They were only going to the end of the corridor, less than three cabins away. As Libby knew only too well, Eluned's voice could easily carry the distance.

They pushed open the heavy door that led to the deck and stood there for a moment, both savouring the cool, early morning air. They were moving slowly out of harbour. Libby already recognised the smooth, silent retreat from land that they experienced every time they left port. She stood beside her mother, listening to the engines hum, feeling the ship turn in its own strong wash of power. The deafening hooters sounded, once, twice, thrice ... and then they were away. The water glittered and rose, and the gulls overhead fell away. They were at sea again, this time on their way to Tripoli. From there, they would take a train to Damascus, stay for a day, and then a long, three-day train journey to Baghdad. The entire journey would take them ten days.

'Why's it called "Bagh-*dad*"?' Libby asked as the driver and Mrs Clarke ferried them from the train station to the new villa on the banks of the Tigris that they'd been told would be their new home. 'Bagh-*dad*. It sounds funny.'

'It *is* funny. It was the name of one of their godless idols,' Mrs Clarke shouted over the noisy engine. 'Typical. Heathens, the lot of 'em.'

'It's not a funny name at all,' her mother said calmly. 'In ancient Persian, the word *"bagh"* meant "God", and the word *"dad"* meant "founded". Baghdad was founded by God, not by godless idols. Or heathens.'

'Hmmph. Well, that's not the story *we* were told,' Mrs Clarke said haughtily.

'Then whoever told you the story got it wrong,' Mother said pleasantly. 'Oh, look ... is that it? How beautiful.' She pointed ahead to a long white wall with the sort of brickwork edges that Libby associated with fairy tales.

Libby gazed at it in disbelief. Beyond the wall there were two turrets, in the same style, in soft pink sandstone. It wasn't a house ... it was a palace!

They stopped directly outside a small wooden gate, set deep into the wall. She'd already noticed how narrow and crooked the streets were. Everything in Bagdad appeared higgledy-piggledy, full of streets with high walls on either side and tangled ropes of telephone wires strung just above their heads, like a giant, celestial spider's web.

The driver leaped out to open Mother's door first, then ran around to a clearly miffed Mrs Clarke. To Libby's delight, he bent down, pulled off one of his long-toed Ali Baba-style shoes and rapped loudly on the gate with its heel.

'*Aiwa,*' a female voice shouted from behind the wall. '*Ahlan!*'

The gate opened and a wizened old woman, draped in black, stood in the entrance. Only her face showed; the deep wrinkles in her brown, leathery skin were as deep and wide as the folds in her burqa. Libby stared at her. Her eyes, deep in their folds of skin, twinkled. Libby liked her at once.

'Your mother is correct,' the driver said suddenly in a low voice, as he followed them into the courtyard.

Libby whirled around in surprise, but he'd already slipped away. She turned back to the garden. It went on as far as she could see, unfolding slowly, tree by tree, blossom by blossom, in front of her, stretching all the way across the inner courtyard to the pink palace that she now understood was their home.

Her mouth parted on a sigh. From the moment she'd stepped through the gate, like Alice in *Through the Looking-Glass*, and allowed the light of the water in the fountain in the centre to enter into her, and breathed in the sweet-smelling air, and took the dampness onto and into her skin, she was lost.

35

The young girl who'd been assigned as a maid didn't look much older than her daughter Libby, Kit mused, as she watched Miriam pick up Eluned and expertly rock her back to sleep. Where on earth had she learned how to handle a baby like that?

'How old are you?' she asked her.

Miriam, sensing she was being addressed, stopped immediately, a look of guilt on her young face. She looked at Kit and shook her head. 'No English,' she said falteringly.

'*Français?*' Kit ventured hopefully.

Miriam shook her head.

Ah. Well, that settles it, Kit thought cheerfully. I'd better set about learning Arabic, and quickly too.

She looked around the room. The master bedroom was larger than their entire Chelsea flat. It was stunning. Large and airy with ornate, beautiful wooden flooring, whitewashed walls – not quite smooth but with a pleasing irregularity – a high, domed ceiling and painted wooden shutters, which looked out over the rooftops of Karrada on the one side and on the other all the way down the garden to the glinting Tigris at the bottom.

She paused, cocking her head to one side. There was something in the proportioning that was oddly familiar to her . . . Ah, she had it! In its own way, it was the oriental, baronial equivalent of Chalfont Hall, with its lawns and ha-has and boxy, trimmed hedges that gave the impression of endless, timeless ownership.

An old, long-forgotten memory suddenly broke the surface of her thoughts. She was five years old again, standing in the Great Room on the first floor at Chalfont, where her parents occasionally entertained. It was winter and the gardens outside were misty with freezing fog. The three long windows at the end of the room looked out onto the lawns, each with its own framed view of the landscape, like three enormous paintings, each one different. In one of them stood a bevy of grazing roe deer. She knelt on the padded sill, watching them curiously. They lifted their heads from time to time, sniffing the wind. Something must have spooked them, for a second later, they scattered, pale rumps dancing from side to side. In doing so, they passed through the frame of one giant painting to the next, and the next. That was when she understood for the first that it was all one stretch of land out there, all under Father's gift.

'Mummy.' Libby wandered into the room, chewing on the end of one of her pigtails and bringing her abruptly back to the present. 'Can I go into the garden?'

'Of course you can,' Kit said automatically. She tried to remember if Mrs Clarke had said anything about snakes. Were there snakes in Iraq? She had no idea. 'Watch where you put your feet,' she called after her. 'Stay away from the long grass. And make sure you've got your shoes on.'

'Why?' Libby yelled back, already clattering down the stairs.

'In case of snakes,' she called out.

The clattering ceased abruptly. Kit drew in a breath. How would her teenage daughter react to *that* little bit of information? She waited. Libby was digesting the news. Then, as abruptly as she'd stopped, she carried on unperturbed. Kit allowed herself the faintest of smiles. Her daughter would be fine in Iraq. It was Paul who would need looking after.

'Darling, you're here! At *last*! I thought you'd never bloody arrive!' Paul came barrelling through the front door accompanied by two servants, one carrying his briefcase and papers, the other carrying a bunch of rather wilted stems. There was an awkward exchange as neither servant appeared to know which was for whom. She was presented with the briefcase first, then the flowers and finally Paul's large stack of office papers. She calmly took charge as Paul looked on helplessly as she directed operations. *Flowers in the sink, briefcase next to the door, office papers in the master's office down the hallway.* The command of servants was second nature to her.

'Oh, dear,' Paul muttered under his breath once it had all been sorted out and the two assistants had beaten a hasty retreat. 'What on earth did they think you were going to do with a briefcase and me with a bunch of flowers?'

'I honestly can't imagine,' Kit murmured. They kissed briefly. As always, it was she who broke the embrace first.

'Did you have a good trip down?' Paul asked, loosening his tie. 'Journey wasn't too bad, I hope?' He looked anxiously at her.

She shook her head, smiling faintly. He was always anxious.

'And what d'you make of this place?' he rushed on. 'Rather palatial, don't you think? I've been sleeping in the downstairs study. At least, I *think* it's a study... Hard to tell, really. I was just rattling around upstairs on my own. Gosh, I'm awfully glad you're here,' he blurted suddenly.

For a moment they stood looking at each other across the dining room table. Kit fought to resist the momentary impulse to leave the room.

'Me too, darling,' she murmured.

'Where are the girls?'

'Libby's out in the garden exploring and Eluned's asleep. That awful Mrs Clarke practically forced a nanny on me... young girl called Miriam. She seems nice enough. Doesn't speak a word of English, though, so I thought I'd better pick up some Arabic pretty quickly. Do you think the company might have a course I could do? Something for the wives?'

'I'll ask,' Paul said, sounding doubtful. 'Drink, darling?' He held up a bottle of gin by the neck.

'Where do you get *that*?' she asked. 'I thought Baghdad was supposed to be dry.'

He snorted. 'Don't you believe it. I've been here a month and I've probably drunk more than I do at home all year. Well, perhaps not quite. But it's terribly sociable, you'll see. You'll make lots of friends, darling. You'll be quite spoiled for choice. There's so much to do. The club's quite good as well. Tennis courts, swimming pool... that sort of thing. You'll soon get into the swing of things, Kit, I promise.' He was talking very fast whilst pouring them both a generous measure – a sign of his nervousness.

Kit studied him surreptitiously from beneath her lashes. He was a good-looking man. Tall and well built with the strong, muscular legs of a rugby player. He had strawberry-blond hair, blue eyes, fair eyelashes and ruddy skin that spoke of freezing baths at boarding school and an Englishman's ability to take the cold but not the heat. It was funny that they'd wound up in Baghdad where the summer temperatures were regularly above a hundred.

Paul was a kind man. Patient. Decent. He had all the right qualities for a husband. That was what she'd been told. *Don't waste time, Katherine. You haven't got it to waste.* She shook herself quickly. Now wasn't the moment to think about all that. It was Bier's fault. He'd surprised her by joining them on the journey. She hadn't been expecting him. She took the drink he'd handed her. 'Shall we go out into the garden, darling? I bet Libby's fallen in love with it.'

'Hello, Father.' Suddenly Libby's voice broke in on them.

Kit turned around. How long had she been standing there? she wondered.

'Hello, darling,' Paul said quickly, setting his drink on the sideboard. 'I was just saying how much I'd missed you.'

Libby's expression was faintly disbelieving. 'Really?' she asked politely, in that funny little voice of hers.

'How was the journey? Did you enjoy it? Did you help Mummy with Lulu?'

'Yes.' She answered all three questions at once. There was an awkward pause.

'What will we do for supper?' Kit asked, stepping in to relieve them of the burden of conversation. 'Shall I ask the cook to make us something? I've no idea what, but I'm sure he'll manage.'

'We could go out,' Paul said, draining his drink. 'There's a rather good restaurant on Al Rashid Street, just up the road.'

'Can I come?' Libby interrupted, looking questioningly at her mother.

'Yes, of course you can,' Kit said firmly. She met Paul's faintly exasperated gaze squarely. 'Miriam can look after Eluned.' She turned back to Libby. 'Why don't you take a bath, darling? And put on a clean dress,' she called out as Libby tore out of the room. 'You've been in the same one for two days!' She turned back to her husband. 'Don't be irritated,' she said quietly. 'She's been cooped up for days.'

'But I want you all to myself,' Paul said plaintively.

Kit sighed. 'You'll have me all to yourself later,' she promised soothingly. She spoke to him as one might to a child. It seemed to work. Paul brightened visibly. She took a sip of her G & T. It would take her a while to slip back into the order of things. Damn Bier.

36

From the minute the train pulled into the shiny, impressively new Baghdad Central Station, Libby knew she would love her new home. London was hardly a village – it was one of the world's largest cities, after all – but it seemed dull and mean compared to Baghdad.

By the time they'd found the company representative, who explained that her father had been sent to Basra, in the south of the country, and wouldn't be back until later that afternoon, she'd counted seventeen different types of headgear. Turbans, top hats, fez hats, three different types of flowing keffiyehs – white, red-and-white check and black-and-white check – panama hats, army pith helmets, soft berets, straw hats, floppy felt tubes and square medieval-looking hats ... She listed them carefully, wishing she'd thought to unpack her notebook and write it all down. The people were a bewildering mixture of: black-gowned men with thick, black beards; Chinese-looking scholarly men with wire spectacles; dark-skinned men in white flowing robes; men in suits; Europeans; Arabs; and hosts of others who she simply couldn't identify. There were women, too, some in voluminous black robes but others in the latest fashions from Paris and London, wearing full-waisted dresses with hats and gloves. There were strange women, all but lost from view under heavy bundles of twigs and grass roots, and occasionally tall, jet-black East Africans, whose faces were sullen and closed. There were hundreds of British soldiers, too, in dusty-looking khaki uniforms, leaning against the walls, their rifles at the ready, smoking and laughing.

It was bewildering and exhilarating. For a fourteen-year-old whose universe revolved primarily around the axis of a three-bedroom house on Mallard Street, SW1 and her school, located half a mile away just off the Fulham Road, it was the centre of a new, exciting world.

But that wasn't all. As they wound their way through the station to the waiting car, she saw monkeys, parrots, goats, chickens, dogs, donkeys ... even camels! She laughed in delight as they came across one, tethered moodily to a gatepost. Was there no end to the surprises?

The company man, whose name she'd promptly forgotten, kept up a steady patter of shouted instructions. 'Mind your feet! Don't step in that! Watch your elbow! Watch your bag!'

By the time they finally reached the car, she was almost dizzy with excitement. Somehow, Eluned slept through it all. In fact, Eluned had slept almost all the way through the entire journey, which was nothing short of a miracle, given her disagreeable disposition.

The railway station was unlike any other Libby had seen. Part terminus, part bazaar, separated only by a thin strip of tarmac on which both goats and cars drifted along, seemingly blind to each other. Adjacent to the brand-new post office, tacked onto the station at its far end, there was a street of cafés. Little clusters of people sat on island tables raised a few inches from the street, sipping tea, smoking and watching the passengers go by. She caught a whiff of something delicious – sweet, aromatic – and then the company man interrupted by telling them to 'hurry up and get inside or you'll be robbed blind!'

Who by? she wondered, looking around. There was no one anywhere near. She decided he must be A Nervous Sort. His face was a peculiar shade of red and huge patches of sweat showed under the arms of his short-sleeve white shirt, and across his back. Like Father, the heat probably didn't agree with him.

She looked quickly at her mother to see how she was taking it all in. Her expression was carefully controlled. She looked beautiful. You'd never have thought she'd just emerged from a three-day train journey without a proper bathtub, all the way from Damascus. There was only a basin with an enamel jug. After the second day, Libby had learned how to balance on the edge of the toilet seat and let the cool water simply run off her body onto the floor. Her mother was wearing a white linen dress with a lovely full skirt and a shiny black belt. Her hair was very short and in the heat it curled a little around her ears and the nape of her neck. She wore giant black sunglasses and she'd put on lipstick before climbing down from the train. She looked like an American film star. The company man was clearly bowled over by her. That was why he spoke so much, and so fast.

The house was the last – and best – surprise of all. Her mouth dropped open as soon as the wooden gate swung to let them enter and she was quite sure it stayed open for at least another hour.

It was *huge*! Bigger than anything she'd ever seen. It was a wonderful combination of narrow corridors that opened onto rooms of unimaginable size and splendour. There wasn't much furniture, which made it seem all the more expansive. The garden, which sloped gently towards the muddy river, was visible from almost every room. The enchanting courtyard of orange, lime and lemon trees that you had to pass through in order to enter the house was cleverly visible from everywhere. She wandered through every single room, from the enormous suite of living rooms on the ground floor, each connected by a series of splendid arches, to the bedrooms on the first floor. Best of all was the vast library on the second floor, accessed by a twisting, spiral staircase at one end of the hallway.

She devoted the first day to exploring every single inch before deciding on which room was to be her bedroom. It was smaller than the others, tucked away in the furthest corner of the first floor, overlooking the enchanted garden. When you opened the shutters, the smell of citrus flooded the room. It had its own bathroom but it wasn't like any other bathroom she'd seen. Floor, walls, vaulted ceiling, toilet, sink, bathtub . . . everything was a continuous tiled surface that enveloped the room, with you in it. It was like stepping into a tiled, turquoise womb. She stood in the doorway for nearly an hour, staring, trying to take it all in. The heat made her drowsy and pleasurably lazy; it was like being in the middle of one of God's enormous yawns. She felt the pores in her skin and her veins widen, breathing the very essence of the new city in.

'Mother,' she announced seriously, when she came upon her in one of the downstairs rooms, looking down the garden towards the river. 'I think I'm going to like it here.'

Her mother turned. There was a funny, faraway look on her face. 'I'm glad. I had a feeling you would.'

The unexpected words sent a warm glow running through Libby. They looked at each other for a second, mother and daughter. Libby held her breath, waiting for something more. Her mother turned back to look at the river again. Libby stood in the doorway for a moment, the sole of a bare foot rubbing awkwardly against her shin.

'Why don't you ask Miriam to run you a bath?' her mother murmured without turning around. 'Father will be home soon.'

Libby's pent-up breath was exhaled slowly, quietly. She walked back up the stairs to the room that was now her own. There was a mirror that was the middle door of the wardrobe. She walked up to it and stood there, looking at herself. The only sound in the room was her breathing. After a while her face ceased to become hers; it was a face just like other faces in the street. It looked back at her a little longer.

Then the front door slammed and she heard a man's voice. Father's. The sound of it brought a new awareness to her. The house in England where she'd lived until now fell away from her and a new familiarity took its place. This was home now. The beginning of something new, something else.

37

'And what did *you* do in the war, Mrs Kentridge?'

Kit blinked, taken aback. It was their second week in Baghdad. She and Paul had been invited to dine with a group of IPC's top brass and their wives at the Alwiya Club in the centre of the city.

She leaned forwards to accept a light. 'Me?' she asked, blowing out her smoke slowly. 'Oh, nothing much. Secretarial work, mostly. A bit of typing and filing. Nothing out of the ordinary. Girls like me weren't brought up to do anything very useful, I'm afraid.'

There was a murmur of self-deprecating laughter from the women in the group. Then one of the wives spoke up. 'But hang on, weren't you at Oxford? I knew someone – a friend of my brother's, actually – who met you once, at one of the balls. I mentioned you were coming out and he said he knew you. Ruaridh. Ruaridh Macleod. Irish chap.'

Kit waved away her smoke. 'Oh, yes, Ruaridh. I didn't know him well. He married one of the girls on my course.'

'Still, you must be awfully clever.'

'She is,' Paul broke in, beaming proudly. 'Much cleverer than I am, I'm afraid.'

'That's usually the way,' one of the directors guffawed. There was another round of laughter. Kit smiled politely.

But Frances Pollard, the wife who'd spoken to her, was determined. 'He also said something about your sister, I believe?'

'Ah, yes, my sister,' Kit said evenly. 'Lily Algernon-Waters. Nazi sympathiser. She married one of Hitler's aides. He was hanged for war crimes after Nuremberg. She stayed on in Germany, I believe. I don't know what's become of her. We're not in touch.'

There was a stunned silence. Clifford Porter, Paul's immediate boss, looked as if he'd swallowed something unpleasant. One of the wives had her glass of gin halfway to her mouth, where it stopped, hovering. Then the silence was broken by Mrs Clarke's arrival with a harassed-looking Iraqi waiter in tow.

'Now, who ordered the pink gin? And the vodka tonic? With or without lemon?'

'You didn't have to do that,' Paul murmured against her ear as they went into dinner.

'Of course I did,' Kit said briskly. 'It gets it out into the open. And they won't bring it up again.'

'I know, I know... But don't you think you could *soften* it a little? They've only just met you.'

'Oh, Paul.' Kit looked at him exasperatedly. 'Soft's the one thing I'm not good at. You know that. But it's had the right effect. Look at Mrs Everard. She's dying to smother you with sympathy. She's wondering how on earth you cope with such a rude wife. She's on your side. They all are.'

Paul looked at her helplessly. 'D'you know, sometimes I'm almost afraid of you,' he said in a low voice.

'Don't be. I promise I'll behave. Listen, won't you get me another G & T? I'm going to need one to get through dinner.'

'All right, I'll be back in a minute. But be nice. I've my position to think of, after all.'

Kit bit down hard on the urge to snap at him. 'Of course I will,' she said soothingly. 'I'll be perfectly charming. You'll see.'

He nodded, relieved, and hurried off to the bar, giving her a chance to look around. It was an elegant and spacious clubhouse, with all the usual trappings: palm trees, a shiny, well-stocked bar, tables with white cloths and linen napkins. For the British expatriates, it gave off the sense of being at 'home'. With alcohol flowing freely on tap and an abundance of hovering waiters, they were delightfully cosseted and indulged. As they sat down to dinner, she looked with detached fascination at her fellow diners. The men were bluff and hearty, in short-sleeved shirts and panama hats, worn in the evenings as a concession to the heat. The women wore summery frocks and went bare-legged, their shiny faces freed at last of the dreadful powder that concealed and congealed their expressions.

Paul appeared at her side with an already-sweating glass. 'Here you are, darling. Practically had to make it myself. Queue as long as a mile at the bar.'

'We were just saying,' Clifford Porter began as they sat down, 'perhaps Kit might like to join Margery's reading group? It gives them something to do, doesn't it?' He chuckled conspiratorially with the other men at the table. The women looked on brightly, awaiting her response.

'Oh, I've got plenty to occupy me,' Kit demurred. 'I was just thinking I might sign up for Arabic classes. Seems a pity not to.'

'Whatever for? They all speak English.' The woman who spoke seemed genuinely perplexed.

'Well, they *try* to,' her husband corrected her. 'Must say, I wouldn't mind a bit of Arabic myself... It'd make the job a hell of a lot easier.'

'Jolly good idea,' one of the other wives chimed in suddenly. Her husband was sitting to Paul's left, a small, inoffensive man whose size and aura was in inverse proportion to his wife's. 'But God knows where you'll find a teacher. It's quite a difficult language. Apparently.'

'Oh, she'll pick it up in no time,' Paul chimed in proudly. 'She's a natural. Speaks about six languages already. Fluently, too.'

'Really? What else d'you speak?'

'German, French, Italian, a bit of Russian... used to work as a translator. Before the children, of course.' Paul seemed to think it necessary to speak for her. Kit said nothing.

'Gosh.' One of the wives spoke up, clearly not knowing what to say.

'Well, I dare say you'll find Baghdad very interesting,' Clifford Porter said pompously, closing the matter. It was quite clear Kit Kentridge had been paid *quite* enough attention. 'Now, who's having what? I must say, I could eat a horse! It's the heat, I shouldn't wonder. No wonder Iraqis wear those long nightshirts. Hides the paunch. Can't do *that* in a suit,' he said, patting his solid retaining wall of stomach and chest.

There was a guffaw all round. Their laughter and the raised voices had the effect of isolating their table from the rest of the diners in the restaurant. There were a few lonely diners – bachelors, Kit surmised – who looked at them almost enviously. As they ordered their food, with much loud deliberation and questioning, Kit caught the eye of a young man, who quickly looked away, like a child who pretends not to notice a birthday party going on in the house next door.

'You've just had another baby, I hear?' Margery Porter leaned forwards, looking enviously at her.

Kit nodded. 'Yes, Eluned.'

'There's quite a gap between them, so I heard?'

'Mmm.' Kit wondered what else the assembled group had managed to find out about herself and Paul.

'Lucky you,' Margery said, the envy still present in her voice and eyes.

There was a moment's pause. Margery looked as though she were about to unburden herself of something Kit probably didn't want to hear. Someone behind her cleared his throat. She looked up. It was one of the waiters. He bent forwards.

'Mrs Kentridge?'

She nodded, relieved at the interruption. 'Yes, that's me.'

'A phone call for you, madam. At the bar.'

Paul looked up. 'What's wrong?' he asked, pushing back his chair to stand up as she did. 'Is something wrong? Who is it?'

Kit waved away his concern. 'It's Madame Abbayas. I told her we'd be here. I won't be a moment.' She stubbed out her cigarette and followed the waiter to the bar.

'Everything all right?' Paul looked up anxiously as she returned a few minutes later.

'Yes, she just wanted to know how much milk to give Eluned.'

'I thought you'd written it out for her?'

'Probably can't read,' someone growled. 'You know what they're like. They'll say "yes" when they mean "no" and they don't think twice about it.'

There was a general grunt of assent but the food had begun to arrive and their attention was mercifully claimed. Kit accepted a plate and sat back patiently, waiting her turn. Underneath the table her leg tapped the floor softly. It was a sign, had anyone noticed, that her attention was elsewhere.

38

Lord Hamilton followed Sir Evelyn Gore-Brown and Sir Stewart Mackenzie, Section Chief of Division Nine, Inter-Service Liaison Department, into the room reserved for them at Boodle's, Sir Stewart's club, at 29 St James's Park. All three men were lifelong members, but of different clubs. Sir Evelyn Gore-Brown was a member of Carlton's, located just up the road, at 69 St James's Park. Lord Hamilton, a proud Liberal and close friend of Churchill's, was a member of the National Liberal Club, on the opposite side of Pall Mall at Whitehall Street, where both he and the former prime minister could be found after-hours in the library savouring particularly good claret.

'Thank you, George,' Sir Stewart said as the waiter set the silver coffee pot carefully down on the table. There were biscuits and Sir Stewart's favourites: Jaffa Cakes. 'That'll be all for now.'

'Very good, sir.' George discreetly withdrew, shutting the door quietly but firmly behind him.

The three men – so-called 'mandarins' of MI6 – eased off their coats and hats and settled themselves around the table. As was his custom, Sir Stewart himself poured the coffee. When all three were comfortable, and the last of the Jaffa Cakes had been consumed, he turned to the other two. He cleared his throat and began to speak in his distinctive Eton-educated voice, laid over with a soft, sonorous Scottish burr. It was the sort of voice that could – and often did – move mountains. As the commander of a naval frigate during the war, those who'd served under him testified to the fact that he'd often moved his men to tears.

'Gentlemen, you're probably wondering why I've called you here today. Thing is, we're in a bit of a sticky situation out there. After Suez last year ... well, I need hardly remind you that we can't afford another blunder.'

Lord Hamilton inwardly grimaced. The whole debacle surrounding Britain's involvement in the crisis had not only damaged Britain's standing in the international community, it had damaged him personally as well. After all, he was the one who'd penned the infamous 'open' letter to Anthony Eden, where he'd cautioned Eden in no uncertain terms: *So far, what Nasser has done amounts to a threat, but only a threat. It cannot be ignored; but it is not a threat that justifies war.*

Whilst there were many who agreed with him privately, the mood in Britain was aggressive. Nasser's move to nationalise the canal was seen as a direct rebuff to the British, who'd 'protected' Egypt since 1882. Sir Stewart Mackenzie, recruited from the Royal Navy after the end of the war, was a no-nonsense, straight-talking Scot. Although perhaps not *quite* as sceptical as Lord Hamilton, Sir Stewart, being a Scot, had a keener nose for the intricacies of power; the two men got along well. They occasionally hunted grouse together in the damp, wet wilds outside Aberdeen, where Sir Stewart's family kept a country home.

Lord Hamilton met Sir Stewart's eyes. 'So what exactly *is* the situation?' he asked.

'Part of the issue over Suez was about the changing nature of trade,' Sir Stewart said, warming to his theme. 'As you're well aware, by the end of forty-eight, we couldn't rely any longer on our old traditional role as the protector of India.'

'Meaning?' Sir Evelyn interjected. He was now head of Special Operations, responsible for the entire Middle East, though his control over Egypt had weakened considerably under Nasser.

'It means those of us involved in the protection of Her Majesty's interests and people overseas are going to have to reckon with a new world order,' Sir Stewart replied evenly. 'The Americans, as you know, are fixated on the Russians. They see the world now divided between two spheres: capitalism and communism. They're not much interested in anything in between. And that, in my view, leaves *us* – Britain – dangerously exposed.'

'You're thinking particularly of the Middle East?' Sir Evelyn asked, tapping his steepled fingers together thoughtfully.

'I'm thinking *only* of the Middle East. Oil, gentlemen. That's why Suez was so important. Last year, two-thirds of Europe's oil passed through the canal. The source, gentlemen, that's the key. Control the source and you'll control the flow. Our interests in the world will be dominated in the next century by oil, not trade.'

There was a moment's pause. 'Who do we have out there?' Lord Hamilton asked Sir Evelyn.

'Well, there's all the army and air force infrastructure, of course. Mostly centred in Baghdad and Basra. But there are a couple of operatives in the region. There's old Toby Barratt in Amman. He's probably the most senior person we've got at the moment. Then there's Roy Knowland-Hughes. He's covering the Tehran-Kabul-Baghdad desk, only he's mostly in Tehran these days. We *could* get him back. We'd have to do it quietly, though, so as not to arouse suspicion, either from the Iraqis or the Americans,' Sir Evelyn replied. 'We're a little thinner on the ground than I'd have liked, but as you say, the post-war situation's been dominated by the Soviet threat.'

'There *is* one other person,' Sir Stewart said slowly, looking straight at Lord Hamilton.

Lord Hamilton's mind began to race. He looked at Sir Stewart with renewed respect. The wily old fox! 'Yes,' he said slowly. 'Yes, there is.'

'Who?' Sir Evelyn asked, obviously puzzled.

'Your girl.' Sir Stewart nodded at Lord Hamilton. 'Kit Algernon-Waters. Now married to an oil company man. Your doing, I believe?'

Lord Hamilton allowed himself the tiniest of inward smiles. 'Yes, indeed,' he said smoothly. His heart was beating fast. He'd been waiting for this.

'Lord Wharton's girl?' Sir Evelyn let out a sigh. 'Ah. I wondered what had happened to her after Beaulieu. I lost track of her after that.'

'She's right there. In Baghdad. Right in the heart of the city.'

'Is she ready?'

Sir Stewart and Sir Evelyn both looked at Lord Hamilton. He took a few seconds to savour the moment. 'Always. She'll do whatever's asked of her,' he said quietly.

'Well done, Charles,' Sir Stewart said as soon as the door had closed behind Sir Evelyn. 'Very well played. He'll think it was his suggestion all along. But you had her in mind right from the start, didn't you?'

Lord Hamilton didn't answer but got up, pressed the bell for service and pulled open a door in the sideboard. He took out a box of Davidoff cigars and brought them to the table. He selected two, expertly clipped them and handed one to Lord Hamilton. A minute later, the door opened. It was the waiter, bearing two brandies on a silver tray. He quickly cleared away the coffee and biscuits and withdrew, leaving them alone again. It was nearly five o'clock on a wet Wednesday afternoon.

They moved from the table to two plump Chesterfields by the fire. They lit up and the room was immediately filled with the warm, aromatic scent of Dominican tobacco.

'So how did you know she'd be up for it?' Sir Stewart asked curiously.

'Ah. You, of all people, should know. Nothing happens in our world without me getting wind of it eventually,' Lord Hamilton said mildly.

'I see. Question is, though, why'd you wait so long? From what I gather, she was a major asset in Belgium and Norway. She went up to Oxford straight after the war. Was that your doing too?'

Lord Hamilton didn't answer straight away. The truth was, he wasn't sure. She'd done exceptionally well. At first they'd intended to send her to Bletchley Park to train alongside the other code-breakers, but on the morning she was scheduled to leave, Vera Atherton rang up and said they thought she was actually Beaulieu material. Something in the girl had changed, she said. She didn't know exactly what it was, just that she thought the girl could go on to become one of their best spies, if she were handled correctly.

Jerôme Bier had offered to take charge of her himself. Bier was one of their most valuable assets, a Belgian Jew with extraordinary linguistic abilities, and determined to bring Hitler to his knees. Bier seemed to think the girl had similar abilities. He'd signed the order, torn between an odd desire to protect the girl and an ambition to see her succeed. So they sent her to STS31 to see if she would indeed realise her potential. She *did* succeed. Beyond anyone's expectations.

'Yes,' he said finally. 'Yes, that was my doing too. I'm … fond of her. No, not in that way,' he added hastily. 'She reminds me of my daughter, you see. You've never met Daphne, our eldest. Bright girl. *Too* bright, in many ways. I had such hopes for her. Wanted her to go up to Oxford, actually, but Marion had other ideas. She thought it would ruin her chances, you see.'

'Yes, I dare say she was right. Daphne's married, isn't she?'

'Yes, yes. Splendid chap. I like him very much. We both do, and they've got two children – a boy and a girl. We adore them, of course, but I never stop thinking … couldn't she have done *both*?'

'You'll never know, old boy. Best not to dwell on it.' Sir Stewart puffed on his cigar. 'So she's taken your daughter's place, is that it? She's doing what you think Daphne could have done?'

'I suppose so. I've never really thought about it like that.'

'Best not to,' Sir Stewart advised for the second time. 'The main thing is, the girl's out there, she's in place and she's capable. How much preparation time does she need?'

'None. I sent Bier out to Brindisi when she left for Baghdad. Precaution only. Just in case something came up.'

'Good man.'

'I'll ring her this evening and let her know what next to expect.'

'Excellent, dear boy, excellent. Now, how about something to eat?'

39

The sun had shone for seventy-two whole days without interruption since they arrived. Libby knew because she'd counted them. The blinding light was still strange to her. Every morning, Miriam woke her in the same way, coming into her bedroom and opening the shutters, releasing a liquid stream of light that was so vivid it was painful. She would go into the blue bathroom, turn on the taps and draw Libby's bath. Unlike England, in Baghdad you had to bathe every single day, sometimes even twice a day, in fact, on account of the heat. It was hot all day. By the time she returned from school in the early afternoon, her pinafore was sticking to her and her entire body was damp with sweat. School was from eight o'clock in the morning until one thirty. It was only five minutes away by car, fifteen on foot. Sometimes Father gave her and Miriam a lift in the morning, other times they walked, Miriam holding onto Libby's arm so tightly Libby feared it would cut her blood off. She felt a little embarrassed by it – which fourteen-year-old walked to school with a maid clutching at her arm? But Miriam refused to be put off.

At first they could barely speak to one another. Whenever they stepped outside the wooden gate and into the street, the cacophonous din of Baghdad slithered up the tarmac to meet her. Cries, bells, hammering, horns, music, the roar of an exhaust, the stuttering of a motorcycle, the shouts of *'dir balak!'*, which she learned meant 'mind your back!' Slowly, what began as unintelligible noises gradually became distinguishable sounds. With Miriam's help, Libby began to learn how to ask politely for things she wanted – *baklava, zlabia, shubbak el-habayeb* – and how to say '*shukran*' to the vendors, whose colourful stalls crowded the pavements along the edges of the road. It was slow, halting progress but by the end of their third month, she and Miriam were able to have a conversation of sorts as they walked to and from the sprawling bungalow on Arasat al-Hindiyah, which housed the British School.

One day, in the middle of November, when the temperatures were finally cooler and it was possible to walk without feeling as though you might expire at any moment from the heat and dust, they walked together down Karrada Kharidge Street to buy *kanafeh* from the corner shop. As Miriam haggled over prices, Libby stepped out of the shop and onto the dusty pavement, taking care not to step in the mud, and looked down the length of the busy street. The sounds of the bustling city surrounded her in the way the sound of wind in the leaves of a forest might. Baghdad felt almost home now, the way London used to.

The air was cool and crisp, and the light bounced off the corners of the buildings as the sun began to sink. Women brushed past her, infusing the air with their scents. A man carrying a parcel nudged her out of the way. She idly watched two young boys dart forwards and pick up a cigarette that someone had dropped, tussling over who would get it.

Suddenly, out of the corner of her eye, she saw a familiar figure come out of an alleyway opposite. She blinked in surprise. It was her mother. She was wearing a light blue dress and wedge-heeled espadrille sandals, and in the crook of her arm she carried a basket. She was hatless, which made Libby frown. Her mother never went out of the house without one of her wide-brimmed floppy hats.

She lifted a hand to wave excitedly to her, and then stopped abruptly. Her mother wasn't alone. She was with someone. He was wearing a light brown suit and a black hat. They were talking intently as they walked. A few yards further along, they stopped in front of a bookshop. Her companion pressed a bell, waited for a few seconds, then they entered the building, the man courteously allowing her mother to go in first. The door closed behind them.

'*Yalla,*' Miriam said, appearing in front of her with a basket full of goodies. She looked very pleased with herself. 'Time to go home. Here.' Miriam broke off a piece of a *klecha* and gave it to her.

Libby slowly put the flaky, date-filled pastry in her mouth. She said nothing about what she'd just seen.

There was no one home when they arrived. Madame Abbayas was cooking. She let them into the kitchen and scolded Miriam roundly for giving Libby a whole *klecha* before tea.

'But she only gave me half a piece,' Libby said solemnly in flawless Arabic.

Madame Abbayas was so surprised that she burst out laughing. 'Listen to her,' she crowed. 'Soon you'll be an Iraqi!'

'She *could* be Iraqi,' Miriam agreed eagerly, relieved to have moved out of the firing line. 'She's almost as dark as I am, you know. Everyone says we look alike.'

Libby looked from one to the other in a mixture of pride and alarm. '*Ana binti Angleet!*' she yelled. I'm an English girl!

Both women laughed. '*Aiwa, aiwa,*' Madame Abbayas said soothingly, and went back to stirring the large pot of stewed apricots. Their sweet scent hung in the air.

Libby wandered out of the kitchen and was on her way upstairs when the front door suddenly opened. Her mother stood in the doorway. Libby stared at her. She was in her tennis outfit: short white skirt, white T-shirt and plimsolls. Her face was red and sweaty, and her hair lay damp and flat against her head. But how could that be? It was less than an hour since she'd seen her in town, dressed as though for a garden party. How could she have come home, got changed and played a game of tennis in that short space of time?

'Hello, darling,' her mother said, shutting the door against the blinding daylight. 'Are you back from school already?'

'Yes,' Libby said. She looked at her mother suspiciously. 'Where've you been?'

'Playing tennis. I played Mrs Ashcroft. And guess what?'

'What?'

'I won. Is there any lemonade? We played for *hours.* I thought she'd never give up!'

Libby said nothing but felt the slow worm of fear plant itself deep in her belly. Why was her mother lying?

*

Kit watched Libby walk up the stairs. She had seen the flash of disbelief flit across her daughter's face as clearly as if she'd spoken aloud. How could that be? Had she been spotted somehow? No, it wasn't possible. She'd been so careful. No one had followed them, she was sure of it, so why the sudden hostility?

She sighed. Perhaps Libby was just being difficult. She was nearly fifteen, and at that awkward age between worlds – no longer a child, but not yet an adult. She heard Libby close her bedroom door, softly but firmly. She stood for a moment, chewing her lip, uncharacteristically indecisive. Should she go after her? But what would she say? Theirs was a strange relationship, and always had been. They were never fully at ease with one another. Libby always seemed to want more – more attention, more reassurance, more love. But Kit couldn't fulfil Libby's demands, certainly not in the way Libby seemed to crave. Kit could never quite banish the suspicion that Libby *knew*. But how could she? No one knew.

She shook herself and looked at her watch. She had half an hour at the most before Paul came home and she needed to clear her mind.

She turned the handle, letting the full force of the cool water sluice over her. She showered quickly, rubbing herself roughly with the hammam towel when she was finished. She looked at herself in the long mirror against the door. Her hair was plastered flat against her skull and there was a rosy strip down her nose where the sun had caught her. She looked ... *vital*, somehow, as though lit from within. It was hardly surprising. Paul often complained that although she looked at him, he always felt as though her real attention lay elsewhere. She tried to shrug it off, but in his own innocent way, he'd stumbled upon a truth. Her real attention *was* elsewhere. It always would be. The meeting that afternoon proved it. And her daughter knew it, too. But how?

Across the landing and up the half flight of stairs, Libby too stood in her bathroom, looking at her reflection. She turned her head slowly this way, then that, concentrating on the way the light hit her skin. Her face appeared to her as a stranger's face, about which some intimate facts were known. Eyes: light brown; skin: sallow, almost yellowish in winter, in England, but here, in the full glare of the sun, she'd turned nut-brown. Little wonder people mistook her for a local, she thought as she stared at her face. The corners of her mouth were dented but her lips were tightly closed. She put up a finger to touch the soft, curly hair at her temples. It had always puzzled her; the rest of her hair was thick and wavy, falling to just below her shoulder blades, but the hair at the nape of her neck and hairline was different, almost springy to the touch. She had a smattering of permanent freckles across her nose, too, that seemed oddly out of place. She looked down at her legs, lifting up the skirt of her dress. The birthmark that had singled her out for teasing as a child was no longer as prominent, now that she was tanned. She stared at it. It was a large, oddly shaped splash of mahogany on the outside of her left knee. She'd always been terribly self-conscious about it, thinking of herself as having a 'good' side, an unblemished side . . . but not any more. Now she rather liked the mysterious marking that no one seemed able to explain.

'Libby?' Her mother's voice suddenly broke in on her thoughts. 'Are you up there? Lucinda's here. She wants to know if you want to go swimming?'

Libby gave herself a little shake. 'Coming!' she shouted, pulling down her skirt again. She twisted her hair into its habitual loose ponytail, splashed some cold water on her face to cool down and opened the door. She clattered hurriedly down the stairs. There was just enough time to go to the clubhouse with Lucinda before the sun went down.

As she banged the front door behind her, she heard Eluned start to yell. She permitted herself the tiniest of smiles. It served her mother right for lying to her.

PART SIX

ESCAPE

1958
Kit

40

She spotted him as soon as she entered the café. He'd aged, she noticed immediately. He was almost white-haired and his face was lined and drawn. Still, it had been almost two years since they'd last met, she reminded herself quickly. He was sitting with his back to the wall, reading a French newspaper. There was a cane resting discreetly against the glass-topped table. He lowered the paper as she approached and smiled gently.

'*Ça va*, Suzette?' he asked, attempting to rise and offer her a seat. So, it was to be French. '*Comment vas-tu?*'

'*Très bien,*' she replied, hurriedly motioning him to sit back down. She pulled out her own chair opposite him. '*Et toi?*' she asked with genuine concern.

He pulled a rueful face, gesturing to the cane. 'Oh, I get by. Some days better than others.'

She nodded sympathetically.

'What'll you have, my dear? Some tea, perhaps?'

To curious onlookers they might have been old colleagues or an uncle and his niece, perhaps. There was a touching formality between them that was pleasing to observe.

They talked rapidly, intensely, for almost an hour. Twice a waiter approached to offer food but they declined, preferring tea (for her) and water (for him), which they drank almost continuously. Towards the end of their meeting, he offered her a cigarette.

'We didn't think he'd actually go ahead with it,' he said quietly, holding out a light. 'But we underestimated Nasser. We usually do.'

'So what am *I* to do?'

'Shukri al Quwatli's our main concern. He went to the Americans looking for aid. They turned him down, naturally, but our worry, of course, is that he'll start cosying up to the Russians. He's here in Cairo. Nasser's about to announce the union.'

'So where do I come in?' she asked again.

'Disinformation. We need to open a line directly to al-Quwatli and his people. It's no good trying to reach Nasser; he's too far gone. But Syria's a different matter.'

'Do you have anyone in mind?' she asked, inhaling deeply.

'Rafiq al-Dalati. His aide-de-camp. Or at least that's his official title. Youngish fellow. Comes from a wealthy Damascene family. His mother is married to al-Quwatli's cousin. It's the usual tangled web of family and politics. Al-Quwatli doesn't go anywhere without al-Dalati. He was with him in Moscow earlier this year. We've reason to believe he and Khrushchev are about to sign a long-term Soviet loan for Syria, which, of course, is setting off all manner of alarm bells in Washington. We need it confirmed ... and the nature of the so-called loan, of course. As much detail as you can.'

'How will I find him?'

'He's staying at the Courcy. Likely to be there until the end of the month. You'll have to move quickly.'

She nodded. 'Of course. Anything else I should know?'

'Rumour has it he's otherwise inclined, but I've never believed it. And I've yet to meet the man who can resist you, my dear. Well, you know what you have to do.'

'Yes,' she murmured. 'Yes, I do.'

'Good girl. Now, what about something to eat? I missed lunch at the embassy, I'm afraid, and I'm absolutely ravenous.'

After Lord Hamilton had gone, Kit sat alone, watching the pedestrian traffic outside the café as Cairenes went about their late afternoon business.

Finally, around five o'clock, when the sun was beginning to drop and the muezzin's prayers had just started, she got up. She walked back up Aziz Abaza to her *pensione* on Ismail Mohammed, directly across from the Spanish Embassy. She went straight to her room, took off her coat and hat and lay down fully clothed on the bed. It was March and the air already held the promise of heat.

She closed her eyes for a few minutes, breathing deeply. There was a single, deep crease between her brows and her lips were moving as though she were whispering to herself. After a few minutes, she opened her eyes and swung her legs out of bed. She picked up the bedside phone and asked for a call to be put through to a Baghdadi number.

'Hello? Hello, darling. It's me. How are things? How're the girls? Oh, fine, fine. No, dreary as ever, I'm afraid. It's been raining all day. What's that? Well, tell them I miss them too. Yes, of course I will. Me too.'

She put down the phone and sat still for a few moments, her expression blank. Then she got up and walked to the bathroom, pulling off her clothes as she went. She showered quickly, wrapped a towel around her wet hair and walked back into the room. Her suitcase was on the floor. She hauled it onto the bed and unzipped it. Her only evening gown, a long, white silk dress, was wrapped carefully between sheets of tissue paper. She took it out and laid it gently across the bed.

She sat down at the dressing table and did her make-up carefully, finishing off with her trademark red lipstick. She ran a comb through her damp hair, got up and walked over to the bed. She slipped the dress over her head and felt it slither down her body to the floor. It swirled voluptuously around her ankles. She picked a pair of shoes out of her suitcase and slipped them on. She was nearly ready. There was only one thing left to do. She walked into the bathroom, opened the wash bag lying on the sink and took out a little rubber device. She put one foot up onto the toilet seat, lifted up the layers of silk and with a practised hand, inserted the device deep inside her. She washed her hands, picked up her evening purse and left the room.

A young bellhop, delivering a pile of suitcases to the next-door suite, heard her whistling as she walked down the stairs. He wasn't able to identify the tune. Something catchy, foreign. Jazz ... wasn't that what the Americans called it?

41

The taxi dropped her off outside the Courcy Hotel in downtown Cairo. It had been the colonial officers' club in the 1920s and 30s and, until the 23 July revolution, had been closed to Egyptians unless they were invited guests. It still retained its elegant, street-front verandah with thick, gold velvet drapes that were drawn in the evening to screen diners and smokers from the hustle and bustle of Lazoghli Boulevard. Now it was frequented largely by upper-class Egyptians, foreign embassy personnel and senior members of Nasser's elite armed guard.

'Good evening, madame.' The liveried doorman bowed almost to the waist as Kit approached. 'Are you dining with us this evening?'

'Yes,' she replied with a wry smile. 'My husband's already in the bar. Would you be so kind as to tell him I'll be on the verandah? His name is Major Forbes. Colin Forbes.'

'Very good, madame.' He snapped his fingers and immediately a younger doorman appeared. He relayed the instructions and the young man scuttled away.

She was shown to the verandah. She chose a table set a little way apart from the other guests, settled into one of the comfortable wicker chairs and ordered a cocktail. She took a cigarette out of her purse and accepted a light from the hovering doorman. She leaned back in her chair and took in her surroundings. It was early evening; dusk had just fallen and across the city lights began to sparkle. A warm breeze had sprung up, sending the palm fronds trembling. Music from the dining room trickled out onto the verandah. Every now and then the soft fizz of tonic water hitting a glass full of ice or the throaty, low sound of a woman's laugh drifted languidly across the room.

Suddenly, without warning, an image flitted across her half-closed eyelids. It was of Lily sitting next to Hans-Georg in the dining room at Lily's new home in Germany, her hair swept up to one side, with a rose pinned carefully above one ear. She was glowing, basking in the attention paid to her at the table by the men whose talk was centred on things Lily couldn't otherwise have cared less about: war, Hitler, England's impending defeat, which, of course, was the opposite of what had happened. Kit was sitting opposite her, struggling to keep pace, to understand the real meaning of the evening, when she suddenly caught her sister's eye.

Look at me, Lily seemed to be saying. *Look at me at the centre of every-thing.* Kit remembered clearly being startled by the revelation. Was that what Lily had always sought? To be at the centre of events – important, world-shaking events? Instead of being on the periphery, as girls like her always were? Was *that* the reason she'd married Hans-Georg?

Now, the thought had come back to haunt her. In their own vastly different ways, could it possibly be that they'd both sought the same thing?

'Darling.' A man's voice broke above her head. She looked up, still shaken by the memory. A tall, dark-haired man in a dinner jacket stood in front of her. He bent down to kiss her cheek. 'How long've you been here?' he asked solicitously.

She gathered herself immediately. 'Not long. A few minutes.'

'What're you drinking?' he asked, sitting down opposite her.

'A G & T.' She leaned forwards. 'Is he here?' she asked in a low voice.

'Left-hand side of the bar. You can't miss him. He's in uniform. Dark hair, green eyes.' He polished off his drink and got to his feet, holding a hand out to help her up. 'Shall we go inside? You look absolutely ravishing, by the way.'

'Thank you, darling,' she murmured, standing up.

He placed a proprietary hand on the small of her back as they walked inside together, past the ballroom where dancers were circling the floor, through to the dining room. A waiter in white with a splendid red cummerbund and a red fez hat made a great fuss of showing them to their table and ensuring everything was *just so*. He took their drinks order with equal flair.

'What's your name?' he asked as soon as the waiter had withdrawn.

'Susan. And you? Colin's not your real name, I suppose?'

'No, of course not.' He grinned. 'But it'll do for now. Have you spotted him?'

Kit nodded. The man to whom Colin referred was sitting alone at a table a few feet away, just within hearing distance if their voices were raised.

'Good. In about five minutes' time, we're going to have an argument. Halfway through, get up and walk past his table. You know the rest.'

She nodded again.

The waiter appeared with their drinks. She left hers untouched. She had only a few minutes to make the contact required and she needed all her wits about her. She was out of practice. She'd said as much to Lord Hamilton.

'It'll all come back,' he'd said sanguinely. 'It always does. Like riding a bicycle. You never forget.'

*

'I'm not listening to another *word*!' She scraped back her chair and stood up abruptly. Her voice was raised to exactly the right pitch. Several diners nearby looked up in surprise.

'Sit down, Susan! Sit *down*, will you?' Colin hissed angrily, looking embarrassed. 'For God's sake! Stop making such a *fuss*!'

'Don't you tell me what to do! How *dare* you?'

'Susan, you're being unreasonable! All I said was—'

'I mean it! I've had enough!' She glared angrily down at him. 'I'm going and don't you *dare* follow me! Why don't you just go to *her*? I know you're dying to!' She grabbed her purse and turned on her heel. Her long white skirt billowed out behind her.

Every single pair of eyes in the room followed her as she practically ran from the dining room. Including his.

'Here, allow me.' A voice spoke to her out of the darkness.

The man standing in front of her flicked open his lighter and offered her the small, steady blue flame.

'Thanks,' she murmured, leaning forwards. Her breasts strained against the tight bodice. She straightened up and leaned back, looking at him through the thin white swirl of smoke.

'Are you all right?' His voice was deep and oddly English-sounding.

She blushed. 'Was it that obvious? I apologise. We were having an argument.'

'It happens.'

'Too bloody often,' she said bitterly. 'I'm sorry … I shouldn't have said that.'

He hesitated for a moment. 'Can I buy you a drink?'

He was tall, deeply tanned with smooth, waxy, olive-toned skin and mesmerising green eyes. She saw from the insignia on his uniform that he was *moqqadim*, a lieutenant colonel.

'Thank you,' she said. 'That would be lovely. I'm Susan, by the way,' she said, holding out a hand.

'I'm Rafiq.' He took her hand and brought it to his lips. 'What about your husband?' He motioned towards the dining room.

'Oh, he's gone,' she said quickly with a shrug. 'He won't be back. Not tonight, at any rate.'

There was a delicate pause. He broke it first. 'Ah. Well, in that case, won't you allow me the pleasure of your company for the evening?' He pulled out the chair opposite her and sat down. He snapped his fingers and a waiter materialised almost instantly.

Drinks were ordered, and a plate of olives. Almonds? Wouldn't she like some sugared almonds? And pearl onions in vinegar, perhaps? Some bread? He couldn't help noticing she hadn't even ordered before their argument broke out. She really ought to try the olives.

'So, how long have you been in Cairo, Susan?' he asked politely.

'Not long at all. Well, Colin's been here nearly six months. I've only just arrived.'

'And is it your first time? Are you enjoying it?'

'Yes, but I haven't really seen very much of Cairo yet.' She gave a quick, shy smile. 'Colin's always so ... busy.' She let the emphasis linger. 'I've always longed to see Egypt. The *real* Egypt. Not this.' She looked around them at the hotel and its elegant surroundings.

He smiled faintly in acknowledgement. 'What does your husband do?'

'Colin? Oh, he's with the embassy. He's second in command to the military attaché. But that's not what takes up most of his time.' There was another delicate pause. 'Gosh, I ... I shouldn't be telling you all this. I'm so sorry. It's none of your concern.' She put up a hand to dab quickly at her eyes. 'I'm just being silly, I know. It's what all men do, or so my mother always tells me. I just didn't think it would happen so soon, that's all. We haven't even been married a year.'

He regarded her thoughtfully for a moment. 'I can't offer you any advice on that score, I'm afraid. But I *can* offer you something else.'

She looked at him, her eyes widening. 'What do you mean?' she asked, lowering her voice to almost a whisper.

'The "real" Egypt, as you call it. Allow me to be your guide. That is, if your husband won't object, of course?'

She paused, just long enough to let him know she'd understood the offer as he intended. 'That would be lovely,' she said breathlessly. 'And no, he won't object. I don't suppose he'll even notice I'm gone. Thank you, Rafiq. It's terribly kind of you.'

It was his turn to pause, showing her *he'd* understood. 'Then it's settled. My driver will call for you tomorrow morning around ten. Where do you stay in Cairo?'

'At the Windsor Hotel. Do you know it? Colin's been living in the single men's quarters at the embassy, but they're supposedly busy fixing us up a house. I have to say, it's rather odd, living in a hotel… but I quite like it. The staff are lovely. Very discreet.'

His mouth lifted in a slight smile. Yes, they understood each other well. 'Yes, I know the Windsor. Well, Susan, I look forward to seeing you tomorrow.' He got up, kissed her hand again and quickly left the verandah.

She sat for a few minutes more as she finished her cigarette, watching the smoke disappear in long, scrolling drifts. Then she summoned the doorman and asked him to order her a taxi. To the few diners who'd witnessed the earlier argument, she cut a beautiful if rather lonely figure. Just another expatriate wife who had found out the hard way just what it would take to keep a marriage intact in the Levantine heat.

His driver was there at ten o'clock on the dot. The car – a long, silver Buick – was parked, engine gently purring, directly outside the entrance. The doorman escorted her solicitously under a parasol. The driver leaped out as she approached and opened the car door. She was wearing a white summery dress of broderie anglaise, falling to just below the knee with capped, slightly puffed sleeves and a square, low neckline. White, wedge-heeled sandals, a single-strand pearl necklace and a floppy straw hat completed her look. To passers-by, she was the very embodiment of upper-class English beauty and charm.

The driver hurried back to his side and explained in broken English that they would be stopping by his master's offices to fetch him. 'Five minute,' he promised, swinging the car around. 'No long.'

She smiled prettily to show she wasn't concerned and turned to look out of the window. As they crossed the Nile and passed the ornate opera house, the elegant, French colonial city gave way to modern-day Cairo, street after dusty street of boxy, faceless city blocks without any distinguishing features. Here there were as many people on foot as there were donkeys and cars.

They were heading towards Cairo University, she saw. The driver turned onto Sudan Street and pulled up in front of a blank, nondescript build-ing. A uniformed guard saluted smartly and lifted the boom gate. They slid into the side entrance and he turned off the engine. A tiny tremor of disquiet wormed its way up her stomach. Why had they stopped here?

'Master office,' the driver said quickly, sensing her fear. 'Wait here.'

'Oh, yes, of course.' She tried to smile reassuringly.

Suddenly she saw him exit the building via a side door. He was with two other officers. He looked at the car and gave a short, brief wave. One of the men peered at the car, clearly noticing her in the back seat. There was a short exchange between them, then Rafiq broke away from the group and walked towards her. The driver jumped out immediately to open the door for him.

His lemon-scented aftershave curled pleasingly around her nostrils as he got in. '*Marhaba*,' he said with a slow, laconic smile. 'I wasn't sure if you'd actually come.'

'Why wouldn't I?' she asked brightly. She removed her hat and placed it between them. He looked down at it for a brief second, considering her action.

'You'll need that,' he remarked as the driver reversed the car into the main road. 'It's going to be hot today.' He rapped on the window and barked out a quick instruction in Arabic. He turned back to her. 'How long did you say you'd been here? Have you managed to pick up any Arabic?'

'Not a word, I'm afraid,' she said cheerfully. 'I'm absolutely hopeless at languages. My poor Mama. I had a French governess for most of my childhood and I still can't manage much more than *bonjour*, sadly. But your English is *perfect*.'

'It's kind of you to say, but no, it's not perfect. I spent a few months at Sandhurst.'

'Well, it sounds perfect to me,' she said demurely. He was testing her, she realised quickly. Small questions, nothing anyone would notice... but she did, of course. *How long did you say you'd been here?* Did he suspect her? she wondered uneasily.

'Was your husband also at Sandhurst?'

'Oh, goodness, no. No, he went straight from university. He's the linguist between us, actually. He read Arabic at Cambridge. But... listen, do you mind if we *don't* talk about Colin? I do so want to enjoy the day properly. With you.'

'Of course,' he said smoothly. 'I asked the driver to take us to the Pyramids first. It's where every tour of Cairo should begin.'

'How absolutely splendid! Well, if we *begin* at the Pyramids, where do you suggest we end?' she asked, angling her knees very slightly so that they lightly touched his. She felt his whole body stiffen. She pulled away, but carefully, so as not to alarm him, and looked out of the window.

He was harder to read than she'd anticipated. Perhaps Lord Hamilton was right? Perhaps he wasn't interested in women? She didn't think so, somehow. She'd been in the company of enough homosexual men to read the signs and Rafiq wasn't giving off *those*. No, his cautiousness had to do with something else. Again, she felt the momentary uneasy twinge of fear.

They drove south, in the direction of Giza. She pretended to marvel at the city appearing in snatches on either side of the impressive highway.

'It's all so very *modern*,' she said, pointing to new construction sites as they were come upon in a flash then left behind.

'What did you expect? Squalor?' he asked politely.

'No, not at all,' she said hastily. 'It's very beautiful, I must say.'

He turned to look at her. 'And what is it you're *not* saying?'

She was momentarily thrown off-balance. There it was again. He seemed to be probing for something beyond her words and gestures. She tried to make light of his question. 'Oh, it's silly, I know, but I suppose I keep thinking of films like *Lawrence of Arabia* – you know, lots of narrow, twisting streets and carpet-sellers and crowded bazaars ... Old Cairo, I expect.'

'Oh, there's plenty of *that*, if that's what you want to see,' he said dismissively. 'Just go to Al Qasr al-Ayni, right there, just by your hotel. You'll see Lawrences of Arabia everywhere.' His tone was unexpectedly bitter. She'd obviously hit a nerve.

She touched his hand lightly. 'That's not what I meant,' she said quietly.

'I'm sorry.' This time he made no move to reject her touch. 'I'm being unfair.'

'Why do you say that?' she asked, turning her knees towards him again.

He looked down at her hand, pale and slender against his own. Her wedding ring glinted angrily in the sunlight. 'Are we a museum?' he murmured, sliding his hand from under hers and turning hers over, palm upwards. He traced the line of her thumb. She felt her whole body shiver. 'Are we never to free ourselves of our past?' She shook her head dumbly, unsure of how to respond.

'That's how you would prefer to see us,' he said, running a finger along the length of hers. 'Am I right?'

She shook her head again. She struggled against the urge to snatch her hand away. Her entire arm felt as though it were on fire. Then, as abruptly as he'd begun, he stopped, releasing her hand.

'I'm sorry,' he said again. 'Forgive me.'

'For what?' she asked.

He was playing with her, she realised slowly. Disturbingly, she wasn't as in control as she'd have liked. The reticence she'd sensed in him had nothing to do with her earlier suspicion, or Lord Hamilton's passing comment. On the contrary. There was a flammable sexual energy lying below his skin that welled up like oil beneath the earth's crust, heating him. She'd felt it more than once. Now she realised why she feared it. It brought someone else to mind.

'Can I see you again?'

The driver pulled up smartly in front of the Windsor. He waited for the signal from Rafiq to jump out to open her door.

She looked at him in the darkening interior of the car. It was nearly six o'clock. The sinking sun cast long, deep shadows on the ground. *Put some distance between you.*

'I ... I had a lovely day today,' she said slowly. 'Really. I can't thank you enough for—'

'Please. I *must*.'

She drew in a quick breath. 'I ... I don't know. I ... I don't think—'

He put a hand on her arm. She jumped at his touch. 'Don't,' he said quickly. 'Don't think. Just say "yes".'

She swallowed nervously. 'When?' She couldn't think clearly.

'Saturday. I'll send the driver for you.' He made no mention of her husband.

She looked at him. 'I ... I could tell him I'm going to visit a friend,' she began hesitantly. 'I've got an old school friend. In Alexandria. I ... I could tell him I'm going to stay with her.'

He dismissed her marital arrangements with a quick, impatient wave. *That's your business.* He looked at her and nodded. 'Saturday. I'll be waiting.'

42

'What do you mean?' There was a sharpness to Lord Hamilton's voice that she'd never heard before.

She swallowed nervously. 'I ... I think he suspects something.'

'I see.' He waited.

'It's just ... it's just a feeling I have. I can't put my finger on it—'

'This isn't like you, Katherine. I put you onto this job precisely because you're one of the few agents we have who *doesn't* operate through instinct. You've always worked with the facts.'

'It's not that ...' she began hesitantly.

'Then what is it? *Is* the man queer? Is that the problem?'

'No, no, nothing like that. Not at all. It's ... it's probably nothing,' she concluded lamely.

'Do you want me to put someone else on it?'

'No, of course not. I'm just ... I was just a little concerned, that's all.'

'Well, unless I'm missing something, Katherine, you haven't actually communicated your concern to me yet. If there's something concrete to worry about, then by all means do so. If not, I suggest you get on with it. You haven't got much time.'

She collected herself. Now was not the time to drop the ball. 'I'm sorry, Lord Hamilton. I don't know what's wrong with me. I'll ... I'll make contact with him straight away.'

'You do that.' The line went dead.

She stood holding the receiver in hand, feeling uncharacteristically gauche. It was Thursday. Saturday was two whole days away and she was due to return to Baghdad the following week. Lord Hamilton was right: there was very little time.

43

Light from the outside filtered in through the patterned grilles across the windows, casting shadows of solid black onto their skin. Across the city, drifting easily across the rooftops, the call to prayer began. *Allahu akbar. Ash hadu an la ilaha ill Allah.* She knew the words by heart, though she was careful not to mumble them.

Rafiq slept deeply, like a child, one hand flung away from his body, the other resting limply on her stomach. She moved carefully, trying not to wake him, and reached for her wristwatch lying on the bedside table. It was nearly six. Her whole body was aching.

'Where are you going?'

She turned back in surprise. She'd thought him dead to the world.

'Nowhere,' she whispered. 'I was just checking my watch.'

'Why? I thought you didn't have to go back tonight?'

'I ... I don't,' she said quickly, trying not to let her nervousness show. 'I was just wondering what the time was.'

'Come here.' He patted the empty space beside him, still damp from her own body. She moved back towards him, trying not to stare. She had already seen the tough side of him: the deeply tanned, almost leathery skin; the dark hair that covered his chest like a pelt; the hard, calloused hands – soldier's hands. He had a cracked collarbone – a fall from a horse, he told her – and a burn down the side of one arm that had left the skin puckered and raw-looking, but the scars and dents only served to reinforce the sense of a body that had pushed itself to its limits and beyond. But when he raised his arm to shield his eyes from the light and she saw the pale unblemished skin where the sun hadn't reached, she caught her breath. She wasn't prepared for the delicate, almost feminine whiteness of it. To cover her confusion, she turned her face into his chest. A treacherous rush of sweet, erotic anticipation swept through her. He reached out and stroked her cheek, letting his fingers trail lightly against her skin. Her muscles contracted automatically, trembling underneath his fingertips. He paused for a moment, letting her settle, then he suddenly drew a line straight down to her sex. She gasped as he plunged his finger deep inside her. She groaned, straining towards him, her body seeking greedily for more of him, but he held her down with his free hand. He was in complete control. His finger teased its way inside her and slowly withdrew, stopping only to lightly trace her hard nub of pleasure before slipping his finger back inside her again. All the while his eyes were on her face, watching her with a concentration that caused her to close her own, lest he see something in her that she ought to hide. She could feel his whole body tense, not just his penis, which remained magnificently erect, but everywhere … his neck, fingers, lips … everything swollen with need. She had never experienced anything like it.

The call to prayer ended and the night began to swiftly close in and still he did not take her. His finger remained in place, sliding in and out, caressing, stroking, fondling her … until she could stand it no longer. She hurriedly shoved his hand aside and in a single move that surprised them both, she straddled him, taking all of him inside her. He met her hunger, exploding inside her with a growl that seemed torn from his throat. It reverberated deep inside her, long after they were both exhausted and spent.

44

There was no sound in the bathroom other than her breathing. She sat on the floor, a towel wrapped loosely around her waist, with her head in her hands. She'd stood under the shower for so long that her skin had wrinkled. Her fingers discovered the wetness that leaked from her tightly closed eyes onto her bare knees. She lifted the back of her hand and wiped her nose and cheeks impatiently. Snatches of their talk in the early hours of the morning came back to her.

'Your name's not Susan, is it?'

'How do you know?'

She was too slow to react. He knew, then. After a moment, a breathy half laugh against her neck.

'So who are you?'

She didn't answer. His voice in the dark was a vibration through his breast. He made love to her again and it took the place of words she couldn't form. *He knew. He knew and he didn't seem to care.* It put paid to any thoughts she had of pushing him for anything more.

A half-strangled sound broke into her thoughts. It took her a moment to realise it had come from her. She let her knees slide forwards until she was sitting on the floor with her legs splayed in front of her, a ragdoll pose, out of childhood. She began to weep, softly at first, then increasingly loudly, until she was hoarse with the effort of howling. Her hands were balled fists that pummelled her thighs, her stomach, sides of her head. She hadn't cried like that in years... perhaps never. She cried until there was nothing left – not a drop of saliva in her mouth, not a single duct with tears left to fall. Time passed. It could have been five minutes or five hours, she had no sense of it.

A wave of exhaustion broke over her and she rolled to one side, gasping as her cheek touched the cold tiled floor. She lay very still, waiting for her galloping heartbeat to return to normal, forcing herself not to think. In seventeen years she had not uttered his name out loud. Not once. Not even quietly, whispering it to herself. Suddenly her tongue and her body and her heart were thick with his name.

She zipped up the suitcase and lifted it off the bed. She looked around the hotel room. There was nothing left to indicate anyone had ever been there. She bent down to pick a thread off the floor.

There was a discreet tap at the door. She walked over quickly and opened it. The bellhop was standing outside.

'Those two,' she said firmly in fluent Arabic, pointing to the suitcase and the small overnight bag beside the bed.

'Very good, madame,' he said, darting in. She walked briskly ahead and took the lift to the ground floor. 'Your taxi is waiting outside, madame, just this way... yes, that one.' The doorman fussed over her. 'Please mind the step.' He snapped his fingers and the taxi drew smartly up to the kerb. The boot was opened, her bags were stowed, a tip bestowed, the door slammed shut.

'Where to, madame?' the driver enquired as they pulled into the street.

'The airport.' She was running away.

PART SEVEN
REVOLUTION
1958–1959
Libby / Kit

45

The strained, tinny-sounding voice of a BBC newscaster woke them. Paul's little transistor radio was on the bedside table.

'A group of Iraqi army officers have staged a coup in Iraq and over-thrown the monarchy. Baghdad Radio announced this morning that the army has liberated the Iraqi people from domination by a corrupt group put in power by imperialist forces.'

'What was that?' Paul mumbled, raising an arm to shield his eyes from the early morning sun.

'Something's happened in Bagdad,' she replied as calmly as she could. Her heart was beating fast. 'A coup d'état, or some such.'

'What?' Paul sat bolt upright. He reached across and turned the volume up. The newscaster's voice filled the small bedroom.

'According to Major-General Abdul Karim el Qasim, the country's new prime minister, defence minister and commander-in-chief, Iraq will be a republic that will maintain ties with other Arab countries. It is said that some twelve thousand Iraqi troops based in neighbouring Jordan have been ordered to return. Baghdad Radio also announced that King Faisal II, Crown Prince Abdul Illah and Nuri es Saïd, prime minister of the Iraq-Jordan Federation, have been assassinated.'

Paul turned to look at her, his eyes widening. 'Did you hear that? Jesus Christ! What's happening?'

Her mind was racing. 'I ... I've no idea,' she said, trying to appear surprised.

'I bet all hell's broken loose,' Paul exclaimed, jumping out of bed. 'Bloody good job *we* weren't there! What the hell's going to happen now? We're supposed to be going back next week! I'd better put a call through to the office.'

'I'm sure foreigners will be safe,' Kit said quickly. She watched as Paul picked up his trousers. 'You probably won't be able to get through to Baghdad just yet. Where are you going?'

'To get the paper.' Paul was already donning his coat.

She lay back as the door closed after him. Her heart was racing. She listened intently to the broadcast again. Prime Minister Nuri es Said had escaped, it turned out, but his whereabouts were unknown. It had happened much faster than anyone had anticipated, catching them all by surprise. And she was partly to blame.

Paul looked up as she came into the kitchen. He was glued to the television screen.

'Are you off somewhere?' he asked, surprised to see her dressed in a coat and hat.

'Yes, I forgot to tell you. I'm going up to town.'

'Whatever for?'

'The estate agent rang yesterday... it completely slipped my mind. They've found someone for the flat, apparently, for when we go back. I thought I'd take advantage and do a spot of shopping for the girls. You know how you all hate being dragged around the shops. I'll be back at teatime.'

'Oh. Yes, all right. You sure you don't want me to come along?'

'No, darling. You stay with the girls. I'll be back before you know it.' She blew him a hurried kiss before he could question her any further and quickly left the house.

The train was crowded. The carriages were full of men in dark suits and bowler hats, stockbrokers and bankers, she guessed, on their way to work. There were young girls too, smartly dressed in suits with pillbox hats, who chattered non-stop, like birds. After months in the Middle East, England seemed to her like a foreign country.

She was met at Embankment by a man who stepped forwards as soon as she came up the escalator. She'd never seen him before but he seemed to know who she was.

'Mrs Kentridge?' He was young and very earnest-looking with round, wire-rimmed spectacles and large, bony hands.

'Yes?'

'I'm Martin Holdsworthy. Lord Hamilton sent me to fetch you. Car's just waiting outside.'

She followed him without a word. Her stomach was in knots. She had no idea what lay ahead.

Lord Hamilton was waiting for her upstairs in the River Room.

'Up the stairs and through the second door on your right,' the doorman informed her loftily as soon as they arrived at the imposing and elegant National Liberal Club, Lord Hamilton's London base.

Martin Holdsworthy waited discreetly until she'd been relieved of her coat and hat and then stuck out his hand. 'I'll just wait for you here,' he said cheerfully. 'I expect I'll be driving you back.'

She was ushered up the magnificent marble staircase by a smartly uniformed man in a top hat and tails. The room, with its ornate, lofty ceilings, rich mahogany panelling and countless statues, was oddly soothing. It spoke of centuries of tradition and order, of a measured calm in a world that was changing before their very eyes.

'Ah, Katherine.' Lord Hamilton looked up as she approached the table. He was with someone. 'Do join us.'

She sat down opposite him, her knees pressed tightly together. Her hands were suddenly clammy. She'd heard nothing from him since her abrupt flight from Cairo.

'This is Simon Pender. He'll be taking over the Middle East desk.'

Simon Pender nodded gravely. He was young and rather stern-looking. He didn't pretend not to be studying her as he accepted a menu.

'So, how are you, my dear? It's been positively ages since I've seen you,' Lord Hamilton said. He made no mention of Cairo.

'Very well, thank you, your Lordship,' she murmured.

'Oh, I think we can dispense with those formalities, don't you?' he said, chuckling a little. 'I'm assuming you've heard the news?'

'Yes … I have.' She looked uncertainly at him. She had no idea what Simon Pender knew, if anything.

'Bit of a bugger's muddle,' Lord Hamilton said ruefully.

'That's putting it mildly,' Pender murmured. 'Fact of the matter is, we've been caught with our proverbials down. In a manner of speaking, of course.'

She looked quickly at Lord Hamilton. His expression gave nothing away.

'Wh-why do you say that?' she asked, hoping her voice didn't betray her nerves.

'We had an operative out in Cairo earlier in the year. Suzette de Vere. I never met her, but she was apparently a leftover from SOE 1945. Your team were running her.' He turned briefly to acknowledge Lord Hamilton. 'She was supposed to feed back intel on one of the Syrians we've been watching but no one quite knows what happened. She bolted, apparently. Just bloody disappeared. Vanished.'

Kit swallowed. 'Disappeared? Is … is she dead?'

'That's the thing. We're not sure. There's been no body, no reporting of a death … nothing. But no one's heard from her. She just vanished into thin air. Didn't make her last meet, checked out of the hotel and hasn't been seen since. Anyway, that's not the point. It's bad luck to lose a good agent, and all that, but the point is, we've been following Nasser for the past year when it's the bloody Iraqis we should be worried about.' He paused, and then turned to Kit. 'Now, I understand your husband's in Baghdad. IPC, I'm told?'

'Yes, but we're actually on leave at the moment,' Kit said quickly. 'The whole family's in London. I don't suppose anyone's sure what's going to happen now. We were supposed to be going back in a couple of weeks' time.'

'Oh, we'll have him transferred, don't worry. Besides, in a couple of weeks' time IPC might not exist, to be honest. It'll be the first thing they do. Nationalising state assets always seems to follow a coup. We were considering whether it might be better to operate out of Oman for the foreseeable.'

'Oman?' Kit's eyes widened.

'Mmm. Things have quietened down over the past few months. Sultan's deeply grateful to us for helping restore order. He's given us two RAF bases at Masirah and Salalah. It's a relatively safe base. And it'll help us keep tabs on old Talib. I've a feeling we haven't seen the last of him yet.'

Kit remained silent. Lord Hamilton had obviously protected her but she had no idea why.

'It's a good posting,' Lord Hamilton said slowly.

His hands were marked with liver spots, Kit noticed, swallowing hard. Although it had only been a few months since Cairo, he looked even older now, almost frail. 'Remind me again – what's his current position?'

'He's the senior distribution manager.'

'Get onto it, will you, Pender?'

'Yes, your Lordship. Straight away.'

'Good man. Now, perhaps if you don't mind leaving us … we've a fair bit to catch up on. Holdsworthy'll see her home.'

Simon Pender leaped up. 'Absolutely. In that case, I'll head back to Whitehall. Lovely to have finally met you, Katherine.' He turned to Kit with a half bow. 'Heard much about you. All good, of course.'

She nodded hesitantly. She turned to Lord Hamilton as soon as he was gone.

'Lord Hamilton,' she began, her voice low. 'I let you down in Cairo. Badly. I let the whole team down. But you covered for me. Why?'

He was silent for a moment. Then he picked up the menu. 'Would you like a glass? The Bordeaux's rather good, I'm told.'

He waited patiently until they'd been served then turned to her. The expression on his face was hard to read. 'You never met my eldest, did you? Daphne,' he said, almost wistfully.

Kit shook her head. 'No, never. Mrs Arscott mentioned her when I met you for the first time. In Claridge's. You probably don't remember.'

'Oh, I do,' Lord Hamilton said, smiling faintly. 'Indeed I do.'

'I didn't know who you were then. I didn't know anything. It seems an awfully long time ago.'

'It was a long time ago. The world's changed.' He leaned forwards suddenly. 'I'm not going to ask about Cairo, Katherine. I assume you had your reasons.' He brushed aside her gesture of protest. 'No. I meant it when I said you remind me of Daphne. Bright as a button, she was. Not that she isn't now,' he added hastily. 'Just … well, she's got other things on her mind now.'

'She's married, isn't she?' Kit asked.

He nodded, taking a long sip of wine, clearly savouring it. 'Yes, they all are. We've got twelve grandchildren between them. Delightful, every last one.'

There was a hesitation in Lord Hamilton's voice that prompted another question. 'But …?'

He sighed. 'I'm just being sentimental. When you began working for us, I often used to look at Daphne and then at you … and wonder. What makes this sort of life possible for one and not the other? There were quite a few of you, you know … young girls from very good families … doing the unthinkable. Did you never regret it?'

Kit took in a deep breath. They were in unfamiliar territory. During the war years, she'd seen him only intermittently, and only ever on assignment. At the time, they'd both been careful not to allow the shared bonds of their families and class to interfere with the job at hand. But the truth was he knew as much about her as anyone with whom she'd lived and worked over the past fourteen years did ... probably more.

She took a sip of her wine, 'It wasn't for me,' she said quietly at last. 'I just didn't want what everyone seemed to think I'd want. You know, a husband, a family ... a home. It just didn't seem ... enough, somehow.'

'But you've managed to have both. It might be an indelicate question, forgive me ... but it's been a good marriage, hasn't it?'

She nodded slowly. 'I suppose so.' She looked down at her hands. 'If SOE hadn't arranged it ... I don't know if it would ever have happened.'

'May I ask why?' Lord Hamilton was watching her intently.

She drew in her lower lip and waited a few moments before answering. 'Something happened to me,' she began carefully. 'A long time ago, when I was still in my teens.'

Lord Hamilton signalled discreetly for another two glasses of Bordeaux. 'You don't have to tell me if you don't want to,' he said, momentarily covering her hand with his. She stared at it for a second.

'No, I want to. I've ... I've never told anyone. Not the whole story. Just ... bits.'

'What really happened in Germany?' he asked gently.

She looked across the table at him, her eyes widening. 'How did you know it happened in Germany?' she asked, her voice suddenly low.

'Faunce,' he said simply. 'Oh, he wouldn't give any details, of course not. But it doesn't take a genius to work it out. What happened to the child?'

She swallowed. It took her a few seconds to compose herself. 'I don't know. I gave him up when he was a few weeks old. Mrs Arscott arranged it.'

'Ah.' Lord Hamilton nodded as if confirming something he already knew. 'But there's something else, isn't there?'

'Yes,' she said simply. 'After it happened and I came to London, I didn't think I could ever ... well, be happy again, I suppose. But I ... I then met someone during the war. Just after I started work, actually. He was in a band. He was the trumpeter.'

'Café de Paris?'

'How did you know?'

'It was hard to miss the news. American chap?'

She nodded again. 'Yes. From Chicago.' It hurt to say the words.

'A Negro chap?'

She nodded again. 'Yes.'

If there was another question to be asked, he chose not to voice it. 'You never cease to surprise me, Katherine,' he said finally. 'Now, on to the matter at hand.' He leaned forwards. 'I don't know what happened in Cairo and I don't want to know. I just want to be sure that it won't happen again.'

'It won't. Ever.'

'Good.' He reached down and pulled his briefcase onto the table. He opened it and slid out a manila envelope. 'Inside you'll find a dossier on the man we're looking to cultivate. Talal bin Said Al-Said. He's the nephew of the current Imam. Eton, Sandhurst, Geneva... very erudite. We need to be sure he's on our side before we make our overtures.'

'Where will I find him?'

'He'll find you. You know how it's done. Keep me posted.' Lord Hamilton finished off the last of his wine. 'Now, my dear... if you'll excuse me.' He got up stiffly, reaching for his cane. He waved her concern aside. 'No, no... I'm quite all right. Don't get up. Finish your wine. That nice young man will be back – what was his name? Holdsworthy, that's it. He'll run you back to the Underground. Good luck, my dear. And do keep your wits about you. It's a delicate and dangerous time.'

And with that, he turned away and walked slowly out of the room, nodding stiffly to an old acquaintance on the way out.

Kit remained where she was, her half-empty glass of wine standing on the white tablecloth in front of her, but she made no move to pick it up. Her mind was a dark, terrible swirl of emotions.

She must have closed her eyes for when the voice broke through her thoughts, she shot up, startled. It was Martin Holdsworthy. He bent down, concerned.

'I say, are you all right?'

She nodded, dazed. 'Yes, yes... I'm fine. I... I must have just dozed off for a minute,' she stammered, looking around for her bag. 'It's the wine, I expect. Not used to it at lunchtime.'

'Yes, that must be it,' he agreed, still looking concerned. 'Can I carry anything?'

'Oh, no … I'm fine, honestly. I'd better get going … My family will be waiting.'

'I'll run you back to the station.'

'No, no need.' She waved him away. 'I'll walk. It's hardly any distance at all.'

'Are you sure?' He looked at her doubtfully.

'Quite sure,' she said firmly. 'I'm perfectly fine.'

'Well, I dare say you can't come to *too* much trouble between here and Embankment,' he said cheerfully. 'Goodbye, Mrs Kentridge.'

'Goodbye,' she murmured, picking up her bag.

She watched him thread his way back through the tables until he disappeared from sight. Then she shouldered her bag and followed suit. She stopped at the cloakroom and collected her coat and hat, then stepped back out into the mid-July sunshine.

46

Libby looked at her parents suspiciously. 'Oman? Where's Oman?'

Her mother had the bright, authoritative air of a carefully prepared speech. 'It's on the sea, darling. It's absolutely beautiful. It's got lots of long, sandy beaches. It's right on the Indian Ocean. You'll love it and—'

'How do *you* know? You don't even *know* what I like!' Libby interrupted her angrily.

'Libby! That's no way to talk to your mother!' Her father glared at her. 'Anyway, it's decided. We're going. I've been offered a new job and—'

'*You* can go if you want! *I'm* not going!' Even she was surprised by the way it came out of her mouth.

Both parents simply stared at her. She felt the horrid hot prick of tears behind her eyes. The last thing she wanted to do was cry in front of them, so she hastily slid off her chair and bolted from the room.

'What on earth's the matter with her?' she heard her father exclaim as she ran up the short flight of stairs to her room.

'Just leave her be. She'll come round.' That was Mother. Distant, calm and unperturbed.

It only infuriated Libby even further. She slammed the door behind her and gave into the wave of panic that washed over her.

'Damn you!' she muttered breathlessly, angrily. 'Damn all of you!'

She sank down to the ground, hot tears of rage building up in her throat. Oman? *Why?* She was just beginning to *like* Baghdad. For the first time since they'd arrived, she was beginning to find her feet at school. It had taken her almost a year to claw her way into the tight-knit group of girls who ruled the roost. Amongst the Claires and Susans and Joannas who decided who was 'in' and who was 'out', insider status had finally – finally – been granted. She had no idea why the acceptance had come – or even why it had been so long in coming – only that it had, and she was pathetically, absurdly grateful. Overnight she'd gone from being the girl whom everyone laughed at for having the wrong socks, the wrong skirt, the wrong pencil or satchel…

Everything about her was wrong. When she put her hand up in class, Clare Jorgenssen, the spoiled only daughter of the Norwegian supplies director at IPC, would roll her eyes. But if she kept quiet Susan Hetherington, the daughter of the British High Commissioner, would whisper to the others, 'See, that new girl doesn't know a thing. How stupid can she be?'

There was no way to win. Her packed lunches, lovingly prepared by Madame Abbayas, were instantly deemed 'too smelly, too Arabic, too *local*'. Miriam, who walked her to school every day and who was her best friend, was 'a wog'.

'She looks a bit like a wog herself, don't you think?' she overheard two of the prettiest girls talking about her in the lockers one day. 'She's almost as dark as they are. Yuk!'

She was too embarrassed to ask her mother what a 'wog' was. Instead she told Miriam not to come past the school gates when she came to fetch her. It was wrong of her, she knew, but she so longed to be some-one's friend – *anyone's* friend – that she simply allowed herself to drift along on the tide of collective snobbery and racism. She was too young and inexperienced in the ways of international schools to see that she was simply the last new girl in a line of many and that her assignation to the role of class scapegoat had absolutely nothing to do with *her*. She was just the wrong girl in the wrong place at the wrong time.

For the whole of that miserable first year she'd looked on enviously from the sidelines, longing to be included. And then one day, out of the blue, Clare Jorgenssen and Joanna Barrington-Browne asked her if she wanted to come with them to the swimming pool after school.

'Me?' She looked at them suspiciously. '*Me?*'

'Yes, *you*. Why? Is there another Libby Kentridge in here that we can't see?' Clare was loftily dismissive. 'Of course, if you don't *want* to come…'

'No, no, yes, yes. Yes, of course I want to come! I'm just… I just didn't… I…'

'Well, hurry up, then,' Joanna said primly. 'The driver's picking us up after school.'

'I'll just have to go home and get my bathing suit,' Libby stammered, her heart threatening to burst out of her chest.

'Can't your driver just drop you off at the Club?' Clare asked, already looking bored.

Libby jumped on the suggestion as if it were the cleverest thing she'd ever heard. She practically ran all the way home and threw herself at her mother, imploring her to take her to the Club at two o'clock. There was a brief, agonised wait whilst her mother muttered something about the heat and 'wouldn't it be better to go at four o'clock?' and 'why was it so important to go at two?' and 'didn't she know she was only trying to protect her skin?' and 'when she was grown up she'd thank her mother for it' and on and on. In the end, Libby threatened to kill herself if her mother didn't let her go and Kit, too stunned by the outburst to argue, simply gave in. It was the happiest day of her life.

And now her parents wanted to ruin everything by making her start all over again. Who knew if she'd be lucky a second time around?

Oman. She wanted to *die*.

47

Muscat, Oman – October 1958

The house in Qurum sat squarely on a hilltop overlooking the azure waters of the Gulf of Oman. The room faced both north and west. To the north, sweeping all the way around the house in a long, slow curve was the undulating glittering silky blue tent of the sea. To the west were the rocky, arid mountains that bounded Oman on almost all sides. It was a beautiful country, hard, rugged and inhospitable, which had curiously produced an almost inverse hospitality amongst its people. The Arabic spoken here was different but easy enough for Kit to follow. They'd only been in Muscat a few weeks but already she was becoming accustomed to its lilting musicality.

She sat at her desk, writing, her hand moving rapidly across the page from left to right. Her report on the function held the previous night at the French ambassador's residence was due in London that evening and she'd been too busy trying to organise their new household to pay it the proper attention.

Her target, Talal al-Said, hadn't appeared, despite the feverish rumours. Lord Harrington wasn't joking. In the tightly knit, bored-to-distraction community of foreigners and expatriates who lived and worked in the small governorate, Talal al-Said occupied a very particular role. Kit had yet to set eyes on the man, though she felt as though she already had. Amongst the wives of the men who drilled in the Gulf of Oman for oil, the thirty-something-year-old nephew of the ruling imam was a rare thing indeed. By all accounts he was a local who met – and matched – the expatriates on his own terms.

'Unbelievably good-looking,' was the whispered aside. 'I mean, just *unbelievably* good-looking.'

Kit had seen a photograph. A proud, haughty face looked out at the world from beneath his officer's cap.

A sudden burst of laughter from the street below broke her concentration. She sighed and got up from her desk. She pulled back the flimsy net curtains and looked down. Just visible through the bougainvillea was the enormous blue convertible American car that made Kit nervous just to look at it. It was Libby. She was back. Her friend Chip had brought her home.

She sighed. Libby had just turned fifteen and was already running wild. In Oman, she'd fallen in with a different crowd at school. Unlike the snobbish, rather docile English girls in Baghdad, whom she'd been desperate to befriend, here things were different. There were a good deal many more loud and ridiculously confident Americans, for one thing, and boys had suddenly started to notice her, including Chip whatever-his-name-was.

Libby was already as tall as Kit. She was lean and athletic, with Kit's languid grace, or so everyone said. But there the resemblance ended. Where Kit was icy-blonde with piercing blue eyes, Libby was the opposite. She was dark, almost sultry, with smooth, olive-toned skin that brought Mediterranean girls to mind. She'd grown into her looks, Kit thought, having gone from a rather awkward, too-tall-for-her-age teenager into a rather striking girl on the cusp of womanhood. She had Kit's wide mouth and perhaps something of her bone structure, but that was all. It was hard to believe they were mother and daughter. Eluned was completely different. She'd inherited Paul's strawberry-blond colouring, with brows and eyelashes as fine and pale as her hair. She had nothing of her elder sister's temperament either. Libby had been a quiet child, content with her own company, and aside from those imploring, beseeching eyes that followed Kit wherever she went, she hadn't demanded much. Eluned was her exact opposite. Almost from the minute she was born she claimed more attention and space than was her due. She could barely talk but the first words out of her mouth were 'I want'. It was partly the age gap, Kit knew. Thirteen years between them ... it was a lifetime. She rarely allowed herself to compare the relationship between her daughters to that of her and Lily ... Sometimes months went by when she didn't think about Lily, but every once in a while she was brought up short. Neither girl was anything like her or Lily ... and yet ... somehow, the odd trait slipped through, slipped out. Libby's habit of beginning a sentence and never finishing it ... that was Lily through and through. The way she turned inside herself when she thought no one was listening – it was thirteen-year-old Kit all over again. Usually Kit steeled herself against the memories; it was the only way to cope. But sometimes her steely will was no match for a memory that surfaced seemingly at will.

The car below idled throatily. She watched as Libby opened the door and got out, leaning against it to chat. She seemed reluctant to leave. Kit frowned. There was an impulsive flamboyance in Libby, just as there had been in Lily, stemming from the deep-seated desire to be liked, even loved. She knew that the first year in Baghdad had been hard on her, even if Libby said nothing. She'd gone out of her way to be likeable with the dreadful set of girls who'd been her classmates – pointless, really. They would never have let her in, not properly. Kit could see it clearly, even if Libby was blind.

Don't, Kit longed to tell her. *Just be yourself.* But how could she? The statement was absurd, coming from her. *Be yourself?* She wouldn't have known how. There were times when she had no idea who *she* was, much less her teenage daughter.

48

'Go on, don't be such a scaredy-cat. Hold it properly, like this. Okay, now take a small puff... not too much. Yeah, cool. Lean back. Wait for it to hit.'

Libby did exactly as instructed, leaning back against the hot sticky car seat. A few moments later, she was rewarded with a rush of pleasurably woozy light-headedness. She began to giggle.

Chip grinned at her. 'Take it easy. Here... give it to me.'

She passed the joint and closed her eyes. She inhaled deeply. All was right with the world once more. She'd flounced out of the dining room earlier that afternoon after another heated row with her mother but she couldn't remember what had started it. These days, it was all she seemed to do – argue with her mother. She was always sorry afterwards but she just couldn't help it. Mother was so ... *controlling*, so always in the right. And lately, the way Mother treated Father had begun to upset her. Once or twice she'd glanced up to catch a look on Mother's face when she thought no one was looking that sent a chill running straight through her, in spite of the relentless heat. Now, more than ever, it was as though her mother wished to be anywhere but there. Old, painful memories surfaced suddenly. The day she'd been caught in her mother's study; the sea-crossing from Cyprus when she'd seen that funny little man; and the afternoon in Baghdad when she and Miriam had gone to buy sweets. Her mother didn't quite add up, somehow. There was something missing, some essential element that would have made her whole and complete, like the other girls' mothers. It frightened Libby, as though she could see her mother but never have her within reach.

But now, none of that mattered. The joint was passed carefully around the car. Chip had 'scored' the dope from Musah, the night watchman at the compound in Muttrah, where most of the Americans lived.

Chip's father was one of the offshore rig managers. Chip was the most impressive person Libby had ever met. He feared nothing and no one, not even Mother. When he came to call for her in the light blue Chevrolet Impala, which was the only car of its kind in Muscat, he simply stood up in the driver's seat with the hood rolled all the way back and yelled out, 'Howdy, Mrs K,' which Libby thought was just about the bravest thing she'd ever seen anyone do.

The first time she'd brought him home with two of the other girls in her class at the American High School of Muscat, which was the only school available that wasn't a boarding school back in England or one of those dreadful Swiss schools to which some of her friends from Baghdad had been sent, she looked closely at her mother's face for what she was sure would be her reaction – distaste. But Mother took Chip calmly in her stride. It was on account of his looks and charm, Libby decided. No one else could possibly have got away with it.

Chip was tall and rangy with golden brown skin like hers and eyes that seemed permanently creased in a smile. He was bored with school, he declared as soon as they met. He was seventeen, two years older than Libby, and marking time until he could 'get the hell outta Dodge'. Libby didn't dare ask where or what 'Dodge' was. He smoked copious amounts of dope, drove the light blue Impala convertible that had been bought for his mother, who'd decided 'out of the blue', it was rumoured, *not* to return to the Gulf with her husband and son after the summer holidays and stayed behind in Warren, Pennsylvania.

'You mean she just left you and your dad all alone?' she asked breathlessly, overcome by a sudden rush of maternal feelings that she couldn't quite fathom at the thought of the two men sitting alone in the big house just down by the port. 'Did they get a divorce?'

Chip shook his head dismissively. 'Are you kidding? She likes the money, honey. She just doesn't like living *here*.'

'Oh, that's awful. I'm sorry,' she said awkwardly.

'What's to be sorry about? My old man's never around. I get to do what the hell I want. I got her car, didn't I?' He grinned lazily at her to show her that her sympathies were entirely misplaced.

Libby stole a sideways glance at him. 'So who does the cooking?' she asked, knowing as she asked it that it was a silly question. Here, as in Baghdad, cooks did the cooking. Servants did the cleaning. Gardeners did the gardening and drivers drove. Maids like their new girl, Salah, looked after the children. Fathers worked and mothers … well, they did whatever mothers did.

Again the fleeting shadow of doubt passed over her. Whatever it was her mother *did*, it wasn't what occupied the other mothers in Muscat. Neither Kerry nor Mary-Beth's mother had ever met Mother, despite several increasingly curious invitations to 'bring her over for tea or perhaps even a cocktail'.

'Is that your mom in the window?' Chip drawled, looking up at the window of her mother's study.

Libby looked up. She nodded. 'Yes, she's probably spying on me.'

'She's hot.'

Libby's mood instantly fell. 'Everyone's always going on about how beautiful she is,' she said sulkily. 'I don't know why.'

'Na, she ain't beautiful. But she's hot, if you know what I mean.'

Libby looked at him uncertainly. 'No she's not. She's just strange,' she said.

'Yeah, whatever.' Chip dismissed her words with a casual wave. 'I gotta go,' he said, putting his hands on the steering wheel to indicate he was moving off.

She opened the car door, too afraid to ask him where he was going. 'Are you … are you coming to school tomorrow?' she said in a rush, one hand hovering on the door handle.

'Maybe.' He shrugged nonchalantly. 'See how I feel. Later, baby.' He gunned the engine and swung the enormous car around. Libby watched as he roared off down the hill.

'Libby?' Her mother's voice stopped her. She looked up. Her mother was standing in the arched hallway that led to her study at the top of the stairs. For a second they stared at each other. 'Did you have a nice time?' her mother asked finally, mildly.

Libby shrugged. 'I guess so,' she said, imitating Chip's insouciance. But for once, her mother didn't take the bait. Libby was seized with a sudden unreliability of her own feelings.

'Hello?' Her father's voice interrupted them. 'Anyone home?' She heard the front door bang shut.

'Coming,' her mother called down.

Libby tensed, waited for her mother to pass so that she could escape

231

along the corridor to the quiet sanctity of her own room and fling herself face downwards on the bed, overcome with the desperate desire to be free of her own family and yet terrified at the thought of what it implied. Suddenly, as her mother drew level, she reached out unexpectedly and took Libby by the arm.

'Ouch,' Libby protested, taken by surprise. Had her mother smelled dope on her breath? Could she? 'Let me go,' she muttered angrily.

'Libby... don't.'

'Don't what?' Libby said, struggling to control her voice.

'Don't push us away. I know what you're going through. I did it too.'

'What are you talking about?' Libby's voice was a croak. It was gloomy in the hallway that was always shuttered against the fierce afternoon sun and she could only just make out her mother's face.

'Oh, *there* you are.' Her father's voice broke the tight, brittle silence that had enveloped them. He came bounding up the stairs towards them. 'What on earth are you two doing in the dark?'

'We're just coming.' Her mother moved off, leaving Libby standing in the hallway, trembling with a sense of having been led very close to something she'd longed to reach only to have it snatched away at the very last minute.

49

The foyer of the Intercontinental Hotel at Ras al Hamra was lit up like a Christmas tree. Ironic, Kit thought as she surveyed the bustling scene in front of her. It was Eid al-Adha, the 'Sacrifice Feast', which had fallen on the 3rd of December when the outside temperatures were anything but Christmassy. It was nearly forty degrees in the shade and the longed-for rains had yet to even form a whisper of a cloud on the relentlessly blue horizon. The hotel overlooked the bay. A kilometre or so offshore was Fahal Island, rising out of the sea like a clenched fist. Behind the hotel, the hard, stony mountains climbed back to the horizon.

She thought for a second of Chalfont Hall and the snowy fields that spread out from the house like a blanket at Christmas time. Very early on Christmas morning, she and Lily would creep down to the enormous pine tree that always stood in the hallway and count their presents before the servants came up to begin stoking the fires. She swallowed. What was wrong with her? For the second time in as many months she'd found herself thinking about Lily.

She shook herself briskly out of the past and turned to look at the gardens. The staff had strung fairy lights from palm tree to palm tree, encircling the gardens like a twinkling necklace of light. It was all very pretty and jolly and, in a much-appreciated nod to his Christian guests, the Sultan had waived the customary no-alcohol ban in the international hotels during the month of December and the expatriates were agog with excitement. She adjusted the straps on her white evening gown and squared her shoulders.

In the far corner of the room, Paul was already happily ensconced with his colleagues and their gaggle of overdressed wives. She looked around her. How much longer could she stand it? She shook herself again. She was being silly. Things were going according to plan. She'd met al-Said twice already and she could tell he was intrigued enough to seek her out when the opportunity might present itself. In all likelihood she would bump into him tonight. What more did she want? She'd dressed that evening with elaborate care, sitting at her dressing table for what seemed like hours, adjusting her dress, choosing her shoes and jewellery and applying her make-up with a steady, practised hand. Her hair was slicked back and fastened with a dramatic dark red silk rose, pinned just above her left ear. The dress was white and fitted, with a dramatic back opening and a thin black silk belt.

'Hi, Mrs K. You look ... incredible.'

She turned around in surprise. It was that boy ... Libby's friend.

'Oh, hello. It's Chad, isn't it?' she said deliberately.

'Chip,' he corrected her. 'But Chad's fine, too.'

His tone was ever so faintly mocking. Or was it? She looked him up and down quickly, caught off-guard. He was as tall as she was in her heels and in his dinner jacket looked a great deal older than she'd thought at first. How old *was* he? She struggled to remember what Libby had said about him. He was handsome, she thought to herself distractedly. And he knew it.

'Are you enjoying yourself, Mrs K?' he asked, a smile playing around his lips. He was teasing her.

'Yes. Yes, I am. Aren't you?' she asked, looking pointedly at the glass he held in his hand.

He waved it away languidly. 'Oh, this is only my first. But that's not what gets me going.' He smiled and patted his jacket pocket. 'A little pick-me-up before the party starts,' he said knowingly.

Her mouth dropped open. She was astounded at his cheek. 'I'm not sure I follow you,' she said sternly.

He looked at her and smiled. 'Yeah. That's what all you ladies say. Well, lemme know if you feel like a little pick-me-up. See you around, Mrs K.' He gave her a faintly mocking half salute and sauntered off.

She watched him go, unsure whether to smile or frown.

'Something funny, darling?' Paul looked up as she joined them at the table. She shook her head, gathering the silk skirt of her dress to one side and quickly sat down. Several pairs of eyes followed her as she leaned forwards to accept the offer of a light. The women at the table jealously averted their gaze. She sighed inwardly. It was going to be a long evening ahead. She hoped al-Said would arrive sooner rather than later.

Suddenly the men all began scraping back their chairs to stand up. She looked up. Her heart skipped a beat. It was the man she'd been waiting for, accompanied by a large entourage of assorted bodyguards and ministers. The women remained seated as the introductions were painstakingly, politely made, one by one. At last the piercing dark eyes came to rest on her. His chin moved downwards in acknowledgement.

'Ah, Mrs Kentridge. We've met before. At the opening of the children's library,' he reminded those present, in the same breath establishing and exposing the harmless expatriate preoccupations in his city that bound them all.

'Have we?' she murmured disarmingly. She looked around. Everyone was watching her closely. She stared boldly back at them.

The conversation, which had been broken by his arrival, hurriedly took up its flow again. Kit leaned back in her chair, listening peripherally to the rise and fall of voices around her, conscious of his glittering black eyes as they came to rest on her, and smoked, holding herself a little apart from the company again. Behind him, just within her view, one of his bodyguards stood, his whole body held stiffly to attention. Their eyes met for a brief second. A small muscle moved in his jaw. She had long ago learned to read the tiny signs that people gave out unwittingly and frowned. The look signalled recognition beyond the blank professionalism of a bodyguard, as if he knew her. As quickly as it had surfaced, it disappeared. He looked blankly back at her.

She turned back to the table and concentrated for a few moments on the conversation drifting around her. When they rose at last to go into the banqueting hall for dinner, she stole a quick look at the bodyguard again. No, she'd imagined it.

She walked in next to Paul but could feel the heat of al-Said's eyes on the small of her back as they went. Yes, he'd noticed her all right.

50

She stood for a moment in the doorway, her hand hovering over the handle. She took a deep breath and opened the door. Paul was lying on the bed with his eyes closed. She walked softly towards him, balancing a teacup in one hand. He looked up as she sat down next to him and placed it carefully on the bedside table. He put up a hand to shield his eyes from the light.

'Here you go. I brought you a cup of tea,' she said, smiling faintly. 'And some aspirin.'

He struggled upright. 'You're a godsend.' He leaned back against the pillows. 'Bit of bash last night, eh? I had far too much to drink.' He swallowed the aspirins carefully, one after the other. He looked at her again. 'Are you going somewhere? You're already dressed.'

She nodded. 'Al-Said's asked me to join him and his family on a picnic at Daghmar. Apparently one of his wives is just back from London and is dying to practise her English.'

'Daghmar? That's miles away. How will you get there?'

'We'll be driving down in convoy. He's sending a driver over to fetch me. You don't mind, do you, darling? I know it's your only day off but the girls are here.'

'Don't you want to take Libby with you? She's been cooped up since the school holidays started.'

Kit got up. 'No, it's an awfully long drive and I think his children are quite a bit younger. I've said she can go to the pool with her friends. That American boy will take them . . . what's his name?'

'Chip. I saw him last night, as a matter of fact.' Paul looked up at her. 'Don't you think . . .' he began hesitantly. He stopped.

'What?'

He seemed oddly shy. 'Isn't he a bit old for her?'

She was surprised. Paul rarely, if ever, commented on the children. 'He's harmless,' she said firmly. 'A bit of a show-off, but harmless.'

'It's not him I'm worried about.'

She stared at him. 'What on earth do you mean?'

'Libby. She's running wild, Kit. Haven't you noticed?'

She put a hand up to her throat. 'No, she's fine. She's just a little . . . headstrong, that's all. She's only fifteen, Paul.'

'Yes, I know, but they're different these days . . . these young teenagers. It's not like it was when *we* were fifteen. We were so . . . well, innocent. It's different now.'

She couldn't speak. At fifteen, her own innocence had been shattered.

'No,' she said finally, in a voice she hoped was steady. 'No, it's not. But she's fine. She's finding her feet, that's all.'

He drew in his lower lip, catching it between his teeth, as though thinking through what he might say next.

She pulled in the wide red belt on her red-and-white polka dot summer dress and picked up her bag. 'I'll be back before tea,' she said quickly, preventing the conversation from going any further. She was gone before he could answer.

There was a burgundy and cream Daimler parked outside. Al-Said's driver was waiting for her. He jumped out as she approached and opened the door with a flourish. He made sure she was settled comfortably in the back seat before running around to his own seat. He started the engine and they rolled slowly down the hill. It was a Saturday morning and the roads were quiet. Changing from lane to lane along the seafront, pausing at the traffic light . . . flashes of sunlight glinting angrily off the sea . . . a whiff of something sweet against the carbon monoxide of a passing car . . . men in white, flowing *thawbs*, sitting in clusters around

236

heavy ornamental hookahs, which snaked around their feet... shop signs in flowing Arabic script...

She took it all in, deep into her lungs and body, like oxygen, lifeblood. Tables outside roadside cafés were like small islands. Occasionally the black-cloaked figure of a woman appeared briefly and disappeared. As they approached the fort where al-Said lived with his extended family of caregivers and takers, the streets narrowed, alleyways appearing like crevices in the white, smooth stone façades of thickly clustered buildings.

There was a brief wait outside the fort's gates. Then the massive wooden side door, studded through with iron bolts, opened and a group of men appeared with al-Said in their midst, deep in conversation. White men dressed in the ubiquitous garb of Europeans abroad – crumpled linen suits, panama hats and florid faces. As the car pulled up alongside, the tallest of the three turned in her direction. She recognised the unmistakable profile of Sir Anthony Eden. The nerves in her stomach began to flutter.

Al-Said broke away from the group and walked towards the car. The driver leaped out and opened the door for him.

'I'll ride down to Daghmar with you,' al-Said said, getting in next to her. 'You don't mind, do you?'

She shook her head. 'Not at all. But who are all these men?' she asked, again hoping her voice was steady. 'I thought this was to be a family picnic.'

He said nothing for a moment. His face was turned away from her. 'Come now, Mrs Kentridge,' he said quietly. 'Let's not pretend. You know who I am. And I know who you are. Back-door diplomacy. I believe that's what it's called.'

She stole a sideways glance at him. 'How do you know who I am?' she asked in a low voice.

'Even if I hadn't been told, I'd have known. You have that sort of face,' he said, settling himself into the plush leather seat. He nodded to the driver to move forwards. 'We'll take the lead,' he said in Arabic. 'The rest will follow. Not too fast. The old English one isn't well.'

'Isn't he?' she asked, surprised.

'Your Arabic is excellent.'

'Thank you, but I don't use it as often as I'd like,' she said as they pulled away from the fort to join the recently completed highway. 'What's wrong with Sir Anthony, if I may ask?'

'Fevers. An ulcer. Who knows?'

'Why is he here?'

'Why are *you* here?' he parried the question. 'Although I should know the answer to that, no? Hamilton wants to know if I'm to be trusted. I presume you're the one to tell him.'

She was quiet for a moment. 'What have they offered you?' she asked.

'Support. Logistics. Troops, if it comes to that. As you know, Britain has been instrumental in helping my uncle maintain rule. And you? What have they asked *you* to do?'

'There's someone they'd like you to meet. I'm supposed to feel you out before they set it up. There's a lot at stake, as I'm sure you know. Iraq took everyone by surprise.'

'Including you?'

She swallowed. How much did he know? There was no way of telling. She nodded carefully. 'Yes, including me.'

'So when is this meeting in London supposed to take place?' he asked mildly.

'It's not in London, actually. It's in Scotland. At Cheswick House, near Berwick-upon-Tweed. It's Lord Hamilton's country home.'

'I see. When?'

'As soon as I give the go-ahead,' she said calmly.

'And will you?' He turned to look at her.

She met his eyes. She had nothing to go on but instinct. She took a deep breath. She nodded slowly. 'Yes. Yes, I will.'

51

Her pen flew quickly over the paper.

I do think we can trust him. It's been three weeks and, so far, he hasn't slipped up once. Sir Anthony and Glubb were here again last weekend and everyone agrees that he's the one we should be talking to.

The phone rang suddenly, shattering the quiet. It was Friday noon and the call to prayer had just been sounded. Everyone was out. Eluned was at nursery and Libby was at school. Not even the maids were in. They'd gone to the market together earlier.

She made a small 'tsk' of annoyance and got up. 'Coming, coming,' she muttered, running down the stairs. 'Hello?'

'Kit?' It was a man's voice, an English-sounding voice, deep, well spoken.

'Who is it?' She didn't recognise the caller.

'You probably don't remember me, Kit, but that's not important right now. I'll explain when I see you. It's an emergency. There's a car outside. Grab whatever you can – passports, papers – and leave. The driver will pick up your family and bring you to the British Embassy. I'll meet you at the gate. Go! You don't have a minute to spare.'

The hairs on the back of her neck stood straight up. There was something in the man's voice, a distant, long-buried note of familiarity, as though she'd heard it before, but she couldn't place him.

'What's going on?' she asked fearfully. 'Has something happened?'

'I can't say over the phone. Trust me, Kit. I'll be waiting. The driver's name is Ahmed.'

'Wait! But I don't know who you are! How do I know this isn't a trap?'

'You don't. But trust me.' He hesitated for a second. 'I was with you that night,' he said, his voice dropping.

She swallowed. 'Which night?' But she already knew.

'The night you met him. D'you remember what we drank? Monopole. Heidsieck thirty-nine.'

She felt her knees begin to tremble. In an instant it all came back flooding back. The cellar. The music. The smoke. Earl.

'*Joel?*' And then it clicked properly. 'It's you!' she gasped. 'You're the bodyguard!'

'Kit, not now,' he cut her short. 'Just get your passports, grab coats for the girls and get the hell out of there. I'll meet you at the gate. Hurry. I mean it.' There was an abrupt click and the line went dead.

She stood where she was for a second, too stunned to move, then her years of training kicked in. She tore back upstairs, grabbed a holdall from the wardrobe and hurriedly stuffed the essentials in. *Joel. Ruth. Earl. Love. Friendship.*

Like miracles and gods, she thought wildly, her heart thumping with fear. They appear not in the places we prepare for them – churches, cathedrals, the sanctity of the home – but randomly, amidst the rabble, in the desperation of crowds.

She swept her desk clean, making sure there were no notes or papers lying around, remembering exactly what she'd been taught – *leave nothing behind* – and ran down the stairs. The driver was waiting, just as he'd said. She flung the two bags in the back seat and jumped in. Eluned first, then Libby. She had no fear for herself, not after what she'd been through. But if anything happened to them... She choked down on the dread.

'Go!' she all but shouted at the driver. 'Just go!'

PART EIGHT

SEX

1961
Libby

52

The cobalt canvas of the sea was pegged tightly to the two jetties, where a cluster of yachts bumped gently up and down, tethered together like animals nosing at a trough. It was the blue hour.

Libby sat with her knees drawn up to her chin, lazily drawing circles in the damp, cool sand with her forefinger. Sitting some way to her left were her parents and her sisters, five-year-old Eluned and the baby, Maev.

The blue hour. She closed her eyes. In an instant she could hear Tim Crick's voice in her ear, as if he were standing next to her, the long, lean line of his thighs encased in tight blue jeans.

'The blue hour is the period of twilight each morning and evening, when the sun is a significant distance below the horizon. The residual, indirect sunlight takes on a predominantly blue hue. The effect is caused by the relative diffusability of blue wavelengths of light, which are shorter than red wavelengths. It lasts on average forty minutes, during which time red light passes straight into space whilst blue light is scattered in the atmosphere and therefore reaches us. Because of its quality, the blue hour has long been treasured by artists ... which is why we're studying it.'

A rill of white-hot pleasure ran straight through her.

She lifted her chin and gazed out to sea. Her eyes held the moving waves; the rocky outcrops with their rings of white froth; the thick, dense green vegetation that ran off the hills, straight into the ocean.

They'd bumped their way down the Paria Main Road towards the sea, the air becoming lighter and fresher with every passing mile. It was a long drive from their enormous house in St Clair but the girls loved it, especially Maev. As hard as it was to give in to sulky, demanding Eluned, it was impossible to deny Maev anything. There was something charmed about Maev. She never, *ever* cried, for one thing. Of course that wasn't exactly true. All babies cried. But Maev only ever cried in moments of real need. Not like Elly, who Libby could scarcely remember *not* crying.

Maev looked like an angel, with the thickest, curliest blonde hair anyone had ever seen on a child. She had enormous china-blue eyes with the thickest dark eyelashes, dark eyebrows and the smallest mouth that made you just want to scoop her up and kiss her until the breath went out of her. Like Libby, she was olive-skinned, a gorgeous, rosy colour that brought sunlight to mind. It was funny how all three girls looked nothing like each other. Everyone always remarked on it. *Those Kentridge sisters.* They were each so different, not just in their looks, but in their personalities and even in their voices. Eluned sounded very English, like their parents, whilst Libby had picked up an American accent at her schools in both Oman and Port-of-Spain. As soon as she set foot in England, she discarded it. It was a useful ability. She was quite the chameleon. And although few people knew it, she was fluent in Arabic as well.

In Port-of-Spain, however, Arabic wasn't quite as useful. One day, she'd been out with her two best friends, Karla and Gracie, when they'd wandered into Salazar's, a café on Maraval Road, near the park. She'd shocked them by speaking Arabic with the Lebanese owner.

'Where d'you learn *that*?' Gracie asked, stunned.

Libby blushed. 'Uh, well, we lived in Oman before... It was pretty easy to pick up.'

'Wow! That's awesome!' Karla was clearly impressed.

'Sounds kinda weird to me,' Gracie demurred. 'Like gobbledegook.'

'Lib?' her mother called out, interrupting her thoughts. 'What's the matter with you? Don't you want to join us?'

Libby shook her head. Playing cards with the rest of the family was the last thing she felt like doing. She slid her legs down, away from her body, and looked at them with a critical eye. *Gorgeous breasts, great legs. You are so eminently fuckable.* Those were his exact words. Tim's words, tipped straight from the horse's mouth. He thought she was one of the most beautiful girls he'd ever seen, or so he said repeatedly. Listening to him as he described her attributes was music to her ears. No, better than music. It was like wallowing in honey, bathing in milk, drowning in champagne. She often pondered the adjectives. She'd been a rather ordinary-looking child, she remembered. No one picked her up the way they did Maev and cooed over her. She'd been coltish and awkward and her hair never quite seemed to know how to behave. But at thirteen, everything began to fall into place. Her legs lengthened and strengthened, and her breasts suddenly developed, even though the rest of her was as lean and sleek

244

as a greyhound. For a while that was what Tim Crick called her – 'the greyhound' – until he started sleeping with her and then he called her all sorts of other things, none of which could be said out loud. Not that you could accuse her of being vain about her looks. Mother was always quick to put a stop to anything that smacked of vanity. 'Stop looking at yourself in the mirror. It'll crack.' She was funny like that. She was beautiful herself but you certainly couldn't call *her* vain either. She was as disinterested in her own beauty as she was in her daughters', or anyone else's, for that matter. No, her mother was too strong to be thought of as vain.

The night they left Oman – which, to Libby, was still the most terrifying experience of her whole entire life – was the night she realised just how strong her mother was. She'd roared up to school with a driver and grabbed Libby straight from the playing fields in front of her stunned friends. Eluned was already in the back of the car, screaming her head off. They reached the British Embassy within minutes. Father was already there but it was Mother who was terrifyingly in command. It was then that Libby realised just how much she needed her mother. Father was beyond hopeless. At the embassy, her mother had immediately been whisked upstairs. Libby was told to look after Eluned whilst Father stood to one side, looking completely lost.

She'd taken Eluned to the toilet when she came upon her father in the corridor, a terrible strangled noise coming from his throat. She froze, not knowing what to do. He was crying, she realised, with dread breaking out all over her skin. He turned and for a second they stared at each other.

She still didn't understand the peculiar strength that came over her so that she was able to say to him, quite commandingly, 'Don't! Don't let Elly see you cry. She'll tell Mother.'

He'd stopped at once.

It was Mother who was in charge. She organised everything. The men at the embassy seemed to know her; Libby couldn't quite work out how. There was a strange scene with a man who'd come out of one of the offices just as they were getting ready to go to the airport. He and Mother had stood to one side, talking in low voices. Libby couldn't hear what they were saying but there was something about the way they stood together that spoke of an intimacy Libby had never witnessed in her mother before. Father just looked on helplessly.

They flew out under the cover of darkness that very same night and landed the next morning in cold, wet London. They stayed at a flat in Bayswater for a fortnight and then moved back into their home in Chelsea. And that was the end of Oman.

Two days after their dramatic escape, Libby heard on the news that there'd been an attempted coup d'état in Oman, and that the man whom she'd seen her mother with a few times – the ruler's nephew – had been killed. None of it made sense.

They stayed in London for two months and then Father got a new job. A fortnight later, they came to Trinidad, which was so different to Oman as to have been another world.

Yes, her mother was equal parts terrifying and compelling, and Libby wondered if there would *ever* be a time when her mother's shadow wasn't upon her.

'Come on, girls.' Her mother's voice broke the calm.

The day was nearly at an end. It was the only thing that reminded Libby of the Middle East here, the way night fell in – suddenly – like a curtain being drawn with the light leaking swiftly out of the sky.

She sighed and got up. The blue hour was over. No, it wasn't like that in London.

'Hurry up. You know Father doesn't like driving back in the dark. We're going to stay with the Tessaros.'

Eluned looked up, recognised the word 'Tessaros' and began crying. She hated it when the unexpected happened. She loved rules of all kinds, all sorts, in all situations. There was a harshness about Eluned that Libby just couldn't fathom. She was forever searching out little giveaway signs in others that indicated a weakness of some sort, some private vulnerability that she could sniff out and hold over them. *So-and-so bites her nails; this one tells lies; that one always wets the bed.* She had a veritable catalogue of the faults of her classmates. She was a bully but for the life of her, Libby couldn't work out *why.*

'Come on, Libbykins. You've had your head buried in your knees all afternoon. Is everything all right?' Her mother caught up with her, leaving her sisters to trail along with Father.

It was a rare moment alone. Libby hesitated. Nestled in the back pocket of her shorts was a small plastic packet containing several pills. Tim had given them to her.

'Take one every morning, poppet. It'll save us both an awful lot of trouble. Don't worry, they're perfectly safe. No side effects. Little white miracles, I call them.'

Did she dare tell her mother?

'No, everything's fine,' she said at last.

'Good. Well, let's get a move on. They're expecting us.'

Libby sighed inwardly. The Tessaros, who were possibly the loudest Americans Libby had ever met, owned one of those gingerbread beach houses set a little way back from the edge of the road, nestled so completely into the vegetation that the house appeared to grow out of the land rather than sit lightly upon it. It was painted in the gay, gaudy colours of the island: a deep pink that had faded to rose and ochre-yellow shutters that matched the sunflowers, whose enormous yolk-yellow heads drooped towards the horizon just as the sun did each day.

Mr Tessaro worked for Texaco, the American rival to BP, for whom Father now worked, but there seemed to be no rivalry between the two men. Mr Tessaro was a loud, bluff man with a grin that split his face from ear to ear. He was from the 'South' – Louisiana, or thereabouts. Even for Libby, his accent was at times hard to penetrate. His wife, Veronica – 'Call me Vera, honey!' – was an equally loud, cheerful woman, with hair that was permanently bound in pink rollers.

When they were not at their beach house, they lived in Laventille, one of Port-of-Spain's southern suburbs, where all the houses looked alike: bungalows with wide flat roofs and sloping front lawns. Laventille was nowhere near as nice as St Clair, where the Kentridges lived, with its mansions and graceful villas and gardens that went on for ever, but her mother didn't seem to notice, or mind. She took as much care with her hair and make-up and the choice of wine or whisky to take to the Tessaros' many dinner parties as she did to everyone else's.

They walked back up the sandy path towards the car, hidden behind a mangrove tree, whose dark, furry leaves brushed their arms and legs as they passed. The sky was soft and black. They all climbed in, the three girls squashed in the back. There was the usual tussle over who touched whom, whose legs had taken up more room, and then Father started the engine.

Her mother lit a cigarette. Elly hummed some indistinguishable school song. The car's headlights picked out shadows randomly that coalesced to become shapes, things... the odd person walking along the side of the road, a figure completely enveloped in night.

*

The conversation in the sitting room flowed around them, rising and falling in laughter and indignation, heightened by the drinks that Vera Tessaro kept refilling.

'Oh, no, no … that's *quite* enough, thank you, Vera.' That was Father.

A snort of derision, followed by giggles. 'You guys are *so* English! So *formal*! Go on, it's Sunday. You've got a whole twelve hours before work tomorrow! *Tell* him, Alfonso.'

The two girls sat somewhat self-consciously on the wide wicker couch, whose cushions had retained the soft indentations of countless backsides. Maev was asleep, swaddled in a blanket, in spite of the heat.

Libby got up, impatient at the separation that forced her into the world of children. She wandered to the edge of the verandah and stood with her nose pressed against the sagging mosquito net, pulling the mothy, fragrant night air into her lungs. She thought she could hear a tinkling sound, perhaps a wind chime? The sound was weak but curiously magnified, like everything in the tropics. Behind her, the small sitting room and open-plan kitchen were all light; the verandah sat between the two, neither inside nor out, opening onto the branches of a coral tree, all scarlet claws now black against the sky. She pushed open the swing door cautiously. The warm square of the night, full of ecstatic insect cries, rose up to meet her.

'Don't go outside!' Eluned spoke up immediately. 'Mummy *said*.' Her voice was full of self-righteous self-possession.

'I'll be back in a moment.' Libby shut the door behind her and stepped onto the gravel path that ran around the house.

She was impatient with the bottles of sickly-sweet Fanta and the plate of already-spongy biscuits that the soft-voiced servant had placed in front of them. For God's sake, she was nineteen years old! Didn't they know she drank *wine*, just as they did? Beer, too. And once, just once, a cocktail that had promptly made her sick.

She walked quickly around the side of the beach house. Far off, the distant roar of the sea, muted to a dull murmur, drifted across the trees. The Tessaros house was perhaps a mile away from the beach; now, in the enveloping blackness in which light from the house spilled out like a stain, the blinding white heat of the day seemed a mirage, something not to be believed in.

She wandered closer to the back of the house and suddenly became aware of voices coming from the kitchen. She moved closer, half absorbed in her own thoughts. Behind her a cricket ceased abruptly and the voices came into sharp relief.

'Galeota's struck gold.'

'How much?'

'Sixty-five million barrels.'

'Sixty-five million? That's thirty per cent over the odds. What's the reaction from the PNM?'

Libby stopped, frowning. It was her mother's voice. She'd been joined by someone else. A man's voice. An Englishman. She wondered who it was. She was directly outside the kitchen door. Her curiosity got the better of her. She raised herself up on tiptoe and peered through the netting. Her mother was standing at the fridge, a bottle of something – gin? – in one hand, an ice-cube tray in the other. Mr Tessaro was standing in the doorway. But there was no one else in the room. The voice she'd heard couldn't have been Mr Tessaro. He was American.

'Did you get to talk to Williams? Properly, I mean?'

'There just wasn't the time. I told his aide-de-camp that I'd be along later—'

'Alfonso?' A shrill call from inside the house broke up the conversation. It was Mrs Tessaro.

Libby watched, spellbound, as her mother's head signalled to him to be quiet. There was a quick little frown between her brows but it was her mother's stance that drew the eye. She was primed, her whole body coiled taut like a spring. There was a moment's hesitation as Mr Tessaro ran a finger under his collar, loosening it, then he left the kitchen without a word. Her mother stood where she was. Libby could see her take a deep breath, steadying herself. Then she closed the fridge door, picked up a bottle of beer by its neck and followed Mr Tessaro through the doorway.

'Now, who asked for a beer?' she cried gaily, all the earlier murmured secrecy banished from her voice.

Libby could see them through the open doorway, her father standing by the gramophone, Mrs Tessaro sitting on the easy chair by the dining table, swinging a leg in time to the low music. There was a vivid strangeness to her mother's face even at that distance. Boldly drawn, somehow, her features still animated.

Libby let out her own breath slowly, moment by moment, only

peripherally aware she'd been holding it in. Mr Tessaro had spoken in another voice. He appeared to be another person. *But that can't be.*

The thought hung there in the thick night for what seemed like ages and then the cricket began chirruping again.

53

A fortnight later, Libby was back in London, back in her own world at art college. The Christmas holiday, with its secrets and puzzles, was behind her. The heat and dazzling sunshine of Port-of-Spain was a mirage, lingering on only in the deepened sun-kissed colour of her skin.

'Christ, you're lovely.' Tim propped himself up on one elbow, lit a cigarette with one hand and with the other traced out a line from the tip of her breast to her navel. Libby felt her entire body – bones, skin, muscle – melt under his touch.

'Am I?' she asked, basking in the attention.

'Mmm. You know you are.' He took a drag and passed the cigarette to her.

'Which bit d'you like the best?'

He made a half snort and rolled away. The spell was broken. Libby could have kicked herself.

'Don't start,' he said shortly.

Libby felt her eyes begin to prickle. Why did she always have to ruin it? It was so hard to know what to say, when to say it, *how* to say it. She tried, she really did, but there didn't seem to be any rules. One minute it was all smiles and slow, teasing banter, the next he was irritable and curt. She was all at sea. Waving, not drowning, but sometimes drowning. Actually, *mostly* drowning.

It wasn't supposed to be like this. In her final year of high school in Port-of-Spain, she'd made the surprising decision not to go to university, but to apply to an art college instead. Her mother's reaction still made her skin crawl with embarrassment whenever she thought about it.

'*Art* college? Are you quite *mad*?'

'Kit, Kit... let her speak.' That was Father, coming to her rescue. Since the night of their departure from Oman, things between them had become even stranger. He tiptoed gingerly around her, almost fearfully. It made Libby uncomfortable but, for once, she was glad of the support.

'Mummy, it's not like that. It's a proper college. It's like a university, only you study art.'

'Well, why don't you *go* somewhere proper, like Oxford or Cambridge? We could get you into the Ruskin, I'm sure of it.'

'But I don't want you to "get" me in anywhere. I want to go to London!'

'What about the Slade?' Daddy put in anxiously, looking at her mother for confirmation.

'Yes, what about the Slade? It's perfectly respectable. It's still a university degree.'

Libby looked from one to the other in disbelief. 'I don't believe you,' she said arrogantly. 'You don't even *work*! What do you care where I get a degree from?'

'Libby! That's enough! Don't speak to your mother like that.'

'But it's true! You've never worked a day in your life! All you do is play tennis and . . . and gossip with the other housewives and—'

'That's enough, Libby,' her mother said quietly. Two spots of colour had appeared on her cheeks. But something in Libby made her press on.

'But it's true, isn't it? Oh, I know you went to Oxford about a hundred years ago . . . who cares? Just because *you* never had the guts to do anything with *your* life, don't try and stop me doing what I want with *mine*! I'm sick of you telling me what to do all the time! I'm not a child!' As the words came tumbling out, a coldness hardened into her mother's face that almost turned Libby inside out with fear. No one else could rouse that sort of anxiety in her. With a rising sense of panic, she tried to turn the conversation, but it was too late. She was in the grip of something that wouldn't let go. 'Anyhow, it doesn't *matter* what you say; I'm going anyway! I can get a grant—' She stopped. Her mother appeared in front of her suddenly. She'd got up from her chair by the window and was standing right in front of her. They were almost the same height. Both women looked at each other for a second and then Kit raised her hand and, for the first time in her life, slapped Libby across the face.

It was the last time Libby ever raised her voice to her mother.

*

251

A month later, without opposition, she enrolled at Chelsea College of Art. Father accompanied her on the flight over. At first it was like landing on Mars. They arrived on a cold September morning, directly out of the Caribbean heat. Although Libby knew her way around London, in the three years since they'd been away it had changed. It was 1961 and the capital was booming. Everything bewildered her. So many people walking purposefully towards destinations unknown! The fashions were astonishing. King's Road, which was a stone's throw from their house, was at the centre of it all. Crossing the road with her father on the second day, she'd nearly been knocked down, staring at a girl in a geometric-striped dress with bright yellow tights. She scarcely knew where to look.

At the end of the first week, Father flew back to Trinidad, leaving Libby behind. She was torn between panic and relief. As the taxi bearing him towards the airport rounded the corner and disappeared, she'd had to choke back a tear. She was on her own for the first time in her life, well and truly alone. Unlike most of the other students she'd met, who all came from places like Surrey and Hampshire, and who were already planning their first weekend home to stock up on food and get their laundry done, for her, 'home' was some six thousand miles away. She wouldn't see her family again until Christmas.

She watched the taxi turn the corner and then walked back up the steps to the front door, wondering what to do next. She'd been allocated a room in The Res, a great, ugly Victorian building just off Fulham Road and within walking distance of the college. There were roughly three hundred first-year art students in Res, with men and women on alternate floors.

She pushed open the front door and stood in the lobby, feeling horribly lost. There didn't seem to be anyone about. The beadle, a rather dour-looking man in his fifties, was behind the reception desk, where he had his own little office, complete with a tiny kitchenette and a rather scruffy but comfortable-looking armchair.

She looked around her. The lobby had a threadbare red carpet, a collection of mismatched chairs and a small television balanced on a three-legged table in the far corner. A huge wooden cupboard for their post dominated one entire wall. Res resembled a hotel reception and a prison simultaneously. There was a tiny grilled and gated lift on the opposite wall, which held *no more than three persons at any given time,* according to the hand-painted sign.

Libby blew out her cheeks. It was four o'clock on a wet Saturday afternoon in September. Classes wouldn't start until Monday morning. She knew no one and she had absolutely nothing to do. She walked over to the lift and pressed the button. It came down, clanking and grinding, and opened to discharge five people, jammed up against each other. They were laughing and talking animatedly. Libby hung back, pretending to wind up her watch. Then she darted inside the cage and pressed '4'.

'Four, please!' someone gasped, just before the doors closed. A girl came rushing in, unwinding her scarf as she went. 'Sorry, it just takes *ages* to come up and down, and I'm certainly not going to climb four flights of stairs every other hour!'

'No, of course not,' Libby agreed quickly, perhaps a little *too* quickly.

The girl who'd just squeezed herself in looked at her sharply.

'It's a bit of a hike,' Libby added nervously.

The girl continued to look at her without saying anything. 'What's your name?' she asked finally, as they creaked their way up.

'Libby. Libby Kentridge.' There was an awkward pause. 'Um, what's yours?'

'Hortense Heatherwick-Hamilton de Hubert.' There was a moment's stunned silence. 'No, I'm only joking. My name's Charlie. Charlie Guthrie, actually.'

'Oh.' Libby wasn't sure what to say.

Charlie was red-haired and freckled, with almond-shaped green eyes and the whitest skin Libby had ever seen on anyone. Her hair was cut in the fashionable Mary Quant 'bob' that Libby had seen on so many girls but would never dare to try herself. It was shorter at the back than the front, with long, pointy ends that curled under her chin and a perfectly flat, squared-off fringe. She wore black eyeliner and thick dark mascara but her lips were pale and lipstick-free. She had on a black polo neck jumper, a short tartan skirt and shocking-pink tights. She was wonderfully dramatic.

'So, what floor are you on?' Charlie asked with a quick, cheeky grin.

'Me?'

'Well, there's no one else in here, is there?'

'No, yes ... I mean, I'm on the fourth as well.'

'What room?'

'Um, 15B, I think.' She hesitated. 'What about you?'

'I'm in 12A. Other side of the corridor. D'you want a glass of wine? I've got some really awful red wine under my bed. You can have some, if you like.'

Half an hour later, sitting cross-legged on the floor in Charlie's room, drinking wine straight from the bottle, Libby suddenly didn't feel quite so lonely. She took a swig, handed it to Charlie and giggled.

'What's so funny?' Charlie asked, her eyes twinkling, as if she already knew what Libby was about to say.

'If my mother could see me now she'd have a fit,' Libby said. 'This is exactly why she didn't want me to come to art college.'

'Oh, mine too. What do your parents do? I'll bet they're awfully exotic.'

Libby was surprised. 'Exotic? What makes you say that? They're terribly ordinary.'

'Bet they're not. Go on, where do you live? When you're not here, I mean.'

'Well, actually, we live abroad.'

'See. Where?'

'Trinidad. We've only been there a couple of years, though,' Libby said hurriedly, in case it sounded as though she were showing off.

'Trinidad? Bloody hell. It's hot out there, isn't it?' Charlie looked at her with widening eyes. 'What on earth are they doing out there?'

'My father works for BP. He's a sales manager, nothing very important. And my mum doesn't do anything. She just plays tennis all day.'

'Wish *my* mum did nothing,' Charlie said gloomily. 'I've got the opposite problem.'

'What d'you mean?'

'They're scientists. My mum was one of the first women to get a PhD in physics from Cambridge. You can imagine how pleased they are with *my* choices. My dad nearly had a heart attack when I said I wanted to become a fashion designer.'

'Mine too. Is that what you're studying?' Libby asked, impressed. Fashion! It sounded so glamorous.

'Yeah. I've *always* wanted to be a fashion designer. Ever since I was little. Me and my sisters used to spend hours making dolls' clothes and stuff. Have you got any sisters?'

'Yeah. Two. I hate my middle sister, though.'

Charlie looked shocked. 'You can't say that. You shouldn't.'

'Why not? It's true. She's horrible. She's my sister and everything, but she's really mean. And my other sister's really only a baby.'

'Isn't that funny? We're exactly opposite,' Charlie said, finishing off the last of the wine. 'I *adore* my sisters.' She pushed the empty bottle back under the bed. 'The cleaners'll come round on Monday morning and report us if they find anything. Will you remind me tomorrow to get rid of it?'

Libby nodded and felt a sudden warmth steal through her. Charlie seemed to think they'd meet again. Was it really going to be that easy?

'Why d'you say we're opposites?' she asked curiously.

'Well, because we are. I'm the baby and you're the eldest. You hate your sisters but I love mine. Your mum's a housewife and mine's a scientist. You see? We're opposites. That's why we're going to get on so well. I'm always right about these things.'

Libby was too pleased to speak. She leaned back against the bed and crossed her long legs at the ankles. She looked at Charlie's tights. The first thing she would do the following morning was buy a pair of bright yellow tights.

Art college was immersion into a world where the only thing that mattered was art. Expression. Creativity. By the end of her second week, Libby was completely drawn in. She and Charlie had become fast, firm friends. Most of Charlie's classes took place 'up town', in the new fashion and graphic design college extension near Baker Street. They spent countless hours sitting on either Charlie's floor or hers, a bottle of wine as often as they could afford it, waiting to be drunk, smoking and going over what they'd learned or failed to grasp.

Drawing, Libby discovered, was a state of being in which her mind was suspended and her hand did the thinking for her. She drew dutifully what was in front of her: a plate of fruit, a body, a head, a hand... She wasn't so much concerned with the objects she drew, though they carried their own burden of feeling and play of light and shadow, but it was the possibility of what might happen when she drew them that really excited her. Every Monday, Wednesday and Friday, at nine o'clock sharp, she sat with fifteen other first-year students in the enormous studios that were flooded with light and drew whatever was presented to them. She loved the thick drawing pads of dense white paper. The whiteness of the sheets always took her breath away. She smoothed the first one over and over again before she dared make the first mark. When the pencil bit into the paper, and she felt it yield to the pressure of her finger, the page was transformed by whatever direction her hand took. That was the real discovery. That she could make and remake the world – the image – any number of times. It was intoxicating.

She'd always been good at art but she saw now that her childish drawings had nothing whatsoever to do with art. *Real* art. Art was life, nothing less. *Her* life. The pages of her sketchbook were her mind and contained everything that was *in* her mind. She had only to let her hand roam free, and whatever was inside her would emerge. It was like learning another language, speaking another tongue, and she'd always been able to do *that*.

And then she made another discovery. One afternoon in late October, she was sitting in the café across the road from college, smoking and waiting for Charlie to arrive, when a shadow fell across her table. It was an unseasonably warm day, the last of an Indian summer, and she was beginning to wish she'd taken off her yellow tights. She looked up. It was Mr Crick, her first-year drawing tutor. *Tim*, she corrected herself automatically. All the tutors went by their first names. Calling someone 'Mr' or 'Miss' or even 'Sir' was now hopelessly outdated.

'Hello there,' he said pleasantly. 'It's Libby Kentridge, isn't it?'

She did her best to appear nonchalant. 'Hi.'

'Enjoying the last of the sun?'

'Yes. Yeah.' She took a drag on her cigarette to cover her confusion. She hadn't quite worked out how to behave with her tutors, especially the younger ones. Tim Crick was somewhere between her age and her parents' age. He wasn't exactly good-looking – a bit too lean and rangy-looking for her taste – but he was certainly interesting, possibly the most interesting person she'd ever met. There seemed to be no end to the facts he was able to summon when talking to his eager students. The fact that he knew her name confused her. He'd barely spoken to her all term.

'Mind if I join you?' he asked, pulling out a chair and sitting down. 'I'm waiting for a friend.'

'Oh. Yes, of course not. I mean, yes, of course.'

He smiled sardonically. Her confusion hadn't gone unnoticed. 'I hope I'm not disturbing you?' He looked pointedly at her book whilst he fished in his jacket pocket for his tobacco pouch.

She looked at it and only just managed to stop herself snatching it away. 'Oh, God no. It's … it's just … something I was reading. I'm waiting for someone too.'

'Some lucky young chap, I imagine?'

She blushed deeply. 'Oh, no. Just my best friend. I mean, she's in Res with me. Not my best friend, she lives—' She stopped herself just in time. 'Sorry. I'm babbling on.'

He laughed at that. 'No, don't worry. It often takes a while to get used to the way things are at college. It's quite different from school. Especially the sort of school I imagine *you* went to.' He had what her mother would call a 'working-class' accent. Northern, perhaps? She couldn't tell. After spending most of her life abroad, she had only the haziest understanding of English geography.

'What sort of school d'you think I went to?'

He smiled faintly and began rolling a cigarette. 'Somewhere posh, safe … cosy. I don't know. You tell me.'

She laughed. 'No, you're wrong. I didn't go to that sort of school at all. You're wrong about me.'

'Am I really?' he murmured, looking at her with narrowed eyes through the cloud of smoke. 'Oldest child, absent father. Possibly even absent mother. Shunted off to boarding school. You don't get on with your siblings. Let me guess – you've got two or three sisters, but no brothers. You've spent most of your life trying to get other people's attention and it's failed. So you've come to college hoping you'll find the answer to your life's own riddle.'

She stared at him and was horrified to feel a lump in her throat. 'It's not … no, it's not—' she began and then found she couldn't go on. Oh, God, she wasn't about to cry, was she?

'Hang on … I didn't mean to upset you,' he said, alarmed at her reaction.

Her heart was thumping. 'It's fine,' she said weakly, dabbing at her eyes. She could have kicked herself.

'No, honestly. That was just thoughtless of me. Let me buy you a drink. A proper one. You look like you could use one. We could both use one.'

He got up before she could protest and walked up to the counter. A few minutes later he emerged carrying two glasses and a bottle of Beaujolais.

'Here we go. I'm sorry. Really I am. Dunno why I said it. I was just showing off. Please. Have a drink. Forget I ever said anything.' He poured two glasses and handed one to her. 'Cheers. Here's to unhappy families. And don't think yours is the only one, my girl.'

She didn't hear the first part. Only the 'my girl'. There was something so outrageously sexy and grown-up about the way he said it. 'My girl.' She *wasn't* his 'girl', she was his *student*. She picked up her wine and knocked it straight back.

'Steady on,' he said, laughing at her. 'It's not orange juice, you know.'

'Sorry. I'm a bit nervous. I don't quite know how to take you, I'm afraid.'

'Any way you like,' he murmured.

She reached unsteadily for the bottle. She had the distinct feeling that things could have gone anywhere at that moment.

But before he could say anything further, Charlie came rushing in. 'I'm so sorry ... I bet you've been waiting ages!' she exclaimed, collapsing into the spare chair. She unwound the bright red scarf from her neck and dropped her satchel of books on the floor. She turned to Tim, her eyes widening. 'Hello, I'm Charlie. Are you on our course?'

'He teaches it,' Libby interrupted quickly, feeling the heat rise in her cheeks. 'He's my drawing tutor.'

'Oh.' For once, Charlie seemed surprised by a piece of news. 'Oh. Well, I suppose *somebody's* got to do it.' She recovered fast. 'What's your name?'

'Tim. Tim Crick.'

'Well, Tim Crick. Nice to meet you. Ah, a bottle of wine, I see. Lovely. Is there any more of that going?'

Two bottles later, when the two girls couldn't stop giggling at anything and everything Tim Crick said, he got up reluctantly. 'Well, girls, it's been lovely and all that but I've got to go.' He waved away their protests and Libby's offer to pay for the wine. 'No, absolutely not. Not at all. My pleasure. Let's do it again some time.' He picked up his small leather tobacco pouch and tucked it away in the back pocket of his jeans. He gave them both one of his funny little sardonic smiles and sauntered off.

Libby and Charlie both watched him disappear down King's Road in silence. Finally, when he was safely out of sight, they turned to each other and burst out laughing.

'So,' Charlie gasped excitedly, 'tell me everything. And don't you *dare* leave anything out!'

'What d'you mean? Nothing's happened. We just—'

'Oh, stop it. You know exactly what I mean. A *tutor*! Well, well, well. He's quite *old*, though, don't you think?'

Libby shrugged. 'I couldn't really tell. Thirty? Forty?'

'Well, I hope it's nearer thirty. Anyway, I'll bet you anything you like he asks you out.'

Libby blushed. 'Don't be ridiculous,' she mumbled. 'He's a tutor.'

'So? It's allowed, you know.'

'What is?'

'Having sex with your students. It's practically the *rule*.'

Libby's face was on fire. 'I'm sure it's not. And anyway, I don't think that's what he's after.'

'Oh, for goodness' sake! That's what they're all after,' Charlie said cheerfully. 'What was he doing at the café anyway?' Then she looked more closely at Libby. 'You *have* done it before, haven't you?'

'Um, no, not really.'

Charlie's eyes narrowed. 'What d'you mean, "not really"? Either you have or you haven't.'

'Haven't,' Libby mumbled, by now thoroughly embarrassed.

'Hmm. Well, in that case, I'd recommend Tim Crick. It's better to do it with someone older, especially the first time.'

Libby stared at her. Whatever confidence she'd managed to rustle up in her first few weeks had vanished. She was left on the outside again, tentatively feeling her way forwards. Was she the *only* virgin left in London?

Charlie must have sensed her discomfort. She slipped an arm through Libby's as they got up to go. 'Don't worry, I'm sure you're not the only one,' she said, accurately reading Libby's mind. 'But it really is best just to get it over and done with. Then you'll see it's not worth making so much fuss over. That's the problem,' she said chummily. 'We spend so much time thinking about it and worrying about it ... wondering what it's going to be like ... finding the "right" boy ... all of that rubbish. Then when you finally *do* it, you realise how ordinary it is and you wonder why on earth you spent so much time agonising over it.'

'You don't really mean that, do you?' Libby asked, half curious, half fearful.

''Course I do. Oh, don't get me wrong. It's nice. I mean, it's fun and everything. But it's certainly not everything they say it's going to be. Quite disappointing, if you ask me.'

'So why do we make so much of it?' Libby asked curiously.

'Haven't you read Simone de Beauvoir?' Charlie asked.

Libby shook her head.

'Don't they teach you anything?' she asked incredulously. 'Anyway,' she continued, warming to what seemed to be her favourite topic. 'What Simone de Beauvoir says, basically, is that men are always trying to make things a bloody mystery so that they can control us.'

'How?' Libby was intrigued.

'It's really quite simple. By pretending that women are a mystery, they don't have to even try to understand us. We're just too complicated and silly and mysterious. And that way, they don't have to help us get ahead.'

'But why do we need to be helped to get ahead?'

'Oh, don't you see, Libby? Everything is based on men. If you're a woman, you have to begin every sentence by saying: "as a woman". But if you're a man, you just assume that everyone's a man. D'you see what I mean?'

Libby nodded doubtfully. 'I suppose so.'

'It's exactly the same for Negroes. Or ... or Jews, for example. They're always seen as different. Not quite *us*, if you know what I mean.'

'I don't really know any,' Libby mused. 'I mean, there's lots of black people in Trinidad but we don't really talk to any of them. Not like friends, or anything. And I don't think I've ever met a Jew, either. How can you tell?'

Charlie stopped walking. She looked up at Libby in surprise. 'You *have* led a sheltered life, darling, haven't you? Well, we're just going to have to change all that. But first things first. Sleep with Tim before you do anything else. That's my advice. And don't take too long about it. He'll find some other innocent to seduce, mark my words. Just don't fall for him. Promise?'

'Promise,' Libby said automatically, wondering how she was supposed to be able to control it.

'And when you have,' Charlie went on earnestly, 'and you've got that hurdle over and done with, then I'll introduce you to some even more interesting people. London's full of interesting people. You just have to know where to look.'

54

That was six months ago. She'd followed Charlie's advice … up to a point. The point where she said 'just don't fall for him', to be more precise. She couldn't help it. It seemed to her to be impossible. How could she not fall in love with Tim Crick? He only had to look at her and murmur, 'Come here, my little greyhound. Why so glum?' and her heart would lift to impossible heights. When he ignored her – which he seemed to do with increasing frequency – it sent her plummeting down into the depths of despair. 'It's for your own good,' he kept telling her, though she struggled to understand what he meant.

Charlie simply rolled her eyes. 'I *told* you,' was all she would say knowingly. 'Don't say I didn't warn you. And, I was wrong, by the way.'

'About what?'

'He's not *supposed* to sleep with his students. They all do, of course, but it's not allowed. I was wrong about that. He could get the sack.'

'Oh.' That explained why he never wanted to be seen with her any-where near college. They always met on the other side of town, near Euston Station, where he took her to the sort of hotel that seemed to have a lot of hourly trade.

'Why can't we go to your place?' she'd asked once.

'I live miles away. It's practically not in London. It would take us for ever to get there and I don't want to waste a precious second on some bloody train when I could be with you. Here. Like this. C'mere.'

She did as he asked. Promptly. Before he changed his mind.

In early December, she was sitting in Luigi's when a group of second-year students walked in. She lowered her book, turned cautiously around to take a look and recognised them immediately. Imogen Wardle-Clegg led the pack. She was the daughter of an aristocrat who'd run off with the children's nanny a few months earlier. Everyone knew about it. It had been in the papers for weeks. Imogen herself had been photographed countless times. Since she was not only aristocratic but tall, blonde *and* leggy, she'd become even more of a celebrity than her errant father. She was purported to be 'fast', which was *ridiculously* hypocritical, Charlie fumed, but whatever the truth of the matter, there was a whiff of louche glamour about Imogen Wardle-Clegg that few people could resist. She was easily the most popular girl in college.

'Darling, do come and sit next to me,' she commanded her table of acolytes. 'No, not *you*, Diana! Move over, you great lump. I want to sit next to Chloë.'

Libby was struggling with Simone de Beauvoir's *The Second Sex*, which Charlie had given her with strict instructions to 'read every single page. And I'll quiz you afterwards, so don't think you can get away with it.'

She'd already had two cups of coffee and three cigarettes and she was feeling rather light-headed from the lethal combination of feminism, nicotine and caffeine. When Imogen arrived with her coterie of female friends, it was a much welcome distraction. Their gossip seemed so much more interesting than de Beauvoir's dissection of women as a 'recessive gender', whatever that was. She kept her eyes on the page but the words had long since ceased to make any sense.

'So, here's the thing,' Imogen was saying, her voice taking on a dramatic breathiness. 'I bumped into Sophie Weston at Café Paradis yesterday and she told me that Crick's *married*.'

'*No!*' One of the other girls drew in her breath. 'How did she find out? Oh, that's just too *awful*. What a *scumbag*!'

'She saw him with his wife *and* their two kids. Can you *imagine*? Poor Sophie. She's got to get rid of it.'

'I never liked him,' someone chimed in self-righteously. 'He was always staring at my breasts.'

'I'm not surprised, Annabel. They're hard to miss. The point is, he's apparently also sleeping with that girl in first year ... what's her name? Libby something-or-other. You know, the tall one. She's awfully stuck-up. Never says hello or anything.'

'She'll wind up like Sophie Weston if she's not careful. I hear she's quite good, though. He only ever picks the good ones and then he completely screws them up. He's terrified that one of us will outshine him.'

'Well, you're safe then,' Imogen said drily, and the table burst into laughter.

Libby was too stunned to move. Her whole body was on fire. She sat very still, praying no one in the group would see or recognise her. Tim was married? *With two children?* Who was Sophie Weston? And could it be true that he only picked out the talented girls so that he could destroy them? The questions went around and around in her mind until she thought she would burst from the painful confusion of it all.

Finally, just when she thought she couldn't possibly sit there for a second longer, the group got up and noisily left the café. No one had seen her. She sat for a few minutes more, trying to take it all in. She got up, paid the bill and left the café, heading back to halls. Perhaps Charlie had some words of advice.

'Didn't I *warn* you? And didn't you read de Beauvoir? It's all in there, Libby!' Charlie said excitedly, sounding anything but sympathetic. 'He's *threatened* by you, it's obvious! The only way he can deal with his own feelings of inadequacy is to finish you off!'

'But he hasn't *done* anything to me!' Libby cried.

''Course he has. Look at you. I hope you've been taking precautions. You don't want to wind up like that girl they were talking about.'

'Yes . . . I am. He . . . he gave me the Pill.'

'Hmmph. Well, at least he's sensible enough to do *that*. Although, I have to say, that's probably more for his sake than yours. If he's got two kids already, d'you really think he wants a third?'

Libby tried to hold back her tears but she couldn't. 'I don't know what to do,' she sobbed. 'I feel so silly.'

Charlie was unmoved. She watched Libby through a cloud of smoke. 'End it,' she said, blowing the smoke out of one corner of her mouth. 'Just end it. End it before he does.'

'I can't,' Libby wailed. The thought made her physically ill. 'I don't think I can manage without him.'

'You will. Trust me. Here, read this.' Charlie reached up onto the bed and grabbed one of the books lying on the bedspread. She handed it to Libby.

Libby looked at it disconsolately through her veil of tears. *The Feminine Mystique.* Another one of Charlie's bibles. She let it fall limply to the ground. Didn't Charlie get it? She was in love. Hopelessly in love . . . and helpless with it. Didn't she *understand*?

55

Tim Crick must have sensed the game was up. She bumped into him coming out of the lecture hall and couldn't quite bring herself to meet his eyes. He stared at her for a moment then turned around without saying anything. She watched his tall, lean frame disappear down the corridor with a sinking feeling in the pit of her stomach.

She didn't hear from him for the rest of the week. She bumped into him twice, but again, he simply ignored her. She wasn't sure which was worse: having his attention, knowing she'd been fed a lie, or being dismissed. She spent a week moping around college, unable to eat, unable to draw, unable to think.

The following Friday, just when she thought she couldn't possibly be any more miserable, Charlie rapped on her door and, in typical Charlie fashion, barged in before she could answer. She stood in the doorway, surveying the evidence of Libby's heartbreak and sighed.

'Right. It's time to stop this nonsense and get you back on your feet. He's not worth it, Libby. *No* man is worth this.' She gestured at the unwashed coffee cups, half-eaten pieces of toast and cigarette butts strewn all over the floor. 'I bet you haven't left this room since morning, have you?'

Libby shook her head. To her shame, two fat tears began to trickle down her cheeks. Again. She hadn't thought she had any tears left.

'He's g-gone,' she began, then had to stop because she was crying again.

Charlie was unmoved. 'Of course he's gone. He probably guessed he'd been rumbled. Bloody good riddance, too. Right. I promised you I'd take you somewhere, and I will. But first you've got to get up, wash your face, put on something other than those rags that you've been living in for the past week and promise me you'll make an effort.'

Libby looked down at her coffee-stained jeans. Charlie was right. She hadn't changed in at least three days, if not a week. Another fat tear rolled down her face. She'd never felt so wretched in her entire life.

'Come on. Get up. Feeling sorry for yourself will only make it worse. Go on … into the washroom with you. I haven't got all night.'

Libby levered herself off the floor reluctantly, knowing it was probably easier to do as Charlie said. There was no arguing with her when she was in *that* sort of mood.

The first thing she noticed as the Hammersmith & City Line pulled out of Baker Street Station was that the number of dark-skinned people joining the carriages seemed to increase exponentially the further west they went. By the time they reached Westbourne Park, there were nearly as many black people in the carriage as not.

'Where are we going?' she whispered to Charlie, who sat next to her with a knowing little smile playing about her lips.

'You'll see soon enough,' was all Charlie would say.

Libby wasn't alarmed, merely curious. It was one of the things she liked best about London, the way whole neighbourhoods existed side by side without so much as a nod to each other's existence. In Chelsea, she'd discovered the Italian and Portuguese communities who ran most of the cafés and restaurants along King's Road, most of whom lived in the council blocks at the end of World's End (an unfortunate name). But this part of London was different.

They got off the train at Ladbroke Grove. Charlie led the way. It was dark and cold and her earlier sense of desolation was beginning to return. They walked up the road from the station.

'Where are we going?' she asked Charlie again, wrinkling her nose. The sour smell of urine and damp wafted up from the gutter. She clutched Charlie's arm. 'Is it safe?'

'Yes, of course it's safe. We're going to a club just up the road.'

'A club? What sort of club?' She tried unsuccessfully to keep the alarm from her voice.

Charlie just laughed. 'A music club. It's a great place, you'll see. We're meeting some friends of mine.'

Libby clutched Charlie's arm even tighter. Who were these friends whom she'd never heard of? And why hadn't Charlie ever mentioned Notting Hill before? It might have been Port-of-Spain if it hadn't been for the narrow houses that looked like the houses in Chelsea, except these were dirty and run-down with broken balustrades and windows. The whole area looked almost derelict.

*

The 'club' was in the basement of a tall Victorian house just off Chepstow Road. Charlie rang the doorbell and a dark-skinned woman in a red shiny dress opened the door. She was smoking and looked the two of them up and down with a faint derisory smile.

'Who you lookin' for, honey?' she asked in a drawl that took Libby straight back to Port-of-Spain. She stared at the woman. She could have been someone she'd passed on the streets of St Clair or Maraval.

'Is Dwayne here?' Charlie asked politely.

The woman looked at her a little more closely. Then she threw back her head and yelled, 'Dwayne! C'mere, boy. Girl here lookin' foh yuh.'

The patois wasn't quite the same as the one spoken in Trinidad, but the lilting singsong was instantly familiar. Libby felt oddly at ease. There was a great clattering of footsteps and the sound of music coming up the stairs from the basement, then a young man appeared, taking the last two steps in a single leap. He was tall and dark, with skin the colour of midnight. He wore a black woollen beret and what looked like a dinner jacket with slightly worn silk lapels and drainpipe black trousers. He was all boundless, restless energy and he greeted Charlie with a smile of genuine delight.

'Didn't think you'd make it,' he said, grinning at them.

'Hello, Dwayne,' Charlie said, looking equally pleased. 'I brought my friend, Libby. I told you about her, remember?'

'Sure I do. Band's not here yet, though. But they should be along pretty soon.' He turned to the woman in the red dress and slipped straight back into patois. 'Ja, they cool. Let 'em in.'

'If yuh say so, Dwayne,' she murmured, standing back to let the girls pass. 'Coats in de second doorway. Just use one of dem racks.'

The basement he led them to was more like a cellar. The floor was stripped and there were small tables and chairs dotted around the room. There was a raised podium at one end with a set of drums, a keyboard and a few empty chairs waiting for the band. There was a makeshift bar at one end, with perhaps fifteen or twenty people leaning against it, drinks in hand. The music was loud and thumping and Libby recognised the beat straight away. Reggae. It was the sound of Port-of-Spain.

She turned to Charlie, her eyes lighting up. 'It's perfect!'

'I thought you'd like it.' Charlie grinned. 'Cigarette?' She handed one to her. 'Come on, let's get a seat. When the band gets here *everyone'll* come down. It gets terrifically crowded.'

'Will there be dancing?'

'Oh yes. That's what everyone comes for. You'll see. Here, let's grab this one. Dwayne'll join us in a minute.'

Libby didn't quite know how to put it. 'Are you two … you know, going out?' she said finally.

Charlie let out a guffaw. 'Oh, goodness me, no! He's *gay*,' she whispered. 'Couldn't you tell?'

Libby was genuinely shocked. A *homosexual*! She shook her head. 'No. I've … I've never met one before. A homosexual, I mean.'

'My,' Charlie drawled, waving away a cloud of smoke. 'Like I always say, you *have* led a sheltered life, darling. No, he's Dino Constanza's lover.'

'Who's Dino Constanza?'

'He's the tutor I told you about. He runs the third-year fashion course. He's Italian and absolutely divine … But he doesn't like girls. He'll probably be here later on. Here, let's grab a seat.'

Libby sat down and looked around her. The place was beginning to fill up. Every few minutes the door opened to admit a new couple or a group. The men wore suits and hats and pencil-thin ties. The women, shorn of their winter coats, appeared in a riot of colourful dresses. There were one or two white girls amongst them. She was oddly relieved to see she and Charlie were not the only ones.

Plumes of cigarette smoke rose lazily towards the ceiling lights and the music slowly began to get louder. The hypnotic throb of reggae blasted forth from the enormous speakers set on either side of the stage. In the middle of the room, one or two couples began to dance.

Libby looked across at Charlie, who had closed her eyes, the better to hear and feel the music. She felt a mysterious tug at her body, as though she were being caught up in something she couldn't quite grasp. One or two people stopped by to say hello to Charlie, including Libby in their conversations and then taking leave with a cheerful 'nice meetin' yuh', before moving on. Like a child at a fairground show, she sipped at her drink, smoked and drank it all in.

By ten o'clock the basement was packed. Two young men joined them shortly after ten, Len and Junior, both of whom seemed to know Charlie. They had to shout to make themselves heard above the noise.

'Nice to meet yuh, Lizzie,' Junior said, looking down at her.

'No, *Libby*, not Lizzie,' she yelled back up.

'What's that?' The music was almost deafening.

She shook her head, smiling. *It doesn't matter.* They smiled rather self-consciously at one another. She liked the look of him. His eyes were a greeny-grey colour – lion's eyes – with thin splinters of yellow in the irises. He was the colour of coffee, dark and rich. He had curly brown hair, cut quite short, and a wide smile that opened onto very white teeth. He looked nice. The other young man, Len, had pulled up a chair close to Charlie.

'Want to dance?' Junior offered casually.

'Yes, I'd like that.' She smiled. It would at least put an end to watching Charlie and Len.

They both got up and he led her into the crowd, finding a space just big enough for the two of them to move. She found the rhythm easily and he was a good dancer.

'You like the music, huh?' He looked at her, seemingly amused. 'You dance well. Better than Charlie, to be honest. She's hopeless.'

They both laughed. There was a sudden commotion at the door and a loud cheer went up. They turned to look.

'Ah, the band's here. The Cats. You ever hear them play?'

She shook her head, watching as the four young men made their way to the stage. The atmosphere in the crowded basement was pulsatingly alive.

'You hungry?' he asked her, as the band began to play. The dance floor was now so crowded it was almost impossible to move.

She nodded, suddenly ravenous. 'Yes. I could eat a horse!' she exclaimed.

'Come on. Let's go.' She followed him dutifully as he threaded his way across the packed floor. As they climbed the stairs, it seemed only natural for him to reach behind him and take her by the hand. He grabbed their coats from the same lady, who smiled at him as they left.

Outside, the street was eerily quiet. They couldn't even hear the music. It was a clear night but the blue light of the police station at the corner of Ladbroke Grove and Chesterton Road shone as though through fog. It was chilly and she shivered a little inside her coat. She looked at him surreptitiously as they walked. He was probably six foot two or three, almost a head taller than she was.

'Why are you called "Junior"?' she asked curiously.

He smiled. 'It's a West Indian thing. The first-born son's always called "Junior".'

'So what's your dad's name?'

'Aloysius Jackson. So I'm Junior Jackson.'

'I like it. It sounds distinguished,' Libby said earnestly.

'Distinguished, eh? Suppose that's a compliment, coming from a girl like you.'

She wasn't sure how to respond. 'Where are you taking me?' she asked finally.

'To the finest roti shop in all of West London. You ever hear of a roti?'

''Course I have.' She laughed happily.

'How so?'

'My parents live in Trinidad. My dad works for BP.'

He stared down at her, amusement breaking across his face. 'You don't say. Your folks live in the *Caribbean*? Who says life's fair?'

'Where are you from?' she felt emboldened to ask. 'Which island?'

'Liverpool, Manchester, London, take your pick. I've been everywhere,' he said, laughing at her. 'My dad's from Jamaica, though.'

'Oh.' She felt rather foolish. 'Have you really never been to Jamaica?' Libby asked.

He shook his head. 'Nah. Britain's all I know. I was born in London, but me dad lives in Liverpool. I'm at college, just up the road, with Len.'

'Oh.' She felt even more foolish. 'What're you studying?' she asked, curious.

'Doing a degree course,' he said, a touch proudly. 'Engineering. And you? You're on Charlie's course, ain't you?'

Engineering sounded a lot more serious than her course. 'Yes, but I'm doing art. She's doing fashion.'

'She gonna be a fashion designer, eh? That's what she's always telling us.' He smiled, establishing an easy familiarity between himself, Len and Charlie. 'There's the roti shop, just up the road,' he said, pointing ahead to a small row of shops. 'Just in case you thought I was gonna kidnap you or something.'

'I didn't.' Libby smiled.

'So how long your parents been out there?'

'Oh, not very long. About two years. I don't know how long they'll stay. We were in Iraq and Oman before that but the political situation made it difficult to stay. Both times we left in the middle of the night.'

'Man, what a life you've had,' Junior said wonderingly.

'It sounds much more exciting than it really is,' she said quickly. She didn't want to appear as though she were showing off. 'Most of the time it's just new schools, fitting in, that sort of stuff.'

'Yeah, I know all about fitting in,' he said, half humorously. 'Anyway, here we are. Mama Johnson makes the best rotis in town. Makes a mean patty too. Come on.' He pushed open the door of a small corner shop and held it open for her.

The warm air burned their cold cheeks. He was obviously a regular. There was a loud, excitable exchange in patois with the woman behind the counter and then a few minutes later, two steaming savoury rotis were handed across the counter. They bit into them hungrily, not even waiting until they were outside the shop.

'Shall we get one for Len and Charlie?' she asked, busy polishing hers off.

He nodded. 'Good idea. Here, hold this. I'll order a couple more.'

Five minutes later, the cold nipping their heels, they were running back down Ladbroke Grove. Charlie and Len were exaggeratedly delighted with the rotis. Charlie held hers away from her as though it might drip onto her dress. They ate in the stairwell, away from the thumping music and the laughter and the smoke.

Libby felt gloriously alive. She turned to Charlie, whose eyes were shining in the dark. 'He's nice, isn't he?' she whispered.

Charlie looked at her and her expression was suddenly serious. 'Yes, he is. But be careful, Libby. You're the sort that'll throw caution to the wind. You'll throw everything you've got at it. But it won't be easy.'

She was a little drunk, Libby saw, but there was something protective and caring about the way that she said it. Libby was excited by this external description of herself as someone who would 'throw everything she had' at it.

She looked further up the stairs to where Len and Junior stood, smoking and chatting. Tim Crick seemed so very far away. Junior looked down at that moment and their eyes met. She held her breath. No words had been exchanged but there was a promise in his light green eyes that seemed to signal something beyond the reach of words. He winked, slowly and deliberately.

It was all it took. She was lost.

PART NINE
BETRAYAL

1963
Libby / Lily / Kit

56

It began with a cold. A harmless seasonal cold that blew up with the change in weather then stubbornly lingered on. It was October, almost two years to the day since they'd met. Libby was in her final year. As a concession, her parents had agreed to let her live in their Chelsea home.

'Just until you finish,' Kit said sternly. 'And you'd better finish with a First.'

Not bloody likely, Libby thought, but wisely chose to keep quiet.

The house was a stone's throw from college with four bedrooms and a living room and kitchen – all to herself. Her parents were currently in Singapore. So now, instead of hurried trysts in the tiny bedsit or suffering the indignity of being smuggled into halls without beady-eyed Mr Sampson seeing, they had a whole house to themselves. Junior still shared a bedsit with Len in the tall narrow house on Oxford Gardens. Their damp, stuffy room, partitioned in two with a sheet, was all the way at the top of the rickety staircase, tucked under the roof. Like most houses in the area, the house was packed to the rafters with tenants, almost all of them West Indian immigrants. In the basement, a family of four were squashed into two tiny rooms, neither as big as the kitchen in her Chelsea house, Libby thought guiltily when she peeped over the railings one day. The two children often bumped into Libby on her way in through the front door. The younger of the two always smiled shyly and called Libby 'miss'. The older child pretended not to see her. On the ground floor, a young couple with a baby and a mother-in-law shared the two-roomed flat and on the second and third floors were an assortment of men who seemed to come and go on an almost weekly basis.

Junior was also in his final year and did most of his studying in the library on Marylebone Road. Len too was studying, but he worked nights as a hospital porter, so the bedsit wasn't quite as crowded as it might otherwise have been. Still, it was hardly conducive to studying – or romance, for that matter.

Charlie had long since dropped her flirtation with Len and the West Indian crowd, of whom she'd once been so proud. Junior sensed it long before she did. Libby came to understand Charlie's enthusiasms for new things, new experiences and new people simply as part of a process of short-lived fascinations that rarely stood the test of time. She was enthralled with freshness and moved from one new fad to another, oblivious to what might be left behind. She had joined up with a new group at college, and seemed to spend most of her time at protests of one sort or another.

She and Libby were still friendly but the friendship was wearing thin. Not that Libby minded terribly. Most of her time was taken up with Junior and the complex hardships he was having to face in order to earn his degree.

'You should just come and live here,' Libby said to him, a few weeks after she'd moved in. It was a Sunday night and they'd been together since Friday afternoon.

'Nah. I'm okay with Len.'

'But this is so much more convenient,' Libby countered timidly. She held her breath.

'No. I'm fine where I am.'

'But there's loads of room here. Why not?'

'I'm fine where I am.' He was uncharacteristically short with her.

'But—'

'Libby, I said "no"!' It came out harshly. Seeing he'd shocked her, he softened. 'Look, I'm not about to sneak around in your parents' house when they're not here, all right? It'd be different ... well, forget it. I'm not doin' it and that's the end of it.'

She didn't dare ask the question sitting on the tip of her tongue. *How would it be different?*

But towards the end of October, just as the weather was beginning to turn, Junior caught a cold, which turned rapidly into a throat infection.

This time, Libby wouldn't take no for an answer. 'It's that bloody room of yours,' she fumed, fussing around him in her parents' double bed, as busily efficient as any nurse. 'It's damp and you never have the heating on long enough.'

'It's expensive,' he wheezed in a hoarse, closed whisper, which was the only way he could speak.

'Well, you don't have to pay for heating here. You're not to go back until you're better. I'm not letting you go back, at least not until you're properly better. I'll make you some broth. And you're to eat every last drop.'

'All right, Matron,' Junior croaked. He was too weak to argue.

She stood by his bedside for a while, looking down at him. There was no further sound. He'd fallen asleep. He had the warm, feverish smell of people who've lain in bed too long. She was overcome with a sudden tenderness. She had never had to look after anyone. Both Eluned and Maev had had nannies to do everything an older sister should do, and she'd never even owned a pet. Her mother wasn't the sort to fuss over anyone, let alone her own children.

She was filled with the desire to nurse Junior, smothering him with her concern. So where had it come from? She had no idea.

She carefully lifted the counterpane away from his face. He was hot again. The fever had risen. The doctor who'd called round earlier had prescribed a dose of antibiotics. If he'd been surprised to see a coloured man asleep in the charming little house at 39 Drayton Gardens, he chose not to say.

Libby picked up the packet and counted out the remaining pills. If he wasn't better by the following day, she thought to herself anxiously, she would ring the doctor again.

She went to the windows and drew back the curtains, looking down onto the garden. It was nearly seven o'clock and the sky was deepening. The noise of traffic floated up to her, along with the mingling sound of other people's radios. Light filtered into the house through the orange and gold leaves of the copper beech trees that lined the pavement. The room was filled with a burnished glow, like candlelight. She let the curtain drop and quietly left the room.

In the kitchen, she fished one of her mother's aprons out of a cupboard and began assembling the ingredients to make a broth. She poured herself a small measure of gin, feeling for the moment entirely grown-up and in command of the pots and pans. But there was only one forlorn onion in the basket under the sink when she bent down to look. She quickly downed the gin and whipped off her apron. There was probably just enough time to get a few vegetables from the greengrocer on the corner before he closed for the night. She grabbed a coat and left the house.

In the shop, she was indistinguishable from the other housewives who, like her, had popped out at the last minute to buy a missing ingredient or two. She enjoyed the few minutes of imposture, selecting her onions, and then carried her purchases back in a blue-and-white striped plastic bag, feeling every inch the little wife.

The following morning, to her relief, the fever broke and Junior slowly began to recover. But the experience of living together had brought out a desire in her to create a life based on an intimacy that she'd never experienced between her parents, with their polite-but-distant accommodation of one another. She craved the closeness in which she and Junior had lived so easily and so naturally. She phoned college to say she was ill. For a week, they existed only for and to each other.

When the week was up and they both descended back into the world, it seemed impossible to her that they would go back to how it had been before. She couldn't bear the thought of seeing each other in disconnected, awkward snatches, spending hours inside cramped phone booths or in cafés where they spun a cup of coffee between them. It was ridiculous, she argued. It just didn't make sense.

So he stayed on.

57

For Libby, the daily preoccupation of living with Junior gave a shape and direction to her life, which had hitherto drifted along. Being reasonably good at art, she'd quickly discovered, wasn't enough. *Everyone* at college was good. In order to stand out, something more was needed, which she knew she didn't possess. So many of the girls on her course were fuelled by a desire *not* to do what their mothers or grandmothers had done. They were often unable to put into words what they *did* want, preferring instead to define the shape of their lives by what they didn't. They didn't want to belong to the world of women. They didn't want to think of marriage as a social rather than a personal bond. There would be no 'I'll have to ask my husband what he thinks'. They would never join knitting or reading groups to pass the time until their husbands returned from work, the way they'd seen their mothers do.

Libby listened to the heated discussions in the cafés and bedrooms with a growing sense of disconnection. For her, the problem was not one of rejection of the values of the previous generation. It was the opposite: she craved them. Unknown to Junior, since she didn't dare speak of it, her dreams for the future centred precisely around those things that everyone else seemed to dismiss. She *wanted* marriage. She *wanted* children. She *wanted* to create the sort of cosy home her mother refused to provide. When she thought about her own family in the dreamy, distracted way that always seemed to occur after making love, it was in a picture-postcard simplicity – one big happy family, where differences of race, creed, class had all disappeared. *That* was the dream. There was no precedent for what she and Junior would create. She would invent it.

58

One Friday morning in early November, Libby woke up later than usual and luxuriously stretched out a hand to feel for Junior. He was gone. The space next to her was empty. She turned her head and forced her eyes open. The small alarm clock on the bedside table showed it was nearly nine thirty. She'd overslept by hours. She sat bolt upright. Her first lecture began at nine – there was no way she would make it in time.

She lay back against the headboard, conscious of a dull throbbing in her left temple. It was the cheap wine they'd drunk the night before, celebrating Len's success in passing the first of an endless stream of exams that would see him qualify one day as a solicitor. Junior had been in a strange, restless mood. They'd all drunk too much but Junior must have had the presence of mind to get up in the morning and make his way to college.

She slid her legs out of bed and picked up the dressing gown that was lying on the floor. It was his. She smiled to herself, pulling it tightly around her waist and inhaling the scent of him that was as familiar to her as her own.

She walked downstairs to the kitchen, shivering in her bare feet. It was November but already it felt like winter had arrived. There was a note to her lying on the kitchen table. She picked it up, frowning as she read: *I'm going up to Liverpool for the weekend. My dad's not well. See you on Monday. J.*

She blew out her cheeks in annoyance. She'd been looking forward to the weekend alone with him. She looked at the note again. It was typical of him. Short on detail. His relationship with his father was complicated, although he said very little about him or the rest of his family. She knew there were two half-sisters in Liverpool with whom he'd recently been reunited. His dad had walked out on his first wife, leaving Junior to grow up alone on a council estate in Canton, one of the roughest parts of Cardiff. His mother had given up when he was six or so, and he'd grown up in foster homes until he'd left at the age of seventeen to make his own way in the world. He said very little else, which only added to her sense of having created something special between them.

She put the note down and stood in front of the stove, her hand going out automatically for the small Italian coffee pot that her mother kept on the second shelf above the range. She felt self-conscious, standing there in bare feet, wrapped in his too-big dressing gown, her hair still tangled and matted from sleep. She put the coffee pot back. She would go out for a coffee, the way she used to before Junior moved in.

She went upstairs, washed her face and brushed her teeth. She pulled back the curtains to have a quick look at the weather – it was cold, grey and damp. She found a thick cable-knit sweater lying on the back of a chair and quickly pulled it on, fished a pair of jeans from the chest of drawers and thrust her feet into a pair of shoes. She grabbed her handbag from the bannisters and let herself out.

The air outside was cold and there was a very fine mist that clung to her fringe. Opposite, the houses were still shuttered and silent. Men left for work around eight but it often wasn't until noon that the women emerged, some as carefully dressed up as if they were going to church, or a party. Occasionally a uniformed nanny with a pram strolled up and down the street, but today all was quiet.

She walked down Drayton Gardens towards the café on the corner of King's Road and Beaufort Street, which she often frequented. As she crossed Fulham Road, she caught sight of the old woman she'd seen several times sitting on a bench just outside the cinema. She glanced at her curiously. She was wearing a fur coat with the collar turned up against her face and she had sunglasses on. Libby had noticed her a few times, either coming out of a shop or crossing the road – an odd, slightly hunched figure, always wearing the same dark brown coat with black fur cuffs and collar. Her hair was white and scraped back into a bun. With her silly oversized sunglasses she looked like an ageing film star who'd fallen on hard times. Her shoes were scuffed and she carried a shopping bag instead of a handbag. For a second the woman's face was turned towards hers but, behind the dark glasses, it wasn't possible to know what she was looking at.

Libby continued down Beaufort Street, her hands shoved deep in her jeans pockets to keep warm.

Stan's Café was packed. She ordered a milky café au lait from the sullen-faced girl behind the counter and took it to the solitary spare window seat, wishing she'd thought to buy a newspaper en route. She sat down, wrapped her hands around the mug and took a sip. The door opened suddenly, emitting a loud jangle.

She looked up briefly. It was the trampy old woman. She watched out of the corner of her eye as she shuffled to the counter and in a loud, perfectly modulated voice of a bygone era, asked the waitress to: 'Give me a cup of whatever she's having.' Libby felt a ripple of something – recognition? – run lightly up and down her spine. It seemed to her that she'd heard the voice before... But where?

She looked at the woman again. She'd removed her sunglasses and was bearing down upon her table, a cup and saucer balanced carefully in one claw-like hand. She wasn't...? Yes, she was coming to join Libby.

Oh, God, Libby thought to herself uncharitably. Why me?

'Do you mind if I join you?' the woman asked, putting her café au lait down on the table without waiting for an answer. The milky coffee slopped over the edge of the saucer onto the Formica top.

Libby looked around her uncomfortably. Couldn't the crazy old woman have found somewhere else to sit, or someone else to bother?

'No, that's fine,' she said, a trifle grudgingly. She scooted her chair over to make room.

'Ah, that's better,' the woman sighed, sitting down. She made a great show of stowing her plastic bag under the table and arranging her coat over the back of the chair.

She wasn't quite as ancient as Libby had thought... Sixty, perhaps? Now that she was sitting opposite and she'd taken off those ridiculous glasses, she was able to get a proper look at her. There was something about the woman's face that was strangely familiar, as though she'd seen her before, but a long, long time ago. Her eyebrows were thin and plucked in the shape of brows before the war, artificially arched, giving her a look of permanent surprise. Her white hair was pulled tightly back and secured with a diamanté pin. The eyes were brilliant blue, like two dabs of turquoise in an alabaster face. Suddenly the woman spoke from underneath the painted mask of her face.

'You're Kit's daughter, aren't you?'

Libby's cup was halfway to her mouth. She lowered it in surprise. 'Do I know you?' she asked.

The woman shook her head. 'Have you got a cigarette?' she asked politely.

Libby shook her head. 'No. I don't smoke.'

'Good for you. Well, I do. And I haven't got a cigarette. Won't you get one for me, my dear?'

Libby gaped at her. She scraped back her chair and walked up to the counter. Two minutes later she returned with a packet of Woodbines.

'Here,' she said, putting them on the table. 'Who are you?'

The woman took her time in answering. She tapped out a cigarette, leaned back and asked the man at the table behind them to light it for her, before she finally turned back to Libby.

'Don't you recognise me?' she asked archly.

Libby shook her head. 'Should I?' Her heart suddenly began to beat very fast. 'Have I seen you before?'

The woman's full gaze came around upon hers. 'No. But I've seen *you*,' she said, blowing the smoke out of the corner of her mouth. She made a sharp, dismissive gesture. 'Oh, not from anything *she's* ever shown me. No, of course not. But I've seen pictures over the years. Not many. One or two. Mother sent them. Father never spoke to me again. Not ever. He went to his grave without speaking to me. Imagine.'

Libby's heart was hammering so hard she thought it might burst. 'What do you mean? Who are you?'

The woman smiled. 'I'm your aunt. Has she never spoken about me?'

Despite the bravado, the sunglasses, the fur coat and the air of self-possession, there was something terribly forlorn in the woman's glance.

Libby shook her head slowly from side to side. She had the terrible sinking feeling her life was about to be turned upside down.

59

In the blood-darkness of her closed eyes, the events of the past few hours seemed impossible, as though she'd dreamed them. But when she raised her hand to wipe her cheeks, she caught the scent of the woman – she couldn't bring herself to think of her as Aunt Lily – on the back of her hand and it set her trembling all over again. She got up from the table, walked into the hallway where the telephone directory was kept and pulled it onto her lap. She unfolded the crumpled piece of paper that the woman had given her and smoothed it out. Her handwriting was remarkably similar to Mother's, all looping curls and remarkably neat penmanship. *Lady Wharton. Chalfont Hall, Hooke, Dorset.* She took the directory back into the kitchen with her and picked up the phone. She dialled the operator and could hear her own breathing, harsh and laboured in her ears.

'Operator, could you connect me to Hooke 732, please.'

'One moment, please,' the operator sang out in a ridiculously cheerful voice. 'Putting you through.'

It rang only once. In the middle of the second ring, someone answered. 'Chalfont Hall.'

'Could... could I speak to Lady Wharton, please?' Libby began in what she hoped was a normal-sounding voice.

'Who may I say is calling?' It was the voice of a young girl.

Libby's heart was racing. In a single afternoon, her world had been thrown off-kilter. She'd been told both her grandparents were dead, that they'd died before she was born. Her mother wasn't an only child. She had a sister. Why had Mother lied?

'My... my name is Libby Kentridge. I'm... I'm—' She stopped, unable to continue. What was she to say?

'Just a moment.' She heard the receiver being laid down on a surface, then the sound of footsteps retreating. After a few minutes, it was picked up again.

'Hello? Who is it?' It was the voice of a century past, with the exaggerated, drawn-out enunciation of the aristocracy. 'Hello?' the woman repeated.

'I ... I ... my name is Libby. Libby Kentridge and—'

'Elizabeth?' the woman interrupted her immediately. 'Elizabeth Kentridge?'

Libby swallowed. 'Yes, I—'

'Are you here? In England?' She was interrupted again.

'Yes, I'm in London. I—'

'Come and see me. Don't waste another minute. I *must* see you. I must see you *at once*. Catch the train down. I'll have the chauffeur wait for you at the station. Oh, my darling girl. Come at once.' There was a click as the receiver was replaced abruptly.

Libby's knees gave way underneath her and she sat down in the chair, hard. She felt as though her whole life had turned upside down, like a great rock on the seabed being dragged along by the current, coming to rest in another place. She was like a startled creature who'd lain under it, suddenly being thrust into the light. She sat there with her face in her hands and waited for the trembling to pass.

60

A chauffeur was waiting on the platform, just as the woman whom she had difficulty thinking of as her grandmother had said. An elderly man, perhaps in his late sixties, he wore a uniform and a stiff peaked cap. As soon as she stepped off the train and onto the platform, he came forwards.

'Miss Elizabeth?'

She nodded vigorously. 'Yes, yes ... that's me. But no one calls me Elizabeth. I'm Libby.'

'I seen you straight off, soon as you come off the train. Ye've the look of her. Yer mother. Och, her Ladyship's beside herself. She's nivver slept a wink since you phoned!' He was Scottish, with a thick, rolling burr.

Libby couldn't speak. Her mind was whirling. Her heart was racing. For the past few hours she'd been on the brink of constant tears.

They bumped down one cavernous country lane after another, sometimes brushing the sides of the hedgerows, now stripped bare in the face of approaching winter. The land was soft and undulating, bringing the novels she'd read in school in hot, dusty places like Baghdad and Oman to mind where she'd tried desperately to picture the England Thomas Hardy wrote about, and couldn't. Oak trees were fringed sentinels scoring the horizon. Every now and then a flock of birds – geese, starlings – blew up out of nowhere and traced lazy patterns in the light blue sky. London had been all fog and mist but by the time the train pulled into Yeovil, the mists had cleared.

The car, a classic, boxy Lancaster of the sort she'd never seen before, bounced its way across a rutted entrance over a small country brook and suddenly, some way off in the distance, she saw the house. Low, pale yellow stone walls on either side of the gate with a brassy plaque that announced the destination. *Chalfont Hall.* A long, straight-backed line of trees led the eye all the way up the gravelled driveway to the house.

'Here we are,' the chauffeur announced unnecessarily, pulling up in front of the main entrance. 'Her Ladyship'll be in the drawing room. I'll bring yer bag around, dinnae you worry.'

Libby's mouth was hanging open. The house was of red brick and cream stone, two wings falling away on either side of an imposing entrance tower. Rows of impressively high and elaborately draped windows on the ground and first floor gave the appearance of a grand dame looking rather coquettishly out. Manicured hedges framed the front steps, leading to the massive studded oak front door.

It opened as she walked towards it. A maid was standing in the doorway, waiting for her. She was very young, perhaps Eluned's age, and with a start, Libby realised she was entering a different world. Her mother's world.

'Afternoon, miss. Her Ladyship's waitin' in the drawing room, miss.' The girl practically curtsied as she spoke. 'Just up them stairs.'

Libby walked into the entrance hall. She stood still. An enormous staircase wound its way up to the first floor. There were antlers and portraits on every square inch of wall and the ceiling was an intricate bas-relief of cornices, ceiling roses and decorated panels that wouldn't have looked out of place on a wedding cake. But, as impressive as it was, if you looked closely, Libby realised as she began to climb the stairs, there was also a rather sad, rather shabby air to the place. The curtains were elaborate but threadbare, the carpet underfoot was frayed, as were the upholstered window seats halfway up the staircase. A grandfather clock with gilded weights the size of sledgehammers chimed the hour loudly as she reached the top, making her jump. The doors to the drawing room at the top of the stairs were open.

From within, the patrician voice boomed out, 'Is she here? Is that her, Mary?'

Libby stood in the doorway. Her heart was thumping. Through the tall windows at the end of the room, the outside light began to deepen. It was nearly three o'clock in the afternoon. It had taken her the better part of the day to get to Chalfont. She hadn't eaten since breakfast and she was beginning to feel decidedly woozy.

'Is that you, Elizabeth? Come here.'

Libby moved forwards slowly. Her grandmother was sitting on one of the enormous leather chesterfields that dotted the room. For a moment, the two women, separated by half a century and a lifetime, stared at each other.

She was so tiny, Libby thought to herself. She looked nothing like her voice. She was dressed almost entirely in black. Her hair was white and scraped into a neat bun at the nape of her neck. She wore a thick string of pearls and there was a cane resting to one side of the couch, which she gripped with evident force, levering herself upright.

'Come here. Let me look at you properly. My eyesight isn't what it used to be,' she said, beckoning to Libby to come forwards. She grasped Libby's arm, pulling her closer.

Libby looked down at her grandmother's hand. It was so thin! The bones folded together as narrow as the slats of a silk-tasselled opera fan that her mother used to have.

'You take after her, you know,' her grandmother said slowly. 'You're darker, of course you are. But you do. You're very alike.'

'Wh-what shall I call you?' Libby blurted out.

Her grandmother looked up at her in surprise. 'Why, Grandmamma,' she said, as though the question were ridiculous. 'That's what I called *my* grandmother. Are you hungry, my dear? Shall I ring for some tea?'

'Yes ... yes, please,' Libby said, sitting down gingerly next to her grandmother.

Her grandmother picked up a little silver bell and jangled it furiously. 'Mary will be up directly,' she said, arranging the stiff folds of her pleated dress as she sank back down into the sofa. 'Cook made a cake. Soon as I put the phone down this morning, I called her in. She only comes in twice a week, that's the thing. Sign of the times, I'm afraid.' A weak, stray ray of sunlight came in through one of the windows. Dust motes began to dance, circling upwards, borne on some invisible current of air. 'Soon as I put the phone down,' she repeated.

Libby felt the prick of tears behind her eyes. 'I don't understand anything,' she said, her voice cracking. 'Why ... why did we never visit you? Mother said you were both dead. Why? Why did she say that? And why didn't she say anything about a sister?'

Her grandmother glanced at her and then quickly looked away. 'She never mentioned us? Never? Not once?'

Libby shook her head. 'No. She never talks about herself or her past. Ever. And Father's the same. It's as if they both only began after the war. Father has a sister somewhere but I've never met her. Why?'

Her grandmother pulled a lace handkerchief from her pocket and dabbed at her eyes. Libby stared at her. She was crying.

'There's been such *grief* in this family,' she said, sniffing and wiping away her tears. 'Such grief. You don't know the half of it, Elizabeth. All that fuss with Lily ... Oh, it was *years* before she was able to come back home.'

'What fuss?'

Her grandmother looked at her. 'Did Lily not tell you?'

Libby shook her head vehemently. 'She just kept insisting I come to see you.'

'Typical,' her grandmother said tartly. 'Typical Lily. Leave it all to me. That's what she's done her whole life.' She dabbed at her eyes again. 'Poor Lily. She lost everything. Everything. They took everything away. She was so young, you see ... and he was so handsome and *wealthy* and everything.'

'Who?'

'Her husband. The German. The count.'

Libby stared at her. 'What happened to him?'

'Oh, they hanged him. Right after the war. There were no children,

285

thank God. And of course she wanted to come home. But Father wouldn't have it. He wouldn't let her come back. There was this list, you see ... She'd named people. She named us, our friends, everyone. It was a scandal. She was just so *young*,' her grandmother kept bleating, as if it excused everything. 'So young.'

'When did she come back?'

'After Father died. I couldn't say "no", could I? And she had nothing. *Nothing!* Just the clothes she was wearing. They took everything. You can't imagine what it was like over there, after the war. They treated them so badly, so very badly.'

'How did she know where to find me?'

'It was Margaret again. Margaret Arscott. She took her in. She did the same for your mother, you know. With the baby, and everything.'

'Baby? What baby?' Libby felt the beating of her own blood, loud and strong. She was very close to discovering what it was that had cast such a shadow upon everyone's lives, including hers.

There was a sudden silence. Her grandmother's bright blue eyes came to rest on Libby's. The same blue as her mother's. As Aunt Lily's. But not her own.

She laid a hand on Libby's. 'My darling girl,' she said suddenly. 'Sometimes, I look back on it all and I wonder what would have happened if I ... well, if I *hadn't* sent her away. I didn't know what else to do. They all blamed me, you see. For sending Kit over there in the first place. But what else could I have done? I never thought ... None of us did. No one could have predicted it. I just did what I thought was best. I wrote to her. Oh, you can't imagine the letters I wrote! You can't imagine the guilt! When Father died, I was all alone, darling Libby. I didn't know myself. I thought I'd have missed myself. I'd have walked straight past myself in the dark. Do you ever feel like that sometimes?'

Libby caught her breath. 'Grandmamma.' She stumbled over the word. 'Please, *please* just tell me the truth.'

Her grandmother was silent for a few minutes. Then she turned her face towards Libby's. 'The truth?' she asked quietly. 'I've no idea what that is any more. Only Kit knows. You'd better ask her.'

61

'That you, Lib?' Junior heard the door shut quietly downstairs. He hurriedly got up and bounded down, two stairs at a time. He'd been worried about her.

'Yes, it's me. I'm back,' she answered weakly, taking off her coat. She turned around to face him and he saw she'd been crying.

'What's the matter? Where've you been? I got back this morning but you'd disappeared. Where've you been all day? What's the matter, Lib?'

She couldn't speak. She could only stare at him mutely, shaking her head. Her eyes were swollen and there were smudges of mascara underneath her lashes. She kept hold of her gloves, gripping them tightly.

'What is it?' he asked again, more gently this time. He walked over and took her by the arm. 'Come here. What's the matter?'

Libby seemed too dazed to speak. He led her to the kitchen table and pulled out a chair. He'd never seen her so distraught. It took her a while to control her sobbing and then it all came pouring out.

62

She was a funny girl, Junior thought to himself as they walked along the Embankment a few hours later, arms tightly linked. He'd listened to the whole story with a strange sense of detachment. Why did it all matter so much? So her mother hadn't told her about her life before she met Libby's father... Why was it such a big deal? Her aunt had been a Nazi sympathiser during the war... Who cared about that now? It was all such a long time ago. There'd been an illegitimate child... So what? He'd tried to make a joke of it. Where he was from, he said, hugging her, it was the *norm*. But it only set off another round of sobbing.

'She was probably too ashamed,' he'd said to her, trying unsuccessfully to staunch the tears.

She shook her head. 'But imagine cutting everyone off like that? Her own *sister*? I had a grandfather I never met! How could she have done that to me?'

He shrugged, at a loss for words. His own upbringing had been so peripatetic. He'd spent the first few years of his life shuttling between his mother's home in Cardiff and his father's in Liverpool, feeling out of place in both ... Until his mother decided she couldn't cope any longer and he'd been shunted into foster care. His father's new wife didn't want him. There was nothing for it. He moved from one foster home to another until he was old enough to move out for good. Family? He barely knew what the word meant. He couldn't understand why it worried her so.

He stroked her hair, wondering if he should go on to make love to her ... Would that help?

It didn't.

Now, walking along beside her, he was relieved that the worst of the storm seemed to have passed. Yes, she was a funny girl. When he first met her, he was struck by her looks, as everyone was. She was so tall and slender, and with such unusual colouring. And those features that didn't somehow add up ... He'd stared at her that first night, trying to work out what she was. Italian? Spanish? Turkish? You couldn't tell. And then she opened her mouth and there was that beautiful voice, the sort of voice you heard on the news and in the mouths of girls from rich homes. Cultured, upper-class girls. She had long, thick hair and the sort of scent that permeated everything but in a light, fresh way, not cloying and heavy like most of the girls he knew. It was one of the first things he noticed about her – her smell. That first night in the club it stayed with him all night. Every time he moved his head, he could smell her. When he woke up the following morning and he went to put on his jacket, her scent was still there. He moved about in it all day long; by the time evening fell, he missed her so strongly it was physical, like a hunger pang, gnawing at him. He got the number to her halls of residence where she stayed with that other girl, Charlie, who was a friend of Len's. He didn't care much for Charlie, all smiles and knowing laughter. He could sense her impatience to get on to the next new thing. For her, the infatuation with Len and all the others – her 'boys', as she called them – would only last as long as she felt herself to be doing something daring or different.

Libby wasn't like that. She didn't care who you were, what you were. With her, none of it mattered. Sitting with her, talking, laughing, teasing, flirting... you were equal to her, no more, no less. Life hadn't changed. You were still the subject of strange looks and the odd, furtive glance to see if there were more of you lurking behind. One black man was uncomfortable. Two was a danger and three was definitely a riot-in-waiting. But when he was with Libby, all of that melted away. It didn't seem much, but it was priceless.

When they started going together, properly, he saw that there was a different side to her. For all her privileges, she was as lonely and rootless as he was. As unlikely as it seemed, they were a perfect match. Other women he'd known – and he'd known his fair share – wanted only to possess him. They wanted to take him, mould him, shape him and own him. Libby wanted the opposite. She seemed to want nothing more than to devote herself entirely to him. It flattered him enormously, especially at first, but it worried him, too. Would he be equal to it? Could he be? It brought out an anxiety in him that he thought he'd long ago successfully conquered. But he had not. It took him straight back to childhood, to the third or fourth foster home; he could no longer remember which one. Nottingham? Birmingham? It mattered little. He'd put on a clean shirt and combed his hair neatly. The woman of the house had come downstairs to meet him. He could read the relief in her eyes. Yes, he was coloured, right enough, but at least he wasn't too dark. That was a good thing. No one wanted a child with skin the colour of midnight. He didn't relax – not yet, not quite – but he saw that she did, and that too was a good thing. He stood very straight and looked her directly in the eye, hopeful that his best qualities would show through. It was that sense of having nothing other than a steady gaze and his clean shirt to go on that he thought would stay with him for the rest of his life. Nothing more. He had only himself to rely on.

And then he met Libby and suddenly a whole other world opened up, full of possibilities that he couldn't yet guess at. A family, a context, a home... All this he wanted to tell her, but couldn't. Some instinct in him that would never quite disappear told him to hold something back. Just a little. Just in case.

And now there was this. A gust of wind whipped her hair across her face, landing on his arm. He reached down and gently brushed it aside. She looked up at him and smiled and then the words were out of his mouth before he could stop himself.

'Marry me.'

63

The house was spotless. She'd spent the entire day cleaning and polishing and cleaning again, as though seeking not just her mother's approval to marry Junior but recognition of her ability to keep house into the bargain. At last it was done. The last plate had been wiped clean, the last surface dusted. It was nearly ten o'clock and her parents were due to arrive any minute. She sat down at the freshly scrubbed kitchen table and tried to calm her nerves. It had been six weeks since the day her aunt had approached her. Six weeks since Junior had asked her to marry him. Six weeks since her whole life had been turned inside out and upside down. She'd rung her parents to break the news of the engagement but said nothing about the other discoveries. That she would have to do in person. Those were not the questions to ask down a crackling international phone line. She wanted her mother to explain everything. To tell her, face to face, what it all meant.

Suddenly she heard the throaty purr of a taxi pulling up outside. She got up from the table and as quietly as possible – she had no idea why she felt she should creep rather than walk – went to the front door. She opened it just as her mother got out of the taxi. She was wearing a trench coat, belted at the waist. She had on a felted hat and a black silk scarf was knotted around her neck. Maev was a tiny bundle of coats and a jaunty yellow hat. She watched as her father paid the driver and lugged the two suitcases out of the boot. Her mother picked up Maev and together they climbed the short flight of stairs. Libby bent down to hug her sister and for a moment they all stood in the doorway, staring at each other. Her mother's skin was very pale with the faintest smattering of freckles. She looked tired but the trademark lipstick had been freshened and a light dusting of powder had taken the shine off her nose. Kit stepped forwards and gave Libby a brief hug, enveloping her in the scent of L'Air du Temps that was imprinted on Libby's brain as belonging to her mother and to childhood. 'Here we are at *last*,' she said, stepping back quickly. 'Hello, darling.'

'Hello, Mother,' Libby said as a sudden wave of shyness crashed over her. She hugged her father. All three looked at each other expectantly. Maev was overcome with unaccustomed shyness. She hadn't seen her big sister for over a year.

'Well, come on, let's go inside. It's freezing! Let's have a cup of tea. Daddy and I are absolutely parched,' her mother said briskly, stepping into the hallway. Libby and her father looked at each other, smiled timidly, and followed her in.

'The house is spotless,' Kit said, coming down the short flight of steps into the kitchen, half an hour later. 'Did you bring in a char?'

Libby shook her head. Her father had gone upstairs to take a nap. It was just the two of them. 'No. I'm perfectly capable of cleaning a house, Mother,' she said sharply. They'd only been in the house for thirty minutes and the tension was already mounting. She knew she was being unfair. It was partly self-inflicted, she knew. For the past six weeks she'd been torn between the most conflicting emotions she'd ever experienced – from complete confusion to elation. Junior had asked her to marry him but her mother was now a stranger to her. She didn't know where to turn or what to think.

'Of course you are. I'm only teasing,' Kit said quickly. 'So, where's this young man of yours? When do we get to see him?'

'I asked him to Sunday lunch tomorrow,' she began hesitantly. 'I ... I thought that would be a good time for you to meet him.'

'Good idea,' her mother agreed. There was a moment's awkward silence. Libby could feel her mother's eyes on her as she got up to refill her mug. Then she spoke. 'Is ... is everything all right, Libby?' she asked in a low voice.

Libby turned around. She faced her mother squarely. 'I don't know what you mean.'

There was another awkward pause. Her mother bit her lip. Libby had never seen her appear so unsure of herself. 'I just mean ... it's awfully sudden, isn't it?'

'No. We've been together for two years. That's not sudden at all.'

'Two years? But ... but you've never said a word!'

'Well, you've never asked.'

They stared at one another. Libby could feel the sudden build-up of tears begin behind her eyes. She blinked hard. She was determined not to cry. Kit's eyes fell first. She looked down at her hands. 'Libby,' she began hesitantly. 'Is there something you're not telling me?'

Libby's mouth tightened. 'What do you mean?' she asked sullenly. Her mother seemed on the verge of speaking, then thought better of it. There was another silence. How dare she ask me, Libby thought. She, of all people – who was she to talk about secrets? 'Well, I'm looking forward to meeting him,' her mother said finally. 'We both are.'

Libby couldn't speak. She looked at her mother's face. Who *was* she really? What had she done? And what had she done with her child? The other one; the first one? Libby's brother?

64

Kit put down her blusher brush and looked at herself in the mirror. Her face stared back at her impassively. To her mind, it was the same face she'd always carried, the habitual expression of wary confidence a particular feature of hers since childhood. She brought up a finger to blot her lipstick and suddenly her composure cracked. Her face crumpled. How could it be that her own daughter had said nothing to her? And what emotion had she sensed in Libby beneath the surface – resentment? Anger? There was something bothering Libby but she couldn't put a finger on it. The way she'd looked at her – as though from a great distance, somewhere far beyond the usual bonds of familial love.

But before she could think about it any further, she heard the doorbell. A few seconds later, a gasp of chill wind, smelling of rain, blew into the house and up the narrow staircase. The door slammed shut again.

They were here. It was time to meet the young man who was about to become her son-in-law.

She stood up and smoothed down her skirt. Paul was already in the living room, organising drinks. She had a feeling they'd be in need of one soon.

Libby and Junior stood together self-consciously in the doorway, looking up at her as she walked down the stairs. She blinked in surprise. He was black! It took her a few seconds to compose her face.

'Welcome,' she called out, her voice unnaturally loud. 'At *last* we get to meet you. Come in. Come through to the sitting room. At least it's warmer in there.'

She was conscious of Libby's eyes following her as she ushered them in. She prayed Paul's expression wouldn't somehow betray him. To be honest, she had no idea how he'd react.

Dear God, was *that* why Libby had kept it quiet?

There was a strange tension running below the surface of the mother's hospitality that Junior picked up on straight away. She was not all she seemed, he decided quickly. He couldn't have said how he'd detected it, but it was definitely there. Years of sitting on the sidelines in one foster family after another had fashioned a keen awareness in him of all the myriad things that could not be said, touched upon or admitted to in families. It was ironic. He, who for so long had wanted nothing more than to belong to a family – *any* family – was now on his guard for anything that struck him as false or amiss. And something was definitely amiss. She was tough, too. Powerful. But the source of her power didn't come, as Libby seemed to think, from a strong sense of what was right and proper in the world. It was the opposite. There was a strong aware-ness of what was *wrong*. She was like a piece of firm and attractive fruit, he decided. Good to look at and to touch ... but then your thumb might suddenly go through a soft and rotten spot.

'So, what's your *real* name if Junior's your nickname?' she asked, getting up to fetch something from the sideboard.

'It's not a nickname. It's popular amongst Jamaicans,' he said with a faint smile. 'You take the same name as your father but no one ever calls you that. You're always Junior.' He was mindful of Libby's instructions not to give anything away of his 'situation', as she'd put it. She didn't want them to know he'd been in foster homes 'or anything like that'.

'So what's your father's name?' Libby's father asked, more out of politeness than interest.

Libby probably wasn't aware of it but the tension emanating from him was easier. It was clean and clear. Hostile. He knew how to deal with *that*.

'Aloysius Jackson. That's why I'm called Junior. He's the senior.'

'He was a musician,' Libby spoke up proudly. 'He used to be really famous. He played at all the top places in London. What was the band's name, Junior? The Chicago Jets or something?'

Junior shook his head, a little embarrassed. 'No. Louie Lejeune and—'

A loud crash suddenly interrupted him. Both Junior and the father jumped to their feet. The mother had dropped the glass bowl containing the trifle. Cream and custard splattered them all. Bits of fruit went flying. There was a moment of utter confusion and the mother sank to her knees, as if she'd been hit. Libby remained where she was, rooted to her seat. He went to help the mother to her feet, slipping on the pooling mess of custard as he went. The father bent to retrieve the largest bits of glass and Libby rushed to his side.

'What happened, Mother? Are you all right? You went down! Just like that!' The worried exclamations bounced off each other.

The mother shook her head, obviously dazed. 'I don't know ... I must've tripped ... I'm sorry. I've made such a mess ...'

'No, don't worry about that.' The father was able to take charge. 'Here, lean on me.'

Together, he and Libby helped her to her feet. Slowly, dazedly, the mother got up. She allowed herself to be led away, murmuring apologies. Junior remained where he was, watching them go. He looked down at his feet. Large globs of custard and hardening cream were splattered across his shoes. He shook his head. They were a strange family indeed. Something wasn't quite right.

Kit brushed aside Paul's frantic attempts to clean her skirt and shoes. 'I'm fine, I'm fine,' she mumbled, allowing Libby to lead her up the stairs and into her study. 'Go and see to Junior. Libby'll help me get changed.'

Libby closed the door behind him. Kit sat down heavily in her chair. Her teeth simply wouldn't stop chattering.

'What happened, Mother?' Libby asked, her whole face tightening in concern. 'Did you trip?'

She shook her head. 'No, I ... I just came over all faint for a minute, that's all. I'll be fine.'

'Shall I ring for the doctor?'

'No, no ... I'll ... I'll be fine. I ... I don't know what happened.'

'Shall I get you some water?' Libby straightened up, prepared to run downstairs again.

Kit shook her head. For a moment, the two stared at each other.

'You don't like him, do you?' Libby said suddenly, the concern on her face vanishing as she spoke.

Kit shook her head. 'No, don't be silly. I ... I don't even know him.'

'No, I can see it in your face. You were shocked when you saw him, weren't you?'

'Libby ... please. You're being overdramatic. I ... it's just a surprise, that's all. I mean, we didn't even know—'

'I don't believe you!' A terrible coldness came into Libby's voice. Kit was aware of the light above her head shining directly into her eyes. 'You *lied* to me.' Libby's voice was harder than she'd ever heard it. 'You've done nothing but lie to us all our lives. All of us! Daddy, me ... everyone!'

'Wh-what are you talking about?' Kit stammered, her heart beginning to race.

'I *know* who you are. I know what you did.'

Dread clutched at her. She opened her mouth to speak but nothing came out.

'Don't you want to know how I know?'

Kit swallowed. 'Know about what?' she whispered weakly. She knew beyond any shadow of doubt what was coming.

'Grandmamma told me. D'you want to know how I knew where to find her? D'you want to know who I met? Right here, in Chelsea? Your sister! You never told us you had a sister! You never told us you had a son!'

'Libby, please ...' Kit could hear herself pleading. She'd never pleaded with anyone before, certainly not her children. But she couldn't stop herself. Her mind was racing.

Libby was crying now, one hand on the door handle as if she were about to take flight. 'How could you?' she all but screamed.

'Libby ... the door! Shut the door!' It was all Kit could think about. She could hear footsteps coming up the stairs.

But Libby yanked it open instead. Her face was horribly twisted with rage and pain, but there was confusion in it too. She couldn't control herself. Kit saw now that the tension she'd sensed ever since she arrived had to do with that, with the dampening down of the dreadful knowledge she'd been carrying inside her.

Paul's face suddenly appeared in the doorway. He opened his mouth to speak but Libby's shrieks drowned him out.

'How *could* you?' she screamed. 'You just *abandoned* him! You just gave him away, as if he was *nothing*!'

'Libby!' He raised his voice. He tried to take her arm. 'Libby! Calm down! What's going on?'

But Libby was beyond hearing. 'You walked away . . . like you always do! You just walk away from everything, from all the mess and the *shit* you cause! And you leave us to mop up after you!' Her face was ugly with rage.

Paul tried to grab hold of her arm. 'What the hell's going on?' he all but shouted.

'Don't!' Kit staggered up from her chair.

Somewhere in the distance Maev began to cry. The whole house was being turned upside down. She heard another set of footsteps. Junior's face appeared behind Paul's. Her mind was in turmoil. Her whole body felt as though it were caught in a terrible vice.

'No, no . . . it wasn't like that. Please believe me.'

'I *don't* believe you! Don't you understand? I don't believe anything you say! You're a liar. You lie about *everything* – about your sister, about Grandmamma . . . And now you want to make sure I'll never be happy either!'

Kit closed her eyes. She shook her head from side to side. 'That's not it, I promise you, darling. That's not it. It's . . . I can't . . .' She couldn't go on. Lily? Lily was here? Libby had been to see her grandmother. *How?*

Junior tried to move past Paul to reach Libby but Paul's arm was blocking the way. It was all going horribly wrong.

'Libby!' All three of them tried to reach the sobbing girl.

'Let me through, mate,' Junior said, trying to prise Paul's hand away from the doorjamb.

'You're just jealous! That's it. You can't be happy yourself because you're such a liar and you don't want me to be happy! Go on, admit it!'

'Libby, stop . . . You're getting yourself worked up about nothing. Look, let me past!' Junior shoved hard against Paul.

'Don't you dare talk to her like that!' Paul's face was suddenly dark with anger.

For a brief, mad moment the two men struggled in the doorway, Paul seemingly determined to stop Junior from reaching her. What was going on? Kit moved towards them, trying to prevent things from spiralling completely out of control. And then it came.

'Get *off* me, you black bastard!'

There was a sudden, shocked silence. Junior froze, as did Libby. Kit looked from Paul to Junior in disbelief.

'I knew it!' Libby hissed. 'I just *knew* it! Well, well, well… That's it, isn't it? All that shit you fed us about everybody being the same, treating everyone as equals. It was all lies! Lies! You're exactly the same as her. You fucking deserve each other, d'you hear me?'

'Libby, don't… He didn't mean it,' Kit shouted, grabbing hold of her arm. 'It just… it just slipped out… He's upset, we're all upset…'

'Yeah? Well, let me give you all something to be *really* upset about,' Libby shouted. 'I'm about to have a black bastard of my own. Yes, that's right, you're about to have a grandchild. A black grandchild, imagine that! But that's not the reason we're getting married! I'm not like you, see?' She turned to face her mother.

There was another shocked silence. Paul's arm dropped. Kit froze. She could feel her own face crumpling.

Libby's eyes were on hers, cruelly narrowed. Her whole face was flushed a deep, ugly crimson. There was a distressing note of triumph in her voice. 'I love him! I don't care if he's black, green or yellow! I love him!'

'You don't mean that,' Paul broke in hoarsely but Kit saw Libby had misunderstood. She saw Junior's face. There was an expression on it that she couldn't read.

'I do!' Libby screamed. 'I *do*!'

Kit closed her eyes briefly, unable to think straight. When she opened them, Junior was gone.

65

Junior had no clear idea where he was going, or why. He'd had just enough presence of mind to lift his coat from the rack beside the front door as he let himself out. He was glad of it. Needles of sharp rain stung his cheeks and the air was bitingly cold. He thrust his hands deep into his pockets and walked as quickly away from the house as he could. His mind was a jumble of emotions – anger, hurt, astonishment ... and fear. Yes, there was fear too. Libby was pregnant. She – *they* – were going to have a child. Why hadn't she said anything and, more to the point, how on earth was he going to keep her ... and a *baby*? He was twenty-two years old with a half-finished degree and no money to speak of. Libby was accustomed to a very different sort of life.

He realised now that he hadn't even begun to think about their future together. He'd asked her to marry him but it had seemed to him to be some distant, far-off event ... at some point in a future he couldn't quite believe in, let alone see. What now? The parents were dead set against it. It hadn't even taken half an hour for the father's true feelings to come out. As soon as the words were out – *you black bastard!* – he realised it was what he'd feared all along, without knowing it. Why did he even *think* it wouldn't matter? Of course it mattered. It had mattered all his life ... Why not now? Just because Libby feigned ignorance didn't mean the rest of the world would. She was different, somehow ... She saw things others didn't, went where others wouldn't. He'd naively thought it was her background. All that travel to exotic places, experiencing the world in a way he could only dream about. But in the end, it boiled down to the same thing. If she loved him so much, why had she kept the baby a secret from him? Why did he have to learn about it that way? It was humiliating. No, worse than that – she'd *diminished* him. She'd made him look stupid and inconsequential in front of her parents. Did she feel the same way as they did? He'd been so sure she wasn't another Charlie, looking for her kicks in the cheapest and most rebellious way she dared ... But perhaps he'd been wrong?

He crossed the street, barely noticing where he was going. He heard a clock strike the hour and looked up. He'd walked all the length of the Embankment and was now in Parliament Square. Big Ben's eerily lit face showed through the mist. It was eight thirty.

He narrowly avoided a bicycle as he turned onto Westminster Bridge. The river flowed beneath him, thick and treacly, its surface pocked by raindrops. He stopped for a moment, looking down. The slick black tongue seemed to mirror his thoughts: dark, ugly, drifting. He turned up his collar and walked on, wanting only for the roaring and confusion in his head to clear. All the old buried childhood fears of not being good enough rose into his throat, choking him. He was six years old again, waiting to find out if the family who'd seen his photograph would agree to take him on. He was thirteen, the lone black child in class. He was fourteen, learning how to defend himself with his fists and always, always being blamed for starting the fight.

'*Oi!* Watch where you're going!' a voice interrupted him.

He stopped. There were three young men standing in front of him. He blinked in surprise. 'Who, me?'

'Yeah, who else, you fucking cunt.'

He blinked again. 'What's wrong with you?' he asked, frowning. 'Just leave me alone.'

One of them reached out suddenly and pushed him in the chest. 'You bumped 'im on purpose, you fuckin' cunt! Watch where you're going, nigger.'

Junior looked quickly to his left and right. He had absolutely no idea where he'd landed up. His heart skipped a beat.

'Nowhere to run to, nigger boy. Not unless you're gonna run back to where you come from. This ain't your country. You wanna just fuck off, the lot of you,' the taller of the three snarled at him. He was wearing a leather belt around his neck, weighted with nuts and bolts.

Junior's heart was pounding now. 'Look, mate, I dunno what your problem is, but I ain't done nothing to you. Just let me pass.'

'You done up one of our mates,' one of the three piped up. 'And we're gonna fuckin' get you.'

Junior swallowed. 'You've got the wrong bloke,' he said, hoping his voice was steady. 'I'm not from round here.'

'Too fuckin' right! Go back to where you come from ... Africa, innit?' They laughed.

One of them reached into his jacket pocket and, that instant, Junior saw the flash of a blade. His heart felt as though it would burst through his ribcage. There wasn't a second to waste. All the muscles in his body drew inwards in a storm of tension that propelled him out of the moment – he ran. The sound of his own body thumped loudly in his ears as he careered away from them, running, running … he had no idea to where. He heard the shouts behind him but he was terrified of what he was running from. He tore down one street after another, blindly, his whole being concentrating fiercely on one thought: *To get away.*

66

'Come on, Libbykins … At least have a cup of tea?' Her father hovered anxiously by her.

Abject desolation burned over her. She was unable to even lift her eyes. A terrible silence had come over everyone as soon as the door closed behind Junior. For the first time, no one was able to look each other in the face. It was as if a storm had just blown up inside the house, scattering everyone and everything in its path.

Her mother had gone upstairs to lie down, leaving Libby and her father avoiding one another's eye. Libby couldn't think straight. Which was worse? Hearing the words come out of her father's mouth or seeing Junior's face as she broke the news? She hadn't meant it to come out that way – she'd wanted to tell him first, privately – but there wasn't time and when the whole ugly scene erupted, it just came out. She couldn't help it. She'd wanted to shock her parents beyond anything she'd previously ever been capable of, yes, but she hadn't meant to hurt Junior that way.

'No.' She shook her head. A wave of tiredness crashed over her, suddenly leaving her drained. She wanted nothing more than to curl up in Junior's arms and to pretend that the events of the past few hours had been a dream, that nothing had happened, nothing had changed.

'Libby,' her father began again, but this time his tone was much more serious. She glanced up at him. His face was drawn. 'Don't be too hard on her,' he said quietly. 'Things aren't always what they seem.'

Libby shook her head. 'You're wrong,' she said stubbornly. 'That's how it always is in this family. Nothing is ever what it seems ... And I want to know *why*.'

Her father sighed. 'It's ... it's more complicated than that.'

'No, it's *not*!' Libby could feel her anger returning. 'That's the whole point, don't you see? The truth *isn't* complicated! It's just the truth, that's all! Did *you* know about it?' she asked him angrily. 'Of course not! But you don't care! I don't know what's the matter with you, it's not—'

The doorbell rang, cutting her off mid-flow. She jumped up, her whole body bathed in relief. It was Junior. He was back! She rushed up the short flight of stairs to the kitchen and opened the door, tears of relief already forming behind her eyes. But it wasn't Junior. Two policemen stood on the pavement.

One of them removed his helmet. 'Is this the home of a Mr Junior Jackson?' he asked, his puzzled expression betraying him.

Libby's heart began to pound. Behind her, she could hear her father coming up the stairs.

'What's going on?'

'Sorry, miss ... Looks as if we might have the wrong address.' One of the policemen held up a small plastic vial. Libby recognised it immediately. It was the antibiotics the doctor had prescribed Junior a couple of weeks earlier.

'No.' She swallowed. 'No, that's his.' She pointed to the vial. 'Those are his pills. What's happened?'

'Evening, sir,' the second policeman spoke, seeing her father appear in the doorway behind her. 'Sorry to disturb you, sir ... There's been an incident.'

'Incident? What sort of incident?' Libby's voice rose dangerously. 'Where's Junior?'

There was a moment's pained silence. The two policemen exchanged a glance. 'Could we come in, sir?' the more senior of the two spoke.

'Who is it?' her mother called down the stairs.

Libby felt dangerously adrift. She stood aside to let the policemen in and it seemed to her that she feared something from them but did not know what it was until it came.

'He was involved in a fight earlier this evening. Messy business. Bermondsey way.'

'Where is he? Is he all right?'

The policeman who'd spoken took off his glasses, pinching the inner corner of his eyes between his thumb and forefinger. He replaced them again and opened his mouth. 'He's gone, I'm sorry to inform you. Stabbed. Didn't stand a chance. We found this in his back pocket.' He held up the vial. 'Now,' he continued, clearing his throat, 'can you tell me what the nature of his relationship is to … er, you? Was he living here?'

Libby couldn't answer. She heard the sharp intake of breath – her father? The sound of footsteps at the door – her mother? Maev's cries … And then a woman's screams – high-pitched, terrifying. Hers.

PART TEN

TRUTH

2014
Kit / Libby / Ro

67

'Libby! Libbeeeey!' Toby's voice carried with it the classic rise and fall of a lament. 'Look at this. Just *look* at this!'

'What is it?' Libby came out of the pantry, drying her hands on her apron. Toby was standing in the doorway to the hall, holding out a lump of clay for her inspection. 'What is it?' she asked again.

'They've been in the studio. I *specifically* told them not to!' He aimed a savage kick at the child's bicycle that was propped up against the wall.

'I'm sorry, darling,' Libby said mildly, inspecting the lump with feigned interest. It looked – to her, at any rate – like all the other lumps in Toby's studio.

He was a sculptor – well, that was to say that he'd recently *become* a sculptor, after a lifetime at the Bar. They were both sixty-five. Toby had retired a year earlier, a year ahead of the schedule they'd always planned for him. He'd sold their London flat and moved to the beautiful home in Kent where Libby had spent the best part of her life raising their family of four. One of the first things they'd done was convert part of the large barn at the rear of the apple orchard, where he could indulge himself in what he always thought of as his true calling: art. There were days during the renovations when Libby stood in the doorway, watching the builders break down walls, install windows, resurface the floor and the thought would pop into her head: shouldn't this be for *me*? Wasn't art *my* 'thing'? But she squashed the thought almost as soon as it surfaced. Her 'thing' was the family. Their children and the home she'd created and maintained for them for nearly four decades.

'Can't it be salvaged?' she asked tenderly.

'No, it bloody well *can't*. Look, can't you see? It's got bits of grass and ... and *stuff* in it. I can't work with it any more.'

Libby sighed. The barn was tucked away from sight of the main house and had probably proved irresistible to Maev's two little ones, Daisy and Zoë. Cameron, their older half-brother, had probably led them there. He was fifteen and still in that no-man's-land between childhood, adolescence and adulthood.

'All right, darling,' she said soothingly. 'I'll tell them off. D'you want a cup of coffee?' she asked, in the tone of voice she often used to placate one or other of the children when they were younger.

She smiled inwardly. She and Ro would have a bit of a giggle about it when she arrived. The entire clan was gathering for Kit's ninety-first birthday. Her heart lifted with almost guilty pleasure at the thought of Ro's arrival. It had been a while since all their children were present at the same time, although Ro, strictly speaking, wasn't Toby's child. She was three years old when Libby met and married Toby, but he'd always been her father. There was absolutely no difference between her and the other three children, she'd always been careful to make sure of that. But of all her children, Ro was the one most like her. It was only in moments like this – of a humorous shared complicity between herself and her eldest daughter – that she ever acknowledged the special bond. Although she didn't allow herself to think about it often, it could all have been so different.

It was to Toby's enormous credit that he'd taken on a single mother with a child who was obviously not his. Ro was clearly mixed-race but Toby refused to allow the fact to alter their circumstances as a family and he worked hard in the beginning to fashion them as one. When she was little, in the years before the arrival of the other children, he'd almost revelled in the confusion it generated.

'This little one's our first, aren't you, chocolate drop? The first and the best-tasting.' He had a whole string of delicious-sounding names for her – sweets and milk chocolates and the like, so that Ro grew up thinking of herself as something rather lovely and most definitely sought after.

She had no memory of those terrible first years when Libby had walked out on her parents after Junior's terrible death. For years she'd blamed them. She'd struggled alone in a string of bedsits in parts of London her parents probably wouldn't have known existed. She'd walked out of the house in the early hours of the morning without waking anyone and without saying goodbye, and gone straight to Len. She gave birth with Len's sisters and aunts on hand, and told herself that it was better that way. She would never forgive them. She had a child to support. There was no going back. She taught herself how to type in between changing nappies and heating milk on the tiny stove in the bedsit in

Mile End that she'd moved to. She wasn't much good as a secretary but she looked presentable and sounded nice, so the firms she worked for put up with her – up to a point.

She was on her third job as a secretary in a law firm, just off Grey's Inn Road, when she met a young trainee barrister called Toby Mortimer, who took a keener interest in her than was perhaps advisable, or at least so his colleagues thought. One or two of the senior counsel had seen baby Ro on the odd occasion Libby had been unable to leave her at home with anyone.

'She's clearly got a bit of a past, old boy.'

But Toby Mortimer didn't care. With his lawyer's instinct to tie up loose ends, he'd been the one to bring about a thaw.

'What's done is done, darling. It's what comes next that matters. We're going to get married and have lots more children and it's not right that this rift exists. You can't cut yourself off from family.'

'But *she* did,' Libby protested bitterly. 'You don't know the half of it. None of us do. She cut herself off completely. I've got a half-brother somewhere in this world I didn't even know existed. I had grandparents... She lied about everything.'

'She had her reasons.'

'I don't care. She had no right.'

'Of course you're angry. It's only natural. But that's in the past now. It's the future that counts. Get in touch with them. Or I will.'

He was as good as his word. He did. Their first meeting after four years was a disaster. There was such anger and hurt on both sides. And then Kit met Ro for the very first time and it was as if nothing else existed. Thick as thieves, those two – partners for life. Right from the start there was a bond that no one could explain. Ro called her Kit, even as a very young child, and never 'Nana', as she was to her siblings who came later. To Ro, 'Kit' was what she'd always been and always would be. It was Ro who'd healed the rift, making it possible to spend weekends together or a Christmas in the same Chelsea house where her life had fallen apart.

By some unspoken rule that they all observed, no one spoke about Junior or the revelations and accusations of that night. In time, Libby learned to accept that there were things about her mother she would never, ever understand or know. And that was that.

So the reconciling was all Toby's doing, she reminded herself often.

And for that, she would forgive him *anything*, even his childish outburst over a lump of clay.

'How about a biscuit?' she said, going over to the window, where she'd just tipped a whole tray of freshly baked gingerbread snaps into a tin. She waited for a moment.

'Yeah, all right,' he said finally, disconsolately.

'It was probably the two little ones. I'll bet Cameron showed them where it was. I'll remind them at lunch, darling, I promise. Now, tell me: what d'you think?' she asked, sliding two still-warm, funnel-shaped snaps onto a plate. 'It's a new recipe but I added a little too much ginger, don't you think?'

He bit into one and she saw the corners of his mouth lift. She was relieved. In over forty years of marriage, there didn't seem to be an incident that a little treat couldn't resolve. Well, perhaps one or two . . . but not many.

'Yeah, a little bit heavy on the ginger,' he commented. 'Nice, though.' He carried the plate over to the beautiful oak table that had been their dining table for nearly two decades, its smooth, warm surface burnished from polishing over the years. 'So, when's Ro arriving?'

'After lunch. She's picking Phoebe up from Heathrow around one, I think, then they'll hop on the M25.'

'What time do I need to go and fetch Kit?'

'Not before four, I don't think. You know how she likes to rest in the afternoon and she'll need it tonight. I know *she* says it's not necessary, but she's over ninety. A party'll wear her out. And besides, it'll give Ro and Phoebe a chance to settle in. You know what Phoebe's like when she's just been in America. It's all "Daddy this" and "Daddy that" and "America's *so* much better than horrid old England". It'll take her a while to settle. And Kit just loves to tease her.'

'Mmm. Did you say there was some coffee going?' Toby asked, his humour just about restored.

She smiled. 'No, I didn't, but I'll make some.'

She untied her apron strings and moved towards the sink. She let the coolness splash over her hands, already thinking beyond the making of the coffee to the radishes she'd just picked and how, when plunged in cold water, they opened themselves up into little pink-and-white roses that were peppery on the tongue.

She ran over the menu in her mind. For starters, there were light-as-air smoked aubergine and yoghurt vol-au-vents, sprinkled with ruby pomegranate seeds and crushed black sesame seeds and one of those enormous blue-and-white ceramic bowls that they'd brought back – in her hand luggage! – from Mexico, filled with a delicious array of roasted spicy nuts and seeds – cashews, almonds, pecans, pumpkin seeds – all rubbed with rosemary and honey and popped into the oven just long enough to harden and brown. There were piles of hot, fluffy pitta bread and three or four thick, creamy bowls of hummus for dipping. She'd made one of her favourite Sunday lunch dishes: tender, roasted lamb with figs, radicchio and chicory. The whole house was redolent with the smell of sage, rosemary and honey, in which the lamb had been smothered and left overnight. It was exactly the sort of feast that Kit would adore: a slew of her favourite Middle Eastern dishes; interspersed with typically English treats like rhubarb fool and Eton Mess; thick, crusty Italian bread; and delicious French and Spanish wines.

It was strange, Libby mused as she watched Toby finish his coffee (and two more of her too-gingery ginger snaps), Kit had never been one to bother much about food. Meals, in the various houses they'd lived in growing up, had been largely left to servants and cooks to organise. The only time Kit ever involved herself in the daily chore of what to eat, what to buy, how to cook whatever had been bought – which had occupied Libby's attention for nearly forty years – was when a dinner party was being laid on. Then another side of Kit came out: one that appreciated fine wine and the way a table might be set; what flowers to put where; what dishes to serve and in what order. Those dinner parties in Baghdad and Muscat and Port-of-Spain, which were the ones Libby could remember, were characterised by a side of Kit that she might not have known existed: charming, solicitous, engaged. Did so-and-so have the right wine? Had so-and-so had enough? It was all so special and delightful, made all the more so to Libby, since she knew it wouldn't last. At the time, she didn't remember resenting it. On the contrary, she was enchanted by this vision of her mother who appeared to others so differently than she did to her children. But when Libby had children of her own, it was one of her deeply buried, subconscious desires that marriage and motherhood seemed to awaken. *Her* children would always see her just as she was to everyone else. Every meal would be made special. Every day would be an occasion of one sort or another.

Libby looked back on it now with a sense of trepidation. Had it worked? She supposed it had. Her own children were close in a way that she, Elly and Maev had never been. But that was Eluned all over. Even now, married and with a child of her own, the same frosty resentment was there between them. It only needed a moment to flare up, as it had the day before when they arrived. Elly made much meal out of the fact that she'd married a Frenchman and that French, not English, was the preferred language of their home. Libby had made the mistake of addressing their son, Loïc, in English.

'Hello, darling,' she'd said, embracing the boy as soon as he got out of the car. 'Oh, it's been too long. I always feel as though I'm seeing someone entirely new every time I see you.' It was an innocent enough remark.

'I do wish you wouldn't do that,' Eluned said, as soon as Loïc and his father, Luc, were out of earshot.

'What?' Libby asked, surprised.

'First of all, we speak French at home and I don't like him speaking English. And secondly, why do you always go on about the fact that you don't see him? It makes him really uncomfortable.'

Libby was too surprised to answer. She shut her mouth firmly down on the retort and moved off to supervise the luggage instead.

But thankfully her own children displayed none of the petty insecurities and desperate fight for attention that she and her sisters did. Ro, Trinity and Emily were as close as could be, and even Duncan, eight years Emily's junior and a surprise late addition, was cherished in the way only a late child – and a boy amongst girls at that – could be.

Perhaps they were too close? Duncan's decision to move to Thailand after university could be read as a way to claw out some space and independence for himself that being the baby brother of three talented, successful and immeasurably bright sisters was hard to achieve. And, God knew, they were bright. Ro was a high-flying scientist. At forty-three, she was one of the youngest professors at King's College Hospital. It still thrilled Libby to read about her daughter's success. With her smooth brown skin, masses of wild, corkscrew curls and her thoughtful-but-playful expression, she was as sought after on the public appearance circuits as she was within the halls of the teaching hospital where she worked. She'd twice been awarded Woman Scientist of the Year. She was a high-flier with a single child, a divorced husband and no pets. Unlike Libby, Ro's energies could hardly have been less directed towards her domestic arrangements. She and Phoebe still lived in the two-bedroom flat in Hammersmith that she'd bought whilst completing her training at St Thomas' and, in all honesty, she hadn't done much to it since.

'It's fine for now,' she said tetchily whenever Libby brought up the subject of hopelessly outdated wallpaper and a sofa that had clearly seen better days. *For now.* That was Ro all over.

Trin was different. She was an architect, an associate partner in one of those global firms that seemed to build the same skyscraper wherever they opened office. She was still renting – much to Toby's disappointment – but valued the fact that she could 'get up and go' whenever she wanted or the job called. She was always on a plane, en route from Singapore to Dubai, or from New York to Honolulu, as the firm she worked for liked to send its young, energetic staff to smooth the way for the next sixty-storey edifice, made out of the same combination of glass and steel, to be erected on prime real estate, invariably at huge profit. She talked of giving it all up and going 'to the countryside', wherever that might be, but in the meantime, she invested the same amount of exquisite love, taste and care on a succession of one-bedroom flats in some of the most unheard-of locations in London – Victoria Park, Exmouth Market, Clacton – that Libby had spent on their seven-bedroom country house.

Emily was similar to Trin: arty and creative. She was a well-known fashion designer with her own boutique in Hampstead and a line of clothing sold in some of London's most prestigious stores – Harrods, Harvey Nicks, Brown's. It tickled Libby pink to walk into Harvey Nicks, head for the second floor and see Emily's eponymous range – *EMILY LOUISE MORTIMER*, in beautifully simple, sans serif font – hanging before her eyes. The clothes were a little too *trendy* for her liking, especially at her age. But there was no denying Emily's appeal or her success. Working women flocked to her shows and she had the sales to prove it.

Neither Trin nor Emily had married, though both had had a string of suitable and unsuitable boyfriends since they were teenagers. Libby sometimes wondered what men made of her daughters. They were so obviously and evidently capable, on almost every front imaginable... If *she* were a man, she thought to herself, she'd run for the hills.

Emily had recently bought herself a Jaguar F-Type, a sleek, terrifyingly sporty thing that looked as though it could – and should – carry one comfortably into outer space. What on earth must a man think when she purred up in *that*? she wondered. It was all so different in her day.

Suddenly a flash of light scored across her vision. It was the emblem on a car's bonnet. It was the F-Type, coming slowly up the driveway.

Speak of the devil. She smiled. It was Emily.

'It's Em, darling,' she said to Toby. 'In that ridiculous car of hers.'

'Ah, it's the Jag!' Toby got up hurriedly. It was sometimes hard to tell which he preferred: his youngest daughter or her car.

Loïc must have heard it too; they met in the hallway with Tim and Cameron hot on his heels. They were all speaking English, Libby noticed with a wry smile. At twenty, Loïc had the exuberance and affability of a teenager.

She followed the rowdy group outside into the bright sunshine. The garden looked spectacular, she noticed. Toby had cut the lawn the day before and the flowers were still holding onto their last-days-of-summer bloom. Hydrangeas, sweet peas, roses, poppies... There was a lovely patch of purple lilac. Beaujolais Bonnets near the Japanese elm, which complemented its dark, bruised-black leaves, and a small cluster of pale blue clematis still flowering nearby. Libby had followed the tried-and-tested principle of ordering her borders and flowering beds according to colour and the results still pleased her, year after year.

'Mum! Dad! Hello!' Emily shouted at them from across the driveway.

The boys had already reached the car and were walking around it in awe, as boys were wont to do in the face of mechanical power.

She'd brought someone with her, Libby noticed. A man unfolded himself from the passenger seat and emerged into the sunlight. Nice-looking, she thought. Would he last longer than the weekend? Given Emily's track record, it was unlikely.

Now stop it, she admonished herself as she made her way across the gravel to meet them. *You never know.*

'Darling,' she said, putting on her widest and brightest smile. 'How wonderful to see you. Did you have a good journey down? And who's this?'

'This is Declan,' Emily declared, a touch proudly. 'He's from Dublin,' as if that explained everything.

'Well, hel-*lo*, Declan-from-Dublin,' Libby said, leaning forwards and offering her freshly powdered cheek. 'How nice to meet you.' Everyone laughed.

Linking arms, she and Emily left the men to organise the luggage and they walked slowly up the front path to the door.

68

The dining table had never looked better. The snowy white tablecloth that stretched over eighteen places still had the crisp crease marks of the cleaning lady, Katie's, hot iron. Libby had taken out her Villeroy & Boch chinaware and the Royal Brierley cut crystal glassware that Toby had bought her on their twenty-fifth wedding anniversary. The pale yellow and silver porcelain plates looked so elegant against the white linen. Pale blue and yellow napkins and huge bowls of Perle d'Azur clematis, freshly picked, were placed at regular intervals down its length.

In the garden, waiting for Kit's arrival, they'd erected a white tent with a long table covered in embroidered linen, with a rather random assortment of garden chairs that gave the whole place a cosy, domestic feel to it, unlike the formal dining room with its rich, velvet drapes and elegant matching tones. The party was to have two halves: one outside, with Pimm's for the adults and lemonade for the children, and lots of rich cupcakes with swirls of cream and buttery icing and flaky pastry tarts that melted as soon as they were popped in your mouth. She and Trin had spent the afternoon baking, perfecting everything. Then, in the early evening, the grown-ups would move indoors and the 'proper' party would begin.

She took one last look around, hugging herself with glee. It was three o'clock. Toby had already set off to pick up Kit from the lovely nursing home where she had lived since Paul's death almost twelve years earlier. She'd refused outright all attempts to move her in with Libby.

'Not a chance, my dear,' she said crisply. 'I won't hear of it. I enjoy my independence too much. You *know* that. If I moved in with you, I'd never hear the end of the fussing.'

For a moment Libby thought of her father, of his pale blue eyes behind customary glasses; his mild-mannered smile that served all purposes, from humour to wry tolerance... For a brief second, the room dimmed and swam before her eyes. She swallowed hard. They had never been particularly close. It had been a relationship marked by distance though not indifference. She'd loved him all the same. His death had come upon them quietly; similar, in many ways, to his life. He'd played second fiddle to Kit all his life – all their lives together – right from the very start. It seemed somehow fitting that his departure should come so many years before hers and be noticed so little, she thought with a pang of guilt. It was Kit's death they all feared, not his. Although you couldn't really call Kit *involved* with her children, her presence was amongst them terribly. She was ninety-one today. It seemed inconceivable that she would die. And yet she would, she must.

'Oh, stop this,' she muttered to herself sternly. 'It's her bloody birthday, not her funeral.'

She turned away from the scene of quiet perfection before her and made her way upstairs. She had just under an hour to bathe, dress and get ready. In her room upstairs that overlooked the barn where Toby worked, shaping dull lumps of inert clay into living forms – heads, busts, torsos, none of which particularly appealed to her, but it seemed to keep him happy – she stripped off quickly and stood for a moment in front of the mirror. Where had it all gone? she wondered, looking at herself. Of course she wasn't twenty any more but the looks for which she'd once been known had all but vanished. Unlike Kit, who'd aged slowly and therefore almost imperceptibly, Libby's decline (which was how she saw it) had happened suddenly, almost overnight. She could still remember the day she'd looked down at her sun-browned legs when they were on holiday – where was it? France? Greece? She'd seen the spider's web of veins begin to spread out from beneath the fatty pad of flesh and loosening muscle just below her kneecap. She'd stared at it. Was the map of decay hers? It had come upon her so quickly.

From a woman in her forties, who'd always had the satisfaction of being able to command the attention of others, to this loose, slightly drooping woman in her sixties, who no one seemed to look at any more ... It was hard to believe it was her, now. She would never have the cool, steely elegance that belonged to Kit. Libby's beauty was the sort that depended on youth, on the firmness of olive-toned skin and the contrast between her dark brown eyes and chestnut-coloured hair, which had grown thin and lifeless at menopause. Kit's, on the other hand, had whitened and lightened in a way that made you think silver was her natural, longed-for colouring, enlivened by her red lips and still beautifully manicured hands.

Libby turned to look at her backside and legs in the mirror. She pulled a quick face. She was seventy-two! What on earth did she expect? She hurried into the white marble bathroom and drew her bath.

The green silk dress that she'd chosen fitted her well. It was years old now, but she'd had it altered when she found herself putting on weight. It suited her. The fashion of that year – 1975 – had been made for her. It had a low-cut neckline, bell-shaped sleeves and a long, full skirt. She stepped into it and pulled up the zipper that ran all the way up her back. It was a *little* tight – too many tarts popped into her mouth when no one was looking – but it was comfortable, although only just. No bread tonight, she thought to herself grimly. It wasn't *quite* Keira Knightley in flowing green silk, but it would certainly do.

She sat down in front of the dressing table and opened her make-up bag. She'd learned to keep things simple: light foundation, a little blusher, touch of mascara... nothing much, nothing dramatic. She thought of Trin and Emily and how, when they were very young and she'd put on a lot of make-up and perfume in preparation for a night out or a party, they'd been entranced by the sight of her all dolled up, scampering around her in excitement as if they expected a sensation. Now the tables were well and truly turned. She pulled a face at herself in the mirror. It was fine; she was fine. It was Kit's big day, not hers.

She stood up, enjoying the feel of silk swirling around her legs. She opened the wardrobe door and chose a pair of dark green high-heeled sandals that she already knew wouldn't last the night. As she closed the bedroom door behind her and began to descend the stairs, she heard a shout from outside. She stopped at the landing and her face creased into a smile. Kit had arrived.

Behind her, in the commotion that followed her arrival, Ro and Phoebe had pulled up. Everyone had finally arrived. The party could begin.

Epilogue

Crabtree Wood, Kent – 2014

Libby put a crimson wheel of red pepper into her mouth and chewed slowly as she cut the remaining green and orange peppers to make the lunchtime salad. The house was still quiet. The adults were all sleeping off the effects of too much wine and Tim had taken the younger children down to the river that ran behind the house, safely out of earshot.

She'd slept badly, her mind and heart full of Kit's letter. Some – not all – of the missing pieces that had characterised her difficult relationship with her mother for all her life had suddenly fallen into place. It was the closest Libby had ever felt to her. But still, there was so much more she had to know.

She finished slicing the peppers and the cherry tomatoes. She cleared a space on the middle shelf of the huge, American-style fridge that took up half the pantry and placed the enormous salad bowl carefully on the glass shelf. She looked at her watch. It was just past noon. She would go upstairs, take a shower and then drive into Benenden by herself. Shopping and lunch with Ro could wait one more day. There were things she had to ask her mother.

Their bedroom was still dark when she walked in. The heavy velvet curtains blanked out the early afternoon light. Toby surfaced momentarily as she opened the door and a chink of light spilled into the room.

'What time is it?' he asked groggily.

'It's nearly lunchtime. But don't get up. I'm just going to pop into Benenden and see Kit,' she whispered, closing the door. 'Sleep it off. I'll take the Land Rover. I'll be back by three or so.'

'Are you sure? You don't want me to drive you?'

She shook her head. 'No, you sleep. Tim's taken the little ones down to the river and there's salad in the fridge. I'll be back before you know it.'

He made a sound that was halfway between a grunt and a snore. Then he spoke up. 'She didn't seem herself last night,' he said. 'Did she seem all right to you?'

She was halfway to the bathroom. She turned, and a cold hand clutched at her heart. 'She was fine. Why? Did she say something?'

He shook his head, suppressing a yawn. 'No, not exactly. But you know what she's like. She just seemed a bit distracted, that's all.'

It was on the tip of her tongue to tell him about the letter, but something held her back. There were still too many unanswered questions.

'She was probably just tired. We forget... she's ninety-one.'

'Yeah, you're right. It's hard to think of her as old.' Toby gave a soft chuckle. 'All right, if you're sure you don't want me to drive you...?'

'Quite sure, darling,' she said firmly.

By the time she reached the bathroom door, she heard the steady rise and fall of his breathing. He was fast asleep.

The Kent countryside was at its autumnal loveliest. The thick trees that lined the winding roads were coming into their mantle of red, burgundy and gold. It was a Sunday and there was little traffic about. She passed the old post office on the corner, which had stood empty for nearly a year – another sign of the changing times. She remembered it from when she and Toby first moved to Crabtree Wood. Back then the little post office had been the hub of village life. It had taken her a while to settle into the slow, gossipy village rhythm, so different from the impersonal, anonymous pace of London. But she'd grown to love it. And the village had taken to Ro in a flash. The thing Libby had been so wary of – the odd glances, the snide comments about a darker-than-average child in their midst – had never happened. It was her *manners* they commented on – impeccable – not her skin colour.

She wound her way slowly around the last bend, just before Rolvenden, and took the first turning on the left towards Benenden. Upton Hall, the graceful stately home that had been turned into a nursing home, was just down Sandhurst Lane. She pulled into the driveway, scattering gravel. There were two or three visitors' cars in the car park, families who'd arrived to spend Sunday lunch with grandparents and elderly relatives.

She locked the car and pulled her cardigan around her shoulders. She pushed open the gate and walked up the damp, stony path, admiring the tiny spray roses that lined the path to the front door. Upton Hall cost a fortune, but Kit paid for it out of her own private income. Libby and Toby could easily have paid but Kit wouldn't hear of it. She had plenty herself, thank you very much.

After her mother and her sister Lily had passed away, years back, she'd sold Chalfont Hall to the National Trust and there were generous trust funds set up for each of the grandchildren and great-grandchildren. Libby had never enquired into Kit's finances. Like all others, it was a subject on which Kit would never have spoken.

The receptionist looked up as she came through the front door. 'Hello, Mrs Mortimer. How are you? No, go straight through. I haven't seen her this morning, but Marek looked in on her just after breakfast. He said she was still asleep.'

Libby nodded her thanks and walked down the corridor towards the courtyard. Kit's suite of rooms – a lovely, large bedroom, a small kitchenette and a cosy living room – were on the ground floor, overlooking the inner garden. She'd chosen them because the bedroom looked out onto a fountain. It reminded her of Baghdad, she'd said once, in passing. Libby had only the sketchiest memory of the garden in Karrada. There was a fountain, yes, and orange and lemon trees, and a thick white wall that opened from the calm of the interior onto the dusty, noisy street. She thought of Miriam, suddenly, and of what might have become of her. In the years since they'd fled the Middle East, how many wars had there been?

She put her hand out to knock softly, letting Kit know she was there, but the door swung open.

'Kit?'

She walked into the room. It was dark and still shuttered inside. The door to the bedroom was partly ajar and one of the bedside lamps was on. Kit was lying on the bed. She could see her feet through the door.

She's forgotten to take her shoes off, she thought to herself. She must have been too tired the night before to undress properly.

Music was playing in the background, very faintly. The radio was on. Classic FM. Something by Mozart, though she couldn't name the piece. There was the faint smell of cigarette smoke still hanging in the air. She walked quietly into the bedroom.

'Mother? You've been smoking again,' she said very softly, so as not to frighten her. 'And you left the door open.'

There was no answer. She walked around the side of the bed. She looked down at her mother. And then it came to her. She put a hand to her mouth in horror.

Kit's eyes were closed. She was still in the elegant midnight-blue silk dress she'd worn to her party, with the camel pashmina wrapped carefully around her shoulders. Her head was slightly to one side and her hair had fallen across her forehead.

She'd hate that, Libby thought absurdly.

She couldn't move, couldn't breathe. She looked down at her mother, at her calm, still-beautiful face. The only sound in the room was her own breath, rising and falling. She stood there, her hand hovering about Kit's face, then she reached down and smoothed the offending lock of hair away with a gesture of infinitely tender care, the sort of gesture Kit would never have allowed her to make when she was alive. Her skin was still warm to the touch but there was nothing else: no movement, no sound of her breath, no rise and fall of her chest. She was gone.

Libby sat down gingerly on the side of the bed. It was so quiet. The music drifted in from the living room in disconnected snatches. She had no idea how long she sat there. At some point she felt cold.

She looked across at her mother. Kit's right arm lay limp against her body. She was holding something in her hand. She peered at it. It was a thin, gold chain with a broken crucifix. Libby frowned. It wasn't the sort of thing she'd ever seen Kit wear. She very gently prised the chain from Kit's fingers. It came away easily, sliding over Kit's hand. Libby caught it and held it beneath her fingers, turning it over. The crucifix was missing one leg – an odd, three-legged crucifix. The gold was almost brassy in colour; the sharp edges of the break had been worn down over time. She put it back in her mother's hand, touching it very, very lightly.

Presently she got up and moved into the living room. She ought to phone Toby. She looked around for her handbag and her eyes fell on the dark mahogany chest standing in the corner of the room, with its lid partially open. She'd never really noticed it before. Like many of Kit's possessions, it seemed to fit perfectly into its surroundings.

She walked over to it and knelt down. She pushed the heavy lid fully open and looked inside. It took her a few seconds to work out what lay in front of her. She gasped. Inside, neatly stacked, row upon row, were dozens of black leather notebooks, spines facing upwards, embossed with gold lettering, which announced an astonishing series of dates. The most recent were on the top: *2011, 2012, 2013*. She drew the first one out with trembling fingers. They were diaries. Kit's diaries.

She began to lift them out in stacks. *2002, 1986, 1977, 1965*. Year after year, the same notebook, the same filigree date stamps. *1958, 1957, 1952, 1948, 1947, 1942*.

The earliest was 1942. Libby swallowed and opened it gingerly. Kit's handwriting sprang up from the page.

April 1942. It's been a month since he died and there are days I can't persuade myself to get out of bed . . .

A bar of sunlight filtered in through the curtains and came to rest on the carpet beside her. Libby looked up, momentarily confused. She was suddenly aware of noise beyond the faint, tinny sound of the radio. Someone was coming towards her. She could hear footsteps approaching down the corridor. All around her lay the piles of notebooks. She looked around her and frowned, as if she couldn't quite place herself. She'd lost all feeling in her legs. She glanced at her watch. It was nearly four o'clock. She'd been sitting, cramped, in the same position for hours.

'Libby?' It was Toby. 'I've been phoning you for ages . . . What's happened? Is Kit asleep? Is she all right?'

She struggled to her feet. She felt the tears welling up in her eyes again. She looked up at him through eyes magnified and blurry with tears.

'No,' she said, her voice catching. 'No, she's not asleep. She's gone, Toby. She was gone by the time I got here.'

Toby's shoulders sagged, as though he'd been hit. '*No!* She was *fine* last night. Where is she? What happened?'

Libby shook her head slowly. 'She was gone when I got here. She's in the bedroom. Still dressed.' She gestured towards the open door. She swallowed and looked down at the piles of notebooks scattered around her feet. 'She left these, Toby.'

'What's that?'

'They're her diaries. I've been reading them.' She stopped, swallowing hard. 'It's all there, Toby. Who she was . . . what she did . . . what happened to her . . . everything. Who my father was . . . Why didn't she tell anyone? Why didn't she ever tell *me*? She was so hard on me . . . on everyone.'

'What d'you mean? You know who your father was . . . What are you talking about?'

Libby bent down and picked up one of the diaries. 'No, it wasn't Dad. It ... it was someone called Earl. A jazz musician.' She swallowed. 'Toby ... he was black. He was American ... A black American. He was killed by a bomb in 1942. It all makes sense now. This –' she lifted a hand to the soft curls at her temple. 'My hair ... my skin ... I've always been darker than everyone in the family ... It all makes sense. He played in a band with ... with Junior's dad. That was why she was so shocked that night. Why didn't she just tell me?'

Toby shook his head mutely. For once, he was at a loss for words.

In that moment, something remarkable happened to Libby. The fear and weight of her life began to fall from her. She felt almost light-hearted, in spite of the terrible feeling of grief. Now, for the first time in her life, she was free of it. She knew who she was. Finally. It wasn't who she'd always thought she was, but her hands were trembling with the strange, overwhelming satisfaction of seeing herself at the beginning of something, rather than at its end.

There was still so much she didn't know. But it was all there, in Kit's fine, elegant script. The whole of Kit's life was laid bare. Her life. Her *extraordinary* life.

Her last gesture had been to make sure it was Libby's too.